Ticia Rani

O-B*TCH-UARY Copyright© 2019 by Ticia Rani

Interior and cover formatting provided by: Nemo Designs
Cover Photography and Author photo provided by:
Chelsea Coad of Chelsea Coad Photography
www.facebook.com/ChelseaCoadPhotography
ChelseaCoadPhotography@gmail.com

ISBN: 978-1795696340

Author's Note: Make a cup of tea. Find a packet of tissues, make that a box. Shut off the world and get comfy. Prepare to feel the entire journey.

Dedication

To Terri C., thank you for long chats, massive bowls of chocolate chip cookie-dough, and ugly crying fits to help get to the heart of it all.

This is dedicated to those who have taken the journey, are on the journey, did not survive the journey, and to those who held the hands of their loved ones, so they weren't alone on the journey.

Kyle —
Love you, Budder —

Tricia Rani

Acknowledgements

Thank you to Tom, or as he likes to be known as, The Great and Wonderful Tom, GAWT for short. You have been my sounding board, support system, shoulder to cry on, and provider of all things caffeinated.

Thank you to Susan B., my best friend, sharer of tons of inside jokes, my partner in inappropriate giggles and side-eyes, and provider of wisdom that I require often.

Much love to my girls, Lorrin and Hannah, you make this mama proud. Keep your sparkle and teach the world to twirl.

Thank you to all of those who willingly took on the task of beta reading my book. Your words and guidance helped to create what others will now hold in their hands.

Without the help and support of many this book would never have made it to paper. Thank you all for your belief in me and encouragement to get it done.

Do you know the difference between "I like you" and "I love you"?

When you like a flower, you pluck it.

But when you love a flower, you water it daily.

-Anonymous

-Let it grow.

Chapter One

~~Dear Diary~~

~~To the Morbidly Curious~~

~~The Great Tata Fairy~~

Dear Friend,

Yes, Dear Friend, that would be you...my friend. My name is Olivia Carpenter and I ~~have~~ had a happy life...until recently. I have an amazing husband who, surprisingly, I still like after all these years. I have two daughters who impress me daily and friends I wouldn't trade for a hot date with Gerard Butler (maybe). Then all hell broke loose. My life took a sharp left turn, and this is where it has led me. To you. I want to tell you my story. My way. I want you to see the events unfold from my side of the journey. Make some popcorn, grab a drink and a box of tissues and strap yourself in...it's gonna get bumpy.

Let's begin with why I opened this document in the first place...

I sent another crumpled up piece of paper flying across the room causing an avalanche around the small trashcan. It had been collecting my rejects over the past few hours. Clearly, I needed a larger container. How can this be so hard? How do you write an obituary? The lowest paid journalists do it every day for God's sake. Did they study it in school? Obit 101: How to crush a life into a paragraph. The thought made me chuckle.

But this is more than that. How do you write your *own* obituary? How do you take the memories and special moments of your existence and reduce them to a small blurb in the local paper? I vaguely remembered being assigned to do this very thing when I was in high school. It was the "What do you plan to accomplish before you die?" assignment. You know the one where all the guys died in bed with a super model at the Playboy mansion, their own personal wet dream on paper. This was real and not nearly as wet. Had I done any of the things I wrote for that assignment? Did I do *the* assignment? I always hated Mrs. Formby's class. Who, in their right mind, tells their class they could earn an extra 100 points in the grade book if they ever noticed her wearing the same outfit twice within the school year? How was that important? How was it grade worthy? I did, however, earn the extra 100 points...and I needed it.

Just a matter of a few months ago, writing an obituary would have never crossed my mind. Then again, I thought I would live forever. Well, maybe not forever, but at least older than 42. It's amazing how you wake up like any other morning. You throw your obnoxious alarm clock across the room, stub your toe on the edge of the dresser, and curse the cat who attempted, once again, to push you down a flight of stairs, but within a few hours everything can change. Things that once seemed important aren't. Priorities change and vacuuming wasn't one of them, thank God. Paper plates worked fine, because doing dishes stole time, and saying I love you was more important than ever.

I couldn't find the rewind button or the script writer for my life. Can we make some changes to my story line? Like, can we say, let me live longer and why did it have to be at the gynecologist's office? Was this Karma's way of laughing at me? The gyno is an embarrassing requirement each woman must endure multiple times in their lives and it sucks. So to have him *find* the Goddamn lumps makes it so much worse. I would have preferred my friggin' dentist or podiatrist found them. How bad can a foot lump be, ya know what I'm sayin'? Hell, make it the bratty kid who picks his nose three doors down, but not the gyno. To top it off, he's hot, like, McDreamy x 2+ a McHottie. See, karma seeking revenge for inappropriate lusting for one's doctor. Just shoot me. This man had to touch me in very intimate ways, for medical purposes, and now it will forever be tainted because of two things the size of nickels. Nickels...not nipples. I know what you were thinkin'. Get your mind out of the gutter.

I guess it might actually help you understand what I'm bitching about if I told you the sorted details, so let's start where this messed up journey started...cue the Scooby Doo flashback sequence.

*****

"Mrs. Carpenter, did you happen to notice the lump under your left breast?"

"Yup, and I checked under the right breast too and felt one there. I figured if it was on both sides it was normal." You know how it is. When you get to be a certain age and you notice weird stuff with your body, but as long as it is a matching set, you didn't sweat it. Little did I know, neither was supposed to be there. With a quick check of my right breast, in a matter of one minute, I went from having one confirmed lump to having a matching set. One lump or two...get it? Sugar? Oh never mind.

Dr. -Way- too- Hot- took a step back and rubbed his chin, all the while staring at my boobs. Yes, look at them. They are lovely, or they were, until they were invaded by the lump twins.

"Mrs. Carpenter, you need to have a mammogram."

I shook my head, "Look, Dr. -Hunk-a-licious-, I had a mammogram a few months ago, and no one called to tell me there may be a problem." I may have said that in an accusatory manner. I may have even offered up some eye rolling and a smirk. I knew I needed to reel in my attitude a bit so I offered an explanation, "The issue is this, Doc, there is no way my crappy insurance is going to cover another mammogram, and I cannot afford to pay for one out of pocket, unless you take gum and lint, and... I don't think I have any gum." Stick that in your pipe and smoke it, my inner bitch screamed and stuck out her tongue like a petulant child.

"I will have a copy of your films sent over. I'll have my office contact your insurance company to explain why another mammogram is required. Mrs. Carpenter, you have two lumps that should not be there. Do you understand what I am trying to say?" He asked with what appeared to be actual concern. Maybe I got a little nervous. Maybe. Kinda.

"Okay. Um… then …I guess," I stammered as I began wringing my fingers on my lap, "You'll call me when you have everything set, right? Once the insurance is straightened out I mean, good luck with that. You will have a chance to look at the films?" I had just noticed the thin gown didn't feel like it covered enough skin. I couldn't seem to pull it tight enough around me. I shivered. I must have been cold. I wanted to pull on my clothes, layer upon layer, and get the hell out of there.

Taking my hand, Dr. -Be*droom Eyes- a*ssured, "As soon as I know, I will call, and we will go from there. We will get you to a specialist, if it's necessary. This isn't something we should wait on. The sooner we get a look the better. Okay?"

I gave an automatic nod and saw the nurse in the corner for the first time. When the hell did she come in? Had she been there the whole time? I didn't need her looking at me like that. I didn't need her pity, and she really needed to back off the red-orange lipstick. It was not her color.

"Can I go now?" I asked while averting my eyes to the extremely ugly linoleum floor.

"Of course, we will get in contact with you as soon as we have some answers," he nodded and dismissed himself from the room.

Nurse –Lipstick- patted my leg and cooed, "Take as much time as you need, sweetie."

Take as much time as I need? To do what, crochet a blanket? Sweetie? That's not very professional. I had a name. It was on the chart she held in her hand. Okay, Olivia, pull yourself together, girl. So, you have a couple of lumps. What are a few lumps? You got this.

I threw on my clothes as fast as I could. As I left the small examination room, it felt like the walk of shame, like I had been caught by the roommate as I snuck out of his buddy's bedroom after a night of sheet tangling. This walk wasn't worth it in the least. The

9

embarrassment and the events preceding my trudge for the exit were not nearly as fun.

I didn't know how long I sat in my little Versa in the parking lot. Si*tting on the Dock of the Bay by* Otis Redding vibrated through the speakers when I finally came to my senses. What now? Do I tell Tom? Do I tell our girls? I didn't have any answers. I didn't even have questions to get answers to, yet. I didn't even have a diagnosis, so maybe I should just keep it to myself for now. No reason to worry them, right? Man, I needed a drink.

I checked the time on the dashboard, "Crap," I am to meet my friends at The Pub for d*ip-n-drinks a*nd I had three minutes to get there. I grabbed my phone to call Trish.

"Hey, chick-a-licious."

"Hey, Liv, where you at?" chirped Trish. She and I had been friends for about six years. Hearing her voice took a bit of the panic that had been rising and shoved it to the back of my mind.

"Sorry, I'm on my way. Order me a mojito and don't eat all the damn dip. Is Alyssa there yet?"

"She called. She'll be here in like five minutes. You sayin' I'm a dip hoe?"

"Yup, that's what I'm sayin'. You be a dip hoe. I'll see you in a few."

I took a deep breath and shifted my car into first gear and then tried to leave the appointment and all it entailed behind in the dark recesses of the parking lot. The problem, I couldn't leave the evidence behind. The lumps went with me, everywhere. Paul McCartney invaded my space as Li*ve and Let Die w*rapped around me like a whisper through the speakers. I cranked it up and tried to let Wings wash away the afternoon's sour notes.

I had no idea how I got to The Pub. I guess auto-pilot is a real thing. I pulled up next to Trish's grime coated black Altima. God, didn't the woman know how to wash a car? Someone had begged her to do just that in the grime of her back window. It made me chuckle.

Alyssa pulled up as I got out of my car. She waved from behind the windshield. She seemed to be beaming. Can a person beam? Well, she was. Alyssa was the newest addition to our collection of crazy, but she seemed to be the missing piece we never knew we lost.

"Hey," I said as I waved, "I thought you would be here already," I said as I walked over to meet her. She was late and I needed details on the school girl grin she was sporting?

"Sorry, I got to talking with someone and lost track of time." I thought I heard a giggle in her voice.

"And..." I nudged.

She grabbed my elbow and pulled me closer, "You can't tell Trish. I mean it." The alarm in her eyes was enough for me to agree. "I met someone," Alyssa whispered as a shy smile slipped across her lips.

"OMG," I about burst.

"Shhhhh."

"Shit, sorry. Who, where, when, how hot...spill," I salivated.

"Later. We can't leave Trish in there by herself. She'll get us banned from another restaurant for being too rowdy," she laughed. Alyssa tried to avoid my insistent look to once again show she was the reasonable one.

"Ugh, fine, but I want all the details, all of them. Not the PG13 version either, 'k? I want all the dirty deets."

Alyssa rolled her eyes, "Of course, Liv, I will spill."

We linked arms and bounced to the door of the restaurant like two teenagers who just found out a boy liked one of us. We found Trish sitting in the bar area facing the door with the sole purpose of seeing us when we came in.

"What the hell took you guys so long? I almost ate all the dip," Trish grinned while a chip dripping with cheesy deliciousness hung in front of her mouth.

Looking at each other we both blurted, "Traffic." Secretive grins crossed our faces as we took our seats at the table. Realizing we were going to need more dip, I waved to get the waitress's attention. They knew us here, all too well. We had been having "dip-n-drinks" night once a week for nearly a year now. With a swirl of my hand over the dip platter, I mouthed "more" and I knew the order was in.

"So, what's up in the wild world of Trish?" I threw out there, knowing she would keep the focus on her and off me and Alyssa, at least for a little while. "How'd the interview go?"

"Hell, I rocked it," Trish shared while reaching for her beer. "You know how it is. I get nearly every job I interview for. My problem is keeping the damn thing."

It was true. She interviewed well, but couldn't seem to hang on to a position longer than a year. She would be on her best behavior for a few weeks and then the outspoken, can't-keep–her–opinion-to-herself side would creep out and bite the first person it saw. Normally it was the person who told her to do something she thought was below her skill level. She didn't understand the concept of making an effort. Nope, she saw it as I was hired to do "ABC," not "XYZ." If it wasn't in her job description, then it was not her job to do. Therefore, she would be let go to find a position best suited to her personality.

Through crunches of chips, Trish sputtered, "I should hear something in a few days."

"What's the interview for?" Alyssa asked as she reached for a chip before Trish could get to it and hoovered it into her mouth.

"Bitch," Trish sneered. "It's a phone bank for a car insurance company, basically I'd be answering questions about claims and shit."

"Well, that sounds boring as hell. But it beats not working," I offered with a snort. "I haven't worked in a little over a year."

Alyssa looked at me with support in her eyes. "True, but you just earned your degree. It can only help when you are out there looking again."

"I can hope for the best, but a degree in the easiest classes a community college offers will get you nowhere. You have to take into consideration, I am 42 and you're 31. Big difference when a company considers hiring someone. The older I get, the harder it will be to find a good job I will love."

"Ain't that the truth?" Trish chimed in while spinning her beer bottle in front of her. "I'm older than Liv, better looking, but older," she smirked, "and I'm still looking for the one company that'll see how awesome I am and look past everything else."

—

I could see this whole work thing bugged her. I knew better than trying to tell her why she couldn't seem to hold a job. She would take it as an attack and not as a friend trying to help.

"Then why don't you start that business you've been talking about for the past five frickin' years? You have dreamt of having your own travel agency, what the hell is holding you back? You're smart, motivated, and bitch enough to pull it off," I stated as the fresh batch of dip arrived. Yummy, it was steamy, bubbly, and screaming for me to dig in. Oh, did I mention it was frickin' HOT?

"Holy crap, holy crap, holy crap," I sputtered as I was dumb enough to have scooped up scalding hot dip and dropped it into my mouth. I proceeded to suck down half my mojito in the attempt to cool my tongue, letting an ice cube soothe the burn.

Alyssa shook her head at my stupidity, "You do that every time. When are you going to learn? If it's steaming and too hot to touch, then you don't shove it in your face," explained Alyssa, in her 'I am talking to a five-year-old' voice while she attempted to stifle a laugh.

"I wanted to make sure I got some before Trish moved in on it," I whined while sticking my tongue out in hopes the cool air would help. It didn't.

"Shut up, it's not like I was circling it like a pack of wolves," Trish whimpered with her lower lip stuck out in a mock pout, raising her eyebrows in my direction.

Our fun-loving taunts went on for another hour and a half before we declared the successful completion of this week's "dip-n-drinks" night. I wish I could say the reality of what was literally sitting in my chest left my mind, but it would be a lie. I felt comfortable lying to myself, at least for a little while. It was time for us to return to our respective lives. We settled up the bill as we usually did. We each threw down twenty bucks, knowing the balance was well below the $60 lying on the table. This offered our waitress/waiter a good tip for putting up with us. We always made it well worth their efforts.

As we said our "goodbyes" with quick hugs in the parking lot, I knew Trish was on her way home to her husband and twin boys. I was on my way home to Tom and my girls and Alyssa was headed home to her dog and maybe this new Mr. Mysterious, which I had to find out more about. As I hugged Alyssa, I reminded her she had some spilling to do and I would be calling. With final waves we got into our vehicles and we were off, each going in different directions.

I felt good about my decision to not say anything about the doctor's appointment to the girls. Alyssa would have tried to reassure me that there was nothing to worry about, and Trish would have gone ape shit crazy while we tried to calm her down. Instead, I got to spend an hour and a half of not focusing on the "what ifs." The question then was should I tell my family? I was thinkin' no. I thought I should wait until I had something to actually tell them. Right then, I had nothing more than a few questions and two lumps. Maybe I should have named the little fuckers, so they didn't seem so menacing, "Thing One" and "Thing Two," or "Righty" and "Lefty," or "Chunk" and "Lumpy?" I felt a small smile slowly creep across my face, and I willingly let it take over. As I pulled into our driveway, I decided it was nothing to worry about until it became something to worry about.

Tom held the door as I stepped onto the porch, "Hey, babe, how were the twin tornadoes?" he asked with a smile and a kiss.

"Ya know, one of these days I am gonna tell 'em you call 'em that," I smiled as I poked him in the ribs. "They are fine. Trish had another job interview, but that's pretty normal." I *love this man. Have I mentioned that yet? I do.*

I tossed my purse onto the entry way table and moved through the house to the kitchen. "Did you and the girls eat, or do you need me to make you something?"

"Lily is around here somewhere, but Shelly got called in to work earlier so I don't know when she will be home," he mumbled with his head in the refrigerator.

"Okay, but you didn't answer my question. Do you want me to make you something?"

"If you want, I won't talk you out of it," he responded with his best cheesy grin.

"I think I have some burger thawed. Do sliders sound good, or do you want something else?"

"Oh no, sliders would be awesome. How about some coleslaw to go on top and baked beans and..." he stopped as he saw the look of annoyance on my face. "What? You asked me what I wanted."

14

I shrugged my shoulders, "True. I did. So, sliders and all the trappings it is. Can you see if Lily wants some too, please?"

As I started to gather up the ingredients for dinner, I heard Tom yell up the stairs, "Hey, Lil, you want sliders for dinner or what?"

A few seconds later, I found Tom leaning on the island with an ice tea. "It looks like we are having sliders with the kid."

"Sounds good, can you help?" I asked as I sat a large onion on the counter in front of him, "Here, cut up the onion while I start the sliders."

He rolled the offending stink bomb back towards me, "How about I *do* the burgers and yo*u do* the onion," he quipped.

What is it with guys? They can kill and gut an animal, but refuse to cut up vegetables. "Fine, if it will make you feel manlier, then go for it."

A look of satisfaction spread across his face, like he won something. I didn't know what he thought he won, 'cause if he messed up the burgers then I got to pick on him every time he wanted to grill something, and I would.

The unmistakable sound of a teenager bounding down the stairs reached my ears as Lily rounded the corner into the kitchen.

"Sup, female parental unit?" she asked as she snagged a soda from the refrigerator.

"Sup? Now I know why your English grades were what they were," I teased as I smiled into those beautiful brown eyes.

Lily was one of a kind, and she would tell you so without thinking twice. She declared herself a we*irdy*. She was artsy, quirky, and sweet to a fault. Her long dark hair and deep brown eyes pulled you in. She had a dark beauty I liked to think she got from me. She guarded herself from outsiders, but once you broke through the barriers you would find her only fault, absolute loyalty. I worried about her sometimes. I feared someone would see her wonderful, loving and trusting heart, and destroy it without knowing. She was pretty, but didn't see it for herself, smart as a whip, when she tried, and had the ability to make you laugh no matter how bad your day had been. I was blessed to be her mom.

"What are you up to tonight, young lady?" I queried as I sliced the onion while trying not to cry.

"The 'boy toy', as you like to call him, will be here in a little while, and we are going to study for an English test. I guess I should put my best stuff on it since you think my grammar sucks. Oh, wait a second. Didn't I just graduate from high school? That's right, I did. I be ed-gu-ma-kaded," she concluded with a smirk.

"So you is," I chuckled, "Grab the bag of coleslaw for me and a can of the baked beans from the pantry."

"Yes, mother," she said in its most proper form. I was amazed she didn't slap a little English accent on it and curtsy. "Darren is coming over to hang out for a while. We will probably watch a movie or something"

"Well, that sounds...not very thrilling at all."

Dropping the items I asked for on the island, Lily proceeded to help me make dinner. Bowls, spoons, mayo and seasonings piled up as we created our masterpieces. I looked out the window overlooking the deck where I saw Tom removing the burgers from the grill.

"Hey, Lil, is it me or do those sliders look a little dark?"

"Crap on a stick, Dad."

"What?" Tom puzzled as he pushed open the door carrying a plate of something resembling bark.

Lily's eyes bugged as she looked at the shriveled disks of meat, "Those look more like rejected hockey pucks. What the heck did you do to them, use a flame thrower?" she taunted. They were burnt, really, really burnt.

"Hey, I just wanted to make sure they were safe for my family to eat. I wouldn't want you to end up with mad cow disease or something."

"We appreciate your undying devotion to your family." Lily said with an over exaggerated bow. "I am so sorry we are such a hardship and a burden for you to bear, oh great and wondrous father o'mine."

"Damn right, and you all would do well to remember it," Tom nodded in agreement with a satisfied grin on his face and arms crossed over his chest.

"All right, we get it. Now set the table, will ya? Does anyone know when Shell is due home?" I wondered out loud. "Will she be home for dinner?"

"Why, yes, I will," Shell sang walking through the back door. "Did you miss me? I know you did. What's for dinner, and what is that God-awful smell?" she asked as her nose twitched at the offending odor.

"Oh, that? It would be Dad's poor attempt at sliders," Lily snorted.

Shell admonished her dad as she offered him a hug, "Aw, Tubs, you ruined the sliders? It is a sad, sad day in the Carpenter house for sure."

"Okay, Uggo, I'd like to see you do better."

"I work at Burger King. Duh, Tubs," Shell quipped as she stuck out her tongue.

"Okay, guys, dinner is on the table. We can torment your dad while we eat his charcoal briquette burgers. I guess you should have sliced the onion like I suggested to begin with." I winked at Tom. I knew he tried, but missed, and I would never let him live it down.

We all took our seats, and within seconds Shell proceeded to regale us with tales of her work antics, which included her co-workers and the ridiculous rudeness of customers. She was such an animated character. She opened all her stories with, "So get this," and barely took a breath until her tale was done. I have to be clear here, she was not asking for advice in anything she said. She just wanted to share the activities of her day. She was our sixteen-year-old spit fire. So active, she ran in her sleep. Shell was the polar opposite of Lily in every way, blonde, blue eyed, vivacious, and as strong as they come. Be warned, if you looked anywhere but her eyes while you were talking to her, she would rip your face off without blinking twice. The only real thing I worried about with Shell was making sure we had enough money set aside for bail. She was something else. She was another blessing to count in my world.

"I asked my supervisor for more hours over the summer. I told him to call me first if someone calls off or doesn't show, so I can buy my own car. I'm sick of having to share," Shell snipped. "I hate having to schedule when I can have the car, especially when I don't know if I'm gonna get called in to work."

"Sounds good to me, that means I get the car all to myself," Lily smirked between bites.

Leaning back in his chair and taking a deep breath, Tom questioned the situation. "Hold the phone there, girls. Lil, what makes you think you would get free reign of the car if Shell buys her own? I don't think that sounds very fair."

Pointing out the facts, Lily stated, "Hey, she's the one who wants to get her own car. I'm cool with the way things are."

"It would also mean you couldn't leach off of the gas I put in the car. When was the last time you filled the tank, Lil?"

With a chuckle and sarcastically sweet smile, Lily rolled out, "Sucks to be you. Why should I put gas in the car if you are more than willing to do it, duh?"

Watching my family joke and argue about such minor things made me fear how they may handle something big, really big. Like, lumpy big. The discussion ended as dinner did, with no real resolution. We all gathered up the leftovers and carried them back into the kitchen to be put away. We cleaned up the mess and loaded the dishwasher in a matter of minutes. We made short work of a menial task, and then we scattered to the four winds, or at least the four corners, of the house. Lily was with Darren, Shell was texting everyone in the known universe and probably a few unknown. Tom was channel surfing like a pro, and I escaped into the shower.

Climbing into the tub I felt the hot water roll over my head and shoulders. I selected the shampoo and began the ritual of washing my hair. I tended to start at the top and work my way down.

I felt them. How could I have ignored them for so long? How could I have pushed aside the events of the day? I ran my hand over one lump, then the other. They were nothing, right? They were just some extra bits of me, right? Kind of like the cellulite that attached itself to my ass, or the unexplainable goat hair that kept creeping out of my chin. Just a couple more flaws were all they were. Why couldn't I stop touching them then? The door opened.

Tom sauntered in and pulled the curtain open with a flourish which would one day rip down the vinyl screen. "Hey, baby," he addressed me with a wink, his fists on his hips. He turned his head to the side and puffed out his chest like the character on a Captain Morgan ad, "I'm checking to see if you need any help washing those hard to reach places. You know quality control and all." He announced with bouncing eyebrows and a wink, he eyed me from my toes to my nose.

"I'm pretty sure I have it under control, but thanks for the offer."

"You sure? I'm a body man after all. I could feel for imperfections in your chassis."

"Imperfections?" I shrieked, "Wow, how does your foot taste? Was there a bit of toe jam in there for flavor? You sure stuck it in your mouth pretty damn quick...and almost all the way up to the knee." He dropped his head in shame.

"Shit, I guess that means I get to go watch TV, doesn't it?"

I nodded my head as I reached for the soap. Tom left in a sulk I knew wasn't real, but whiney none the less. I ran a quick razor over the areas that called for it, and washed the rest of me, all the while making sure to avoid the two things that were hard to miss. I got out and wrapped a big fluffy towel around my body and twisted one turban style around my head. Pulling my pajamas from the drawer, I sat on the edge of the bed and lost myself in a daze of nothingness. No thoughts, just staring at some unseen spot on the wall.

"Hello again, wife, how's you?"

"Hello husband," I blinked into awareness, "I is good, you?"

Flopping back onto the bed and resting his head on the palm of a bent arm, Tom said, "Not bad, not bad at all. What great adventures did you go on today?"

"Same shit, different day. You know, I ran to the grocery store, post office, bank, doctor's appointment, and took Oliver to the vet." I rattled off in no particular order. I shrugged my shoulders as if to say it was all no big deal.

Perking up a bit, he asks, "What's up with the Lolly Monster?"

Wow, he heard vet but not doctor. Should I be offended? "Nothing, he was due for his shots and a physical. Hey, speaking of Oliver, can you tell Lily it is her turn to take care of the litter box," I asked as I bent over to buff my hair with a towel.

"Why me?" he whined. "You know she is gonna pop a cork when I tell her. I don't wanna," he sniveled and stomped his feet like a child.

With my jaw hanging slack, I stared at him in disbelief. "Good Lord, man, how old are you?"

"Twelve, and if you ever wonder in the future, I am perpetually twelve."

"You definitely know how to act twelve."

He exited the room to go torment our daughter with chores as I finished climbing into my pj's. Throwing on a robe, I strolled out to the living room to stare at the idiot box for a little while. Yeah, T*een Wolf* was on. At least I was guaranteed an hour of thought-free entertainment. After an hour or so, I decided to give it up and go to bed. I hoped to collapse into sleep the moment I climbed into bed, and I did just that.

I can't say I had a restful sleep, but it was sleep none the less.

Chapter Two

Normally waking up to Tom wrapped around me would have been a pleasant arousal, pun intended, but that morning it felt a bit much.

"Hey, hey, it's time to get up," he whispered while slapping my butt.

"Why? What time is it," I mumbled into my pillow.

"Don't you wanna go to the gym? Its 6:00, time to hop to it, Skippy."

I snarled as I rolled over and wrapped the bedspread around me like a burrito. "I have all day to go to the frickin' gym. Do you want me to work on those imperfections you referred to last night?" I mumbled into my pillow.

"Fine, if you don't want to go to the gym then don't. We could work out right here, right now if you wanna play." Sliding his hand up my leg he groped my ass.

"No," I snapped with a weak kick in his general direction.

"You're no fun."

"Nope."

With that, he swung himself up and out of bed in a huff. In the noisiest way possible, he got dressed for work. Yanking open the accordion closet doors, slamming drawers, dropping boots, turning on lights, doing anything and everything to ensure I didn't go back to sleep. Jerk. He succeeded, but I refused to unfold myself from my cocoon until he had left for work. I was not going to give him the satisfaction of knowing he got me up. I laid there listening to the events of the morning unfold. I smelled the coffee, heard the rattle of the condiments on the refrigerator door, the rustling of Tom's lunch bag, looking to see what I'd packed, probably adding more cookies, and then the backdoor. I listened for the garage door, then the truck as it backed out, and then... I got up. I shuffled down to the kitchen to pour a much needed cup of coffee. The best invention in the world was the timer for the coffee pot. It was so nice to know I didn't have to wait to brew a pot in the morning. There it was, waiting to hug me with its aroma and warmth. Wow, where did that sappiness come from? It's just coffee.

Moving on, I munched a bowl of cereal and a banana to energy up for my trip to the gym which I really wasn't mentally up for. Drinking down the last of the milk in the bowl, yes I did that, I rinsed my dishes and loaded them into the dishwasher. A concept everyone I lived with hadn't figured out how to do yet. I quickly made the bed and dug around in my dresser to find some shorts and a t-shirt. I have boobs and not little ones, so to prevent a nasty black eye I donned an underwire bra and then pulled a sports bra on over it. It may have seemed like overkill to most women, but those of us who packed higher than a "C" know what we are doing. As I pulled on my tank, I wondered if I would have this problem in the future. I shook the thought from my head and pulled on my t-shirt. The goal was to sweat, and it's what I planned on doing. Shorts, socks, and thoroughly broken in sneakers were thrown on as I picked up my phone to call Trish to make sure her lazy ass was up and heading to the gym.

Three rings, four and, "What?"

"Is that any way to answer the phone when a friend calls? Get up on the wrong side of the bed this morning?" I inquired, but clearly I already knew the answer.

"You're lucky I answered at all," she mumbled, "What do you want, Liv? I am in no mood for your crap."

"Well, fine then. I called to see if you were gonna make it to the gym, but I'm guessing you are in no mood for that either, right?" Bi*tch*.

"Shit. I forgot. Richard and I had a rough night, and I didn't get a whole hell of a lot of sleep."

"Clearly," I bitched. "You paid for this membership and these sessions with the trainer."

"I know. Okay... um..., give me twenty and I'll be there. What time does it start this morning anyway?"

I looked over at my alarm clock, "In a half hour, so if you get to it you will make it with time to spare."

"Fine, but I am doing this begrudgingly."

"Really, I hadn't noticed. See you at the gym."

"See ya, bye," and Trish hung up before I could say another word.

She and Richard were a volatile mix. She wanted to do what she wanted to do, and he wanted her to do what he wanted her to do. They couldn't agree on wh*at* *s*he should be doing. They both wanted control over the same thing, her. The first time I met him it was clear we were not going to get along:

"Hi, *I'm Olivia, but everyone calls me Liv," I offered my hand to Trish's husband in greeting.*

"*My name is Richard and that is what I expect everyone to call me," he replied with a glare, while completely avoiding the hand I had extended to him. "If I were meant to go by another name then my parents would have given it to me."*

Douche. From that meeting on I referred to him as "Richard Noggin," otherwise known as "Dick Head," if you couldn't follow the pun. I wished I could say other meetings had gone better, but sadly it was not the case. He had been a jackass at every turn. Trish said he believed I was a bad influence on her because I spoke my mind too freely. I "didn't know my place." Well, brace yourself ass monkey. I have my own thoughts, feelings, and beliefs, and what were you gonna do about it? Nah-na-na-na-na-nah. Jerk face.

That little mental snit got me ready for a workout. I loaded my towel, water bottle and pass key in my gym bag and scurried out the door. I whipped into the parking area less than six minutes later. I could have walked, but I knew I would be too tired for the return trip after my workout. As I walked across the parking lot, I saw a car waiting for another to vacate a parking space because it was closer to the gym door. Are you so lazy you had to park at the door of the gym? No wonder a third of the country is fat. Then I saw the driver. My trainer. Are you kidding me? I shook my head in disbelief and went inside. The smell of cleaner and sweat invaded my nostrils the moment I crossed the threshold. I could see the bulgy anatomy of the body builders at the back of the gym eyeing themselves in the wall of mirrors. Yes, *those are overworked muscles that look like they want to pop off your body and run away.* I was all for a well-formed, Adonis-type, male body, but it seemed a bit much and for heaven's sake, back off the tanning beds. Their nuts had to look like raisins, shriveled, or maybe they resembled the slider's Tom grilled to death the night before.

I jumped on a treadmill and started to warm up while I waited for Trish and our trainer, Veronica. Just as my mind started to wonder to the shadow that hung, well, around my chest, Trish showed up. Her timing was spot on. It was just in time to start working with Veronica, who began barking orders at us the moment the clock ticked over to our paid time. It appeared she and Trish both got up on the wrong side of the bed, and I had the honor of suffering for it. Veronica barked orders and Trish mouthed back, and I was sweating, trying to keep up. By the end of the session, I wanted to vomit and crawl into the nearest hole and Trish was ready for more.

"Come on, let's get on the elliptical and do a couple miles," Trish insisted.

"I can't. I can barely stand. I did fifteen minutes on the treadmill before you got here," I moaned while bending over and leaning on my thighs for support. I felt a wave of nausea flow through me. Luckily it didn't make an exit.

"Ya big baby."

"I'm aware of my mistake. You are exercising out of anger, so you have more stamina then I do. If you want to stay, then by all means, stay. I, on the other hand, am going home, taking a shower, vomiting again, and then dying on my couch." I crossed over to Veronica and checked the schedule for our next meeting. She was still very cranky, and I made her aware of it. Shit, people, don't take your bad day out on me. I waved to Trish as I made a bee-line for the door. I was glad I lived so close to the gym because otherwise I might have puked in the car. I made it home before the dam broke, and I got to revisit breakfast. Was it the trainer's way to guarantee weight loss? They tell you to eat breakfast, only to work you out to a point of getting sick. So, is it that you get to keep the nourishment of whatever your body was able to digest up to that point, and then the rest has to go? It seemed like a waste of good food, but I was not a trainer. I was a squishy, middle aged woman who wanted body parts to stop wiggling, like the bingo wings attached to my upper arms. You know what I'm talking about. When you wave to a friend and the fat on your upper arms continues to wave after you stopped, those are bingo wings. The flapping reminded me of the old women at the church bingo hall. When they would win, they would yell "bingo" and wave their arms in the air, flapping their wings.

The image still makes me laugh.

I should have taken a shower, but in hindsight, I think I may have been avoiding it. Besides, it would have been pointless. I had chores I could do outside first. I slipped out the back door and went to gather up a bucket of birdseed to fill the feeders. I unfurled the hose to water all the flowers and plants we spent so much time and money putting in. We were in the middle of a dry spell. It was so bad the cacti were dying. I swore I could see them coughing dust. I washed out the birdbath and filled it with fresh cool water and then sprayed off my car. What the hell, I was out there and I had the hose. I did come to realize when you could smell yourself, it was a bad thing. I wrapped up the hose and went in. I kicked my wet shoes off at the door and proceeded to trip over the cat.

"Shit, Oliver," I cursed as I tried to regain my footing, "Out." I held the door and waited what seemed like twenty minutes before he made up his mind to go. Then the big orange fur ball ran for cover like he was being chased by an imaginary dog. He is lucky cats have nine lives because I had wanted to kill him at least seven times over the years. I went to my room to gather some clean clothes and made my way to the shower, picking up Tom's dirty clothes along the way. I did a quick check of his pockets before I threw his laundry in the hamper. I found two bolts, a candy bar wrapper, and some change. Just what the old washing machine needed, more crap to bang around in it. Man, I was cranky. Why? Was it the gym? Trish's shitty attitude or maybe it was revisiting breakfast? Maybe it was wondering about...everything? I threw away the bolts and the wrapper, put the change on the sink and stepped into the shower. As usual, I started at the top and worked my way down. I showered quickly, skimmed over the lingering questions. Once dry, hair blown out, clean clothes on, I checked my phone to see what I had to do that day. Opening the calendar, I saw I had to get the oil changed, buy a birthday card for a friend, and return two books to the library. It would keep me busy for about 8.2 seconds. Then what? Climb inside my own head and drive myself crazy? Sounded like a plan.

I dropped the car off at the dealership to have the oil changed. That gave me about a half hour to walk over to the little strip mall across the parking lot to find the birthday card I needed and drop off the books I had borrowed but never read. I did it all the time. I checked out books with good intentions, but I liked tv too much to give it up for a dusty book. Besides, if the book was any good, they would make it into a movie, right? I would watch it. So, either way, I would know what the book was about without ever cracking the spine. I could justify anything if given a minute to think about it even if I was wrong.

Checking my watch, I saw it had been over forty minutes, so I made my way back to the dealership. My Versa sat by the service bay, so I went in, settled up, gathered my keys, and headed for home, quick and painless. On my way home I passed by Dr. -Nice Ass's- office. Why hadn't they called me yet? Maybe because it had been less than a day, Mrs. -I am so important I deserve special treatment-. Breathe. You would get the answers as soon as they had them to give. It was only Wednesday, if I didn't hear something by Friday, I would call and ask. Plan set, now move on.

Have you ever noticed how time slows to a crawl when you are waiting for something? Like when we were kids and Christmas seemed as if it would never come, and the last 24 hours were the worst. Well, that's how I felt. Except I knew I was not going to like what happened in the end. There weren't going to be any brightly covered packages for me to open. I was trying to keep myself busy.

I scrubbed our bathroom from ceiling to floor, reorganized the linen closet, dusted, and vacuumed. I even refolded sheets. The right way. Do you know how long that takes? Geesh. Still, only a few hours had gone by. So, I grabbed my purse and keys and hit the grocery store. I knew what would keep me busy, making spinach lasagna rolls for dinner. That would kill a few more hours. I ran the gambit of the store, and loaded up the cart with the ingredients I would need to make my family's favorite dinner. I bought stuff for a large tossed salad and garlic bread, too. Dessert? Hmm, but of course, but what to make? Cake, Tom loved cake. What kind of cake? Do you have any idea the number of combinations of cake you can make? I think I spent more time deciding cake and frosting for this one dinner than I did on my wedding dress. I wandered around and stood in the chip isle forever. Do you have any idea how many types of chips there are? Not just potato, but chips in general. A lot. There are a lot. I finally made it to the check-out where I waited reading the glaring front pages of the tabloids while pretending not to read them. I have never bought one. I have never witnessed a purchase of one either. I was too good, in my own head, to buy them or maybe too embarrassed to admit I wanted too. Yup, that's the reason. Chicken.

I loaded my groceries into the car and eyed the liqueur store across the street. Hmm, maybe I would pick up some wine. For whom, Tom and me? No, it would just be a waste of good wine or bad wine. I didn't know the difference either way. I had enough to keep me busy. I didn't need to get tanked on top of it. I went home to start the laborious job I had elected to do. By four that afternoon, I had the salad made, cake cooling, garlic bread ready to bake, and lasagna spirals in the baking dish ready to hit the oven when everyone made it home for dinner. Now what? Shell went to work while I was gone and Lily was...who knew? I decided to send the girls a text to let them know about the massive dinner menu I planned to eat away more time:

Lily, Shell: Hey, I wanted to let you know I have a regular banquet ready for dinner. When you gonna be home?

Lily responded first, letting me know she was hanging out with friends and would be home by six. Shell followed by telling me she got off work at 6:15. Cool, that meant everyone would be home for dinner. What could I do for two hours? Crap. Ummmmm... my phone rang. Saved by the bell or should I say, saved by Alyssa.

I loved that girl. We met nearly two years before when I had been laid-off and unemployment was running out for me. Tom and I had talked and decided I should look into going back to school. It had always been my dream, but life, and its many obstacles, got in my way. We didn't know if we could actually pull it off. Paying for college was going to be the main hurdle. I met Alyssa in the Financial Aid office. She had the honor of being the counselor I talked to about following my dreams, and she helped clear the path for me to do it by finding grants and scholarships. Not only did she help find funds to cover courses and books, but also managed to get me a little extra cash the first semester to buy a computer and a Kindle in my third semester. Needless to say, Alyssa was the angel everyone looked for, but I was lucky to have found her. To thank her for that first semester the best way I knew how, I brought her homemade chicken and dumplings and cookies for lunch. That sealed it. We were friends from then on. Whenever classes and her schedule allowed, we would have lunch together somewhere, anywhere: in the Commons, on the grounds somewhere, or down the road at one of the many fast food joints. She preferred to spend her lunch break as far away from the Financial Aid office as possible. Even during holidays or summer breaks I would pop in with lunch to share with her from time to time.

"Hey woman, what's up?" Caller I.D. rocked.

"Not much. I figured you would have called last night to interrogate me about my guy," Alyssa said sarcastically.

"How was I supposed to know if he was, for lack of a better term, v*isiting y*ou last night," I offered as defense.

"Good point, and he did come over later." I could hear the smile in her voice.

"Okay, so spill. Who is he? How'd you meet him? Where does he work? How hot is he? You know all the good stuff."

"God, calm down before you give yourself a coronary."

"Shut up, I've been married for forever. Take pity on me, will ya? This is the closest I get to fooling around," I whined.

"All right, geesh, well his name's Neil and get this: he's a doctor. Can you believe it, a doctor? I am seeing a doctor," she squealed into the phone. I had to yank the phone away from my ear before she burst an eardrum.

"You're kidding, a real, honest to goodness doctor?" I sounded shocked. Why was I shocked? She was very pretty and extremely smart. Why shouldn't she bag, or bang, a doctor?

"Yup, a living, breathing doctor," she said coolly. "I met him at work. Neil came in to do a class for the nursing students about two weeks ago. We met in the cafeteria lunch line. It's kind of odd because you know I never eat in the cafeteria. Anyway, he was behind me in line, and we started chatting. By the time we checked out with our plates, we were in a full-on conversation and just sat down together. It was so different from any of the other guys I've dated," Alyssa said with wonder.

"No kidding. Normally it involves some guy buying you a drink and you thinking you have to sleep with him to thank him for the $4 purchase."

"You make it sound like I'm a slut."

"Are you trying to say it's not true," I taunted.

"I didn't say that. I am just amazed you actually said it." Thankfully she had a giggle in her voice or I would have been in deep shit.

"Shocking, I know. Have you slept with him yet?"

"Yes, last night. I guess taking anatomy class has its benefits in the bedroom. WooHoo. I didn't have to fake anything. It was all real and all awesome."

"I guess it's a good thing I didn't call. Does he give classes? You know tutorials for the 'not so talented' or 'lacking something' guy out there?"

I told her I was happy for her and she deserved to be happy. I warned her I would be asking a lot more questions. We laughed and joked a bit longer, and planned to have lunch the following day. Sadly, Dr. Neil would not be joining us. I would have to remember to ask if Neil was his first or last name.

Tom came home while I was on the phone. He reeked of old motor oil and gas when he leaned in to kiss me "Hello," then just as quickly exited to hose off. Just one of the many joys of working in the automotive repair business, not only did you get the stench but ruined clothes too. The girls would be home soon, so I put the lasagna in the oven and set the timer. I set the table, gathered all the necessities for salad, the fresh grated parmesan, and warm bread.

By the time the buzzer went off, everyone was already gathered around the table chattering about what they had done during the day. Dinner was enjoyed to its fullest extent, and just knowing there was a chocolate cake sitting on the counter kept Tom grinning.

"What's the occasion? Did I miss the memo," Tom asked while eyeing the cake in lust.

"Occasion? No, I was kind of bored, and I knew this would keep me busy for a while," and keep my mind off of things that were going to drive me bat-shit crazy.

Maybe I should have told him.

"You should get bored more often," garbled Shell with a mouth full of garlic bread. "I love this stuff."

"Ain't that the truth," agreed Lily.

It didn't take much to make my crew happy, good food and cake. Cake was Tom's favorite food group. I remembered a conversation we had many years ago that still made me smile.

"I want my headstone to say 'He Ate Cake'," announced Tom while stuffing another bite into his mouth. He didn't even cut a slice and put it on a plate. He was eating directly from the cake dish. He explained how it was pointless to dirty another dish when he might eat the whole damn thing. The sad thing was, he just might, and it wouldn't be the first time.

I chuckled and pointed out, "You have never been one to turn away cake, even bad cake."

"Hey, cake is cake. It's like sex. Even bad pizza is still pizza."

How could you argue with that? He had a logic all his own.

When we had eaten way too much and were stuffed to the gills, we cleared the table, scraped and rinsed the dishes, put things away, and loaded the dishwasher. God, I loved how they all rallied to get it done. What would have easily taken me an hour or more we managed in a matter of minutes. I wondered how they would rally in other situations, real Earth shaking situations.

Our evening progressed like any other Wednesday. Lily was getting ready to go hang out with the boy toy. Shell didn't have to work the next day, so she was making plans to spend the night with her friend, and God only knew what those two would be up to. This left Tom and I sitting in our respective spots in the living room watching animated stupidity dance across the screen. I often wondered how he could possibly enjoy that crap, but I was reminded by his uproarious laughter that he did. I found a magazine and blindly flipped through it. I don't think I actually looked at anything on the shiny pages. Ugh, I wished I could shut off my brain, or at least choose a different topic to focus on, like winning the lottery, shopping for clothes in a smaller size, or having a root canal. Nope, I focused on lumpy boobs. My debasement was interrupted by Tom trying to get my attention.

"Pssst."

With a brow raised in a "what in the hell do you want" slant I asked, "What?"

"Have you noticed the girls are gone? That means there is no one here but us," he whispered while a mischievous grin slid across his face.

"I am well aware that if they aren't here, then we are alone."

"So... you wanna?"

"Seriously, is this your idea of foreplay?"

"Yup."

I quickly jumped to my feet, startling Tom a bit, and hit the floor running to our room. I heard his thunderous foot steps behind me as I started to giggle. I dove on the bed, pulled the covers up to my nose, and watched over the edge of the sheet as he entered the room. He puffed up his chest and did ridiculous body builder moves in the door way.

"That's right. You want me. You can admit it."

"Like the plague baby, like the plague," I teased.

He closed the door with a flourish. I am leaving you outside wondering what we were up to. Hey, this wasn't Fifty Shades of Grey for goodness sake. Perv.

Twenty minutes later we found ourselves naked at the breakfast bar dunking Oreos into large glasses of milk. It's all good. He was relaxed, and I thought I might sleep that night because of our…not love making so much…what did Tom call it… "Monkey fucking." Yup, sweaty, loud, and fast, maybe a bit too fast, but hey, what could you do about it? I guessed it was like Tom's feelings towards cake, even bad sex was sex.

I broke the silence by stating, "We need a bigger bed."

"What's wrong with the one we have?" he asked between a bite of cookie and sip of milk.

"It's a double bed. I thought something a little bigger would give us more room to move around. Don't you want more room?"

"I don't have a problem with this one. Besides, the way I see it, it's like a gold fish and its tank. Gold fish will only grow to the capacity of the tank, the bigger the tank, the bigger the goldfish."

"Excuse me," I sputtered. "Are you trying to tell me the only reason you won't break down and get a bigger bed is so I won't get fat?"

"When you put it like that it sounds bad, but I was thinking of you, babe." He desperately tried to back pedal. I thought I saw a trickle of sweat running down his temple.

"Well, babe, I want to help you stay thin too, so I recommend you sleep in your recliner for a while. It is much smaller than our bed, and should ensure you don't become a bigger ass than you already are," I declared with annoyance and a bit of humor.

"I fucked up."

"Ya think? That is an understatement." I finished my last cookie and downed my milk as he did the same. He took the glasses, rinsed them, and put them in the sink. It was proof he was sorry for being a dumbass, by doing some menial labor as a form of ass kissing. I smiled at him, took his hand, and led him back to the bedroom. I went in to the bathroom to brush my teeth and smear on some *youth in a jar to* get ready for bed. He had pulled out his clothes for the next day and laid them on the chair in the corner. It was yet another way to pucker up and kiss my hiney. That way he wouldn't wake me in the morning when he got ready for work. I sighed with satisfaction and climbed into bed.

"You could have been romantical and said something like, I like the smaller bed because it means you are closer to me. Now that might have gotten you laid again tonight. Oh well, your loss." I rolled over and took the covers with me.

He cursed under his breath and rolled to put his arm over me and admitted, "Sorry, babe. I'm an ass."

"Love you, too. Night, babe," I whispered as he nuzzled his head down into his pillow.

Within minutes I felt his steady breathing on my neck and his heartbeat against my back. I wished I could fall asleep as quickly. My brain refused to shut off.

Chapter Three

I couldn't sleep. After the fourth time my eyes popped open I called it quits and climbed out of bed as carefully as I could. I didn't want to wake Tom from whatever dream he was having that plastered a goofy smile on his face. Slipping out of the room, the clock read 3:52 a.m. Great, I was gonna be a hot mess all day. I shuffled my way into the kitchen. It was too early for the coffee pot to have woken up, unlike me, so I opted for a cup of tea instead. I filled the kettle, grabbed a cup, a tea bag, and sat and waited for the whistle to blow. With tea in hand I moved toward the computer.

Should I have done this? Would I just make myself crazier than I am already? I had to know what I could be getting into. I fired up my computer and hoped for the best. Do I Google it or WebMD? I typed "breast lumps" into Google and soooo many pages came up. Some gave me hope that these were nothing more than cysts or maybe an infection, but in the back of my mind I was trying to be realistic. As much as I wanted them to be nothing more than an annoyance, I knew they were more, much, much more. With reality rearing its ugly head, I looked up "biopsy of breast lump" and read about my options, if it was needed. Fine-needle aspiration biopsy, Core needle biopsy, Vacuum-assisted core biopsy, Open (surgical) biopsy...Holy Shit-balls, Batman. Okay Olivia, you are freaking yourself out. Should I have been freaked out? I didn't know. My heart started to pound. I felt tears trying to escape and I let them. Quietly, I cried. I cried because I didn't know what I should cry about. Were they nothing? Then I could have cried in relief. Were they cysts, nothing bad, but they need to come out? Then I could have cried in relief and because there will be scars on my breasts. Tom liked my breasts. That's what made me want to crawl under my desk and howl in anguish, anger, fear, selfishness, and vanity. What if they really were "the worst case" that these web sites wrote about? *Push it out of your head Olivia. Quit making a mountain out of a mole hill or a mass out of a lump. Okay, let's look up something that wouldn't hurt. Hmmm, why didn't the mammogram catch these nuisances?* Within minutes I found a plethora of information telling of how mammograms can miss cancers. I found this on RadiologyInfo.org:

Mammography is the only screening tool for breast cancer that is known to reduce deaths due to breast cancer through early detection. Even so, mammograms do not detect all breast cancers. Some breast lesions and abnormalities are not visible or are difficult to interpret on mammograms.

Why didn't I know this?

In breasts that are dense, meaning there is a lot of ducts, glands, fibrous tissue and less fat, many cancers can be hard to see on mammography.

Many studies have shown that ultrasound and magnetic resonance imaging (MRI) can help supplement mammography by detecting breast cancers that may not be visible with mammography. MRI is more sensitive than ultrasound in depicting breast cancer, but MRI may not be available to all women.

Why?

If screening MRI is performed, then screening ultrasound is not needed, though ultrasound may be used to characterize and biopsy abnormalities seen on MRI. When ultrasound is used for screening, many more abnormalities that may require biopsy are seen than are seen with mammography or MRI. These abnormalities usually are not cancer (false positives), and this limits its usefulness.

Did I miss some breaking news on breast health or something? At least I knew there were other tests we could do before poking me with anything sharp if the need arose. It didn't make me feel any better.

The aroma of coffee invaded my nose, waking me from my blank stare. It was 5:30. Tom would be up in no time. I cleared the screen on my laptop and went in search of something mind numbingly stupid...Facebook.

I guess it was time to check in on the "friends" I didn't actually talk to. I had several hundred people who have requested me as a friend. I managed to whittle the number down and be selective. I didn't know how many times I had cleaned up my friends list by deleting people I am not close to, only to get another friend request from them within 24 hours. Did they not get the hint? If you have been deleted, why would I want you back? Oh well, life went on. Right?

Did you know there are very few people on Facebook at 5:30 in the morning? It was like they were asleep or something. Geesh people, I needed to be entertained and you were mauling your pillows. How careless of you to not bend to my will. I updated my status:

How dare you all be rubbing up against your mattresses while I am up looking for entertainment? I am crushed. :-) (5:45am)

That would teach 'em not to be there for me. I logged off and closed my laptop with a little too much sass. Oops, I checked it quickly to see I hadn't broken it. Whew, no damage.

"Hey, what are you doing up so early?" Tom asked over the edge of his coffee mug.

"Couldn't sleep."

"You sick or something?"

"I'll go with the 'or something.' Do you want anything for breakfast?"

Dumbass, I could have told him then.

"Nah, the guys and I will hit some drive-thru later this morning. I gotta go, babe. Tons of work waiting for me since that hail storm last week," he murmured while he leaned in for a quick nuzzle of my cheek. He needed to shave. "Last night was...fun," he offered with a wolfish grin and bouncing eyebrows.

"For you, I on the other hand felt short changed," I snipped and stuck out my tongue.

"Oh, tongue, I like. Maybe we can practice a little more tonight."

"Go to work perv boy."

I walked him to the door, handed him his lunch and kissed him goodbye. How very June Cleaver of me. I saw the girls shared car in the driveway. I didn't know which one or if both were home so I went to take a peek. It looked like Lily was drooling into her pillow and it appeared Shell had spent the night at her friend's place. I could have made French toast for breakfast. Lily would have liked that. Then I remembered it was only six in the morning. She would have blown a gasket if I woke her up early. I needed to find something to do to keep my mind occupied. I walked from room to room in my house and a list of chores started to form in my head and laundry was at the top. Man, I hated laundry, but I sure do love clean clothes. So it began.

The list of chores shortened with time. By the time I looked up from my mop it was nearly 11a.m. I got a lot done in the last five hours and managed to get Lily's lazy butt out of bed. A lot of good it did since it then landed on the couch with the remote firmly in her grasp. I didn't have the energy to fight with her today. My cell rang which brought me out of my inner tiff with Lily that she wasn't even aware of. It was Alyssa on the line.

"Hey, Alyssa, what's up?" I asked as I put the mop in the bucket.

"Not much. Checking to see if we are still on for lunch, and where do you want to go?"

"Oh, yes, we are," Crap, I had completely forgotten about our lunch date, "how does the Mexican place on 4th street sound? I could really go for some good guacamole." Was I really excited about eating dip? I placed my hand on my belly and realized I had not eaten breakfast and my stomach was reminding me in a rather grumbling way.

"Yeah, sounds good. See you at about 12:15. 'k?"

"See ya then. Bye."

"Bye."

I pushed the mop bucket into a corner out of the way. I ran to the bathroom. I jumped in the shower for a quick wash that was so short I barely got wet. Hell, I didn't even think the soap had time to lather up. Oh well, I would do better next time. I scurried out, toweled off, and rummaged through my closet to find something to wear. Huh, I guess it was a good thing I did laundry this morning, I chuckled to myself. I threw on some mid-thigh length khaki shorts, a belt, an *American Eagle* t-shirt, and gladiator sandals. Good enough for lunch with a friend. I lightly blew dry my hair and ran some styling wax through it. I loved having short hair. It took just seconds to do it up right. I added a touch of mascara and Chap Stick. I took a second look. *You'll do,* I nodded to myself. Spinning around I set out for the living room to gather my purse, keys, and cell.

Eyeing me quizzically with her head tipped upside down over the arm of the couch Lily asked, "Whatcha doin?"

"I'm going to lunch with Alyssa at Senor Salsa's," I mumbled as I looked for my keys.

"Awe, I wanna come."

"No, you just barely got out of bed. You aren't dressed and I'm not going to wait. Where are my keys?"

"Why would I know where they are?" she snarled. Did she honestly think I was going to reward her with lunch for waking up? *Hell no. Look for a job, clean your room, do some of your laundry, do something around here besides channel surf, then, and only then, I may consider taking you to lunch. So there.* Of course I didn't actually say it out loud, but I felt satisfied I said it to myself.

"Found 'em," I stated with a shake of my keys.

"Good for you." Could she have smeared any more sarcasm on those few words? It was so thick it dripped on the floor.

"Well, I am going."

"Hey, bring me back a couple tacos and some guacamole and chips," Lily added with a pout and puppy eyes.

"Too little, too late, little girl. You shoulda thought about that before you got pissy with me."

"Mooooooommmmmm, awe, come on," she whined, even getting up on her knees to beg. It was kind of funny.

"Nope, bye." I snatched up my purse and coasted out the door with the tiniest of a slam. Which felt good.

I pulled into the parking lot at Senor Salsa's. Alyssa's car wasn't there, so I went in to get us a table and chips, guacamole and sweet tea. Just as the waiter stepped out of the line of sight between me and the door, I saw Alyssa step in. With a small wave I caught her eye and she made her way toward me with a smile.

"Hi," I offered with a goofy grin. "You look...tired," I added with a sashay and smirk. "What have you been doing that has put bags under your eyes and a sly grin on your face, hmmm?" The waiter stopped by with our tea and chips.

"I don't know what you are talking about." She faked innocence while shoving a tortilla chip bursting with guacamole into her mouth. I looked up at her as she offered me a full toothed grin covered in green goo.

"Agh, that's so gross," I admonished while laughing at the same time. She washed the mess down with a big gulp of tea.

"Yes, I spent the evening tangled with the good doctor and," with a cheesy school girl smile on her face added, "most of the morning." My jaw hung slack at her admission. I never saw her like this.

"Are you in lust," I asked as I pointed accusingly at her. "How long have you known Dr. Neil," I asked. "It's Neil right, is it his first name or last?"

"I met him a few weeks ago at the school, like I told you. He didn't really ask me out until a week later when his section of class ended. I guess he figured he had to because we may never have seen each other again." She paused long enough to wedge another chip into her mouth.

"Have you ladies decided what you want?" The caramel colored waiter asked. He couldn't look less interested. He may have wanted to rethink his career choice.

"I'll have the triple taco plate, hard shell, with a side of refried beans and Spanish rice." I explained with as much indifference as he showed us, "and a refill on my tea."

"Oh, sounds good. I'll have the same," chimed Alyssa. You could tell by her tone she wasn't aware of the little snit going on between waiter boy and me.

"I'll put your order right in. Shouldn't take long," Giving me a sneer, waiter boy walked back to the kitchen. Great, I wondered if he was going to spit in my food, or worse. The vision in my head made me gag inwardly and stick out my tongue in a disgusted fashion. I did it to myself. My attitude got me into trouble sometimes. Okay, it got me into trouble a lot.

"Neil is his first name, Neil Mathews," Alyssa seemed to melt as his name slipped from her lips. Pull yourself together woman.

I was picking up a chip when I realized something was off. "Wait, what's his name?" Why did his name sound...no, no, oh no.

"Neil Mathews, why?"

With a pained look on my face I asked, "He's a gynecologist isn't he?"

With a furrowed brow she answered with curiosity, "Yes... his office is in town, a couple of blocks from here. Why?"

I just looked at her with panic in my eyes.

"Okay, what are you getting at, Olivia?"

I sharply inhaled through my teeth and carefully announced, "He's my gynecologist." I crushed my eyes closed and turned my face away in shame. I must have looked like I was bracing for a punch. When none came, I carefully peeked out of one eye. Her mouth was gaping, once again showing me the food in her mouth. Ugh.

Pulling herself together and straightening up in the booth she declared, "Okay, so he's your doctor, so what." Wiping some imaginary crumbs from the table, I could see she was trying very hard not to make this weird or weirder. I couldn't help myself. I burst out into involuntary giggles. She looked at me like I had lost my mind, only to join in a few seconds later. The reality was her boyfriend had seen most of the women in this town, including me, in the most intimate and embarrassing ways. She was just going to have to process that and get over it if they were going to work out.

"Have you thought about the 'doctor with only women patients' thing?"

"Not until now, thanks for pointing it out." Her disgust evident on her face.

"Think about it this way, Alyssa, he asked you out and he can't get involved with his patient's, so it's good, right?" I shrugged my shoulders, "Besides, how many crusty old vaginas can you look at before you just don't care anymore?"

"Hey, he seemed to enjoy mine just fine last night and this morning." There it was. The humor had found its way back.

Our food arrived at the table and I looked at waiter boy for any hint he may have messed with my food. He put the plates down in the middle of the table in such a way either one of us could have taken either plate. Cool, I thought I was safe. With a nod and a smile I thanked and dismissed him. I peeked in my tacos anyway. You never knew what people were capable of. It looked safe and Alyssa had already stuffed one in her mouth. I added some taco sauce and took a bite. God, they made good food there, phlegm or not. I sighed with satisfaction as I chewed.

I swallowed my mouthful and took a sip of tea. "Of course he enjoyed you, and he likes you. He asked you out," I offered.

"It's not like I slept with him on the first date. I slept with him last night. It was our *fifth date*." Why was I shocked? Oh, probably because Alyssa didn't wait. She thought if the sex sucked, find out right away. That way you don't waste time pursuing a relationship.

"Don't look at me like that. I can wait you know. It's not like I wanted to wait, but he was worth it." She seemed annoyed and ecstatic all at the same time. "Being a gynecologist, seriously, has its benefits," she dripped in a very carnal way.

"T.M.I. Alyssa. This is the guy I have described to you and Trish as Dr. Hottie, remember?" I realized I would never be able to look at him the same way again. I may have to find a new gynecologist. No, he was the one who found, shit, did he tell her what he found? Get real, Olivia, doctor patient confidentiality, duh. He didn't even know we knew each other.

"Shit, that's right. He is hot, isn't he?" It was more of a rhetorical statement than a question.

"It's what I've been saying for the last two years. I swear you guys never listen to me." I huffed and stuffed a fork full of refried beans in my mouth. Tom was going to suffer because of my dietary choices that day.

With a sarcastic look she disclosed, "We listen. We don't care nearly as much as you think we should." She laughed, and I followed suit and laughed, really laughed. I dropped my fork to the table which then bounced to the floor. It made me laugh harder. There was no way I was picking it up and using it. I pulled myself together as much as I could and waved the waiter over telling him I needed another fork. All the while trying to stifle giggles that popped out whenever I opened my mouth.

With a fresh fork in hand I played with my food while thinking of some witty, snarky thing to say, but decided it was too funny to mess with. Score for Alyssa. Lunch flowed without a hitch for the remainder of her hour. I decided to not ask any details of her sex-capade with the doc. I did not need those images in my head. I did, however, ask how he had treated her so far, and if she was happy. You know, the questions a good friend asked. What I really wanted to know was the nitty-gritty of it all, but with him being my doctor and Alyssa being a friend, I thought better of it. I waved to the waiter for the check. I refused to let her pay, so she demanded she leave the tip. Hell, go for it. I had no intention of tipping waiter boy. You had to actually do more than take my order and give me a fork for me to tip you. He never checked on us once during our meal. Maybe I would have given him a single penny as a tip, to get my point across. Mean? Absolutely.

We walked out into the parking lot and gave each other a quick hug. As I climbed into my car, I felt my phone vibrate in my purse. I dug it out and saw Trish's face on the screen.

"Hey woman, what's up," I chirped as I started my car. Air conditioning was a wonderful thing.

"Are you home?"

"Um, no, I met Alyssa for lunch. I will be home shortly. What's up?" I could hear something in her voice.

"Can I come over?" Her voice was low, guarded.

"Of course, my door is always open. Are you bringing the boys? I can pick up some subs or something?"

"Gage and Warren are at camp. They left early this morning. I'll be at your place in like five minutes."

"'k, I'll be there. Bye." She hung up before I finished my sentence. This wasn't good. Trish had a volatile marriage. Richard was a very domineering, controlling asshole. I never understood how they even got together. Trish wasn't the kind of woman you controlled. She did what she wanted when she wanted. They were like oil and water, not a good mix. I didn't know if Richard was crazy enough to have ever hit her, but I did know she wore a lot of long sleeved shirts when the weather dictated otherwise. I had asked her many times if she was good, but she had always given vague responses and cryptic information. I wondered and I worried and I wanted to be there for her.

I pulled into the driveway as Trish pulled up to the curb. As she started walking to the house, I could see she had been crying. Normally she had her sunglasses on, but they were absentmindedly resting on top of her head. I saw her eyes. They weren't so much misty as they were… swollen? Her lip? What the…that son-of-a-bitch.

Chapter four

Ushering her through the door, I held up a hand to say not to speak. I checked around for Lily to make sure the room was clear and to give Trish the privacy and security she needed. I took her hand and led her to the couch. "Sit. Do you want anything to drink or eat?" I asked as she gingerly slid onto the couch.

"Water and an Advil if you got it?" I saw her wince. What the fuck happened? I would kill him myself, the fucking...must calm down, be there for her.

"Advil good?"

"Yeah, it's fine."

I hurried to the kitchen and got the water and Advil. As I made my way through the rooms I paused in the bathroom for a box of Kleenex. I entered the living room and put everything down in front of her on the coffee table. I settled down sideways beside her with my leg tucked up under me so I could face her. I took a deep breath and put it out there. "What happened, Trish?" She popped the Advil and chugged half the bottle of water. I saw her shoulders hunch and start to shake. She attempted to hold whatever it was back. She tried to keep her feelings caged. I reached out and took her hand from her lap. "Let it out. Don't try to hold it in. Just let the tears fall where they may. I will cry right along with you, friend." The cage broke and the tears came. I pulled her into a hug and let the sobs fall on my shoulder. I caught a bit of movement out of the corner of my eye and glanced up the staircase. Lily had stopped half way down the stairs and was gaping at the soggy mess on the couch. I waved her on and pressed a finger over my lips begging her to remain silent, so Trish wouldn't see her. I knew Trish. If she saw Lily she would have clammed up and I would never have gotten her to talk. Lily slipped down the rest of the stairs and circled around to the side door without as much as a squeaky board. How'd she do that? She knew where every loose board was, hmm. I needed to file that information away for later.

After a few minutes of tears, the tremors started to slow. Gasping for air, Trish wiped at her face trying to scrub away the evidence of her moment of weakness. I turned her toward me and as I wiped her tears and the black river of mascara that ran down her cheeks with the tissues, I whispered, "Tell me."

"Richard," she cringed as the name fell from her swollen lip. "He...did this," she stated then ran her tongue along the damaged lip.

"I can see," I breathed with a sympathetic smile. "Tell me what happened, sweetheart. I'm here."

"We were sitting on the back porch last night having a couple of beers and talking, ya know. It was kind of nice, just relaxing." I nodded, acknowledging her words. Twisting a tissue in her fingers she continued carefully. "Things started to get heated when we were talking about work. I haven't heard from the insurance place yet, and he heard there may be another lay off where he works at the end of the summer. He started to get really pissed, but not at me, mad in general, then he really started to drink. I tried to calm him down, but he got madder. So, I went into the house. I hoped he would calm down if I left him alone... I was wrong." Her lip started to tremble as the memory of what happened flickered behind her eyes. It's when I started to notice and make note of what I saw: a bruise had formed above her right eye, while I rubbed her hand I saw broken nails and scrapes on her fingers, she wore a long sleeved t-shirt and jeans. It was hot outside, really hot, and here she sat dressed for cooler weather.

"I was doing the dishes when Richard came in looking for more beer, but we already drank what we had left. I didn't go to the store yesterday. He started yelling saying I was worthless and lazy. I don't do anything around the house but eat and get fat." More tears fell, hers and mine. "He said he should have never married me. He had women around him all the time that would willingly spread their legs for him that aren't fat and disgusting." I could feel the embers deep inside start to glow red. "Women who got him hard, not like me."

"Trish, you know you are not fat, right? You know he said those things to hurt you, that's all."

"It doesn't matter. I tried to tell him he was wrong about me and he shoved me into the counter and I think it's when I hit my head on the cabinet, right here." She rubbed the bruise above her eye. "I started to scream at him about his drinking and getting pushy with the boys and it's when he grabbed me by the arm and started to shake me, saying I'd ruined his life, and he never wanted to have kids. He said I trapped him in a marriage he never wanted. I tried pulling away from him because he was really digging his fingers into my arms." She ran her fingers over her swollen lip. "That's when he backhanded me in the mouth. It knocked me clear to the floor." I could see her pain. "He kicked me and kept screaming. I crawled up under the kitchen table to try to get out of reach of his feet. I was so scared because the boys were up in their room. What if he went after them?" Pure fear screamed in her eyes and hot tears flowed from mine.

"But then he heard sirens. Someone called the cops. He said I needed to keep my fucking mouth shut. Tell them I ran into a door or something, or he would fucking take off with the boys and I would never see them again. So, that's what I did. I told the cops I did it to myself. There is no way they believed me. How do you run into a cabinet with your mouth? They had to take him in anyway." She rested her elbows on her knees and cradled her head in her hands.

"Do you want to lie down? Honey, you look haggard," I cooed and pushed her hair back out of her face. "Let me get you a pillow and blanket and you can lie down and rest. I won't leave you, I promise." She nodded her head and hummed her agreement. I slipped to the linen closet as quickly as I could to gather up a pillow and throw for her.

I helped her slip off her sneakers and settle down on the couch. I curled up in the chair across from her so she could see me. "Go to sleep, friend. I am right here," I whispered as I saw her eyes start to flutter. Within minutes she was asleep. I quickly grabbed my cell phone and set it to camera. Turning off the sound I took pictures of her face. I sat with her for what seemed like hours. As she moved and rolled, I caught glimpses of bruises on her lower back. I took more pictures. Everything I saw, my camera held deep in its memories. I would take that son-of-a-bitch down one way or another.

Trish was still asleep when I got up to start dinner. Tom was due home soon and his anger would be unmistakable when he saw Trish. I had my hands, up to my wrists, deep into the meatloaf as I tried to mix it all together when I heard the truck come up the drive. I caught a glimpse of the tailgate as Tom pulled into the garage. The house phone rang on the wall, but I was still covered in gooey meat. Crap, I tried to wipe off one hand to answer the phone just as it stopped ringing. Tom must have picked up the line in the garage. A minute later I saw him coming up the back steps.

"Hey, babe," he greeted me as he came breezing in. "Playing with your meat I see," he chuckled and kissed me. "Where's Trish? Richard's on the phone for her."

I shushed him and guided him to the living room where Trish still slept. "He beat her last night," I whispered and before I knew it Tom was out the back door. I ran after him so he wouldn't go to Richard's and do something rash. Tom was on the phone when I reached the garage. I made it in time to catch Tom's side of a very heated discussion.

"No, Dick, you can't talk to her, she's not available… I don't care if your name is Richard. I'm calling you 'Dick' because it's what you are, you son-of-a-bitch…Yeah, it takes a real man to raise a hand to a woman…Really? If you think it's a good idea to come over here and get her, bring it on 'Dick', I'd like to see you, too." I could see sweat had formed on Tom's face. His eyes were glacial and jaw tight. The veins in his neck were bulging and his fist was clenched. I didn't know if I had enough cash in my checking account to bail him out if he did something completely warranted. "Okay, you gather up the friends you don't have and come on over… Fuck you, you piece of shit. I'm right here." Slamming down the phone he spun around and his eyes caught mine. I was crying. I don't even know when I had started to cry. He crossed the garage in no time and wrapped his arms around me. I awkwardly put my arms around him and tried not to smear him with my meat covered hands. "Are you okay baby?" he asked.

"Yeah, it's Trish I'm worried about."

"Well, it's my job to worry about you. How's Trish?"

With my arm still around his waist and his wrapped around my shoulder, we walked toward the house. I gave him the run-down of what Trish had told me, and once inside, I showed him the pictures I took. We stood in the kitchen talking as I finished prepping the meatloaf and put it in the oven. Tom was leaning against the breakfast bar drinking a beer, talking about his day when Trish appeared in my line of sight.

"Hey, how'd you sleep? Do you want a drink?" I asked while cutting veggies for the salad.

"I could use something cold."

"Well, ice tea, cherry Kool-Aid, milk, water or beer?"

"Beer me, definitely beer me," she said matter-of-factly. Tom grabbed a beer from the fridge, handed it to her and put his arm around her shoulder. She winced at his contact, but with a little squeeze, Trish knew Tom knew and was on her side. Looking down at the floor she leaned into him placing more of her body weight on Tom's side.

With a reassuring smile, Tom vowed, "We gotcha, kiddo."

"Thanks, guys. Now, what's for dinner, and what do you want me to do?"

"You can set the table for five and get the butter and stuff from the fridge. After dinner we will sit outside, watch the sun set and figure out what's next," I said as I popped open a can of ready-made biscuits.

"Sounds good to me."

As dinner was coming out of the oven I spotted Lily from the kitchen window. She was standing on the side walk by the driveway. Wondering what she was doing I watched. Shell pulled into the drive and Lily greeted her with a wave. I saw them speak briefly then immediately head for the front door. Bounding through the door, they both followed their noses toward the aroma of food. They laid eyes on Trish. They walked to her and each placed a small kiss on her cheek and gave her light squeezing hugs. Without as much as a word they clutched their plates and proceeded to pile on the food. Gotta love these girls, they never stopped amazing me. We all gathered around the table and enjoyed our dinner and each other's company, completely avoiding the bruised elephant in the room.

The girls made short work of the kitchen clean up. Tom went in for a shower, and Trish and I exited out to the back deck. Claiming seats at the large table, we settled in and got comfy. Silence sat comfortably with us for a while, unlike Oliver, who wanted attention and didn't hesitate to scream at you to get it. Trish picked up the robust cat and settled him in her lap where he was more than content to be. The sun hadn't set yet, but it was clear evening had arrived. It was warm, but not hot and an intermittent breeze tickled our skin. I leaned my head back to rest on the back of the chair and stared at the inside of my eyelids. I wasn't tired physically, but emotionally I was wasted. I was trying to take advantage of this moment of silence to think about the spot Trish was in and what I could offer to help. Nothing...I would have given her the shirt off my back, but I knew she would wear it on her way back to him. I couldn't make her wake up to the reality that was her life. There would be a breaking point. I hoped it was before there was irreparable damage. You don't know what people are truly capable of until they are tested. It also went for abusers. When they started to get sloppy by leaving evidence which couldn't be covered by clothing, then they no longer cared what they were doing was wrong. They were losing what little control they had left. That was when someone really got hurt, and more often than not, it wasn't the abuser. It wasn't just Trish caught in an inferno, though, she had two young sons who could get burnt in the process. How could I get her to understand before it was too late?

"What do I do now?" Trish murmured so low I nearly missed it because of the argument going on in my own head.

"Sadly, my friend, that is up to you. We are here to help, no matter what you choose, but ultimately it's up to you." As much as I wanted to tell her she must pack hers and the boys' things and get the hell out of Dodge, I couldn't. I knew all too well this was something she had to decide all by herself. I had been there in more ways than one, not with Tom, but, long ago, I was faced with that very decision, twice. "I've been there and I know what's going through your head. I know you're scared. I know you're confused, and I know you think you don't have a choice in what happens… but you do. You have something I didn't have. You have people who will back you every step of the way." I never told anyone what I went through except Tom. It wasn't something you add to your yearly Christmas letter or chat about on "Dip and Drinks" night with the girls. It was saved for the scripts of nightmares, after school specials, and horror flicks.

I could see I had gotten her attention. I had given her new information about me, something she didn't already know. She was shocked. "Why didn't you tell me?"

"Why would I? It's not a good thing you want to share with all your friends. It was a foul and violent time which I try not to relive or wallow in."

Trish's shock seemed to twist into skepticism. "Yeah right, I bet you know about it as much as you know about small engine repair."

Wow, I got mad. No, pissed. I got really pissed. I didn't know if it was from her attitude or her doubt in what I said. She basically called me a liar. If only I was, it would have made my life so much easier. Leaning forward in my chair and placing my weight on the table in front of me, I braced myself. My eyes and emotions now glacial, I started. "I know abuse. All forms of the vile word, and I know it intimately," I spat out in anger. "You are not the only person on the planet who has had to face questions about a black eye or fat lip, but try doing it when you are a child and no one believes you." Trish straightened in her chair and tried to put some distance between us. We both turned as we heard the door open. Tom stepped out carrying a bottle of wine and three glasses. He felt the tension the moment he laid eyes on us.

"What the hell did I step into?"

"Trish here seems to think I couldn't possibly have experienced abuse because I was what, born under some magical star or something?" I smothered it with all the distain I could muster. Tom admonished me with a look.

He sat down, opened the wine, filled our glasses, handed me mine and said, "Tell her."

I jerked my head to look at him so fast I thought I pulled something in my neck. "Tell her? Are you kidding?"

Tom nodded his head as he passed Trish a glass of wine.

"Tell me what?" she provoked.

I huffed, slumped back into my seat, and grabbed my glass. I drank...all of it. Tom poured me another as I breathed. "Haven't you ever wondered about my family? Not Tom and the girls, but where I came from?" She nodded as she sipped from her glass. "Contrary to popular belief, I am not an orphan. I have blood relatives wandering out there in the world. I choose to have nothing to do with them and I refuse to allow their filth to touch my girls." I looked to Tom for support and there it was as clear as the nose on my face. It was in his eyes, the way he sat facing me, leaning in to catch me if I started to fall. He reached for my hand, gave me an encouraging smile and nodded to continue. "I learned very early in life I had a place. It was at the lowest of rungs. I was told my sole purpose in life was to clean litter boxes and scrub toilets, nothing more. I learned that 'assume the position' meant to pull down my pants and lie across the end of my bed and let my legs dangle to the floor. I spent more time like that, not because of what I did or didn't do, but because my mother had a bad day at work." I couldn't look up. I couldn't bring myself to look into Trish's eyes, so I stared at Tom's hand holding mine. "She beat me so bad on one occasion I could not sit down without being in excruciating pain. I couldn't wear jeans. They hurt so much I had to wear dresses and skirts for a week. I was in grade school at the time, second grade I think, and got into trouble because I kept fidgeting in my seat. It hurt so much to sit down. My teacher got mad and made me stand in the corner." With a little reprieving chuckle I continued, "Little did she know, it was what I was hoping for. I remember even going to the school nurse and showing her the welts and bruises. As far as I know nothing came of it. I got to live with it over and over and over. If that's not bad enough, I was molested by one of my mother's boyfriends and she knew... it had an even more twisted effect on her. Through the years whenever one of her relationships failed or was in the crapper, she accused me of trying to steal her boyfriends. I was five years old the first time." An icy finger seemed to rake down my spine. I did my best to shake it off. "I wish I could say he was the only one, but there were others and some were family... my mother was some kind of scum magnet. She would bring 'em into our lives with open arms, which meant I was thrown into the cesspool she created and forced to sink or swim." I found the courage to steal a look at Trish. Her arms were crossed tightly over her chest protecting herself from my past. I continued in a quiet murmur, "I remember when I was very little, before I was even old enough for kindergarten. She would lock me in my room, using hook and eye latches on the outside of the door. She would put me in there for hours. She put a coffee can in there as a make shift toilet so she wouldn't have to let me out if I needed to go. All so I wouldn't bother her and her friends while they were getting stoned." With a dismissing wave of my hand and a smirk I added, "Don't get me wrong, I've got good memories too. My favorite times were when she refused to talk to me for weeks at a time. I lo*ved her* silence. It was… almost like a vacation – the only thing better was when she went on vacation without me. Now that was bliss." I continued to tell her tales of beatings for obscure reasons, punishments lasted weeks, having to learn how to cook at the age of seven if I wanted to eat, and of being touched in ways no child should. All the while, Tom never let go of my hand. He kept my wine glass full to make the words fall from my lips a little easier. They still stung, but fell just the same. It was like bile on my tongue. Nearly an hour later, Trish threw up her hands and groaned she couldn't take any more. She said she could feel the nightmares taking notes and prepping for the evening's show.

"You said you understand what I'm going through, too, but how?"

"Well to answer that question as simply as possible, it's like this: I got into a relationship with a guy who said all the right things and promised me peace and happiness. I packed up all my shit and moved in with him. The reality he showed was different. The moment he got me where he wanted me, he became no better than my mother. It turned out he liked to hit, a lot. But I swore to myself when I was a little girl no *one would* raise a hand to me when I grew up… ever. So, when he was passed out one night from drinking way too much, I took a ball bat to his knee. End of story. I walked away and haven't communicated with anyone who knew what he did to me and what my mother did for all those years, and did nothing to stop it. I could be standing in front of you bruised and bloody, and somehow my mother was able to make people believe I was a trouble maker or an attention seeker. My mother somehow was able to convince everyone I was lying. It didn't help that she thought the sun rose out of my boyfriend's ass. I swear she had a thing for him. No matter how bad things got, it was always my fault."

—

"What about your dad? What did he do?" Trish asked in disgust.

"I don't know my father. My mother refused to tell me who he is. For all I know, she might not even know who he is. She didn't even put his name on my birth certificate. She told me the only reason she bothered to keep me was because she wanted to prove she could do it on her own. She was stronger than all the 'Nay Sayers' believed she was. I was in foster care for a short time when I was really little, but she managed to get me back. Oh, Joy."

Trish downed the rest of her wine and slid the glass over to Tom. "Damn, girl, you should sue the state for letting her get custody back." Tom tipped the bottle for us to see it was empty. He got up to get another. He placed a warm hand on my shoulder and gave it a little squeeze, then went to the kitchen for more liquid courage.

With a snicker I retorted, "'What doesn't kill you makes you stronger' is what my grandmother use to say." I rotated the wine glass on its base. "Bullshit, it killed my spirit and my self-esteem and stole my childhood. Gone. Now that is sad," I growled as I slammed my hand on the table in front of me as Tom stepped back out onto the deck holding another bottle of wine and munchies.

"Hey, don't go breaking our table. It's the nicest one we have ever had," he scolded and pushed the plate of meats and cheeses in front of us. He snagged a piece of salami and through a mouth full of meat demanded, "Eat some, or you both will end up toasted tonight and worthless tomorrow." He winked at me and held another piece of salami between his lips like he was sticking his tongue out. Well, he had warned me he was perpetually twelve years old. I shook my head at him, but smiled and filled all our glasses. Trish and I each got a chunk of cheese and clinked them together like you would a glass of Champaign. Well done, Tom, cheese and wine. Yummy.

Eager for more, Trish pushed. "You got away from the guy, how?" The question was not only on her lips, but you could see it in her eyes and feel it in her body language. She wanted to know. She wanted the directions in writing as to how to walk away unscathed.

"It wasn't easy. I'm not gonna lie to you, and I only had to worry about me. It was well worth it, but there were some serious struggles along the way."

53

"Until she met me, ag*ain,*" Tom grinned with such satisfaction you needed sunglasses to look at him. "I was the best thing to ever happened to her." How cheesy could he get? He was right, though.

"Babe, yo*u are,* as in present tense, the best thing that ever happened to me – besides our girls." I swooped in and pinned him with a kiss.

"Ewe… get a room. Good Lord, you two." Trish faked a gag and barfed over the side of her chair. "You'd think you were teenagers or something."

"He does claim to be twelve."

Tom leaned over the table as if he were to impart the winning lottery numbers or something. "We were when we met the first time. She was every guy's wet dream walking the halls, and I was the grease monkey who worked on cars. I don't even think Liv knew my name back then, but I knew hers. Every guy did."

"Hey, now, I knew who you were. I may not have known your name, but I did know who you were." I tried to defend myself, but we all laughed at the feeble attempt. "It's not like I was allowed to hang out after school or date. Shit, cut me some slack will ya, God."

"So, you guys went to school together, but how did she meet you 'again'? I mean, how do you meet someone twice if you already know them?" I thought we confused Trish, or we had two bottles too many of wine. Nah, that couldn't have been it.

"I got this," announced Tom waving off my words. With a nod of satisfaction at the chance to tell his tale, he began, "Once upon a time…I went into the Army right out of high school. When I decided to get out after my four year enlistment, I came back home. Olivia was waiting tables at the diner down in old town across from the theatre at the time. I was looking for work. It was before my brother and I took over the garage. I stopped in to snag some lunch and there she was, looking as good as I remembered." What a load of crap. I looked like death warmed over. "I was in there every day for a week before I got the nerve up to ask her if she remembered me." Not taking his eyes off me, Tom continued to regale us with his version of our tale of love, or was it lust? Who could tell the difference? "Finally, Olivia was waiting on me, again, and asked me if I was a glutton for punishment because the food there wasn't great. I agreed, but I told her the company was well worth the heartburn. That's when she fell in love with me, but who could blame her." He chuckled with the most arrogant smirk on his face. I slapped at him and he defended himself by flapping his hands like little girls slap fighting in a playground, and he had the nerve to laugh at me. "You know it's true, admit it. Come on, you can tell us. We're all friends here." We were laughing by now and trying to make light of what had happened that day.

"It's all well and good, but you still haven't told me how *you* got away from the guy," demanded Trish. She wanted answers, an easy answer, but it was going to be anything but, even if she got the strength and balls to do it.

"Like I said, I waited until he passed out one night. He liked to drink. I contacted a friend of mine earlier in the day and told him I was going to get out and needed his help. I packed all my shit. He was already drunk when he got home and, of course, we got into it, again. He split my lip and got in a good back hand to my cheek before he crawled into bed. When I was sure he was out I called my friend, and when he got there, I threw all my stuff in his truck. But, I was still pissed about him hitting me, so I grabbed the bat he had by the back door. I marched into the bedroom and swung the bat as hard as I could at the son-of-a-bitch and watched him scream and squirm and beg for help." I could feel the sweat trickle down my back and saw my own hands clenched as I remembered that night. "My friend came running in to see if he was beating on me again. I think he was shocked to see I had the upper hand for once."

"You didn't get into any trouble with the cops?"

"Nope, that was because he had already knocked me around earlier. He wasn't gonna call the cops. They would say I was defending myself, and that's what I told him. No one was going to believe I hurt him. I gave him the phone to call whoever he wanted and I left. I heard he called his mommy and told her he was drunk and fell or something. I busted his knee cap." I could feel the smile on my own face. After all that time I still felt satisfaction at standing up for myself, and making him feel what he liked to dish out to people smaller than him.

"Have you seen him since," Trish was eating this up like cheesecake.

"I've seen him," chimed in Tom. "He still drinks himself stupid, but the big difference is the noticeable limp. My baby knows how to use a bat." A touch of pride was in those words, and I felt shy when he looked at me.

"How did you survive? Where did you go? How..." Trish shot questions at me like bullets fired from a gun.

"Simple, friends, I bounced from couch to couch for a while until I got the job at the diner. The owner, Mr. Zinkman, let me stay in a little apartment above the restaurant until I could get on my feet. I wouldn't tell anyone where I lived," I winked at Tom. "I didn't want my ex to find out where I was, and I certainly didn't want my mother to get word either. She knew I was working at Zinkman's diner, but the one time she came in Mr. Zinkman threw her out. So, I lived and worked and that's about it until Tom pestered me for a date."

Tom sat back and folded his arms over his chest and looked at me with false astonishment. "Me, I did no such thing. I recall it was you who chased me, and that's the story I will tell anyone who asks." He stood and emptied his glass in a gulp and said, "And ladies, I have to throw in the towel. Some of us have to work in the morning."

I jumped up quickly to stop him. "Let me get some stuff for Trish, so she can shower and have something to sleep in." I was in the house and across the kitchen before anyone had a chance to say anything. I ran up the stairs to our room to gather up a clean t-shirt and shorts. I pulled some things from the linen closet and set off back down to the office/ spare room. I made up the hide-a-bed quickly and put the clean clothes in the bathroom across the hall. Just as I finished and was walking back out, Tom and Trish came in the back door with the wine glasses, food, and empty bottle. Tom set his arm load on the counter, crossed the kitchen, took me in his arms, and gave me a loud, wet goodnight kiss, then slipped up the stairs to get intimate with the bedspread.

"I made up the hide-a-bed for you and put some clean clothes in the bathroom so you can shower if you want."

"Thanks, I really appreciate everything. I don't know what I'm going to do tomorrow."

"We will worry about it tomorrow. Let's get through the rest of today and go from there. Do you need anything?"

"No, I'm good. I think I need to wash the crud of the day off and hit the sheets," Trish moaned. She looked so tired, and I bet all the wine didn't help. I showed her where everything was in the bathroom and gave her a new toothbrush from the linen closet. I gave her a squeeze, told her I would be right upstairs if she needed anything, and I climbed up to the warmth of a shower.

It had been a very long day. I told a secret, a secret I had been mute on for nearly two decades. Those who knew my story were as few as the fingers on one hand. Now, I had to add another finger to the count. I hoped to never have that evil pass over my lips ever again, but the events of the day required its telling. I only hoped it had done some good. I felt as though I was dragged behind a truck. My body ached from the tension of telling the tale. I was nauseated and was plain exhausted. As tired as I was, I feared my pillow. I had opened the box and it was going to take a lot of time to shove the ugly back into it. The bad dreams would come.

Chapter Five

I woke with a start, sweaty and haunted. I realized I was looking into the concerned blue eyes of my hero.

"Hey, you okay?" he whispered as he stroked my brow.

"Hmmm, I will be. What time is it?" I asked, allowing my eyes to flutter close.

"Ten to six, I woke you cuz I thought you should know Trish is gone, and you looked like you were having a nightmare."

"I figured it would happen."

Tom looked at me with the question written all over his face. "You knew she would leave or the nightmare?"

"Both. She wasn't ready to run yet. She's too scared and doesn't know how to run with the boys. She needs to find her safety net."

Tom settled down beside me and engulfed me in his arms, with his chin resting on my head he asked, "Safety net?"

"The people she can turn to. You know, like my friend Brian who helped me leave. Not everyone has that." I tried to free myself from his arms and roll out of bed. "Ugh, is there coffee? My head is pounding."

Tom held up a finger to say "wait there" and he disappeared from the room. I could hear him go down the stairs. I flopped back onto my pillow which had been a traitor to my head last night. It didn't protect me from the boogey man who invaded my dreams. I threw my arm over my eyes to try to block out the brightness of the overhead light and laid there listening to the rhythmic click of the ceiling fan. Soothing, but I doubted I would be able to go back to sleep knowing she had slipped out during the night. What could I do? Could I do anything at all? Damn, didn't she know I had my own issues to worry about right now? No... no one knew, not yet. I smelled coffee and peaked under my arm in time to see Tom glide through the door holding a glorious steaming cup of joy. I sat up to take my mug of morning's blood and enjoyed the first sip. Tom handed me two Advil. He knew me so well.

"I gots ta go, babe. We have so much work piled up," Tom said as he leaned in for a kiss. The hail storm that rocked this town about a week and a half before had a great financial effect on every business around here. It had done wonders for everyone. Yes, there was a lot of damage, but it brought in a lot of money. Tom and Wayne's body shop was booming. Roofing companies, siding, window repair, you name it, it was busy. Not to mention all the checks pouring into our neighborhood mail boxes. It was funny to think we were thanking God for the storm that did so much damage, but we were. I admit it scared the crap out of me. Tom and I had left the house to go to dinner when it started. We were trapped in the truck trying to find cover. We drove toward the car wash hoping to get inside out of the barrage of hail stones, but everyone else on the road had the same idea. They arrived there first. So, we sat it out in the parking lot. I thought for sure the windshield was going to end up in my lap but it held, and we survived. The vehicles in town had more dimples than a golf ball, but thankfully no one had been hurt.

"Have a good day, babe. What do you want for dinner?" I took another sip of coffee while downing the Advil. 'Make it something simple, pleeeeease,' I begged in my mind.

"How about we go out for dinner?"

"God, I love you," I exhaled with relief. "How did I get so lucky?"

"I don't know, but maybe you should buy a lottery ticket, or share the good fortune and let me get lucky later," he dared while his eyebrows bounced in a 'wanna' kind of way. "Okay, gotta go.

Bye." With another quick peck he was nothing but a gust of wind out the door. He was backing out of the garage within mere minutes.

I nearly spilt my coffee when Oliver jumped up onto the bed. It would have been a sin this early in the morning. Shame on you, Oliver. I reached over and scratched his back as he made his way to one of Tom's pillows. He knew what he liked. I sat there and scratched Lolly Monster and finished my first cup of the day while I debated whether or not to get up. Up won. I had so much weighing on my mind I couldn't even remember getting dressed, but there I stood in the kitchen pouring another cup of coffee fully dressed in my workout gear. Workout gear? Did I really want to do that to myself? No, but I needed it. Those "Bingo Wings" needed to go. I ate a quick bowl of instant oatmeal and made my way to the car, munching on a banana.

Today was not a trainer day, so Veronica could keep her nasty attitude on the other side of the gym. There was no Trish in sight, and I had no intention of calling her. I would send her a text later but right now I would let her be. I claimed a treadmill and climbed aboard. I loved those new ones with the TV built in. I could sweat and watch VH1 all at the same time. I plugged in my ear buds and got my rock on. No, I meant got my work out on. Who was I kidding? No I didn't. I climbed off after about 30 minutes and headed for the free weights. I did a quick cycle and decided I had enough of all this healthy crap and went out for a doughnut.

I stood in my kitchen with a box of doughnuts, even though my intention had been to buy just one. I indulged in the chocolate covered delight. Closing my eyes I savored the joy in my mouth. When I opened them I saw Shell's hand reach into the box. Shit. She's sneaky...and quiet.

"Morning, Bug, you're up early."

"Hmmmm," was all she could work up as a doughnut dangled from her lips. She got the gallon of milk and poured a glass. Slumping back to the breakfast bar she sat and chewed.

"Geesh, calm down, you are going to wear me out with all the exuberance you are exhibiting." I could be so sarcastic at times. Shell looked at me with a raised eyebrow and a tilted smirk on her face while shoving more doughnut in her mouth.

"I'm not complaining, but what are you doing up this early? I thought you closed at Burger King last night?"

She swallowed and chugged some milk. Wiping her mouth with the back of her hand, she was such a lady. "I closed, it sucked, and now I have to go in for the early lunch shift because my manager is a dumb-ass and doesn't know how to schedule people. I worked until after one and now I am up at 8:30 and have to be to work by ten. Tell me my life doesn't suck." I love teenagers...not.

"At least you get to start your day with chocolaty goodness and me. I don't know which is better."

"That would be the chocolaty goodness."

"Brat." I was proud of the girl and her work ethic, but even I knew she needed to, as they say, stop and smell the roses from time to time.

Shell fished another doughnut out of the box and refilled her glass. She kissed my cheek, and with a tired smile, went back to her room to get ready for a fun-filled day at work. I yelled after her to wake her sister for me. I started to unload the dishwasher when Lily arrived in all her splendor. Throwing herself on a barstool, she crossed her arms on the breakfast bar and dropped her head onto them with a thud.

"Why am I up?" she yawned.

"Because there are things to be done, and you are going to help do them," I answered in my Mom voice.

"Why can't Shell do it? Is she too good for crap chores?" I could see she was in a mood this morning.

"Shell has to go to work in about an hour. That's why she is up, and why I didn't tell her to do anything. You, on the other hand, are available to do whatever it is I need done. Now, I am going to go get a quick shower. You need to get dressed and ready to go cuz we have grocery shopping to do, understand?"

"Fine, I have a life too, ya know. I have plans this afternoon. Can you get me a glass of milk, please," she sneered while picking through the doughnut box.

"Not with your attitude. Get your own milk. I'm going to shower. Get moving."

I turned on the radio in the bathroom and hummed along as I danced around under the warm rain. I had to stay busy today. It had been three days since my appointment. Should I call this morning or wait until after lunch? Should I wait for them to call me? That was when Aretha chimed in and reminded me that I was a woman. Ha, perfect song when you were talking about boobs. More music filled the room reminding me to hang on and that's what I was gonna do. I was gonna hang on to my peace of mind and go grocery shopping. I toweled off and got dressed.

I was writing my list for the store when both girls appeared. Once again they reached for doughnuts, so I helped myself to one too. Such a healthy meal, not.

"I need deodorant and razors," announced Shell pointing at the list. "I could use some new socks too."

"I'm going gro-cer-y shopping not clothes shopping."

Throwing up her hands in defense, she said, "I was just sayin'. Don't get all bent outta shape. Chill."

"I'll take you on your next day off to get what you need."

Lily damn near choked on her mouthful of doughnut. "I need stuff too. Are you going to take me shopping?"

"It depends on what you need? I'm not going to buy you stuff just cuz Shell needs something. If you have a need, then so be it, but this isn't a 'she got something so I should too' situation. Got it?"

"I see. Shell is this, Shell is that, Shell has a job, so you kiss Shell's ass. Yup, got it."

"Are we going to do this again, Lily? I don't know what crawled up your ass and died this morning, but I suggest you pull it out, now. I am not going to put up with your pissy mood today. You know as well as I do we do not favor one of you over the other. Period. Now, get your shit and grab the shopping bags and let's go." When would they realize they held equal parts of my heart? Shoot me, please.

Shell put on her hat and tossed her purse over her shoulder and she declared, "That was fun, but I have to head to work."

"Bye, Sweetie. I hope it goes by fast for you today."

"It's a five-hour shift, so it's not too bad, and I get to hang out tonight," she said with a smile as she left me with Brooding Lily. I was not in the mood to deal with her mood because mine was bad enough.

It was amazing how my girls acted when the other was not there. Lily's attitude did a complete 180° when Shell wasn't with us. Separately, they were a joy to be with. It was only when you put them together all hell broke loose. It was like mixing chemicals for a bomb. On their own they are harmless, docile even, but mix them together and it is a weapon of mass destruction.

We hit the grocery store with a mission and walked out less than an hour later with everything on my list and then some. We decided to check out the local farmers market and left there with a bag of fresh veggies and a watermelon the size of a tire. Lily even suggested we swing by Wally World and grab Shell some socks.

No, I'm not kidding. She actually wanted to do something for her sister. What? I know, right? It made me look at her twice too. Did I miss the invasion of the body snatchers somewhere along the drive?

I went along with it and enjoyed the change. We stopped to get Shell some socks and the weirdest part was Lily didn't ask me to buy her anything. Seriously. Once at home, we unloaded our conquests and put away the groceries. Because she didn't bitch the whole time we were out, I gave Lily some money and the keys to my car and sent her out to hit the drive-thru to snag us some lunch. I took those few minutes to check my phone to see if I missed any calls or texts. No calls missed, which meant the doctor's office hadn't called. Damn it all. No texts either, which meant no word from Trish. I decided it was long enough and sent her a quick message:

I *understand. I will not judge. I am here and always will be.*

I hoped she would see we were here for her if she ever decided to leave. I didn't expect to hear from her right away, but I hoped. Lily was back with calories in paper wrappers and cold caffeine. Mmmmm, I was hungry. We wolfed the burgers and fries and talked about what had been going on in her world. Hoping to hear what I wanted to hear, I asked her if she still planned on going to the art college about two hours away. I wanted her to go, but I knew her boyfriend, Darren, wasn't crazy about the idea. She didn't give me a straight answer and I tried not to push, but at least she didn't say

"No." I needed to know within the next five weeks so I knew whether or not we had to send in the tuition. I had to remind myself not to push or it would guarantee she wouldn't go. My phone rang. My skin crawled. Trish...caller i.d. was "unknown..."

"Hello," I answered. I could feel the fear in that one word.

"Mrs. Carpenter?"

I got up and walked into the living room. "That's me."

"This is Nurse -Lipstick- from Dr. -OMG's- office. I have a referral from him to another physician for you."

"Oh, okay. Let me find a pen." I scrambled for a pen and scrap of paper. The grocery receipt would have to do. "Okay, go ahead."

"He would like you to see Dr. -How many letters are in your name-. His office is in our building, suite 201, across the corridor from here." Corridor, who the heck used the word corridor these days, it's called a hall. Geesh.

"What does Dr. -I can't say his name right- do? Is he a specialist?"

"Yes, Mrs. Carpenter. He specializes in breast pathology. Let me give you the telephone number and you can ask them any questions you may have and set an appointment. Okay?"

"Okay," I murmured. I scribbled down the number and thanked Nurse -Lipstick- for the information. Should I have called then or...

"Who was that?"

Pull yourself together, now. "Oh, I had some blood work done. I'm old, remember? They had to reassure me I'm still alive." Shit, shit, shit. I needed to call this other doctor's office, but, not while Lily sat there. Crap.

"I'm gonna go hang out with Jessica before I meet up with Darren later. Did you need me to do anything else?" Had she read my mind? I loved her so much at that very moment.

"No, I think I can handle the rest. Here..." I reached for my purse and handed her a twenty, "...thanks for going along with me. I know it wasn't your idea of a good time."

"Thanks, Mom. No problem. If you are gonna give me cash every time, I may help more often."

—

"I wouldn't bet on it if I were you," I gave a smile. "Please, think about college. We need to know soon, okay?"

"Yes, Mother. Later," Lily blew me a kiss as she crossed the street to Jessica's.

Breathe, Olivia. I laid the receipt out in front of me and dialed...hung up...dialed...hung up...Oh for God's sake, just call. Exhaled, dialed, rang...

"Dr. -What *did you say's*- office, how can I help you?" an unknown female voice asked on the other end of the line.

"Um, yeah, hi, I was given a referral from Dr. −Yes- to see Dr. -I *can't roll my tongue like that-*" I stammered.

"May I have your name, please?"

"Carpenter, Olivia Carpenter."

"Yes, Mrs. Carpenter. I see the referral in the computer. Would you like to set an appointment?"

"Um, yes, please. The sooner the better," I affirmed.

There was silence on the other end of the line for a moment. "Okay, Mrs. Carpenter, Dr. -*Garble & Mumble*- has an opening at 11:15 on Tuesday. Would that work for you?" asked the sing song voice on the line.

"That'll be fine."

"Okay, I will put you in that slot. Now, please arrive at least 30 minutes early to fill out the new patient packet. Please, bring with you your insurance information and your co-pay. Do you have any questions?"

"No, I think I am good for now, thanks."

"Mrs. Carpenter, don't worry about something that hasn't been given a name. This could be nothing. Enjoy your weekend and we will see you Tuesday," she tried to reassure me.

"Thank you." She tried to ease my mind, but my heart was pounding and my fingers had gone cold. More waiting, this was going to drive me bonkers, and it was a very short trip from here to there. I put the appointment into the calendar in my phone. The text alert whistled at me. It made me jump.

Thanks, friend. I'm good. Don't worry.

Trish. I stared at the text not knowing what to say and I realized I had nothing to say, so I didn't. My mind wasn't in any condition right at the moment to deal with her problem.

I found myself on the couch staring off into space an hour later. I didn't know if I was even thinking about anything. It was blank when the phone rang. The caller ID showed it was Molly, my sister-in-law. What now? Argh.

"Hi, Molly, what's up?" Could I sound any less enthused?

"Hi, Wayne and I are having a barbeque tomorrow. Would you and Tom like to come? We can hang in the pool, eat some hot dogs and have some drinks. What do ya say?"

Did I really want to put myself through that? I needed to get my mind off of the answers I didn't have so... "Sounds good, I will have to see if Tom is up for the excitement."

"He already said yes. I had Wayne ask him a little while ago."

What? Then why the fuck did you call me to ask a question you already had the fucking answer to. Dumb-ass. "Well, then why did you ask me if you already had an answer?"

"I don't know. Just thought I should check with you too," Molly giggled. Could I get any more pissed?

Yes I could. Watch.

"Okay, um, do you need us to bring anything?"

Here it comes...

"Could you bring your deviled eggs and potato salad? Also, bring whatever it is you want to drink and maybe a dessert or something. 'k?"

I told you I could get more pissed.

"Sure, would you like me to clean the pool, too?"

"What? No, Wayne will do it. But, hey, can you bring some of your lawn chairs, too? We are having a few other people coming."

ARGH!!!!!!

"Fine, what time should we be there?" I could feel my face getting hotter. I walked into the dining room and was holding on to the back of the barstool so hard my knuckles had actually turned white.

"I guess around noon-ish. I'll call you if I need anything else."

"Oh, goodie," you arrogant, self-centered piece of...breathe... my mind ranted. "Is this invitation for the girls, too, or adults only?"

"Well, I hadn't counted on them, but they could watch the other kids. That would be awesome, that way we don't have to," she giggled. Did she really think I was going to bring my kids so she and her friends can have free babysitters? Oh, hell to the NO.

"I'll have to see if they are busy. They do have lives, you know. I have to go. I have groceries to put away, and apparently deviled eggs and potato salad to make." I was so fucking mad I could barely see straight.

"Cool. You get on that and I will talk to you later. 'k?"

"'k," I said with the most sarcastic tone I could muster and hung up. Shit, why didn't she just ask me to throw the fucking party for her? What the hell was I, a caterer? Party planner? I texted Tom.

So *we are going to a party I get to cook for and provide seating and drinks? She was even hoping for free babysitting. WTF????*

I had run a stream of curse words and judgments through my head when the phone rang. If it was Molly, I would throw the phone across the room. I could care less if it shattered into a thousand shards. Screw the fucking contract. Oh shit, it was Tom.

"Hey," I snarled.

"Hey, what's going on?"

"Oh, the usual, your sister-in-law decides to have a barbeque and I get to cook and bring drinks and our lawn chairs and...if the girls come, they get to watch all the kids, so everyone else can have a good time and not be responsible for their own children," I huffed out all in one breath. I wondered if he could tell I was a little perturbed. Duh.

"No one said we have to go."

"Wait, what? She said you already said we would go."

"Wayne asked, but I told him I would check to see if you had anything going on first."

"She is such a bitch."

"Wow, you're in a foul mood. What's the deal?" Man, I needed to chill out. I couldn't take this out on him. He didn't do anything.

"Sorry. I'm tired. I didn't sleep well, as you know, and," think, think quick, "this thing with Trish is bugging me."

"You can't do anything about it, babe. It's on Trish now. She knows we are here for her if and when she needs us. Hey, I gotta go. Shit ton of work still waiting."

"Okay, I love you. See you later."

"Ditto. Bye."

I sat down at the breakfast bar and held my head in my hands and cried. I had no idea why I cried. Was it Trish? The doctors? Being run over by Molly or...what? I decided not to fight the tears and just let them come. After a few minutes my eyes ran dry, and I ran my hands through my hair. I needed a nap. I hit the couch, turned on the boob tube and barely made it through a commercial before I drifted.

I am stuck behind a locked door...Mommy... mom... I have to go potty. Mommy can I come out... "Mom... mom...mom, wake-up."

"What?" My eyes popped open.

"Hey, you okay?" asked Shell with a slight look of concern. "I wanted to let you know I was going out tonight," she explained as she stood over me. "Really, are you okay? You don't look so hot."

"Gee thanks."

"You know what I mean. Are you sick?"

I don't know yet, Shell. I don't know. "No, I got hit by the Molly train that's all."

Shell rolled her eyes and nodded, "Ohhhhh, nuff said. What'd she hit you up for this time? Clothes, cleaning her house, oh, I know... your liver?"

"Gross, no, she is having a barbeque I get to do all the work for. You're lucky. She said if you and Lil want to go you get to watch all the kids. I told her you guys may be too busy to come. You can kiss my feet now." I raised my leg up and wiggled my toes at her.

She slapped my foot away in disgust and exclaimed, "Talk about gross. I think not. Thanks for covering for us. I have no intention of taking care of a bunch of brats while all the adults drink themselves into oblivion." Shell went for the fridge, opened the door, and stared at the items that lay before her. "Get anything yummy to munch on?"

"Depends on what you think is yummy. I got some really good grapes from the farmers market in there."

"Ooooooo, sign me up." With the bowl in hand, she popped one into her mouth and smiled. "Now those are good. Dang, that is one big watermelon. Better not let Molly know, or she will want you to bring it too. It would be sad cuz I won't be there to eat it."

"I am not taking the melon anywhere beyond our property line," I announced as I reached into the bowl. I popped a grape into my mouth. "You said you were going out. Where to? Who with? Am I paying? ...Wait, disregard that last question because I'm not paying."

"Just hangin' with my bestie, Hanners. Might go to the movies. Don't really know. I gots my own cash, so there. All I know is I don't have to work tomorrow, so I am gonna have me some fun."

"Sounds like a well-made, non-plan, kinda night."

She handed me the bowl of grapes and sniffed at herself. "Yup, but now I must shower cuz I offend."

"I agree," I announced while holding my nose as she walked by. Shell stuck out her tongue at me as she took the stairs two at a time. It was nearly five o'clock. Tom was getting off soon so I needed to get cleaned up and ready to go to dinner.

Chapter Six

I woke early, way too early for a Saturday if you ask me, but I had a party to throw. I mean cook for. How did I get myself into these things? Oh, I know, I was married to a guy whose brother married someone 19 years younger than him that's how. Mrs. "The world revolves around me" just had to have the *house* with a pool in the *n*eighborhood near th*e s*chools and th*e b*est shopping. Whatever, right? I was still standing in my kitchen, while the world slept, peeling potatoes at 7 a.m. so her majesty's party would be "the" party of the summer.

"What are you doing up this early," grumbled Tom, scratching in ways he shouldn't near a kitchen full of food, as he made his way to the coffee pot.

"Cooking for her majesty."

"Bitter much?"

"Duh."

"How do you really feel? Don't hold back," he cooed in a sarcastic Freudian kinda way. "You want some help? I can peel some taters."

Who was he kidding? He would hack those potatoes within an inch of their sad little spud lives. "Thanks, but no thanks. What you can do is get the two biggest pots out of the cabinet and fill 'em with water. Grab the eggs out of the fridge, put 'em in one of the pots, and get them started. Her majesty wants a dessert too. What should I make?"

Digging around in the cabinet making more noise than a bull in a china shop, Tom stopped for a moment appearing deep in thought. Pulling his head out from under the counter he gasped with hope in his eyes, "You got the stuff to make a slush cake?"

Were you frickin' kidding me? It took way too long to make and it wouldn't be set up by the time we had to go over there and cater her fucking party. Was everyone against me?

"Yeah, I have the stuff to make it, but it would never be ready by the time we have to be there," I huffed.

"Hey, don't bite my head off. You asked me, remember? I was trying to help," he mumbled from under the cabinet. "Why don't we just buy something at the bakery? No one said you have to make everything," he grumbled while pulling out the pots.

I was shocked he would even suggest such a thing. He knew I was the best cook around. Well, at least in this kitchen- illiterate family. Molly asked me to cook this stuff because she knew it would be good. Wait, why the hell am I defending her? Tom's right, I could just buy something.

Setting one of the pots in the sink and turning on the water, Tom looked at me, took a swallow of coffee and wondered aloud, "Where is it written Olivia mu*st m*ake everything from scratch an*d b*itch about it the entire time?"

"I am not bitching..." I stopped dead in my tracks. "...Okay, maybe I am bitching, but she wants my *food*."

"No, she wants you to pro*vide f*ood. That doesn't mean you, yourself, must make it all."

Oh, he was such a smartass and he was right...again, but I would never, ever, admit it. Ev*er.* "Fine, we will buy something somewhere, but it can't be crap." Why should I care if it was crap or not? This wasn't my party.

With a flourishing wave of his arms, Tom bellowed, "Ta-da. There, the eggs are on," with a bow and with his best Elvis impersonation, "Thank you, thank you, thank you very much."

"All right, Elvis, pour some vegetable oil in the pot. It will stop it from boiling over," I whispered in his ear and placed a small peck on his cheek. He was a good guy and was trying to help. I was not looking forward to all the fakeness I was going to have to put up with at this party. Cutting up some more potatoes and tossing them into the second pot I wondered how many people would be there. Molly never told me how many I was to cook for. Crap. Was I making enough? "Hey, Tom?"

"Yeah?" I heard wafting from the living room.

"Do you know how many people will be there? I don't know how much to make."

Coming around the corner, Tom was chugging the remainder of his coffee. "Make what you are making, if it's not enough too bad for her. She can carry her butt to the store and buy some from the deli." Leaning over, Tom and I were nose to nose. "Don't worry about it, okay?" With a stretch and a yawn he added, "I'm gonna go out to the garage and get some lawn chairs and wash out the cooler. What do you want to take to drink, booze or sodas?"

"Yes and yes."

"So, do you plan on drinking at this thing?"

"I might. It depends on how pissy I get," I added with a smirk.

He opened the kitchen door and turned to look at me. "Just remember you can't take back what you say while you are stupid drunk."

Oliver scurried into the kitchen before Tom could pull the door shut. He made figure-eights around my feet while I finished cutting the potatoes and turned on the burner. "What do you want from me, huh? It seems like everyone wants something." I picked up Oliver and walked over to where I kept his cat food. I scooped up some and dumped it into his bowl. I set him down and went to fill the water dish. "At least you show me love and affection when I do things for you. I bet I won't even get a thank you from that horrible woman." I set down the water dish, ran my hand down Oliver's back then turned to get another cup of coffee. Shit. That was when it dawned on me: this was a pool party, which meant bathing suits. I had to wear a bathing suit. For a 42-year-old woman, I wasn't in bad shape. Round is a shape, right? I wouldn't call myself an M.I.L.F., but I was still kinda cute. The sad reality was, Molly was 26, spent ho*urs p*erfecting her "look no stretch marks" body. You know the ones, boobs that gravity and pregnancy had not touched. You could bounce a quarter off her abs, and could still tell where the butt ends and the thigh started. You know the butt-slide that we older women have. It's kind of like a land slide, but it is your rear-end running down the back of your leg. Let's not forget the bingo wings I have been constantly fending off. She has no idea what is coming her way with age. This was a party, one of her parties, which meant there would probably be other 26-year-old "Barbie's" lying and prancing around the pool, too. I may as well have worn a parka and ski pants. Like my life wasn't bad enough at that point. God had to help me get through the day.

The potato salad was done and in a lovely bowl, and the 36 deviled eggs were safely stowed in the carrier in the fridge. Tom and I hopped into Caroline, his 57 Chevy and left for the bakery for desserts and then to the liquor store for booze, sodas, and ice. Luckily the stores were all located in the same strip-mall. I walked to the bakery while Tom darted into the liquor store. While perusing the selection of cakes, pies, cookies, and other concoctions which caused me to gain weight just looking at them, Alyssa and Dr. -I'*m panting*- sauntered in. How do you handle that kind of situation? Should I have said something, or pretended I hadn't seen them? How weird was it going to be looking the good doctor in the face, knowing he knew?

"Hey, Liv, What's up?" Alyssa greeted me with a little hug and HUGE smile.

"Hi," I said in an, I *didn't see you come in, I swear, k*ind of voice. "I need to grab something for a party this afternoon. What are you up to today?" I asked, but I really didn't care because I was waiting for Dr. -Oh *shit he knows*- to say something.

"Neil and I," she oozed while looking up at him as though he was the cover model for any modern romance novella, "are here to bow to our addiction to chocolate. You know how it is," she said while nodding her head at the collection I had piled in my arms.

I stood there holding two cakes, a pie and half a dozen doughnuts, yes, I knew how it was. "Well duh. Um..., hi, Dr.

Matthews, nice to see you outside of the office and not wearing a white jacket," I said without really being able to look into his eyes. Someone had to break the awkwardness there, right?

"Mrs. Carpenter, nice to see you too, but I think you can call me Neil since I'm not in a white coat, and you have on more than a sheet."

Silence, what the hell? Had he just blurted it out? With Alyssa standing right there!

Alyssa burst out laughing. "Girl, you should see your face right now, priceless. I wish I had a camera ready for that moment."

Dr. -I *want to punch you in the face right now*- had his arm around her waist with a shit-eating grin on his face.

"Sorry, I thought it was kind of funny." He tried to defend himself.

You sorry sack of shit.

"Oh, really it's fine. I'm glad I get to brighten up your day. You caught me a bit off guard, you know, coming from a doctor and all. It's the kind of crude joke I would expect from you, Alyssa," I bit out. I knew it would shut her up because she acted as though she was above talking like that. She always complained when Trish did it. Alyssa's cackling stopped and she gave me a look, the fu*ck you look*. I smiled.

"Well, I have a lot to get done for this pool party. It's nice to see you both. Have a good weekend. I'll see you later, Alyssa." I spun around, turned toward the register, and paid for my selections. Giving a small wave and nod of my head, I got the hell out of there. I met up with Tom at the car as he was pouring the bags of ice into the cooler.

"What's wrong now," he asked as he looked up at me.

"What do you mean?"

"When you got out of the car you were finally calming down. Now you look like someone licked your doughnuts." Tom stood up, looked at me with his hands on his hips and waited for an answer. He seemed to gaze past me when he asked, "Is that Alyssa? Who's 'The Dude?' He looks new."

Without even turning to look, I stated, "Yes, and yes. His name is Neil Matthews. The icky part is he is my gynecologist, weird right?"

A shiver shimmied its way up my spine causing me to tremble slightly.

"He's your wha… it's just… yeah, let's go with weird. Does she know he's that kind of doctor and you are one of his… you know?"

"Patients, I'm one of his patients. She knows."

Climbing into the car he quizzed, "And she's cool with it? You know, him seeing women naked and spread out like, well like…?" I thought I could actually see his skin crawl.

"She knows and 'spread' is not the word I would have chosen. I would really like to talk about something else, anything else, please."

We sat quietly in the car on the drive back home. I collected the sweets from the back seat when we parked in the driveway and went into the house to prepare everything for transport. I changed into my one piece bathing suit. Lily was sitting at the breakfast bar eating a bowl of cereal when I went back into the kitchen. I laid out the treasures from the bakery on the counter to rearrange them on a tray for the train wreck to come.

"Yippee, real food," she bellowed while tearing into a box.

"Finish your cereal before you stuff your face with crap." Man I sounded so motherly, funny because I had every intention of stuffing a doughnut into my mouth, too. I smiled at her. She knew.

"Don't worry, Mom, I'll save you one."

"Save me one, too," hollered Tom as he came in through the kitchen door. "You guys want any milk?" he asked as he got a glass from the cabinet and the jug from the fridge. We both nodded at him cuz our mouths were full. The three of us stood around the bar and enjoyed our doughnuts and milk.

"You coming to the pool party with us, kiddo?" asked Tom while catching a breath between bites.

"I don't know. Mom said the only reason Aunt Molly even agreed to let us come was so we could babysit for stupid drunk people," Lily complained while popping the remainder of her éclair in her mouth, tipping her head and raising her eyebrows at him.

"She can't make you watch anyone if you don't want to. You can come. Drive the other car so if you wanna leave, then leave, it's that simple." He seemed so satisfied with himself, but it was very hard to take him seriously with a milk mustache.

"Your dad's right. If you want to come, you better get a move on because we are leaving here in about a half an hour," I stated while tapping the imaginary watch on my wrist.

Forty-five minutes later Lily finally joined us in the driveway where Tom was buffing Caroline with a cloth diaper in gentle circles. He looked as though he was in his own little world. He loved his car. Caroline, as he called her, was a red and white '57 Chevy. She was beautiful, fully restored by Tom and his dad. I wondered if his connection to her was more than her perfect body, maybe the memories connected to his dad. Tom found her in a junk yard while hunting rabbits with his dad, Mitch, when he was younger. Mitch went back sometime later and bought her. He brought her home the winter before Tom left for the Army. They worked on her in the evenings and over the weekends, restoring and rebuilding her until she was a vision of perfection. I thought it was the nostalgia of the time Tom got to spend with his dad who drove him to care for her the way he did. I swore he loved the hunk of rolling metal more than he did me. It's okay because he could always sleep with her when I was mad at him, and he had.

"You ready?" huffed Lily. "You told me to be ready and here you are rubbing all over the car like you are putting suntan lotion on it. It's kind of disturbing."

"Don't be talking shit about Caroline. She's a good girl," Tom scolded as he snapped the cloth at Lily.

"All right, you two. I swear I have three kids instead of two. Come on, we have to get all this food over to Uncle Wayne's before it goes bad." Wouldn't it have been funny to see? I imagined a slew of perfect bodies blessed with professionally done hair barfing in Molly's neatly manicured yard. I smiled at the thought.

Tom called ahead and told Wayne we were driving Caroline and to clear a spot in the driveway for her. So, when we pulled up I was not surprised to see a space for her. There were cars everywhere. How many frickin' people did this nit-wit invite? I swore she needed a good shaking to get the bee-bee moving around in her empty skull. We got out of the car to gather up the feast I had been ordered to provide. Wayne threw open the front door, "What the hell took you so long? Do you have any idea how hard it was to keep Molly's lazy ass friends out of your parking space? God forbid they walk ten extra feet."

With a cheesy grin, Tom explained, "I had to buff her down and make her shine."

"I hope you are talking about the car and not Liv. That could hurt."

"Might have been more fun, but then we would have been even later." Tom pulled out the cooler. "So where does the 'lil woman want all this stuff?"

"I don't know. I could tell you where I think she would want it, but I would be wrong. Here, let me help you." Wayne took one of the handles and they disappeared through the front door, leaving Lily and me to manage the rest of the food.

"Oh, there you are. We were wondering when you would show up with the food." Molly's voice was like nails on a chalk board. I would have preferred she not speak. Ever.

"So sorry, I had soooooo much to make for *your* party. I didn't want to disappoint you and not make it perfect." I knew she couldn't be so stupid not to get the gist of the statement.

"Oh, I understand. I wouldn't want you to mess it up."

She *was* *d*umb enough to miss what I had said. Wow, I was actually shocked. "Um, well, okay, where do you want everything?"

"You can put it all on the table under the tent-like thingy. You know, so it's not in the sun. I wouldn't want the potato salad to go rancid out there." She grinned like a fool. Did I look like "the help"?

"Here," I handed her the large bowl of potato salad, "you can help us unload the stuff we brought." Ha, her face was so worth it. You would have thought I had just handed her a shitty diaper.

"Unload? Unload what? I thought you guys had it all?"

"You did ask me to make potato salad, deviled eggs, and desserts for everyone. Oh, and let's not forget all the beverages. What exactly did *you* provide?"

"I bought hot dogs and those ready-made frozen burgers. How convenient is that and cheap too."

"Have you ever eaten any of those burgers before?"

"No, this is the first time."

"You're about to find out why they are so cheap." This woman infuriated me. Just her existence pissed me off. I stormed off to the car to gather what was left, to get the hell away from her. As I walked back around the house with the tray of deviled eggs, I got a look at the people who were there. Holy shit, I was blinded by the number of belly button piercings reflecting the sun. There were tramp stamps on every female and maybe even a few of the males. It looked like some kind of Ho*llister a*d and here I was, old enough to be these kids ... younger...cool aunt.

Cut me some slack here, okay?

I unloaded the rest of the food and saw Molly had Lily cornered near all the screaming kids the mommies and daddies didn't want to take care of. Oh. Hell. No.

"Lily, I need your help," I yelled over to her, "Now." I hoped I didn't scare her. I didn't want her being used by Molly.

"Yeah? What do you need?"

I placed my hands on her shoulders and leaned my forehead against hers. "I don't need anything. I don't want Molly making you feel like you have to take care of other people's kids. You know you don't have to, right?"

"I know, Mom. That's what I was telling her. I told her I didn't come to babysit, and I think she got mad."

"Screw her, kiddo. You do not have to do a damn thing. You should have brought the other car so you could escape when you wanted."

"Who would keep you company then?" She was laughing at me, the little snot, but she was right. There was no one here besides Tom I would even have considered talking to.

"Come on, smartass. Let's try and find a spot to sit where we won't be blinded by these oiled up bodies."

Lily and I wanted seats far enough away we could hear the laughter, but not be subjected to the stupid comments that caused it. We could see the shine of the body oil, but not be nauseated by the coconut scent. We wanted to sit as far away as possible, but still be able to watch what was going on without actually having to be involved in any of it. So, we crossed to the furthest side of the pool and sat facing the land of stupid. It was like watching An*imation*

Domination on Sunday nights. Little ones were running around the pool, stuffing their faces with everything they could get their nasty little hands on and drinking way too much soda. These young mommies were going to regret not watching their children by the end of the day. I prophesied vomiting, sunburn, and hyper-active craziness in their futures. Lily was laid out next to me preparing to turn red. Tom and Wayne were burning meat, and Molly was walking around with her ass hanging out from either side of a string no wider than dental floss.

Yes, a thong. Really?

You had to be kidding me. That was it, time for a drink, and I didn't mean soda. I marched to the cooler and made sure whatever I snatched was cold and contained alcohol. I saw Tom eye me from the grill area. Before he could say anything or make it over to me, I downed an entire beer and grabbed another.

"What are you doing?" he asked between clenched teeth. Oh, he seemed a bit peeved.

"What does it look like? Correct me if I am wrong, but I believe this is a party. I am partaking in the drinks we *provided*, and then I am going to get some food I *made*. Then, if I run out, I may get another drink. I don't know. It depends on how thirsty I get."

Taking me by the hand, Tom led me a few feet away from the crowd which had formed at the food tent. "I told you earlier, you can't take back what you say or do when you drink. If you plan on drinking then you need to be smart about it. I don't need you causing any problems."

"Problems, I..." I snatched back my hand from his grip, "...being here is a problem for me. I am only here for you and your brother, not for the twit he married. He's such a fool." I left him standing there gaping. I made my way to the food tent and forced my way through. I piled on twice the amount I would have normally gotten and sauntered back to where Lily and I had taken up camp.

"Lil, hey," I nudged her, "I stole us some food. They are like a pack of frickin' wolves over there. I am waiting for someone to get bit." I moved a small cooler between our lawn chairs and set the food on it. We sat and watched the show. It was a whole lot of skin to see all in one place. It almost looked X rated. Then I saw someone which made my jaw drop. Red hair, no, bright red hair, skin so pale you could see veins, her name was Charlotte. She was Irish from the word go and proud of it. I looked to the heavens with a smile. I was saved. She was a proud, loud Irish woman who was married to a lil' Hispanic dude named Miguel Quiles. They were a contradiction in every way. He was 5'5" and maybe a buck and a quarter whereas she was 5'3" and easily a buck fifty. He was quiet and polite where she was loud and in your face. There she was, in all her glory, wearing a bikini and letting it all hang out. Charlotte Quiles was so comfortable in her own skin. I was jealous. She saw me, squealed and bounced over to me and Lily to claim her spot on the end of my lounge chair.

Chapter Seven

Charlotte came to a screeching halt mere inches from me and scooped me up into a hug. Even though I had at least six inches on her, she encircled me in her vitality. I could feel the joy just radiating from her skin.

"Let me take a gander at you." She smiled as she reached for Lily. "Give this big gal a hug."

Lily grinned and jumped to her feet to greet this powerhouse of a woman. "You look awesome," giggled Lily as she accepted the hug that was ordered.

"Awesome? Well I will take it and raise you a "fabulous," Charlotte quipped while claiming a seat. "So what are you fine gals doing all the way over here all by your lonesome?"

"Avoiding the *Hollister* ad on the other side. This is our little oasis from the land of fake, naked, and body oil," sighed my lovely daughter as she settled back onto her chaise.

"In that case, you's best get your ad perfect body over there with all those pretty people."

I think Lily had whiplash as she jerked to look at Charlotte as if she had lost her marbles and they were rolling around on the concrete. "Thanks, but I don't think so."

Had she declined because she didn't want to go over there, or because she disagreed with Charlotte's observation? Hmmm, something I will have to talk to her about when we aren't surrounded by prying ears.

"It's good to see you again, Charlotte. Where's Miguel?" I asked as I settled back down into my seat.

Moving to the chaise next to me, Charlotte gestured toward the grill area and explained, "He took the Scotch eggs and chalupas over to the food area and is talking to the boss men."

"Scotch wh*at and* chalupas? What the hell kind of combination is that? I thought you were Irish not Scottish?" My eyebrows had crawled so far up my forehead they got lost in my hairline.

"What? You don't like Scotch eggs and chalupas? I thought they would be good for a party. I am Irish. Where is it written I can't make something I like? I made chalupas and you don't question it."

"What the hell is a Scotch egg?" I quizzed, "and why are you mixing it with a chalupa?"

"You've never had them? A Scotch egg is a hard-boiled egg wrapped in sausage and deep fried and a chalupa is…"

I waved her off, to say I knew what a chalupa was.

"You know they," I waved my hand in the direction of the land of the young and slow-witted, "aren't gonna eat it, right?"

"They might not, means there is more for us."

"True. Let's go get you a plate before all the food is gone and I can get me one of them there egg thingies to try."

We left Lily in supplication to the sun and went in search of food. We stopped by the grill to see if our men folk wanted anything to eat. They stood there proudly as they ritualistically burned meat over an open flame. I regaled Tom with the tales of the Scotch egg. With lust in his eyes and a secret desire on his lips he whispered, "Bring me two" and Wayne nodded his head and begged, "Bring me more." Molly had brought food for Wayne but neglected Tom and Miguel. Annoyance bouncing around in my head, Charlotte and I walked off to the food tent and marveled at the remains of the carcass that was once the buffet table. Shocked at the carnage, but even more shocked anything remained. We proceeded to gather up food for our men and ourselves. I had already been in there and filled a plate for me and Lily. It wasn't likely I was going to get in the pool and show off my middle aged jiggle anyway. I was happy and somewhat saddened to see most of Charlotte's gifts remained on the table, but I was more than happy to gather a plateful for Tom and Wayne to enjoy. Piling two plates way too full I exited in the direction of the grill to pass off the food. On the way back to our designated oasis Molly grabbed my arm and steered me to the side. What was it with people thinking they could pull me around like a fucking wagon? "What?" I snapped as I tried to resettle my plate.

"What is that?" Molly hissed.

"What is what?" I looked at my plate and assumed she was questioning the food. "You mean this?" I gestured to the egg. "It's a–" before I could get out the words, she waved them away.

"No, I mean that thing over where you are sitting. That thing in the bikini with red hair."

"I know you didn't just call my friend a 'thing,' because if you did we are going to have a real issue right here and right now." My food hit the pavement as my stance stiffened and I leaned into Molly's space.

"She is an eyesore at my party. It is embarrassing."

As my hand came up I felt Tom's hand on my shoulder and Wayne's bulk at my side.

"What's going on?" Tom asked just millimeters from my ear.

"Your sister-in-law," I explained as I jabbed my finger in her face, "just called our friend a 'thing'," I clarified by using my fingers to put quotation marks around the word "thing."

Wayne ran his large hands threw his perfectly styled hair and sighed. "Did you say that?" He asked his wife. "No, I know you did. Who did you call a 'thing'?"

"Charlotte," I threw in.

Wayne dropped his head into his hand and asked, "Why would you call her that?"

"Wayne, honey, she looks...she...look at her," blurted Molly folding her arms over her tiny frame. "She is a bit of a shock to look at."

"So are you. Why don't you go and cover your ass instead of showing it to the world," I spewed. "You have also been quite successful in showing how much of an ass you can be, too." I stormed away from this huddle and got another beer from the cooler, popped the top and put the cold can to my lips. I eyed Tom as I stalked by. Wayne and Molly were still in a discussion, but if you didn't know what they were talking about you would think he was seducing her the way he petted her arms and held her face. Shit, why couldn't Tom and I fight that way? It would end in bed instead of him sleeping on the couch.

I made it back to my seat still clutching my beer. Charlotte looked up, tilted her head, and asked with a straight face, "Who's the wee slag prancing around like a peacock?"

"The what?" Most of the time I could make out what she was saying, her accent wasn't too bad, but it was the things she said which completely threw me off.

"Wee slag," declared Charlotte.

"Once again, what the hell is a wee slag?"

"Um...it's a...hold on." Charlotte waved Miguel over to ask him how to explain the statement.

Miguel's eyes widened a bit, but the smirk made me curious. He looked at Charlotte turned to me, and stated in the most gentile way, "Skank." He nodded his head and walked away to rejoin Tom at the grill.

I spat beer. Yup, all over my legs. Nice. "Who are you calling a slag again?"

Charlotte eyed the crowd and gestured with her chin in the direction of her target: "The one wearing band aids and twine." My eyes followed her directions and found Molly perched on her throne in the middle of her adoring fan club.

"She, unfortunately, is my sister-in-law."

"What did she want when she made you dump your plate?"

"To piss me off."

"Looks like she was successful in her venture," Charlotte chuckled and stuffed another deviled egg in her mouth. I nodded my head and drank the rest of my beer.

"Ta hell with her," Charlotte sneered with a wave of her hand, "Tell her she can give you an Aussie kiss and let's get our lash on."

"Aussie kiss? Lash? Will you speak fucking English, please?" I begged.

"Lash is getting' drunk and think about the words "Aussie kiss" and you will figure it out," she said with a knowing look.

"I am all for the lash part, let's do it." The remainder of the day passed in a haze of red hair, laughter, and beer.

Lily stuck it out with us throughout the entire party and even drove us home. I thought she may have started to have fun when some guy started talking to her by the coolers when she got up to get a drink. The next thing I saw was her head bobbing above the water in the pool playing volleyball. It was nice to see her enjoying herself. Her boyfriend, Darren, never took her anywhere unless she paid, drove, and forced him to come along. He was such a douche pickle. Maybe she was seeing there were other opportunities out there. Maybe this would show her the fun she could have if she went away to college. Maybe I had had too much to drink and needed to go to bed. I could still cross my fingers and hope for the best. Right?

Walking in our front door we saw a sea of bodies pooling in the living room and Shell was heading the wave. There were at least a dozen teenagers playing Wii and sitting around eating pizza and drinking what better be non-alcoholic beverages.

I was greeted with the melodic sounds of my Shell, "Hullo, Madre."

"Did I miss the conversation where you asked if you could invite a small nation into our living room?" I asked as I dropped my purse on the entryway table and fished out my cell phone to put on the charger.

"What you missed, Madre, were the texts I sent you asking if I could have a small nation over," she was a smart-ass, "but since you let your phone crawl down to the endless abyss that is your purse, I texted Dad."

"Cool. I am going to take a shower and pour myself into bed. Let's be clear. No guys stay the night. Do you understand?"

"Yavol,"she responded with a backwards salute. How could you not love her smart-ass attitude? I wondered where she got it from.

"Night all," I yelled above the rumble, "Don't burn down our house," I added. I was awarded with a united, "Good night, Mrs. Carpenter."

I treaded up the stairs wanting a hot shower and cool sheets. Tom was in the shower before I got there so I decided to do what he does. I slipped into the bathroom and jerked the shower curtain open and eyed my husband. Sometimes I forget why I fell for the man. Sometimes I forget how precious he made me feel. Sometimes I was a bitch. He was looking at me and waiting for a response, a response to what? "So, are you?" he asked again.

"Huh, am I what?"

"Are you gonna get in and wash my hard-to-reach areas?"

"Yup," I climbed in without even bothering to strip.

"Impatient, are you? Come here so I can get you out of those pesky clothes."

Tom fingered the tail of my tank top and worked it up over my head. He made short work of my cut-offs leaving me standing before him in the one piece bathing suit that never even met pool water.

"Do you want to talk about today?" Tom asked as he played with the straps of my suit.

"You want to talk? Now?" Was he kidding? I stood there in the shower with him and he wanted to talk?

"Yeah, I think we need to talk about Molly and what you did."

Pushing him away I stuck my finger in his face, "What I *did*? What the fuck did I *do*? Huh, come on, tell me what I did." I put my hands up in an attempt to stop him from speaking, I continued, "No, let me tell you what I did. I got food and was pulled to the side and asked what that 'thing' was. Turns out that thing, was our friend and funny enough I got mad. I wanted to defend my friend from a hateful, vile, disgusting person who cares about purses and shoes, but not about people. So please tell me what I did." I rested my crossed arms over my soggy bathing suit and waited for his justification.

"You made a scene. You could have handled it a lot better."

"I made a scene? I did not scream. I did not bitch slap her like I wanted to. I did not drag her by her hair. I stood there and listened to her degrade Charlotte and before I could do anything you were at my shoulder. So please tell me how I made a scene."

Reaching behind him, Tom turned off the water and took a towel from the shelf to wrap around his waist. He handed one to me to dry off but I hadn't even showered yet. I threw the towel to the floor, turned the water back on, and pulled the curtain shut. I tossed my wet suit to the end of the tub and stepped under the water.

"We need to talk about this, Olivia."

"I tell ya what. You stand there and figure out why I am pissed and then we can talk. But, until then, don't say one fucking word to me." A few seconds later I heard the door close. I turned my face into the jet of water and cried. I let the shower wash away my tears and contain my anger. After going through the motions of washing, conditioning, and soaping, I rinsed off and got out. I wrapped a towel around myself and went to our room to get some pajamas. Tom was under the covers with the lights off and not speaking. Screw him. I secured my pj's, my pillow, and exited to the spare room. Here I tried to have a special moment in the shower, and I got hit with a cold shoulder instead.

I needed to sleep. I pulled on my Pillsbury Dough Boy lounge pants and t-shirt, and sought out the comfort of my pillow.

I'm hungry, but Mommy will get mad if I bug her when her friends are over to play. But, I am really hungry. Maybe she won't get too mad. "Mommy, can I come out? I'm hungry, Mommy." I hear feets. They aren't pounding loud so maybe she's not mad. My skin feels all prickles. It's not Mommy, it's Myles.

"Come on, pumpkin. I'll get you something to eat and then we can play."

I was curled into the arm of the hide-a-bed screaming when Tom flew into the room. He folded me into his arms and swiftly carried me back to our bed. He rocked me and wiped my tears and talked the sleep out of my eyes.

"It's okay, baby," he soothed, "I'm right here. You're safe. It was just a bad dream."

I sniffled and waited for my heart to return to its natural rhythm. I took a deep breath. It *was only a dream. It was only a dream. It was only a dream. I* figured if I chanted it enough then it would wipe it all away. I could never say it enough to wipe the slate clean. Without letting go, Tom pulled me down further into the bed and covered me with the blanket and his protection. He smoothed the hair from my face and kissed away what was left of my tears. "Do you want to tell me about it?"

Why did he think talking about it would help? I had gone to therapy and still had the frickin' nightmares, so sitting there talking about them was going to do no good. "Nothing I haven't dreamt before. Just as scary and just as crappy and just as real."

"Was it the fight that triggered it?"

"Gee, I don't know, Dr. Phil, but maybe you can ponder it out in the middle of the night instead of going back to sleep. Back off the psychobabble bullshit and let me sleep."

"Okay, we can talk about it later. Let's get some sleep. Maybe being in your bed where you belong will help. I love you, babe." He turned off the light on the bedside table and wrapped me in his arms.

"I love you too...sometimes."

With a snort, Tom pulled me in closer and relaxed into our mattress. Within minutes I could hear his breathing become slow and steady, and I knew he was asleep. I laid there listening to the cadence of his breathing and prayed I would be lulled back into a less scary dream, but I was clearly not so lucky. Every time I closed my eyes I saw demons, demons I would rather have forgotten. I swear I could even smell the past. Shit, what time was it...4:37 a.m. I couldn't lay there and get inside my own head. I needed to focus on something else. I carefully extracted myself from Tom's bear hug and slipped out of our room.

Coffee was what I needed. I was half way down the stairs when I saw bodies, lots of bodies. None of them better pee standing up or he will forever pee sitting down. With a quick scan of the room I determined there were no weeds among the flowers. Flowers? Could those girls smell any worse? Between nasty sneaker feet and whatever God awful stuff they ate during the night, it smelled more like fertilizer than a bouquet of fresh flowers. I tip-toed through the mess which was my living room and made my way to the kitchen. I quietly set up the coffee pot and slipped out onto the back deck to wait for it to brew. It was so quiet, maybe too quiet for me to escape my own mind. I headed back to the coffee pot to grab a cup and to get my phone off the charger. Oooo...looks like I was popular. I had six messages and two missed calls.

Two texts were from Shell asking if she could have friends over and one saying she asked Dad since I wasn't answering in a timely manner. One text was from Charlotte asking if we could get together for lunch. Cool. The last two made the hair on the back of my neck stand up. They were from Trish:

He's bad tonight. 8:44pm

911 10:01pm

Fuck, one missed call from Trish, one voicemail from Alyssa.

"*Liv, I'm at Bayview Hospital. Trish was brought in. Richard really messed her up. Call me as soon as you can.*"

I could hear the tears in her voice. I knew it was bad.

I hit the floor running. I snatched clothes out of the dryer and threw them on. I think the shirt was Tom's. Who cared? Cell, purse, what else, anything...? Keys! Flip-flops. I was in the car within minutes of hearing the message. Wait. Do I call Lys? It was only like five in the morning. Screw it. I hit dial.

A groggy voice answered the phone, a groggy ma*le* voice. "Hello?"

Surprised and annoyed I stated the obvious: "I need to speak with Alyssa."

He cleared his throat and responded with the typical, "She's asleep right now."

"Look, I am aware of the time. This is Olivia, and I need to talk to Alyssa, now." My impatience was showing and I didn't care.

"Olivia, this is Dr. Matthews...Ne–," I cut him off before he could continue with the unneeded introduction.

"I know who this is, and I know it is not who I want to talk to. Put her on the phone please." I could hear her voice ask who it was on the line. Dr. -Dumb-ass- explained it was me and finally handed over the phone.

"Liv? Why are you calling so early? What's wrong?"

"What's wrong? I don't know. Maybe because you said to call you when I got your message. Maybe because our friend is in the hospital. Maybe to wake you up so you can screw my doctor again. You pick and let me know which." Yup, I was pissed.

"What the fuck is your problem?" she yawned. "It's not like the hospital is gonna let you in to see her until visiting hours or anything."

"Fine. Don't tell me what happened, or why you were crying last night. I will go see her later and find out for myself." I disconnected the call before I had to listen to one more syllable from her mouth. Fuck, fuck, fuck! I hated people. I crawled out of the car and slammed the door behind me. What do I do now? I stormed back to the house, but remembered as I was about to slam the door there were a shit ton of girls playing carpet in my living room. Argh, I closed the door cautiously and headed for the coffee pot. As I poured another cup I fumed about everything: not getting the messages, Trish going back to that piece of shit, the douche bag husband putting his hands on her again, Alyssa not helping at all, and having to hear Dr. -I'm in bed with your friend's- voice so early in the morning knowing what he knew about me. How could Alyssa date my doctor? Maybe she was just using him for sex. It wouldn't be the first time she did that to some poor sap. For someone so put together, she was a hot mess when it came to the male persuasion.

I carried my coffee out to the deck and took my position at the table. I took a much needed sip and stared off into the oblivion which was my mind. I turned my head slightly and saw Tom sitting next to me staring. "What?" I asked because I knew he had said something while I was swimming laps in my brain.

"How long have you been out here?"

"Few minutes, I guess," as I took a sip of now cold coffee, "or more," I added when I realized how cold my coffee was. Wow, how long had I been lost in a daze?

Tom raised his mug to his lips, but hesitated to ask, "Do you wanna come back to bed or are you up?"

"Does it look like I want to go back to bed?" I sneered as I pulled at my pant leg. "I am up, dressed, and have consumed coffee. Why would I go back to bed now?"

Swallowing a large gulp of Folgers' best, Tom inquired, "So, who pissed in your corn flakes this morning? I would appreciate it if you wouldn't bite my head off this early."

He had a point. This wasn't his fault, but the night before was. "So you think I should forget last night? Do you plan on telling me what I did to cause a 'scene' as you called it?"

"Hey, you're the one who got in Molly's face and threw food all around."

"Excuse me," I screamed way too loud. I leaned my body in his direction so he could get a clear look at my anger. "You seemed to have skipped over the part where she pulled me to the side. Where she referred to our friend as a 'thing'," I spit out using air quotes. "As for the food, I did not throw anything. I dropped it when she said something so shocking and vile I was surprised by it. Get your fucking story straight before you come at me with stupid accusations."

"Look, I am asking questions based on what Molly and Wayne told me."

"Wayne didn't see anything. He was with you, if you remember correctly. How the fuck would he know what was said or done." Flinging my hands in the air I squealed, "Oh wait, I know. Molly told him. Therefore it must be so truthful we can call it gospel. God forbid what I say is true. Why? Because my ass is bigger than a size four and I wear clothes that actually cover my ass...etc."

Leaning over the table in defeat Tom grumbled, "I don't wanna fight. It's too early to fight. All I wanna do is eat."

"I'm supposed to forget any of this shit even happened. That you questioned my actions? Is that it?"

"Fine, you're right, okay? I was wrong. You were right. Can I take you to breakfast now?"

"No, it's not fine, but we will shelve this conversation for now because I want waffles."

"Mmmm, I'm thinkin' biscuits and gravy."

Tom went back in to the house to get ready to go to our friendly local Maria's restaurant. I decided to warm up my neglected cup of coffee. I realized I had a raging headache starting, so I got the Advil off the refrigerator and popped two with a swallow of my much warmer coffee. What was going on with my world? So much I didn't know what to focus on first. I had my doctor's appointment in two days, Trish was in the hospital because Richard was allowed to breathe, and Alyssa was doing Dr. -S*cratch my Itch*-. Why does it bother me she is playing naked with the good doctor? Weird. It's not like I had a thing for him. He was hot, but that was all. Why did it bug me?

Tom interrupted my inner psychoanalysis with the probing question, "You ready for food?"

"Let's do it."

We exited through the back door and went to the garage to take Caroline for a spin. Tom led the way and opened my door to let me slide in first. How sweet. Proof he knew he screwed up last night. It was all good. I would add it to the list of stupid shit he had done over the years.   As I settled into the seat I could smell Armor All and Windex. It was a wonderful smell that brought back memories of summer drives and make-out sessions in the back seat. There were so many things I wanted to do again or do for the first time. I was shaken from my whimsy as we backed down the driveway and sped off toward food. Maria's was only a few blocks away and we could have walked, but I would have missed out on a chance to be noticed in Caroline. Men drooled when they saw her and women always took notice. Women tended to pay more attention to the driver, but that was cool cuz he was all mine, bitches. Maria's was normally packed but since it was only quarter after six, the crowd was light. As we slid into a booth, the waitress greeted us with her normal unenthusiastic banter: "The usual, Hon?"

"Nah, I'm gonna venture away from the norm today, Alice. I am gonna go for the biscuits and gravy with a side of cottage fries, coffee and water, please," drooled Tom. Geesh, get a bib.

"And you's, Sweetie?"

Never glancing at the menu I ordered up my morning's desire. "I am thinking waffles, bacon, crispy please, coffee and water."

Alice scratched our orders onto the worn memo pad and slid her pen into the wadded up bun on her head. As an afterthought she asked if we needed cream and sugar before she toddled into the galley style kitchen.

"Guess what happened last night," I anteed up while I waited for my coffee.

"What? At the party?" Tom cocked his head and I could see the events of the previous night tick through his head.

"No, I got a couple texts and a voicemail. Alyssa left a voicemail to let me know Trish is in the hospital. Dick Head beat the crap out of her again."

Silence hovered over us as Alice brought out our coffees and water. I busied myself with sugar and cream, while Tom's face heated with anger.

I blew across my coffee cup and took a hesitant sip. I looked at Tom over the rim of the battered cup and said, "I figured I would go by the hospital this morning to see how she is and if she needs anything. You know, like pamphlets of every safe house within a fifty mile radius and a ball bat."

"So, is the piece of shit in jail? Is she gonna press charges this time?" The venom in his words was evident.

"Don't know..." I paused long enough to allow Alice to put our food in front of us and vacate, "...that's why I want to go to the hospital to see her and talk some sense into her. If she hasn't, statistically she probably won't."

"So, what's the point in going?"

"I can be hopeful, can't I?"

Silence took its place across the table from me. I sat and waited for a response but Tom ate his breakfast with a sprinkling of wrath. Why was he so pissed? He dropped his fork to his exhausted plate and looked me in my eyes.

"Not everyone is you," he pointed out, and with his fingers he began to tick off the reasons why. "First: not everyone is strong enough to wade their way through a childhood of shit. Second: not everyone can battle an abusive waste of skin, who claimed to love you, and third: not everyone can do all of that and still come out with a heart."

"But-"

Cutting me off he continued with conviction, "No but's. You can't assume Trish can walk away from this. I know she's your friend, but you can't make her be what she's not ready to be." Tom raised his hand and waved to Alice for the check.

"That's fine, but I can't write her off either," I huffed. "She's strong and will see Richard for what he is."

"When? When he puts her in the hospital again, or maybe when he puts one of the boys in there or worse?" He reached for his wallet in the back pocket of his time-bleached jeans and pushed away from the table to pay for our meals. I sat and sipped at my coffee and prayed for some kind of magical answer to the ugly reality poking me in the face. Tom was right. You couldn't make someone be strong.

Tom stepped up to the table and laid down a tip way more than Alice had earned, but that was Tom. "You ready?"

"Yeah, you gonna go to the hospital with me?"

Without looking at me we turned toward the exit. "No." I knew better than to push it. I would go on my own.

It was still too early to go to the hospital. We went home, and went our separate ways at the door. Tom went to vent in the garage, and I attempted to clean up even though there were still snoring girls covering every surface of my living room. That was when I decided the extra room in the basement would be turned into a hangout for the girls and their horde of friends.

I collected a cup of coffee and my thoughts, and went up to our room. I sat on the edge of the bed and stared out the window at nothing but the past, present and possible future which was my life. Why couldn't my world leave the past where it belonged, in the past? It seemed to find ways to poke out its thorns at every turn. The little pricks. My present seemed to be in a limbo all its own. I had no way of knowing where each moment would take me. Didn't the great wide open know I had my own problems to deal with? Why were the issues of my friends creeping into my daily worries?

"Quit worrying about her."

I nearly launched right out of my own skin. Where the hell did he come from?

"What? Worrying about who?" I asked as Tom walked into the attached bathroom.

"Trish, who else? You have more than one friend in the hospital?"

I avoided the opportunity to tell him my little issues: "Oh, no. I was just zoning out there for a minute."

"Wayne called and asked me to come and help him move some crap around in his basement. Is that cool with you?" Tom grunted as he pulled on a clean t-shirt.

"Sure, I'll be leaving here in a few minutes anyway to go see Trish." I glugged the last of my coffee and collected myself and scattered thoughts, which seemed to hang on the periphery of my mind. "Have fun, don't hurt yourself, and please don't drop anything heavy and breakable on your dear sweet sister-in-law," I instructed with loathing in my tone.

"I'll try not to." Tom stepped into my path and pulled me into his embrace. "Hey, come here. You can't fix the world. All you can do is be there for your friend. Okay?"

"I know." I allowed myself to huddle there, if only for a moment. I tipped my head up, kissed him on the corner of his mouth and slipped from his grasp. "Okay, I'm gonna go and so should you."

"Yup," he smirked while placing a ringing smack on my backside as we took the last step on the staircase.

"Hey, that hurt...a little. Jerk."

"That's me. Jerk, Tom Jerk," he said in his best Bond British.

I found my purse and rummaged through it to ensure I had everything, because God knows women literally kept everything in their purses. "I'm off," I smiled. "Love you...bye."

"Bye, babe."

I exited the safety of my home to venture into the abusive world of a friend. On the short drive to Bayview I mentally prepared myself for what I might see. Alyssa didn't tell me the extent of Trish's injuries. Actually she didn't tell me a damn thing. So, I was running with a worst case scenario outlook.

Chapter Eight

Karma was having a bit of fun based on the music that was playing on my drive to the hospital. Rhianna and Eminem crooned about lying and loving and burning down houses. What a fitting song to have sung along to while I drove to see an abuse victim. It had always amazed me the music you listened to during a particular moment in life carried the sentiment of that moment. When you were heartbroken all you heard were love songs that reminded you of the one who done you wrong. Coincidence? A sign? The Fates spewing their version of a twisted joke?

My teeth were on edge. I could feel my breakfast fighting with my stomach. My tears slid from my eyes like lava. It made me angrier I had cried, which only fed the anger I had already started cooking inside.

"Pull it together, Olivia," I hissed to myself as I pushed the tears aside and pulled into the parking lot at Bayview Hospital. It was early on a Sunday morning, so the parking lot was hungry for visitors. I was able to slip into a parking space fairly close to the main entrance. I gave myself a once over in the visor mirror to wipe clean the tears from moments ago. T*rish has enough to deal with. Don't make her deal with you, too, I* reminded myself. I threw the door open of my simple little car and placed my foot squarely on the ground. I hated hospitals. Even when gracing the world with the arrival of my children, I hated being in there. I had seen the inside of these walls one too many times in my younger years. But, this time, I was here for her. I crossed the parking lot listening to the echoes of my flip-flops bouncing off the side of the building. A gust of air conditioned, antiseptic-scented air hit me as the automatic doors opened. It made my nose burn and brought goose bumps to my flesh.

"Good morning," I greeted the woman manning the welcome desk. She was long in mileage, but quick with a smile. "I am here to see Patricia James. Could you please tell me what room she is in?"

"Certainly, now let's see here," she seemed to jest as she poked her glasses back up her nose. "What was the name again?" she asked as she started to peck at the keyboard in front of her.

"Patricia James, she was brought in last night."

"Oh, there she is. She is in room 542 on the fifth floor. The elevators are right over there, dear," she instructed pointing a twisted finger down the hall.

"Thank you," I offered over my shoulder as I walked toward the silver doors. I slipped inside after little to no wait at all and pushed the button for the fifth floor. I leaned back against the railing and thudded my head off the metal wall. Breathe in, breathe out was what my brain forced me to do. Y*ou can do this. This isn't about you. Focus on Trish. T*he elevator slowed and jerked to a stop at my destination. I stepped out and looked at the "You Are Here" sign across from the open doors to find Trish's room. I turned on my heel and headed to the right of the elevator and scanned the room numbers in search of 542. I knew it before I could even see the door. There was a man in a bad suit standing just outside of a room near the end of the hall talking on a cell phone. I slowed my advance and stopped a few feet short of him as not to disturb his call. When he disconnected he looked at his notebook and scribbled something on a marred page.

"Um...excuse me, is this room 542?" I asked while I leaned as far forward as I could to try to see into the room.

"Yes it is, and you are?" The man eyed me with a question mark between his eyebrows.

"Olivia Carpenter. I am a friend of Trish's, Patricia James."

"You'll have to stay out here while Detective Nichols and I finish up with Mrs. James," Detective -Ey*ebrows*- stated as he stepped back into the room.

I perched myself on the edge of a very uncomfortable chair against the wall next to Trish's doorway. I could hear muffled voices and could make out a bit of what was being said. The detectives were asking questions about what happened and if this had ever happened before. "If *this had happened before"* what did they mean by th*is?* Th*is w*ould be called spousal abuse. I couldn't hear Trish's response. I prayed she told them the truth. You didn't fall down. You didn't walk into a cabinet door a dozen times. Pl*ease,* I prayed, t*ell them what he did.* I stiffened when I heard the obligatory, "If you have any questions or remember anything, my number is on the card."

Seconds later the two police detectives stepped from the doorway. They both eyed me and slid prefabricated smiles onto their faces. With military precision they made their way to the elevators I had exited minutes before.

Should I? Would it help? Decision made. "Wait," I jumped from my seat and nearly ran to catch up with them.

The men stopped and turned as I reached them. "Yes, ma'am? Can we help you with something?" asked the man who had been in with Trish when I arrived. I looked at his shiny name tag that showed his name: Detective J. Nichols.

"Did she tell you the truth? Please tell me she is going to press charges against that piece of-" I hissed.

Raising a firm hand, Detective Nichols cut off what would have been a rather nasty rant, "Miss, we can't disclose anything," he grumbled solemnly.

"Look, I get it. You have to be all official, but what if I have pictures of what he did to her a couple of days ago," I asked with concern and hope in my shaky voice.

"Did she press charges after that incident?"

"No, but I know there was a domestic violence call made by a neighbor. She came to my house the next afternoon. When she fell asleep on my couch I took pictures of the bruises and scrapes I saw," I explained as I dug through my purse in search of my elusive phone. "I have them on my phone and on my computer at home. Do you want to see?" I asked as I held out my cell phone to them.

With a nod from Detective Nichols' I opened the picture gallery on my Galaxy and handed it to him. -Eyebrows- looked over Nichols shoulder at the photos before them. They skimmed through the pictures and, as Nichols handed me back my phone, -Eyebrows- handed me his card. Typed in masculine print across the top was his name and it wasn't Officer -Eyebrows-. His name was Detective C. Arnold. Hmmm...it didn't work for me. He will remain Detective -Eyebrows- to me.

"We're gonna need you to email those photos so they can be added to the report. I can't say they will help, but it couldn't hurt," -Eyebrows- requested. "My email address is on the card along with my contact number at the station."

"Okay, I can do that when I get home. Is that good?"

"Yes, ma'am, that would be fine."

"Olivia, my name is Olivia or Liv," I clarified.

"Right, Olivia, please email those," he emphasized by pointing to my phone, "as soon as you can."

"I'm taking a chance that may cost me my friendship, but save my friend at the same time. I just want to help her."

"We do too."

I turned back toward Trish's hospital room to visit my friend. My flip-flops squeaked and made an annoying clapping sound as I made my way to room 542. I didn't bring flowers. I didn't bring candy or a gift. This wasn't something you celebrated or reminisced about over a trinket that was bought to commemorate the day. This was the kind of day you swallowed down deep and used as mortar to build the wall of protection around your sanity. It was the kind of event you referred to as that day, the day things changed.

She lay in bed with her eyes focused on something on the outside of the wall of windows. She was in the bed closer to the door, so there was no way she was able to see what was on the ground, but she had a clear view of eternity.

"Hey," I whispered as to not violently upset the silence.

Trish turned her head to face forward, but not toward me, and responded with a simple "Hey."

"How are you?" Well, wasn't that a stupid question. She was in the hospital for God's sake. It's not like she sprained her ankle doing the Mambo.

"I am fine," she snipped. "It's not like it's the end of the world."

I stepped closer to the side of her bed and looked at the end result of Richard's stupidity. My friend looked like a broken china doll. Her lips were swollen and split so deep that they required stitches. The entire side of her face was the darkest purple I had ever seen. Her eye was so swollen I couldn't tell if she was able to open it. Her broken nails were twisted around the thin blanket that covered the rest of the evidence. I could see tape and the edge of a bandage on the top of her head that was leading down the other side of her face. I chose not to walk around to the other side of Trish's bed. I knew how hard this was for her and how embarrassed she had to be. I slid one of the visitor chairs closer to where I had been standing and sat next to the bed.

"Do you want to talk about it?"

Keeping her head turned slightly away from me she whispered, "What is there to talk about?"

"How you ended up in here, what or who caused all the bruises and cuts and what you are going to do next?" I tried to keep my tone as even as possible, but I'm sure I failed miserably.

"I fell."

"Fell. Where? Into Richard's fists, boots, belt...what did you fall into?" The calm was gone.

"Don't judge me," she hissed through her stitches. "You don't know what you are talking about. I fell down the basement stairs."

"Carrying a bag of what? Bricks, wrenches, ...his work boots?" I stood with so much force the chair tipped backward into the wall. I stomped around to the other side of the bed demanding she look at me. I stopped dead in my tracks when I came face to face with a demonstration of pure hatred. The bandage edge I had seen from the other side of the bed covered where her ear was. A large bald patch was visible at the back of the bandage and a gash with jagged stitches interrupted the flow of skin at her jaw. "Jesus Christ," I gasped as my hand flew up to my lips. "Oh, Trish," I sighed in agony for my friend.

"Don't."

My throat tightened as I tried to swallow past the ball formed in my throat. "How can I help you? Let me do something to help, please," I begged.

"You wanna help. Leave." She sounded so angry...at me.

"Why? What did I do? Why does it sound like you are pissed at me?"

"You and your husband pissed him off. Tom made threats. You pissed him off." Trish was breathing hard and spittle was stuck to the dried blood that caked on her lips. She was blaming us for what that worthless sack of shit did to her.

"Are you blaming this on me?" I asked gesturing to myself.

"If you had just left it alone he would have calmed down."

"You are blaming me," I stated with total shock screaming off my face. "I didn't do this..." I gestured to all of her, "...I was there when you needed a place to go. I was the shoulder you used to cry on, and I will be here for you whenever you need me. But, I will not carry the blame for what your poor excuse for a husband did to you." I was on the defensive.

"Just go," Trish demanded and turned her face away from my line of sight.

"If that's what you want. If you need anything call. I will be there for you."

"I don't need your help."

My spine straightened as I stepped back into her line of sight. I leaned toward her so that she could get a good clear look into my eyes and said, "When you realize that this is not going to stop and your beautiful boys see this," I gestured toward her again, "you will need someone. If you think for one minute that Douche Bag won't touch your kids, you are sadly mistaken." I straightened and took a deep breath. "I know you are scared and confused and need someone to blame, but I am not the one to carry that load of shit. I don't blame you for being upset, and I will not hold this against you. When you are ready, I will be there." I stepped back around to where the chair was still leaning against the wall. I righted the chair and walked out of the room. I turned right and took a few steps when I immediately reached for the support of the wall. I turned my back to it, slid down to the floor and cupped my face in my hands. The damn broke and the tears came. A nurse appeared in front of me. She placed a warm hand on my shoulder and offered me a small box of tissues. She said nothing. She gave me a sympathetic I *understand* kind of smile and stepped away. I took the tissues, mopped up the down pour and blew my nose. I tipped my head back and listened to Trish cry. I couldn't go to her side. I couldn't wipe away the tears and tell her this would pass and we would help her regain control of her world. I wanted to, but she didn't want me. I picked myself up off the floor and walked down the long hallway toward the elevator. As I passed the nurses' station I set the box of tissues on the counter and thanked her for her kindness without missing a step. I poked the button to call the elevator and waited for the ding. It felt like an eternity standing there, but it was only a minute. As the doors slid open I stepped to the side to allow two people to exit. I stepped in and pushed the button for the lobby, moved back, and wrapped my fingers around the railing for support, not for the elevator ride but for the roller coaster that my emotions were on at that moment.

When the elevator descended to the lobby and the doors opened I was greeted by a face I knew, Alyssa. I pushed past her and walked right out the front door.

"Wait."

"Go fuck yourself...no, wait," I sneered as I spun around, "go fuck the good doctor while your friend sat in a hospital alone all night."

"What the hell? It's not like you were around to be here for her."

"True, but I also didn't know anything about it until this morning." I stepped right up into her face and continued, "You fucking knew and left her here. What? You wanted to play doctor with the doctor? Is he more important than being there for your friend?"

"Where the hell do you get off judging me? I was here when she came in last night."

"Wait, you were already here? So you weren't here for her? You just happened to be here, or were you under a desk somewhere having a quickie?" Silence. Busted. "That's what I thought." I turned in my spot and stalked toward my car. "I hope all three of you will be happy together, and let the good doctor know I will be finding a new physician."

"Why would you do that? Because you are pissed at me for dating him," she asked as she closed the distance between us.

"You don't date, Alyssa. What was it you said...?" I halted to try to remember clearly. I opened my car door and white-knuckled the top as my memory found the correct path. "Oh, yeah," I spun around so I was looking at her as I spat out her nasty truth. "You treat dating as if they were interviewing for a job, and it wasn't your fault none of them me*asured up*. That's why none of them lasted longer than a good orgasm. Wasn't that what you said? I'm pretty sure it was. You've been seeing him for a couple weeks now, right? He must measure up. But for how long?" I swung myself into my car and yanked the door shut.

"Are you really gonna leave like this?" she asked as she stood there with her mouth gaping open in a very unattractive way, arms slack at her sides, shocked and defeated.

I lowered my window slightly and snarled, "Close your mouth. You're drawing flies. Or are you just practicing for later. Stretching out those jaw muscles?" I started my car and drove away. Within seconds my tears were burning a blazing trail down my cheeks, and my cell phone was ringing from the bottom of my purse, and that was where it was going to stay...for now. I said some terrible things I will regret more and more as time goes by, but at the moment I was angry and hurt. I tried to reach out to help someone, but got slapped in return. I needed to go to my safe place and lick my wounds. Where was my safe place? Tom was with his brother and her. *My* friends were the reason I needed my safe place, so they weren't going to be it this time. Huh...I have no safe place without the people I considered as my armor. Great. Why the fuck was all of this shit hitting me? Fuck them, all of 'em.

I skidded into my driveway, just missed the girls' car by inches. I sat there for a few minutes and tried to get my anger under some semblance of control before I faced Shell and her cohorts. I knew I could handle all of this shit. I needed to remind myself. I gathered up my stuff and my nerve and wandered back into the home.

"Nice entrance. Are you gonna be trying out for the next Fa*st and the Furious?*" Shell asked with a snide grin on her face. "I would be more than happy to practice with you."

"I don't think that would be a good idea, for either of us. But, thanks for the offer." I dropped my bag and keys on the entry table and turned back to my conscious daughter. "I'm shocked to see your eyes open."

"Lanie had to go home early and wasn't real quiet about it. So here I am...awake, while everyone else snores." Shell scanned the room filled with her friends and noticed, "Man, did you hear them snoring. God, it's loud."

"Oh yeah, I heard. The smell wasn't that great either. You hungry? What do you think everyone would want to eat?" I asked as I hurdled the bodies between me and the kitchen.

"I don't know about them, but I could so go for some French toast and bacon...mmmm...baaaacon." A serine smile sped across her face as her eyes drifted closed at the thought of, yes, bacon.

"You need help. Like doctor type help for your obsession with porkie products," I joked.

"I get it from Dad."

"All right, I will start breakfast, and you, gently wake your friends. Okay?"

"Sure," she chuckled. "Wake up," she bellowed only to be greeted with groans and flying pillows. I chuckled softly and told myself, My *safe place is where I make it.*

Just as I finished piling the French toast on a plate, the last of the zombies made her way to the table. I carried out the French toast and tray of bacon only to be greeted with grunts and hands snatching at the food. I dropped the victims into their ravenous grasp and stepped away before I was bitten.

I needed to get out of there. I went up to my room and put on comfortable walking clothes and slipped out for a walk in the park. As I left my world behind, I slid my earbuds in and cancelled out the whines of the world, so I could focus on my own whining for a while. I walked the three blocks to the park under the cover of the shade trees which lined both sides of my street. The maple trees were relics of decades past and sweeping in size. Wide and tall, they created a canopy that tunneled my path. They were a blessing in the heat of the day and a torment in the winds and snow of the cold. Either way, I loved the scent they shared, the piles of leaves I watched my children dive into, and the safe haven they provided for the creatures that lived near us. I needed the serenity of being alone, alone with my thoughts and heartbeat. Sunday would allow just that. At this time of the morning most people were gathering in a church somewhere, and I was in my own private session with God and nature. I walked the paths while running issues through my head. What was up with me? Why was I so quick to anger these days? Why was I so pissed at Alyssa and Dr. -I *saw you first-?* My world seemed to be imploding, and I didn't know how to stop it. Hell, I didn't even know why it was happening, or did I? How cryptic could I get? You knew you were good when you could confuse yourself while soul searching. I think I needed a map.

I came upon my favorite place in the park and drifted to a bench to be still. I laid claim to the place that allowed me to put my back to the rest of the lives out there and focused on the beautiful fountain before me. I sat and watched as some droplets of water bounced onto the concrete surround of the fountain. That was how I was feeling at that moment. I wasn't good enough to be in the pool. I was being cast off and left to fall to the side and sear away, alone. What was I supposed to do? Trish was mad at me for reasons that made no sense at all, at least to someone who didn't understand what she was going through. I knew how bad things could get, and until she saw it for herself, I couldn't help her escape the landslide she was about to be covered in. I would be there no matter what. All she would have to do was give me a sign she was ready and needed me.

I turned up the volume as Adele sung of scars and despair. That didn't have to be her story. Trish could still have it all if she were ready to take hold of it, like I did. In that situation I knew not to grab at her hand, but wait until she reached out. The reality was, she may never extend herself far enough to want the help, and I would have to accept it and walk away. I could not let myself get sucked into her personal hell. I shifted my position, lay back on the seat of the bench and swung my left foot up so my heel was perched on the seat back. With my right arm bent and behind my head I took a deep breath and slowly let the air escape my lungs. What could I do about the blow up with Alyssa? I treated Alyssa like shit on my shoe and had no clue as to why. My eyes were staring at the leaves over head when my line of sight was invaded by a very large snout.

"Shit," I screamed at I flailed my body to get upright as quickly as possible, yanking the buds from my ears. "What the fu...Matilda?"

"Sorry, I didn't know anyone was over here," Alyssa stated as she reached out her hand to grab her Great Dane's collar.

"It's fine. I know she's harmless," I said as I reached out to pet the huge puppy.

Silence. Awkward. Uncomfortable. Extended...silence.

While clipping the leash to Matilda's collar, Alyssa lobbed the bomb that we were both tossing around in our heads, "So, are we going to get this straightened out, or will we do this every time we see each other?"

"I don't know," I shrugged. "To be honest with you, I don't know what to say." I sat on the bench bent at the waist supporting my upper body with my elbows on my knees. I couldn't bring myself to look at her. If I looked, I would either give in to my anger, or cry and forget any reason I may have had to be upset to begin with. True, I wasn't really sure why I was mad at her all I knew was that I was.

"You weren't lacking in words at the hospital," she sneered.

I guess I got to hang onto the anger. "True, and that statement didn't help in putting out the fire, now did it?"

"Why are you pissed off at me? I haven't done anything to you. This is bullshit!" she bit out. "Where do you get off being shitty? Trish said all this was your fault. What the fuck did you do to make Richard do that?"

I was on my feet and in her face before I could finish a blink. "Excuse me? What did you just accuse me of? You have no fucking clue about any of this." My hands were shaking as I pointed my finger in her face. "Richard would have found a reason to beat the shit out of her or make one up. Did Trish mention that he had a good head start on the bruises just a couple of days ago?"

"What? No."

"Of course not," I clarified as I stepped back toward the bench. "In comparison to now, he slapped her around a bit a few nights ago. She came to my house the day you and I had lunch and stayed the night. She was bruised and scared, but more afraid to stay away. So she snuck out in the middle of the fucking night and went crawling back to that piece of shit. And...now she is blaming me for what that waste of skin did to her." I was pacing at a pretty good clip, with every word enunciated with a jerky movement of my arms ...and I was furious. "I understand why she's doing what she's doing, but where the fuck do you get off putting the blame on me. You had no clue about any of this. What did I do, Alyssa, grab his fists and make him beat her to a bloody pulp? Explain to me how you think I somehow did this to her."

"I'm relaying what she said to me."

"It didn't seem odd to you she blamed someone other than the bastard who did it?"

"Trish told me you and Tom got Richard all pissed off, and that was why they got into a fight and he pushed her down the stairs."

"Are you really that stupid?" I faced her dead on. "You believe... that the injuries she has... are from a fall down carpeted stairs, onto a carpeted floor. Is that what you are saying? One fall caused all those bruises, gashes, and breaks?" I couldn't believe she was so naive to think that was what happened. "Just how stupid are you?"

Alyssa stared at me. I could see her connecting the dots, and finding the picture Trish drew lacking way too many details. She shifted her posture and looked to the trees for divine guidance. Matilda sat on Alyssa's feet, leaned her massive body into her and seemed to wait for her to riddle it out. "I don't understand?" she whispered. Holding her forehead in her left hand and Matilda's lead in the other, "This has happened before... and you knew... and you let her go back to him?"

She was accusing me! "Hold the phone. We did not let *her* go back to him. She chose to go back, in the middle of the night, I might add. We couldn't tie her to a chair and make her stay. That would have made this shit worse than it already is." I ran the fingers of both hands threw my hair and left them intertwined at the crown of my skull. "What would you have done, Alyssa? Would you have nailed her feet to the floor and forced her to stay? Would you have tried some psychobabble bullshit on her to try to make her see the light? Is that what you would have done?" I asked as I stepped into her personal space. Dropping my arms I leaned in. "You would have been wrong. Every. Step. Of. The. Way." I tossed myself back down onto the bench, leaned back and spread my arms out along the top of the seat back. I put my right ankle on my left knee and waited for some kind of response to the questions I just laid out at her feet. Nothing.

With a bitter tongue I asked, "What? No magical answer? No divine wisdom?"

"So, what do we do now?"

"What do you mean? We can't do anything. This ball is in her court. She has to decide to press charges for anything to be done to the Dick Head, or... leave him," I explained as I offered her the seat next to me. "I don't think she's ready to run yet. She's afraid, but what she needs to be is angry. Anger is more of a motivator to do something, where fear will keep you rooted in one place," I turned to look at her. "It's the 'if /when' factor. 'If' is an excuse and 'when' is a timeline? Like, 'If this happens then I'll do that. 'When' is what I like to think of as a destination, you know. 'When' I get there... life will be better. Does that make sense?" I asked. "Trish is still stuck in if"

"But, if what? What is she waiting for?"

"I have no clue. She probably doesn't know either."

Matilda jerked Alyssa right out of her seat. Clearly the dog wanted to get moving and was tired of listening to us bicker about things we had no control over. Alyssa steadied herself and Matilda, and then pivoted toward me. Gesturing with her hand to the open space between us she mumbled, "We good?"

"I want to say 'yes' but...," I shrugged my shoulders and clasped my hands together on my knees.

"Yeah, I get it. Maybe we can get together and talk tomorrow?"

"We'll figure it out. Call me later and we can plan something."

She nodded and allowed Matilda to lead her away from our conversation. That could have gone better, but it wasn't like I had any time to think it out before it happened.

I laid back down on the bench the way I had been before Matilda stuck her nose in my business. I continued to lay there for a while. I watched the leaves move above me and wondered if I had ever really noticed them before. The sun light filtered through the miniscule openings between the mosaics of leaves. It was beautiful. I felt the breeze skim over the hairs on my arms and smelled, what, what was that? Soil, I could smell the soil cradling the life around me. I listened. I really listened. I heard birds. I heard a bee buzzing nearby, and children at the playground on the other side of the park. I heard people walking on the sidewalk on the other side of the bushes. Even silence isn't silent. The world played white noise, like background music, everywhere and always. Why had I never heard it before? I knew. I was busy having a life. At that moment, I was busy worrying if I would still have one, and if Trish valued hers enough to do something to protect it. It was ridiculous to think I was frightened for mine, while she devalued hers. I was vibrated back to the moment by my cell in my pocket. It was Tom. "Hey, babe" I answered.

"Hey, where are you?" he asked.

I sat up and placed my feet firmly on the ground. "I went for a walk. I'm at the park."

"Shell said you left around 11:00. It's 3:45. You coming home or have you run away to build a fort in the park?" he jested.

Although, it was an intriguing idea, "As good as the fort sounds, I guess I will come home," I answered with a small smile. I got to my feet and pointed them in the direction of home. "Any ideas for dinner?" I asked as I exited my bench and my time surrounded by white noise.

"I am in the mood for burnt hot dogs with lots of mustard, potato salad, and cole slaw. Well, that's what I brought home at least," he snickered.

"Awwwww, honey, you're making me dinner. How romantical of you," I cooed as I rounded the corner of my canopy-covered street. "I'll be home in a minute."

"Cool. See you in 59...58...57...,"and he hung up the phone. I picked up my pace to see if I could make it before my time ran out.

I threw open the door with a flourish and collapsed on the cool tiles by the door. "I ran." I panted. "About ten yards." I rolled to my back, giggling, and looked up into the deep brown eyes of my Lily.

"What the heck did you do that for?" she asked as she tried to pull me up from the entryway.

"Cuz your dad was counting down from…"

Tom interrupted my amusement. "14…13…12…oh, you made it," he smirked as he leaned his shoulder against the archway. Crossing his arms he interjected a bit of nasty: "I may have slowed my count a bit to give you a chance."

Ass, he can be such an ass sometimes, but he's my ass. "You can be a jerk, you know that right?" I wheezed.

"Moi?" he asked placing his hand on his chest as if I hurt his feelings. "I would never…admit to such a thing."

Yeah, right.

With a belly laugh Lily chimed in, "Ha! You don't have to admit it, Dad. We already know it's true."

I was home, wrapped in the sarcasm and love of my people. The remainder of my day was filled with the tales of activities, dismays, broken nails, and horror stories of the nasty sister-in-law. I hoped this love would be my umbrella for the shit storm that had been raging and the forecast wasn't looking any better. Two days…

Chapter Nine

Monday...I could understand why people hated Mondays. I may have different reasons but the hate was still there. I had a lot of time to kill and no plans to do so. I stood in my backyard hanging on to my coffee cup as though it held the answers to...to what? Why we were here? What was my purpose? Why are government officials chronically stupid? Why do some get lumpy boobs and others get *happily ever after?* I drank what was left of my cold coffee and stared at the empty vessel. Nope, no answers lay at the bottom, only a sad brown ring. Boobs, bongos, hooters, airbags, fun bags, knockers, rack...so many ridiculous names for the two things that were causing me so much turmoil. Let's hope the name k*illers* *w*asn't added to the list. Coffee, I needed more coffee.

It was only ten in the morning and my house was empty. Only the shadows that my thoughts were casting kept me company, the guests from hell. I sat at the breakfast bar with a freshly poured cup of love and tried to figure out something to do to keep my sanity for the next 36 hours when the doorbell rang...saved by the bell. God I hated that show...as I crossed the living room to the front door. I knew who it was before I opened it. I saw the red locks poking up above the arched window at the top of the door. God was looking out for me.

"Hi!" I was overjoyed to see Charlotte's face.

"Hello, sweet girl. I am bored, and need something to do before I get myself into a bit 'o trouble, or well a lot 'o trouble," Charlotte beamed. "So either we plan something, or I am going to get you into trouble too!"

I held the door open and grinned from ear to ear. "Get your ass in here, and let's plot the day." T*hank you, thank you, thank you,* I murmured looking to the grace above. "Do you want some coffee?"

"Is my hair red?" she responded with one eyebrow quirked up and her lips pursed. Of course she wanted coffee, what a stupid question.

We walked back toward the kitchen and gathered up our mugs. I suggested we sit on the back deck and enjoy what was left of the morning's welcome cool. I shooed Oliver off of one of the deck chairs and offered the other to Charlotte.

"So, what's the story?" Charlotte asked while avoiding Oliver's advances.

"Oliver! Go!" and off he went with his tail held high. "What story?" I asked, wondering what the hell she was talking about.

"Story...what's going on."

"Oh, how many times do I have to tell you to speaka da Engrish?"

She chuckled and sipped at her coffee. "What's the story with that gowl...Molly?"

"Gowl?"

"I just called her, um... stupid. Moving on," she waved away any other questions and continued, "what's her problem?"

"How long do you plan on staying? That could take all day," I chortled.

"Like I said, I'm bored. I couldn't leg it outta there fast enough after you left the other night. I couldn't bear to hear the crap that fell from her gob," Charlotte fell silent for a moment and I could see there was more to that statement than the value of the words she chose. Do I ask or let her tell it on her own? I chose to let her speak on her own. I had pried into the lives of others enough over the past week. "*I swear the woman is thick.*"

"Now thick I understand. Molly is a piece of work, that's for sure." I turned my full attention to Charlotte. "Did she say something after we left?"

Bringing the coffee mug up to her lips, she paused and thought for a moment. "Say somethin'? Not to my face, but I'm not as thick as she may think I am." She sipped at her coffee slowly. It was like she was trying to hide from me.

"Screw her, Charlotte. She isn't worth the time or effort to worry about." I reached across the empty space and took her hand. "So what kind of mischief would you like to get into today, friend?" The clouds cleared from her face and excitement caught the corner of her eye.

"I was thinkin' we could go to lunch and then go to the pictures. What do ya think? You up to hangin' with this lass?" She held her coffee mug up as if she were waiting for me to raise mine in acceptance of her plan. What the hell? It's not like I had any plans other than to drive myself crazy, and we all knew that was a short trip from here to there.

"Let's do it." I smiled and briefly raised my mug and chugged the rest of my coffee. "Let me go change really quick while you figure out where you want to eat, 'k?" She saluted me with her mug as I left her on the deck chair, all the while being stalked by a fat, orange cat.

A few minutes later I found Charlotte rinsing her mug in the kitchen sink. "Are the dishes in your washer clean or dirty," she asked.

"Dirty," I responded as she took my mug and did the same with it. "Would you like to come live with me? No one in this house seems to know how the dishwasher works."

"I would, but Miguel would run out of clean dishes and food too fast. We would find him mummified in his favorite chair in a matter of days." We both laughed at the visual of a leather-skinned Miguel in his lounge chair with a death grip on the remote. Charlotte had a way of putting me at ease. No matter what might be plaguing me, she could shake away the crud and make me enjoy the moment.

"Where are we going for lunch?" I asked while I dug through my purse for my list of needs: phone, wallet, keys, Chapstick...

"How does Chinese sound?"

"From an Irish woman who is married to a Mexican, why not have something exotic," I stated as a laugh hung from my tongue. "Do you want to ride together or separate?"

I once again held the door for Charlotte, this time as we left. "Let's ride together."

Since Charlotte's car was at the end of the driveway, we took her Grand Cherokee. It was funny to see the seat so close to the steering wheel. "How do you reach the pedals?" I asked laughing as I saw her try to maneuver herself into position to drive.

"It's not like I have to sit my ass on a telephone book. It's a pillow, for Christ's sake," she asserted as she straightened the pillow at her lower back. I couldn't help but laugh. It was funny.

"Are you sure you don't want me to drive?" I snickered.

"Shut chur puss! I can drive just fine, thank you very much," and we were off to the restaurant and an adventure. Thankfully it was a short drive to the restaurant, but long enough for my cheeks to ache from giggling.

I talked to Charlotte about the incidents with Trish and Alyssa. I bitched about Molly. I talked about Lily and her boyfriend, and whether or not she would go to college. I talked about Tom and Shell and even the cat. I talked. She listened. She offered kind words and advice when I asked, but never overstepped and never pushed. She made me laugh and I her.

"Is there something else bothering you?" Charlotte quizzed with narrowed eyes. It felt like she was trying to see through me, to search me inside and out for the story I wasn't telling.

"Isn't that enough? I talked to you about everything but world peace. What about you, Charlotte? What's the story?" Deflect! Get the attention off of me and onto her!

"Not much to tell, ya know. Miguel works so hard he comes home shattered. All he wants to do is bathe, eat, and fondle the remote." That last bit came out laced with need. She was feeling neglected because of the guys being so busy. I could relate. Tom was right there with Miguel every day, after all.

114

"I know what you mean. The hail storm was a blessing and a bitch all at the same time." I waved to the waitress to get a refill on my drink and continued, "It won't last forever. But you gotta admit the money has been great."

"It has." She smiled, "I went shopping and bought some fanciful things to wear in the bedroom." She was grinning like the Cheshire cat.

"Um...I really don't need that vision running around in my brain..." I shivered and tried to shake off the image. Blah!

"It's not like you would have to take a gander, don't cha know."

Oops, I think I offended her. "I didn't mean anything bad, Charlotte. It's just the general idea of picturing..." I leaned in closer so none of the other patrons could hear, "those kinda moments between other people...it creeps me out, okay?"

She crowed with laughter, full on table slapping laughter. Not some gentle chuckle or trill. I mean the hold your sides, ugly faced, rocking in your seat kind of roaring. Needless to say, people were looking at us as if we were bonkers. Maybe we were, and maybe this was what the doctor ordered.

Hours later we returned to my house carrying leftover buckets of popcorn with way too much butter and soda cups that held enough liquid to require two pee breaks during the movie. I still had a smile on my face as Charlotte backed down my driveway. She leaned out of her window and bellowed, "Don't miss me too much, girly. It might make Tom wonder what we were up to." With a shit-eating-grin and a smirk, she was off. I could still hear her laughing three houses away.

We had gone to a matinee, so it was still early. Tom wasn't home. I was so full of Chinese food and popcorn there was no way I was going to be able to eat dinner. Bu*rp*...*a*nd an idea struck. I slid into my little Versa and made my way to Subway and picked up a few different subs. Dinner was ready and I didn't have to do anything. The lazy way out worked fine for me.

Tom found me napping on the couch when he got home. "Rough day?" he asked with a twinge of jealousy.

I peeked out of one eye and sighed, "You have no idea how difficult my day was: waking to an empty house, having coffee on the deck with Charlotte, lunch at the Chinese place down town, then to finish up my day with a chick flick." I swung my feet off the couch and settled into a sitting position. "Such a rough day," I smiled.

"It's nice to see that," he commented.

"See what?"

"That smile." Tom sat down next to me and wrapped his arm around my shoulders. "I haven't seen it in a while."

"It's been there. It's just been hiding under all the shit that has piled up over the last few days." I leaned into him and put my head on his shoulder ...then jerked it away, fast. "Dude! You reek! Argh!" I hollered as I jumped up and away from his pits.

Sticking his nose into his pits he jerked his head back with his face scrunched up in what appeared to be pain. Yes, he smelled so bad it was painful. "I didn't realize it was that bad."

"Bad? That's not bad. It's a felony." I pointed toward the stairs. "Take that stench up to the shower and do *not le*ave those nasty-ass clothes in our room. Put them in the laundry room so our bedroom doesn't stink to high heaven."

Tom leaned over and untied his work boots and toed them off. "Yes, dear," was all he could muster.

"Um...don't leave these stink bombs in my living room either," I demanded, bending to retrieve his boots. "Those can be set out on the deck to air out for a while...like a week."

Tom held the boots out and wiggled them in front of my nose with a chuckle. "Yes, ma'am. Anything else madam requires?" he asked with a small bow.

"Yes, I need..." and I ticked off items on my fingers, "...the winning numbers for the lottery, to win Publishers Clearing House, a hot husband, and to lose fifteen pounds. Not necessarily in that order."

"Is one out of four good, cuz that is all I can manage?"

"I guess the fifteen pound weight loss will have to do then." His eyes bulged out of his head with shock. Ha, it was satisfying! "Gotcha!" I hollered and skirted around him as quickly as possible.

I claimed my chair out back and was sipping a cold iced tea when my cell vibrated across the deck table. I reached over and picked it up to see who it was dared bother my peace. It was Alyssa. Did I want to talk to her? Ring number two...I'm still ticked at her...ring number three...do I want to hear what she has to say...Ring number – I answered, "Hello."

"Hey, Liv," Alyssa droned.

"Whatcha need?" I asked not wanting to know the answer.

"I was checking in to see how you are."

"How I am? Shouldn't you be checking to see how Trish is? Not me."

"I just left there. She's ...well, she's the same."

I shifted forward in my seat and leaned my body against the table. "Did you expect a miraculous recovery?"

"No, of course not! Shit, Liv, why are you being this way?"

"What way? Realistic? You're the one who doesn't get it. Why don't you have the good doctor explain it to you. Maybe then you will get a fucking clue."

"Christ, Liv. I don't need Neil to explain anything to me. Trish told me all I need to know," Alyssa hissed. "She still thinks you and Tom caused this, and now she doesn't want to see you at all because of some pictures you gave the cops."

Defeated, I sighed and leaned back into my chair. "The pictures I gave the cops were of the bruises she had the day she came here and stayed the night. She was covered in them. Look, when an abuser no longer cares if the marks are seen there is no telling what they'll do."

"I know you thought you were trying to help, but maybe you need to stay out of it."

"You don't know a damn thing about it. You wouldn't know abuse if it slapped you in the face. He won't stop unless something is done."

"Really? How do you plan on helping when she doesn't want you around?"

"Screw you," I hissed. "You have your own shit to deal with, so don't play Miss 'My Shit Don't Stink' with me." Alyssa knew how to piss me off just by opening her mouth. "I'm sure the good doctor doesn't know your trashy track record, but then again maybe he can tell. He is a gynecologist after all."

"Fuck you, Olivia. I happen to like Neil...a lot. Not that it matters to you."

"No, it doesn't. Well, I have major shit of my own to deal with right now, and you don't fall high enough on my list to care. Later." It was moments like that when I missed old house phones. I missed being able to slam it down...hard. It doesn't have the same effect on a cell phone. Instead, I got to poke En*d Call*. Where was the satisfaction in that? I opened the messages on my cell and began to type:

So I hear I'm not welcome. I would...delete, delete, delete

Screw that! I am going to make Trish say it to my face. I deleted the message and went inside to get my purse and shoes.

"What's up? You look...determined," Tom asked as he stepped off of the bottom step smelling a thousand percent better than before.

"I'm going to the hospital to see Trish," I said through clenched teeth.

"Do you think that's wise? She wasn't receptive yesterday when you stopped by."

"From what I understand she won't be receptive this time either," I grumbled while tying my shoes. "She had her watch dog call and tell me I'm not welcome, and all of this is our fault."

"Watch dog? Dick Head didn't fucking call you did he?" he asked as I watched his jaw clench. "Cuz I will fucking kil-" I stepped into Tom's chest and placed my hand over his heart and shook my head to calm him down.

"No, he didn't call me. He's still locked up as far as I know. Alyssa called to tell me I'm not welcome."

"Then what's the point? If she doesn't want you there, why go?" I could feel his concern in the way his fingers tightened on my hips.

"I have to go, no matter what comes of it." It was hard to explain, but I needed Trish to look into my eyes and tell me she didn't need or want my help. She needed to see even if those words fell from her lips it didn't mean I wouldn't be there for her when she finally realized she needed help.

"Want me to come?" Tom asked as he wrapped his arms around me to pull me in closer.

"I don't think that would be a good idea. You don't need to see what he did to her, or hear what she and I might say to each other," I whispered while my forehead rested on his shoulder. I could smell the clean he wore like cologne. I inhaled deeply and nuzzled a bit closer to rob him of some of his warmth. Stiffening slightly, I pushed away from him. Instantly I felt the void of his protection. "I better get this over with." I kissed him lightly on the cheek and picked up my purse. "I bought subs for you and the girls. They're in the fridge. I'll be back sooner rather than later," I sighed. I was reaching for the door as it burst open.

"Sup, peoples!"

Gotta love our Shell. "Bye. I'll be home in a bit," I bellowed as I slipped out the door. "Hi, Shelly. Bye, Shelly."

"Where ya goin'? Can I come?" she asked as she poked her head back out the door to follow me.

I was walking across the yard to the car when I hollered back, "Nowhere you need to be and hell no. Bye! Love you!" I waved at her through the car window as I backed down the driveway.

I was greeted by the lyrics of Concrete Blonde asking the same question I had been asking myself for days. What in the hell is going on? I screamed along as the melody thumped from my speakers. I whipped into the parking lot at Bayview, and I went on a scavenger hunt for a parking space. Unlike on Sunday, there were no open parking spaces close to the doors on a Monday evening. I ended up parking about as far away as you can get while still being in the parking lot.

That added to the anger I already had brewing at the time.

I trudged my way to the automatic doors and inhaled that noxious smell of sanitizer they used to sterilize the place when they woo*shed* open. Maybe I could use some of that cleaner to scrub away the crap which has been thrown at my feet. I nodded my head at the older gentleman who manned the courtesy desk. I wondered briefly where the woman was I spoke with yesterday. Sh*e can't work every day, ya dumb-ass,* I reminded myself.

Duh! Right.

I slipped over to the elevators pushed the call button, and waited.

Chapter Ten

I don't know how many trips up and down I took in the elevator. I stood at the rear of the car with my back pressed against the wall and my hands grasping the handrail like my life depended on it. I watched dozens of people get on and off as the doors slid open and closed. Each had a destination, a loved one to see, or a job to do. I was going to see someone who didn't want to see me. I was trying to help, but was I really? Does it help anyone to be pushed into things they aren't ready for? I needed to let Trish come to things in her own time. She needed to see it in her time. I could only let her know that when that moment came, I would be there for her, but until then I had to walk. I looked up as the doors slid closed on the third floor. I took the two steps to the control panel and pushed the button to go down. It's time to walk away.

As I trekked the expanse from the hospital to my car, I dug my cell and keys from my purse. I unlocked my car, slid in and opened the messages on my phone to send a text to Trish.

I understand you don't want 2 c me. That's ur choice & I will honor it. When u c things clearer and need a friend, who understands, and one u can't lie 2 I will b here. As long as he is still

in ur life, u aren't welcome in my home. I will not put those I luv at
risk. It's bad enuff u and the boys are in that position. Take care of
urself. U know where to find me.

My finger hovered over the send button like it would set the
nukes free to bomb Cincinnati or something. I knew if I sent it all
hell would break loose...or maybe I would never hear another thing
from her. I dropped my thumb to the button. I silenced my phone
and shoved it back into the great black hole and started the car. I
backed out of my parking space and said goodbye to my friend with
one last look back at the sliding emergency room doors. I hoped she
would never have to go through that pain and fear again, but I was
realistic.

Hope in one hand and shit in the other...which will
fill up first?

I don't remember the drive. I found myself in my driveway
pulling the key from the ignition. Now that's kinda scary. I stepped
from the car, pushed the button to lock the doors, and shoved the
keys into my pocket. I walked to my porch but couldn't bring myself
to go inside. The anger was starting to build. How dare she push me
away? Who the hell does she think she is? I had always been there
for her. I gave her a place to go and a shoulder for support. Where
does sh-

"Hey, whatcha doin' sittin' out here all by your lonesome?"
quizzed Tom as he took a seat on the step below me and handed me
a beer.

"Just needed to be alone."

"Hmmm...wanna talk about it?"

"What part of al*one* i*s* too difficult for you to comprehend?" I
snarled as I raised the beer to my lips. Why is it when I want silence
I get noise, and when I want solitude I get a crowd?

Tom slowly unfolded himself and stepped back up the stairs. I
heard the door open and quietly click shut behind me. I took a long
draw off my beer and wondered if it held an answer...any answer.
Maybe it was at the bottom of the bottle. So I drank. Nope, no
answer, just an empty bottle, I knew the feeling all too well.

"Mom? What are you doing out here all by yourself?" asked Lily. Where did she come from? I didn't hear the door, but then I was arguing with the voice in my head, and it was a rather heated one.

"Sitting."

"I can see that," she laughed as she claimed a plot, "but the question is why?"

"Because it was quiet and I was alone." I put a little emphasis on alone and hoped she would catch on. Nope, no such luck.

"And why do you want to be alone when there is an awesomely cool person right here in front of your fabulous face?" Her grin spread like a rash, bright and irritating.

"What is it with people? Is the word, alone, foreign? Do you not understand the combination of those five letters?" I turned my eyes to meet her waiting on a response and got none. Lily stood quickly and stomped to the door. This time I was awarded with a good hardy slam and a slight rattle of the glass.

Cheers! I thought as I raised my empty bottle to no one. *Here's to silence.*

"What the fuck, Liv?"

Jesus Christ!!! Can't I sit alone for five fucking minutes? "What?!"

Tom bounded down the steps and stood in front of me. "What did you say to Lily?"

"Asked her if she understood the word, alone. Just like I asked you minutes before. Why?" I didn't care, but thought I should ask why he was in my face.

"Because she's upset," he snipped as he bent to come eye to eye with me. "I don't know what crawled up your ass and died, but you don't dump your shit on the kids. If this is about Trish, I'm sorry it is all fucked up, but you can't bring that battle here and bite our heads off. Get it?" I gave a slight nod and nothing more. "Are you coming in?" he asked as he climbed the stairs a second time.

"No."

"Fine." SLAM.

Damn, I should have asked him to bring me another beer. I had no idea how long I sat there. I could see the neighborhood children riding bikes and playing catch in their yards. Why couldn't life be that simple again? Why did what if's have to ruin tomorrows? Why couldn't people see what was right in front of their noses? Why did I wait so long to have a checkup? What would tomorrow bring? I'd shoved my own mess into a dark room and slammed the door. I blocked it with other people's crap thinking it would magically disappear. That didn't work, duh. Could be nothing. Could be nothing big. Could be the answer to world peace. Could be something I don't want to face...but have no choice. I could just be scaring the crap outta myself for no reason. Maybe I had lumpy boobs. Not all of me can be perfect. As I sat there contemplating things I clearly didn't have answers to, I watched children play. When did I stop playing? Is there an age or a moment in life when playing was no longer allowed?

Behind me I heard the door open, again, "It's almost 10. Don't you think it's time to come in?" advised Tom in a not so happy tone.

"Fine," was all I could muster as I climbed the steps. At that point, I really didn't care about much of anything. At that point, I had declared the day over along with a friendship. At that point, I didn't look forward to tomorrow. At that point, I wanted to sleep. I carried my war torn body to the bathroom for the comforts of a shower to wash away the remnants of a lost battle.

Washed and weary, I wrapped myself in my large pink robe and crawled into bed. Tom lay quiet within arm's reach, but I wasn't reaching out to anyone any time soon. With a huff, he rolled away from me and stated, "We didn't hurt you. Don't hurt us."

The alarm clock read 2:43 a.m. when my eyes drifted open. I had been in a dreamless, fitful sleep for about four hours, but no rest was actually in my possession. It was one of those sleeps where you are fully aware. I heard the neighbor's dog, a car driving by the house with an amazing sound system, and many thoughts of the day wandering behind my eyelids. Crashing together and making more noise than my brain could handle. So, I gave up. I listened to Tom's steady deep breathing as I slipped from a bed I didn't feel quite welcome in. Still wrapped in the warmth of my robe, I slipped from our room and made my way downstairs where I was greeted by Lily who was channel surfing.

"Hey, what are you still doing up?" I whispered.

"Couldn't sleep. You?"

"Same." I paused by the couch where she sat, "I'm sorry about earlier. I didn't mean to hurt you."

"You didn't. It's all good."

"Want some hot chocolate with extra marshmallows?" I bribed.

Shifting from the couch, Lily stood and hooked her arm with mine and said, "Lead the way."

She took a seat on one of the bar stools and watched as I busied myself making the cocoa. "So what's up with you? I haven't really seen much of your face lately."

Popping a marshmallow into her mouth she replied in a garble, "Oh, you know, same shit, different day."

I looked over at my daughter who was clearly hiding something.

I wonder where/who she got that from?

I stood stirring the milk that was slowly warming on the stove and asked the question I knew she didn't want to hear. "Do tell. What shit and on which day has caused you to look like the World is sitting on your shoulders?"

"Did you know guys suck ass? Really suck ass," Lily began. "They think with the head with less brains than the one attached to their shoulders." She sat in a way that declared her defeat. She released a breath she appeared to have been holding and continued, "Why is it when they don't get what they want from you, when they want it, they will creep somewhere else to get it?"

I remained silent as I poured the hot chocolate into mugs and heaped marshmallows into hers. I placed the mug in front of her and took a seat. "Are you really asking these questions for future reference, or are you questioning something that has already occurred?"

"He's a lying, cheating, piece of shit!" Lily's hands shook as the rage started to work its way out. "That fuck-tard went to a party the night we were at Uncle Wayne's pool party and hooked up with some skank. He said if I had gone with him it wouldn't have happened. If I stood by him he wouldn't have..." Lily choked on the word that hurt her most.

I finished it for her between clenched teeth. "...cheated." She quickly nodded her head and sipped from her mug-o-marshmallow.

She wrapped her long fingers around the mug as if she needed the warmth to survive.

"Do you think he's right? If you were where he wanted you to be, whenever he wanted you to be there, would it have stopped him from cheating?"

"No. that's proof he is a fucking idiot," she bit out. "How stupid does he think I am to fall for the it's your fault that I stuck my dick in some other girl crap?" She followed with a soft chuckle and a sickeningly sweet voice, "yes dear, run on over there and have sex with the local ho. Oh, it's okay, I'll take all the blame, and then you can come back to me and everything will be fine...what a moron."

"Sweetie, you...um...don't seem...hurt. I don't know if hurt is the right word. Do you understand what I am trying to say?"

"I'm not hurt, mom. This isn't the first time."

"What?!"

Lily took my hand. I'm guessing for moral support or for something to squeeze, and explained, "I felt like there was something going on, but never had any proof, ya know? It's not like I caught him doing it. Something felt off. But, on Saturday he was dumb enough to think he could flaunt it around, and a few of my friends saw him and let me know. He tried sayin' they were lying and were jealous of our relationship until I showed him the pictures they snapped and sent me," she closed her eyes and tried to un-see the images. "He still tried to explain them away. How the fuck can you explain away having sex with another girl? How?"

"You can't. It is what it is." I looked down at the last of my marshmallows floating in my mug praying they would be able to give me some answers, but they melted away. Bastards. "What now? Have you decided to break up or talk or...?"

"It's hard, ya know. Darren and I have been together for over a year. I don't know what I am going to do."

I walked over to my daughter, my child, my blessing, and wrapped my mother arms around her and held her to me. "I love you, and no matter what you do, I will stand with you." With a squeeze I added, "Just get the truth from him. How many times he has done this? Talk to your friends and see what they know. You can't fix it if there are lies and doubts stuck in your head." I placed a kiss in her hair and held on.

"Thanks, mom. I have a lot of thinking to do. I think I am gonna try to get some sleep. I am going to hang out with some of the girls tomorrow and find out what I can before I move forward." Lily stood and hugged me back. "I love you, mom," off to bed she went. I had to stop myself from following behind her to tuck her in. She's not little anymore. All I wanted to do at that very moment was to castrate the little fucker and turn his tiny testicles into a charm bracelet. That would scare any other idiot boy that came sniffing around. You mess with my girls and I will wear your manhood on a hook around my wrist.

I was now alone. It was 3:48 a.m. and I was making coffee. Alone.

*****

A warm mug in hand I went in search of a distraction...Facebook. How much more can you ask for? It had drama, comedy, stupidity, and from time to time, a touch of wisdom (not really). At this point it was better than Google or WebMD. I spent the next hour and a half losing myself in random nothingness. I scrolled, I read, I don't remember a word of it. None of it seemed to matter. I avoided Trish's and Alyssa's posts, if there were any. I didn't want to read a bunch of crap. Maybe I should delete them? I felt deleted. I felt...sad, mad, confused, but mostly scared out of my mind. Where the hell were my friends when I needed them? Well, how the hell were they supposed to know, ya dumbass. You hadn't told anyone. *Tough Olivia*, she can handle whatever is thrown at her. She doesn't need anyone holding her hand. Yet, I whined I was alone. Well, to myself. I really needed to learn to make up my mind. Or, accept the choices I have made. Nope, I chose, *Tough Olivia*. With that realization I stuck my tongue out at the wishy-washy woman reflected back at me and closed my laptop. I made up my mind to have another cup of coffee. So, there.

As I added the caramel macchiato creamer to my cup, Tom crossed the living room moving in a straight line to the coffee pot. He wore blue camo pajama pants and the shadow of sleep. He ran his fingers through his hair, but never looked in my direction. He kept moving. His bare feet slapped against the tile as he entered the kitchen. He stood there quietly as he poured his coffee and added more sugar to one cup than I use in an entire pot. Made my teeth hurt just watching it. I leaned my ass against the counter directly behind him with my arms crossed over my chest holding my cup to my lips. I watched and waited to see if I could determine his mood. I could see the tension that gripped the muscles in his neck and back and there was a slight tic in his jaw. He was still mad. He stood with his back to me long enough to take a sip and left me standing there in the echo of silence. I had nothing to apologize for, not to him...er, maybe a little. I made peace with Lily last night. For the sake of silence, and not making things worse, I decided to leave him be. Oooo...I made another decision. I went to the living room and made myself comfy in the recliner. It was just me, Gayle King, and coffee.

Twenty minutes later, I still had no idea what the news was because my mind kept wondering about things unknown. I was drawn to the sound of Tom's footsteps on the stairs. I made myself not look at him, to remain in the position I was in. Let *him come to me*, I thought. He was being shitty for no reason. Right? *Maybe I should say something. J*ust as I moved from the chair, I saw the back door closing. I was too late. I watched him back down the drive from the dining room window. Gone without a word. I stood there staring out the window at the invisible tire tracks the truck left in the drive as Tom backed out. In my mind I was sitting shotgun and could see and feel every turn and stop until he pulled into the auto shop parking lot. He really was mad at me. Shit. I guess it didn't help I have been a bit on edge for... seven straight days.

Over the course of the next 90 minutes I showered and dressed, three times, did my hair and hid my face behind a layer of spackle. All that and I would end up sitting in a cold room wearing a paper napkin with my ass hanging out. Yup, I needed make-up for that. I found my sandals in a box in the closet and did one last quick check. I exited my room and proceeded to go down the stairs. "Morning, mom."

I halted my descent and looked up over my shoulder to see Michelle closing her bedroom door still sporting her bacon and eggs fuzzy pjs. "Morning back," I smiled. "Where are you off to this early that you are up?"

"Nowhere, yet," she fell in step behind me. "I have to work at eleven." Crossing the living room Shelly made a bee-line to her favorite spot. She plopped down into the recliner and caressed the remotes as if she hadn't touched them in ages. "Where are you going?" she bellowed while finding entertainment that wasn't me.

"Oh...um...I have an appointment."

"Cool. Can I come? What's it for? Not the DMV, right? I hate the DMV."

I chuckled at the idea. "No, not the DMV, I have a doctor's appointment." I cringed a bit and waited for a response.

"What time? Maybe we could get breakfast before." She still hadn't looked beyond the television.

"Um...sure. I think we can do that. I have to be there at 10:45 so we should drive separately. I wouldn't want you late to work."

"God forbid someone not get a greasy ass burger quick, fast, and in a hurry," she snorted. "Give me five. I need to put on my classy uniform." She took the stairs two at a time and was out of my sight within seconds. While she got ready, so did I. Insurance card, cash, phone, keys...where the heck did I put my keys? I skirted around the room in search of the blasted things. I finally dumped my bag on the dining room table and sifted through eight pounds of crap. I really needed to clean that thing out. I bet Hoffa's body could be lurking in this mess. Keys! Found 'em. I swept the rest of the mess back into the bag and waited for Shelly.

"Let's do this," she yelled as she bounded down the stairs.

"Shhh! Christ, Shelly, Lily is still asleep. She was up pretty late."

"That's her fault not mine."

"She was up with me, smartass." I gave her a sideways glance followed by the very mature move of sticking out my tongue. "Let's eat!"

We met up at Maria's and shuffled our way into a booth at the back.

"Good morning, ladies. Can I get you something to drink?" prompted Alice. She seemed to be in high spirits this morning, or just awake.

"Hi, Alice. I'll take a large chocolate milk aaanndd," Shelly hesitated as she skimmed the specials board on the wall, "...a short stack with a side of bacon."

"And you?" Alice asked as her pen stopped and she eyed me.

"Coffee, water, and a bowl of oatmeal. Can I get a side of brown sugar and butter with that?" Alice nodded as she scribbled down my order. "Thanks, Alice."

"Oatmeal? You could have had that at home."

"I could have made pancakes too."

"True, but where's the fun in that?" Alice chose that moment to bring our drinks. Shelly shoved a straw into her chocolate milk and downed at least a third of it. "Ahhhhhh...now that's good stuff right there."

It's moments like that when I had to remind myself she was sixteen and not six. She had the ability to cross between a child and an obnoxious teen in mere seconds. That's what made her fun. You weren't gonna shove her into some labeled box. She was her own creation, and I was in awe of her. Her smile had a way of melting away the cold, calloused acts of others. I would do anything to ensure that smile stay within reach.

"So is it a 'fend for ourselves' kind of night?"

"What do you mean?" I asked with confusion causing my eyebrows to try and touch.

"Isn't it 'dip and drinks night' with Alyssa and Trish?" she quizzed as Alice placed her plate of pancakes in front of her. "Fooooood!" She snatched up her knife and spread butter like it was frosting followed by a river of syrup. Yup, she is her father's daughter. Sweet tooth from hell.

"No, I don't think we will be doing that any time soon." It took the remainder of our breakfast together for me to explain the situation. It was easy explaining why Trish and I were taking a hiatus, but trying to explain the rift between Alyssa and me was another story. I couldn't seem to figure it out, which made explaining it much harder. Yes, her stupid comments and assumptions about the problem with Trish was definitely on the list, but was that severe enough to have caused the split? I didn't know. Michelle listened, chewed, and offered up snarky comments and mildly wise observations through the duration of the conversation. She sided with me when it came to Trish's situation, but was just as confused as I was about Alyssa.

"Hey, no one said this crap would make sense," I declared. "You wanted to know what was goin' on, so there it is. In all its fucked-up glory."

Shelly chuckled as she observed, "It's nice to know even adults act like stupid teenagers. I have so much to look forward to."

"I see what you mean." I glanced at the time on my phone. It was 10:20 and I needed to get moving. "Okay, sweet cheeks, we gotta go." I waved to Alice to bring the check and proceeded to search for my wallet.

"I got this," Shelly declared as she dropped a twenty on the table. "I gots me some monies and I be spendin' it on yous."

She had such a cheesy grin on her face. I loved her so much.

"Keep the change, Ms. Alice!"

She slid from the booth and waited for my decrepit old butt to get out as well. I slipped my arm into the crook of her elbow and we exited arm in arm. When we got to her car I pulled her into a hug and told her how awesome she was. I placed a peck on her cheek, and we went our separate ways. I really needed to start paying attention to the blessings that surrounded me every day and everywhere. I didn't think we did that enough. We were able to point out the things we didn't have, but not the amazing things we did.

How was that for deep thinking? Impressive, right?

It was time to go. I waved to Shelly as she took off down the road in the opposite direction than I was going. My life seemed to be going in the opposite direction, too. I slipped onto the road with ease and made my way into the unknown. Cue dramatic music...Nope, I got Billy Idol questioning the purity of a bride instead. Good enough for a trip I didn't want to take. Minutes later I was parking my little Versa in the lot at the doctor's office. The specialist's office was in the same building as Dr. -S*trip me down and oil me up's-*. Yuck! I can't even seem to enjoy the memories I had of Dr. -D*rool-tastic-* anymore because of Alyssa. Well, shit. I slammed the car door and schlepped my way into the building. I approached the communal reception desk and gave my name to the young, very young girl behind the glass partition. She handed me a stack of papers to fill out that would give Wa*r and Peace a* run for its money. And, of course there was no table to sit at to fill out my life's story. I had to balance the clip board on my lap instead. For God's sake, these were educated people, and they didn't think to put a frickin' table in there. About twenty minutes later I trudged my anthology back up to the reception desk and warned the young lady to pick it up with care. I wouldn't want her to sprain her wrist. She didn't get it. She told me to take a seat, and my name would be called when the nurse was ready for me. I moved back across the lobby and sat in a cold plastic chair. I guess they wanted you to be prepared for the discomforts of the examination rooms which were just as cold and impersonal. There was a flat screen hanging on the wall at the far end of the room with some ridiculous program on. Why do they put on such boring programs? There were kids in there. Why not put cartoons on? Educated idiots. The children were bored and agitated, which made the mothers, yes mothers, there was not one daddy in the bunch taking care of a child, frustrated and pissed. That made for a wonderful waiting experience. There were young pregnant girls and old people with dull eyes. There was a boy in a cast and another hitting it with a magazine asking if it hurt. The parents sat there ignoring the events around them. That's when I saw her. She couldn't be older than I was. Her eyes were a shocking green. I wondered if she was wearing colored contacts. Her skin was the color of the oatmeal I had for breakfast, and her lips were devoid of any color at all. But, that wasn't what drew my attention. She had no hair. She wasn't covering her head with a pretty scarf, ballcap, or wig. It was there for all to see. There was just skin and soft peach fuzz that indicated the start of regrowth of her auburn hair. She was beautiful in a shocking way, and she scared the hell out of me. The door across the room opened, and a name was called, her name, Tracy Pearson. The man who sat next to her, which I hadn't even noticed until that very moment, took her gently by the hand and helped her stand. He gathered her things and walked with her until they disappeared behind a closed door. I felt tightness in my throat as my eyes remained on the door. I didn't want to go into that room. Only minutes later, the man exited the room and left the building. Where was he going, and why wasn't she going with him?

"Olivia Carpenter."

I jumped in my own skin. "Yes, coming." I grabbed my purse from the chair next to me and stood. I looked at the nurse who stood holding the door and a chart, my chart.

"This way, Mrs. Carpenter," she prompted. I nodded my head and followed. Thankfully we did not go into the room Tracy appeared to be abandoned in. We entered a room further into the office building. We made a few turns to get to where we were going, and I knew I was going to need a map to get back to the reception desk.

"Mrs. Carpenter, there is a dressing gown there on the table. The doctor needs you to remove everything from the waist up, please. You can keep your pants and shoes on. When you put the gown on, please ensure that it opens at the front. Okay?"

"Okay."

"I will be back in a few minutes." She gave me a soft smile and pulled the door closed behind her.

I took a deep breath and let it escape. At least I didn't have to worry about my ass hanging out for the entire world to see. That thought gave me a tiny bit of peace as I dropped my bag to the floor and began to remove my top. I was sitting on the table with my feet swinging when the nurse knocked and entered. Why do they knock if they are going to throw the door open anyway? It's not like they wait for a response. I could have been...naked. They wanted me naked, so what difference did it make. Anyway...

"Mrs. Carpenter..."

"Please, call me Olivia."

"Olivia, I am going to take your temperature, blood pressure, weigh you and ask you a few questions, okay?"

I shifted forward on the table, offered my arm for the blood pressure cuff and stated, "It sounds like a plan."

Nurse Nancy, no really, her name was Nancy, took my blood pressure, my temp, and put my flabby ass on the scale. She then sat with my file out in front of her and wrote the numbers into the designated boxes. "Why are you here today, Mrs...Olivia?"

"It's a referral from Dr. -*I can't think of him that way anymore-*."

She scribbled down a note and inquired without looking up, "Why were you referred?"

"Dr. Matthews found two lumps, one in each breast." *Look at me!* She kept her head down as she scribbled further.

"When was your last mammogram?"

"About a month ago," I felt I should explain. "There was nothing visible which is why I was given the referral." Finally, she lifted her head to look at me.

"Okay, get comfortable. Dr. Khudiadadzai will be right with you," which was medical speak for I *hope you brought a snack and water, you're gonna be here a while.*

"I'll wait right here," I joked. Once again, she didn't get it. Didn't anyone in this office understand humor? Nurse Nancy smiled, a little, and closed the door leaving me in a dangerous position. I was trapped with a very active imagination.

I looked at the gross posters that covered the equally gross wall paper. I looked out the window. I swung my feet from side to side and counted the ceiling tiles. I was moving onto the floor tiles when I heard the rap on the door and the knob turn.

In walked absolute perfection in a white coat, Dr. -What's his *face*- across the hall had nothing on this man. He stood before me in his pristine white lab coat with a light blue collar visible from underneath, the most amazing fitted khakis, and boots. Were those motorcycle boots? His black licorice hair was long. Not shoulder length, but past his shoulder blades long. He had it slicked back into a tight ponytail that laid down the center of his very wide back. His skin was the color of caramel and his eyes were a deep, dark chocolate brown. My doctor was a candy bar. Licking him would be wrong, right?

"Good morning, Mrs. Carpenter. I am Dr. Malik Khudiadadzai, but you can call me Dr. K or Malik, if you prefer." His voice was sex. Pure. Primal. Growling. Sex. I am toast.

"Um...okay. I'm Olivia," I reach out my hand to shake his. Every doctor I have ever had had ice cold hands, but his were warm and silky and were going to touch me. Ge*t a grip Olivia! "I* like to be on a first name basis with anyone who is gonna feel me up," I said with a smile.

He gave a soft chuckle, "Hello, Olivia, I guess it would be good to know the first name of anyone doing that. So why have you come to see me today?"

Wow, that was a quick change of topic.

"Referral from Dr. Matthews. I apparently have two lumps that should not be there."

"And where are these lumps?" he asked while opening my chart and shifting through the pages.

"I have a matched set, one in each breast." He raised his eyes to meet mine and gave a tight smile.

"I see. Let's take a look shall we," he rose from the stool near the sink and walked to me. "Please, lay back and raise your arms over your head." I did as instructed. "I'm going to untie your gown and examine your breasts." He seemed to be asking my permission in a statement.

"Okay," I whispered and turned my face slightly away from his intense eyes. I felt his warm hands move across my flesh but didn't find it to be pleasurable in the least. He was looking for my flaws, for the invaders. His hands stilled and pressed into the tissue of my left breasts. He found number one. He lingered there rolling the lump under his fingers. Cold air was all I felt. He moved his hands to my right breast and replayed the events of the left. He found number two.

"Olivia, you can sit up now," he prompted by placing a hand gently behind my shoulder and assisted me in regaining the seated position. I pulled the gown around me and protected my breasts behind my crossed arms. Dr. -Mr. *Good-bar-* resumed his seat on the stool and began making notes and marks on a likeness of the female form. Each mark was on the breasts. My breasts. "Olivia, the mammogram failed to catch these lumps because you have very dense breast tissue. What I would like to do is send you to have an MRI, do you know what an MRI is?"

"Not really." Dr. -Ch*ocolate fantasy-* slid his stool closer to where I was hugging myself on the table.

"An MRI is a test that uses a magnetic field and pulses of radio wave energy to take pictures of the internal structure of the body. It's not painful. You will be lying on a table that slides into the MRI machine. All you will do is lay still, and the machine will do the rest."

"Okay. When do you want me to do this?"

"Now. You can do it right here in the medical center if you like. Our radiology department is downstairs. I will give you the order, and you can go right down and have it done. You may have to wait, but they can get to you quickly."

I felt the tears pushing at the back of my eyes, fighting to get out, but I held on to them with a death grip. "How bad is it?" I ask in a voice choked with fear.

"That's what the MRI is for." He turned to the counter and gathered my chart. "I will always be honest with you, Olivia. I will not say it is something until I know, and I will not say it's nothing until I know." He placed his hand on my arm and gave a gentle squeeze as an act of support. "We will find out together and go from there. Yes?"

"Yes," I croaked.

"You can get dressed, and I will send the nurse back in to get you. Once you have the MRI, Radiology will email the films directly to me. After I get an opportunity to review them, we will call and set another appointment for you."

"Okay." What more could I say? Was I going to argue with the man? Nope.

"I will have the radiology order for you at the reception desk, okay?" I nodded my head in acceptance without meeting his eyes. He slipped from the room, and I put my things back on. I was sitting with my purse in my lap when Nurse Nancy came in.

"I'll take you back to reception," she said as she held the door for me. We walked in silence until we reached the front. "You can check with the desk to see if the order is ready. If not, it will be shortly." She reached out and touched my arm as Dr. -Caramel Bliss- had done minutes before. I turned toward the desk and walked away.

"Olivia Carpenter, I'm supposed to get an order for radiology," I told the faceless person behind the partition.

"Who is it coming from?" droned the voice.

"Dr. K."

"It's not here yet. Have a seat, and we will call you when it gets here."

I found myself in a cold plastic chair again, looking at nothing but the air in front of me.

"Mrs. Carpenter...Olivia..."

"Wha..." I went to stand thinking that my order had been brought up when a hand settled on my shoulder and guided me back down in to my seat. My eyes slowly shifted up to see Dr. Neil Matthews. "Dr. Matthews?" He handed me a handful of tissues. That was when I realized the tears fighting to be free, were in fact, free.

"Are you okay?" He asked as he stooped down next to my chair. Why do people ask such a stupid question when clearly there must be something wrong to ask it in the first place? Duh.

I blew my nose and looked at him. "You know as well as I do. What do you think?"

"What are you waiting for?"

"An order for an MRI. Dr. K wants me to go down now and have it done." I was looking at my hands that were wadding and tearing at the tissues in my fist. "It hasn't made it to the desk yet."

"Do you need anything?" Why was he asking? What was he gonna do for me?

I stiffened up, took a deep breath, wiped my eyes, and stated, "No. I don't need anything. I can handle this all on my own. Thanks." He dropped his head and placed his hand on the armrest of the chair.

"All right then," he said as he used the chair for balance as he stood to his full height. "She misses you, ya know."

Where the fuck does he get off?! I'm stressed enough. "And telling me that is supposed to help me how?"

"I thought you should know she is hurting, too. I would hate to see you end a friendship over me."

Say What?! I gave a silent chuckle at the thought. "Well, Captain Ego, it's not about you," I snapped, "or did she not tell you she believes I had something to do with Dick Head putting Trish in the hospital?"

"What do you mean?" He seemed truly confused.

"Did you really believe it was because of you?" I laughed. "I guess you two are made for each other cuz you are both self-centered and dense. Why don't you ask her to tell you the *truth.*"

He looked hurt, really hurt. "I'll do that. Goodbye, Olivia."

Dr. -Dumb Ass- turned and walked back to his hallway without a glance in my direction. I felt bad for saying the things I did, but at least they were true. I let more tears fall.

"Olivia?"

Oh for fucks sake! Who now? Is this some kind of reunion or something? I looked up to see the last person I wanted to see, Molly. Crap!

"Molly."

"Are you okay? Why are you crying? Are you sick?"

"Which question do you want me to answer first, Molly?" I sat back in my uncomfortable seat and turned my head to look at her. She claimed the seat next to me putting my purse on the floor. *Don't put my purse on that nasty-ass floor!* I snatched it up and held it on my lap. "No, because, and maybe."

"What?" She asked with a look of absolute confusion. Wow, just like Dr. -Ego-.

Counting them off on my fingers, I re-answered her three questions, "Are you okay? No. Why are you crying? Because. Are you sick? Maybe."

"Maybe? What does that mean?"

"Means I don't know yet." As the last word crossed my lips I heard my name being called again, but this time from the front desk. "Excuse me, I have to get that." I picked up the order and paid my co-pay for the appointment. I was looking down at the order when I realized I had no idea where I was going. I scanned the walls to see if there was a "You Are Here" map.

"What are you looking for?" Molly asked. I thought she had left. Not my lucky day.

"Radiology, it's down stairs somewhere."

"I know where it is. I'll take you." She took me by the arm and guided us to a bank of elevator doors.

"You don't have to," I stated as I tried to squirm out of her grip.

She turned to me and looked me dead in the eyes, "I know where it is, you don't. You are upset. Don't lie. And, I want to help."

Don't lie. She said not to lie. Okay. "What do you care? It's not like we're friends. We can barely stand to be in the same room together for more than ten minutes."

"No," she agreed with a shake of her head. "We aren't friends. We are family," and with that declaration she pulled me into an open elevator and pushed the down button.

Chapter Eleven

"Let me see that," Molly demanded as she reached across the elevator and snatched the doctor's order sheet from my grasp. "You are going for a...MRI. Why are you going for a MRI?" she asked with a quirked eye brow as she scanned me from head to toe.

"Because Dr. K wants me to have one."

"For fucks sake, Olivia, answer the damn question."

"I have two lumps. Okay? The mammogram didn't catch them, so he wants the MRI," I snarled. "Happy now?"

"No, Liv, I'm not happy." She stepped closer and took my hands in hers. Just as I found the courage to meet her eyes the elevator slowed and came to a stop. The doors had barely opened when she pulled me out. "Okay, let's do this." She read the minuscule piece of mangled paper again and compared the information with the chart on the wall. All I saw was a list of names and numbers. It may as well have been Korean cuz it was all Greek to me.

"This way," she directed as we turned left down the hallway. The Radiology suite was a few doors up on the right. "Here we go. That wasn't so hard to find, now was it."

"Yeah, I guess." I took the order from her hand and went to check in at the desk. There were four people in the waiting room, but I think some were there for moral support. Unlike Molly, who I thought was there out of morbid curiosity more than support. She needed to leave.

"Thanks for helping me find the place. You don't have to wait around for me. They aren't sure how long it will be."

"It's all right. I didn't have any real plans after my appointment. I can keep you company."

She gave me a wide grin as if we were BFF's just hanging out. We weren't BFF's, and we weren't hanging out. "Molly, go," I almost begged. "I can manage on my own, really." I tried to show her I was fine, and did not need her, of all people. "I'm sure you could be out with your friends buying a new purse or something," I blurted.

Molly stiffened in her seat, and it was clear I over stepped some line. "Look, I get you don't like me. I get we aren't friends, but what you need to understand is we are family. Family. I may not be the person you want sitting here, but I am the person that is sitting here." She hung her head in frustration. "You and I don't know one another. I don't know your story, and you sure as hell don't know mine, so don't make assumptions, okay?"

"Like I have a choice." She had me by the arm and was dragging me to the door faster than I could register what she was doing. Out in the hallway she shoved me up against the wall and had a go at me.

"There are times in a person's life when it is cool to be brave and stand-alone, but then there are those times when you have to learn to ask for fucking help, or at least accept it when it is offered, even if it is from someone you don't like," she poked her well-manicured finger in my face as she continued to call me out. "This is not the time to be alone. I know you are scared, but are too damn proud to admit it. Where is Tom, Olivia? Does he even have a clue about any of this?"

"No, I haven't told him anything because there is nothing to tell." I shook my head and stared at the floor, "What could he do anyway?"

"He could be sitting in that waiting room with you." Molly turned away and took the few steps to the other wall. "You don't realize how good you've got it, do you? He would climb Mount Everest for you," she leaned her back to the wall and rested her head against the cold tiles. "Shit, all he did was talk about you, and defend your actions at my party the other day when he was helping Wayne. '*Liv was trying to defend her friend.*' '*Liv was upset.*' '*Sunshine pours out Liv's ass.*' *It* was annoying," she piss moaned while making talkie faces with her hands.

"Mrs. Carpenter?" both Molly and I looked at the figure standing in the doorway. "We are ready for you."

"Yes, thank you," I stammered as I straightened myself away from the wall and followed her back into the waiting area.

"I'll be right here," affirmed Molly as she staked a claim on what appeared to be the only seat with a cushion. I gave an eye roll and followed the radiology technician through a set of doors and into another room.

"Mrs. Carpenter, I need you to remove your jeans, and if you are wearing an underwire bra, you will have to remove it as well. There are gowns in the cabinet, and you can put your belongings in one of the lockers," she instructed. "When you are ready, step through that door way and we will get started. Do you have any questions?" I shook my head and moved to the cabinet to get a gown. The tech exited through the door I would be emerging through in a matter of moments. I removed and folded the required clothing and stuffed my bra between the folds of my jeans. What, was someone going to sneak in and judge my Target bra? It *was on sale. Don't judge. I* shook my head and crammed my things in a locker and pushed open the door.

I stood rooted. It was cold. It was unnerving. Across the room was a very large...tube, for lack of a better word. Other than the table sticking out from it, there were no be*lls or whistles T*hat I expected there to be. It didn't look like the USS Enterprise, no flashing lights, big shiny buttons, or beeping noises. It was, however, deep.

"This way, Mrs. Carpenter," the tech drew my attention to the table. "Are you claustrophobic?"

"Um...I don't know. I have never been stuffed in a manicotti shell before."

She laughed, finally, someone with a sense of humor. "Okay, well, we are actually going to place you in the MRI feet first. Hopefully it won't be too uncomfortable for you, okay?"

"'k." The tech helped me on to the table and made me as comfortable as possible.

"You are going to have to remain still once you are in the tube. Any movement can cause distortions in the images which means we would have to do it again." She started pushing buttons I didn't see and the table/bed I was on began to move toward the tube. Slowly I was swallowed by this large gray mouth. If that wasn't bad enough, the bed began to move closer and closer to the ceiling of this nightmare I was stuffed in. Going in was bad, going up was unnerving. I was within a fraction of an inch of the ceiling. I could feel my own breath as it bounced back at me. I had to keep my eyes shut. Being that close was starting to freak me out.

"How're you doing in there so far?"

"Not my idea of a good time, but I think I will survive."

"Good, now it will get noisy once we start the process. I have headphones here you can wear. You can try to nap, or we can play whatever kind of music you want." She slipped the headphones over my ears.

"Classic rock, please."

"You got it. Remember, remain still, okay?"

"Believe me. I don't want to do this again." Static and...*Survivor* started singing about rising up to challenges. Well, wasn't that the perfect anthem right at that moment.

The headphones didn't help. It was loud being stuck in that thing for what felt like forever. I could swear a group of kids stood outside the tube and clanged on pots and pans the whole time. The music helped distract me, but how on God's green earth could anyone nap in there. I was helped out of the MRI and off the table about forty minutes after it all started.

"You can put your clothes on and toss the gown in the bin by the door," directed the tech.

"Cool, thanks." I slipped back into the tiny changing room and removed the gown. I pulled my things from the locker, and sure enough, no one had disturbed my Target bra. Go figure. I returned my clothing to where they belonged, on *my body,* and tossed the gown in the bin. I exited the room and the tech was standing in a doorway a few feet away.

"Is that it for me, or do I need to do anything else?"

"Um…No, Mrs. Carpenter, you are good to go," she glanced over her shoulder at a wall of computer screens with images appearing on them in what looked to be different viewpoints. "Once the radiologist finishes up with your images he will email them to Dr. Khudiadadzai."

"Do you know how long that will take?"

As we talked she edged me further out into the hall so she could close the door to the imaging room. "No, I'm sorry. I can't give you a definitive time frame. As soon as Dr. K has reviewed the results, he will get in contact with you."

I guess that was the best I was gonna get. "Thanks," I said as I turned to leave. I found Molly sitting in the same seat reading a Glamour magazine that looked to be at least two years old and dog eared. "You ready?" I asked as I approached her chair.

"Oh, thank God. You were in there forever," she moaned as she tossed the magazine to the side and retrieved her purse. "Let's get out of here."

"I told you to go."

"I know and it delights me so to tick you off by being nice."

"Ni*ce,"* I chuckled and swung open the door to the hallway. "Do you even know what that word means?"

"Shut up and let's go," Molly demanded as we walked back to the elevator. "Wayne and Tom will be at your place for dinner soon. So we need to figure out what you are going to cook us."

"Wait, WHAT!?" I stopped dead in my tracks. I ran my hands down my face and back up into my hair and held on for dear life. "What do you mean they will be there for dinner? Why is Wayne coming to dinner? What did you do?" The more questions I asked the tighter my throat became.

Molly stopped, took a deep breath, and spun to face me. "I know you haven't told Tom yet. I know you are scared. I even know that you don't have any details to tell, but you need someone to lean on because I won't always be around to hold your hand." She walked to the elevator doors and pushed the up button. "Let's go. The smell is getting to me. Would it kill these people to find a cleaner that doesn't smell like they are trying to kill us?"

I walked over as the doors opened. We stepped aside as a small herd of people dressed in scrubs disembarked. "You never said why you were here today?" I inquired as we entered the now empty box.

Molly selected the ground floor and the doors began to close, "You never asked."

*****

"So what are you going to make for dinner?" Molly asked as we walked to the parking area in search of our cars.

"What do you mean?"

"I told Wayne you were cooking. So what are you going to cook?"

"Fuck, Molly!" I jerked to face the bane of my existence. "What the hell is your problem? What right do you have to decide to invite yourself and your husband over for dinner?"

She looked at me with a huge shit eating grin, "It's not like you ever say no, when you do then maybe I will stop."

I opened my mouth to rip her to pieces to only snap it closed again for the lack of words needed to even start. She was right. I had never said no. I always did what others wanted me to do. I would piss moan to myself and crab at Tom, but I never declined.

"No."

"Too late, I already told you, they know we are going to be having dinner at your place."

God, I hated that woman. I stomped the rest of the way to my car and thought about what to make for dinner. I got in and sat for a moment trying to pull myself together. I took out my cell to check for messages. I had three.

1.   *From Charlotte:Hey lady! What r u doing today? I'm bored.*

2.   *From Lily:Hangin' with Jess tonight. Won't be home for dinner. <3 U!*

145

3.   *From Charlotte:If I didn't know u was secretly in love with me I would be thinkin u r ignoring me.*

I smiled. I thought it may have been the first time in a few hours. I sent out a *quick 'I love you, be safe'* to Lily and the same to Shelly for good measure. Then to Charlotte I replied *with, Ur right. I do <3 u and I feel dirty for it. Lol...was busy today. I'll call u* later. Moments later I was honored *with, I knew it! No reason to feel dirty, love. Talk to you* soon. I started the car and drove over to the butcher's shop to find something for dinner with a person that made me want to barf. Maybe I could make her barf. Tripe? Pig's feet? Tongue? Nope, I didn't want to eat anything that could taste me while I tasted it. Gross! I had given myself a chill with the thought of it. I stood in front of the butcher's counter and looked at nothing. Then she came in.

"Mmm...please tell me you are getting those beautiful steaks. They look delicious."

I attempted to get the butcher's attention, "Excuse me, sir."

"Yes, ma'am, what can I get for you?" He asked while he wiped his hands on the bloody apron that barely fit around his beach ball of a belly.

"May I get four pork steaks, please?"

"Of course."

"Pork steaks? Why pork steaks?" she wrinkled her nose at the very idea. "You could get those sirloins," she pointed while gawking at the meat in the glass cases. "You got a problem with beef?"

"I have a problem with people who think I should spend our money on them in the way they want. If you don't want pork steak then I suggest you go home and cook whatever you want for dinner."

The butcher stepped back to the case where he handed me my white wrapped order, "Will there be anything else?" He asked while eyeing Molly and me.

"No, thank you. That's all," I gave him a small embarrassed smile and went to check out. Back in my car I cursed her and myself for responding to her. Why did I let her get to me?

Beer, yes, I need beer. This was a case of, "It's five o'clock somewhere." Although, it was nearly three, so screw it. I stood in my kitchen with that cold elixir press against my lips when the wicked witch strolled in to judge me.

"A beer? You do know what time it is don't you?"

"Nope, I never learned, like you have never learned to knock." Fuck you!

She dropped her bag on the breakfast bar and smoothed her long beautiful hair. Yes, it was absolutely beautiful. Molly eyed me as if she were my mother and did not approve. Too bad sweetheart, I hated my mother, too.

"What do you have to drink that isn't filled with alcohol and empty calories?"

I eyed her over the beer hovering near my lips and responded simply, "Water." With a smirk I tipped the bottle the rest of the way and took a very long, satisfying gulp. "Ahhhh...that was good. What else does your highness want for dinner?"

"God, why do you hate me so much, Olivia?" she sighed. "What did I do to deserve your wrath?"

I looked at the invisible watch on my wrist, "Do we have time? Do you really wanna know because I will tell you?"

"Yes, tell me," She slid onto a stool and laid her hands neatly on the bar.

I crossed the kitchen and sat myself across from her. "You are a self-centered, entitled bitch who doesn't think before she opens her mouth." I saw her wince slightly but correct herself just as quickly. "You don't seem to care if you hurt people with your words or your actions. You only care about you," I sneered. "How's that for starters?"

Molly rolled her lips into her mouth and looked off briefly. She took a deep breath and then focused her eyes on me. They almost looked...hurt. "So, that's how you feel, but you didn't tell what I did to make you feel that way," she clarified. "You feel this way, but can you give me a reason?"

"Is that a challenge?" I taunted as I went to the fridge for another beer. She nodded her head and entwined her fingers together that still rested on the bar in front of her.

"Okay then. Do you want it chronologically or random?"

"Whatever suits you."

"Let's start with your party last Saturday..." I listed my grievances about the treatment and comments made about Charlotte and then moved on to her using me for food and the girls for free babysitting.

"Now, hold on," she interrupted with the wave of a hand. "You did not say no to cooking for the party and the girls did not babysit, so what's the problem?"

"You assumed I would, and they would."

"Because you have never said otherwise, if you didn't want to cook then why did you agree to?" God, she was right, and I hated her for it.

"Let me point out that we are family, and it is what we do for family," was the only defense I could come up with.

"What you're saying is," she straightened up in the barstool, "if I call you at any time to come and cook for me and Wayne, you will because we are family?"

"No!" Shit... "That's not what I meant."

"What did you mean?"

"Er...you were having a party...and you asked...fuck!" She got me. With my elbows on the bar I dropped my head into my hands. Crap. I looked up at my sister-in-law and expected to see an arrogant smirk, but none was to be found. She sat there quietly, waiting.

"Fine, I could have said no, you're right. But, that doesn't clear you of the way you treat people." I sat up and looked Molly square in the eyes. "You can be a true bitch."

"I can."

"Why?"

"It's a very long story, but all you need to know is I had to learn to protect myself from the actions of others."

What the hell was I supposed to say to that? I knew how she felt. We sat silent for a few minutes. She kept her eyes down, and I drank the rest of beer number two.

I broke the silence with a simple question that did not have a simple answer, "Now what?"

"I don't know," she mumbled with her eyes fixed on her manicured fingers that still lay on the bar. "It's not like I can take back the things I have said and done. Some, I don't regret and others are unforgivable. So, you tell me, now what?" Her eyes slowly rose and pinned me where I sat.

"I don't know." What now? What could we do? "I want to offer a clean slate, but some of the shit you have done..."

"Was pretty shitty, I know." She stood and walked into the kitchen and got a glass of water. She stood staring out the window into the back yard.

"Maybe, not a clean slate, but we can try to be a bit friendlier?" I suggested.

"Not BFF's?"

"Not any time soon."

"I guess I can settle for that." She turned and rested her scrawny ass against the counter. "Now, what else are you cooking for dinner?"

And...she's back.

*****

Tom and Wayne got to the house a little after five and were greeted with the most bizarre sight they had laid eyes on in...forever. They stood slack jawed as they watched Molly and me in the kitchen preparing dinner...together. And no one was bleeding, crying, or throwing anything, not yet at least.

"Are we facing an apocalypse?" Tom beamed. "I never thought I would see this day. Unless the world was coming to an end and you guys had no choice."

"Didn't you see the zombie horde in the back yard?" I replied, straight faced. Smartass! "Oh my God, Molly, they must have broken out of their pen again, damn it!"

Molly gasped in her best damsel in distress, "What ever will we do?"

"All right, we get it," grumbled Wayne. He never did have much of a sense of humor. "Let's enjoy it while it lasts." He was such a party pooper. Molly sidled up to her husband and placed a sweet kiss to his cheek and whispered something in his ear that placed the brightest smile I have ever seen on that man's face, ever. He put his arms around his wife and seemed truly happy. Hmmm...? What was I missing?

"What's for dinner, woman?" Tom nagged as he poked me in the side.

"That," I pointed to Molly and Wayne as she was still in his arms, "is the way they *say 'Hi, honey, I'*m home' and I get poked and a*sked, 'what's for* dinner?'" I grumbled. "Look around you and see for yourself." I exited the kitchen door to the deck to work on the pork steaks. Nothing beat a properly grilled pork steak, which was why I was doing it and not Tom. I loved that man, but sometimes I would have liked to kick him...in the nuts. I was vibrated out of my vengeance by the cell that was stuffed into my back pocket. I unlocked the screen to see I had a text from Alyssa.

I think we need to talk.

She could be right, but not right now. So I replied:

Not in the mood.

That should go over like a lead balloon. I silenced the damn thing and shoved it back into my pocket. Do you remember the days when we could leave the house without a phone? We used to be able to live life each day without a vibrating, chirping reminder that life was going on, with or without you. I flipped the last pork steak onto the platter and moved to the door where Tom was standing holding it open. I slid the platter onto the counter when he pulled me into his arms.

"Hi, honey. I'm home," and he kissed me senseless.

When he released me I gasped for air. "You're forgiven," I choked out. "Let's eat."

The four of us gathered around the table and began to pile way too much food on to way too small plates. We ate, talked, laughed, and threw rolls across the table at each other. I didn't know if Molly and I would become best friends, but I could, possibly, see us getting along better. Maybe.

"Where did you two run into each other today and decide we should have dinner tonight?" Wayne asked. Why did he go there?

"We saw each other at the medical center," Molly responded without thinking. Her eyes jumped to meet mine with an 'Oh, shit' look.

Tom turned to me and tipped his head and narrowed his eyes, "Medical center, why were you at the medical center, Liv? Didn't you have a doctor's appointment last week?"

And that was where my world crumbled.

I took an unsteady breath, looked at Molly who gave me a slight nod beckoning me to tell him. "I had to have a follow-up appointment with another doctor today," I muttered. "I had to see..."

"See who?" he pushed.

"I had to see a specialist," I was looking at Molly for strength. Odd. *"Dr. -Tie Me Up Tie* Me Down- sent me to see a specialist because he found...he found two lumps at my appointment last week." I was shaking. I was uncomfortable in my seat, in my skin. I didn't realize that my hands were balled up into fists with my nails digging into my palms. I turned and looked at Tom and waited for some kind of reaction.

"Why am I just hearing about this now?" he murmured placing his fork on his plate. "Why, Liv?"

"I ...there was...I had nothing to tell you. All I had was a date for an appointment." I tried to justify with the shrug of my shoulders. I was trying to explain why I had left him out of my...what...my life, my fear? Molly reached across the table and took hold of my shaking hand. "I was going to tell you if there was something to tell." I hesitated to continue until Molly squeezed my fingers and motioned for me to look at him. The look on his face was dejected. I pulled my fingers from Molly's grasp and reached for Tom's instead. "I didn't want you to worry if there was nothing to worry about."

"So, you have worried for both of us. Is that it? Did you feel like you couldn't tell me?"

"Tell you what? Hey, Tom, I have another doctor's appointment." I was reaching for a reason he could understand.

"Exactly, that is exactly what you should have said." He ripped a hole in my heart. "What did this doctor say?"

"He sent me for an MRI. Molly and I ran into each other in the waiting room and she..." I was running out of steam. I got so tired all of a sudden. I wanted to curl up and disappear. The look he was giving me was so...he looked hurt.

"I showed Olivia where the radiology department was and stayed while she had the MRI," Molly finished. "That's when I told her she owed me dinner for sitting in the waiting room." I know she was trying for levity but missed the mark.

"What now?" sighed Tom, *"what do we do now?"* he asked while waving away the space between us.

"They will call when Dr. K has had a chance to look at the images and set another appointment," I shrugged. I didn't know what was next any more than they did.

"I'm going to that appointment."

"Okay," I squeezed his hand but got nothing in return. He looked at me like I had run over his dog or wrecked his baby, Caroline.

Wayne, the master of understatement, noted, "Well, that was some depressing dinner conversation." He pushed back from the dining room table a bit and looked at Molly. "Should we brighten the room a bit, my dear?" He asked as he took her hand and kissed each knuckle.

Yup, that made me jealous. A LOT.

"Why not? They are going to find out soon enough," she beamed at him.

"What?" I asked as my mind wandered back to seeing her earlier. We were at the medical center and she was behind Dr...*No shit!*

"We are pregnant!" declared Wayne with so much joy. This was big. Tom told me they had been trying for a long time. She was pregnant once before, but lost the baby when she was only a few weeks along. It devastated them.

"Congratulations!"

"Congrats for what?" asked Michelle as she swung into the dining room and came to a stuttered halt when she saw Molly and Wayne. "Oh, hey, Uncle Wayne, Molly."

"Uncle Wayne and Aunt Molly were telling us they are going to have a baby," Tom stated.

"Cool! When? What is it?" Michelle asked as she bounced in the excitement that only someone so young could pull off.

"I am only about ten weeks along," offered Molly, "and we don't know what we are having, yet," she smiled as she looked back at Wayne who was grinning from ear to ear. To think, she had kept that to herself all day. I guess it was only right Wayne get the news first.

I was finishing up the dishes when Molly and Wayne came in to say goodbye. We actually had a good time, minus the half hour of hell between me and Tom, and I had a feeling it wasn't over yet. Molly and I agreed to get together and have lunch later that week, and off they went, arm in arm. I returned to the last of the dishes when Tom came in. I felt him standing there, but he said nothing. I finished what I was doing and was toweling off my hands when I turned to face him.

"We need to talk about this," Tom acknowledged the very thing I had been avoiding.

"What's there to say? I had an appointment and am waiting on a phone call."

"Why didn't you tell me?"

"I told you, there was nothing to tell you. It was an appointment. That is all," I threw my hands up in the air, "what more can I say?"

He closed the distance between us, but did not touch me. "You have two lumps, and you didn't think that was something I should know about?"

"They could easily be fibroids. Nothing more, nothing less," I insisted as I crossed my arms over the topic of conversation. He stepped closer, reached out and moved my arms, and wrapped them around him instead.

"True, and let's hope that is the case." He placed a chaste kiss on my lips and pulled me in tight to him, any tighter and he might have been able to feel those little bastards pressed against his chest. "I'm going to take a shower," he said as he placed a kiss to the tip of my nose.

"'k," was all I had. He released me and walked away. I could see the stress creeping up and sitting on his shoulders already. That's why I didn't want to drop that bomb on him. It's nothing until it's something, and right now, it's nothing.

If I had said that enough would it make it true?

Once I was finished with the kitchen chores, I slipped up the stairs and opened the bathroom door to see Tom supporting his weight with his hands pressed to the wall of the shower and his head held lower than his shoulders. The water was pounding down on him with an unforgiving heat. He didn't move. I don't know if he knew I was in there with him. His head started to shake from side to side and "no" slipped from his lips. It was a whisper, a plea, and not meant for my ears. I slipped out as quickly and quietly as I entered and hid myself from view as I cried. I had fought the tears so many times over the last week, but I let them create a river on my cheeks, but they washed away nothing. Nothing changed when the tears stopped. Nothing.

Chapter Twelve

I sat pushing the page down button on my keyboard as pages and pages of Fa*cebook "look at me's," "feel happy for me's," "feel sorry for me's,"* and stupid ass joke posts rolled by. I could have wri*tten a 'feel sorry for me'* that might have impressed them enough to delete some of their whiny shit. Nope, none of them needed to know what was going on in my world cuz, well, there's nothing to tell, yet. I scanned the television for something, anything that could take my mind off of the things going through my *mind. P.S.I Love You* appeared on the guide. Do I want to watch something sad but funny. Would I do those things for Tom, if I knew I was…going to live a very, very long time? I planned on torturing the men who sought out my girls, and laugh with my grandbabies, and kiss Tom for at least another 400 years. I pushed the button and watched Gerard Butler dance around in suspenders. If that didn't make ya smile then nuthin' would. I sat in silence and watched and cried and watched some more. As the credits rolled I glanced at the clock to find it was after two in the morning, and I still couldn't bring myself to go to bed. I couldn't bring myself to wrap my arms around the man I hurt by keeping him in the dark. Was it so wrong? To him it was.

I woke from the smell of coffee that hovered near my nose. I pried my eyes open to find Tom standing next to the recliner and placing the coffee cup on the end table.

"Why'd you sleep here?" He asked with a hint of hurt in his voice.

"I didn't mean to. I guess I fell asleep watching tv." I sat up and scooped up the mug and drank. "Sorry."

"I have to go."

I slid out of his favorite chair and tried to put my arms around him. He hesitated at first but then wrapped me tightly in his arms. "I love you," he whispered into my hair.

"I love you too."

He looked down into my eyes, gave me a half smile and left me standing alone as he walked out the door for the day. I felt lonely. I felt cold. I felt like I needed more coffee. I refilled my cup and went up to my room to try to pull myself together to get through the day. I stood at the foot of the bed a little shocked. He made the bed. In all the years we had been together, I don't remember him ever making the bed. Who cares? It was just a bed. I shook myself out of my shock and went and took a shower. In, out, dressed, and standing in the kitchen pouring cup number three, I heard my phone chirp letting me know I wasn't the only person on the planet. Good to *know.*

Did you forget that you were gonna 'talk to me later?' How much later?

Crap! I forgot about Charlotte.

Sorry! Got busy.

The cell chirped *again.*

I didn't need to know u and Tom "got busy." Lol Can I come drink ur coffee?

Please, please, please!

Puttin on a fresh pot now. See you soon.

No sooner had I sent that she was standing at my front door knocking. What the hell?

"Well that was quick."

"I was sittin' in yer drive when I texted," she grinned.

"Clearly. Come on, let's get you some coffee." I led my friend into my home and prayed she'd stay a while. Help me feel not so alone. The weather was not so pretty today, gray skies and wind. I heard Oliver scratch at the kitchen door to be let in and rescued from the elements. He meowed up my leg then stretched.

"Hey, buddy. Did ya eat another bird?" I asked as I scratched his head and worked my way down his back. "I hope not."

Poking around in the fridge, Charlotte asked, "Got anythin' to eat, or do ya wanna go get breakfast?" She lifted her head to barely above the door.

"How about we go to the donut shop?"

"Ooooo...let's!"

We were out the door and in her car in record time. I think she may have even broken a few road rules driving to the donut shop. We went in, found our spot, and ate way too many donuts and drank more coffee than should be legal for any one person. We chatted about some things, laughed about nothing, but didn't really talk about anything. I really wasn't in the *mood for talking* anyway. We whittled away a few hours and took my mind off the things chipping away at my sanity. I laughed with and at my friend and loved her for rescuing me from me. When lunch time rolled around, we switched restaurants and beverages, but continued the chuckle-fest we started hours before, and before I knew it three o'clock was smiling at me from the face of my cell. It was time to go home and plan for my family's evening. Charlotte dropped me off and declared her everlasting love for me...as loud as she could so that the neighbors would have something to talk about over dinner that night. I shook my head and laughed.

Alone within the walls of my home, I dropped my crap on the table by the door and dug for my cell in the suitcase I drag around with me. The little blue light notifying me I had a text was blinking. It was from *Alyssa.*

WE NEED TO TALK! WHAT DID YOU SAY TO NEIL? Trish was released from the hospital today.

I wasn't in the *mood.*

I told him to ask you what the TRUTH was. Good luck to Trish and to you.

Send. I didn't need this. My cell chirp, that didn't take long, did it?

Alyssa: The truth. What do you care if I tell him the truth or not?

Me: I don't. Not anymore. He ASKED me, so maybe he's catching on to you. Later.

I tossed my phone on the dining room table and went in search of dinner. Then the damn thing rang. Fuck! I didn't want to talk to her. I grabbed my phone with the intention of silencing it when I saw it wasn't Alyssa. It was the doctor's office.

"Hello?"

"Mrs. Carpenter?"

"This is she."

"This is Nurse Nancy from Dr. Khudiadadzai's office. Dr.K. would like to set an appointment to meet with you."

Cotton mouthed, "Um...okay. When?"

"Are you available tomorrow at 1:30?"

"Yeah, sure. I can be there then. Do I need to bring anything with me?"

"No, just yourself."

"Okay, see you then."

"1:30 tomorrow. See you then, Mrs. Carpenter."

I ended the call, ran to the bathroom, and vomited donuts, lunch, and maybe a lung because I couldn't breathe. Tom found me rocking and hugging my knees on the bathroom floor. I didn't know how long I had been there. He scooped me up into his arms and carried me up the stairs to our bed. He laid me in the middle, crawled on to the bed behind me, and pulled the quilt up over our heads. Many moons ago when we were a young couple, we did that. It was our way of blocking out everything but us. Just Tom and me and nothing else, we would talk and cuddle and well, cuddle more. This time it was to focus on peace, giving me peace in knowing Tom was there for me and was willing to block out the world for me.

"Talk to me," he whispered and pulled me closer. "Talk to me. Let me in."

"The doctor's office called to set another appointment for tomorrow."

"They called. Already?" He tried to keep his tone calm, but I heard the slight shake.

"Yeah," I shook, too, "already. Tomorrow at 1:30, did you still want to come?"

Tom nuzzled even closer and turned me to spoon with him. His cheek was pressed to my cheek. "I'll come home for lunch, get cleaned up and we will go, together." I nodded my head, closed my eyes and let one lonely tear fall.

*****

We clung to each other for a while until I pulled away with the excuse I needed to make dinner. I wasn't sure if the girls were home, or even if they were going to be. But, I was going to make dinner for someone. I found some fish fillets and homemade tator tots in the freezer that would do. I busied myself in the kitchen.

Tom came down about thirty minutes later, damp and smelling of soap and clean laundry.

"Need help?" he asked as he opened two ice cold beers. He slid one across the counter toward me.

I raised the beer in his direction, "Thanks. What else do you want with fish?"

"Ice cream." He smiled.

"You want fish, tator tots," I tipped my beer at him again, "beer, and ice cream."

"Yup, unless you want pie."

A soft chuckle escaped me as I shook my head. "No, ice cream's good." We looked at each other for a few quiet moments before the silence was replaced by the door swinging open and our girls strolling in.

"Hi! What's for dinner?" asked Lily as she rubbed her tummy. "I'm a Starvin'Marvin."

"Me, too," Shelly chimed in. "Whatcha cookin' good lookin'?"

"Fish and tots, you in?" asked their dad while handing them sodas. I smiled at the interaction. They had such a wonderfully beautiful bond. Those were two very lucky girls. I wondered if they knew it.

Lily popped the top on her can and awed, "Mmmm...fried food and sugary drinks. I'm in." She clinked cans with her sister and moved in to help.

Our girls jumped right in dipping fish into batter and tossing it into hot oil. They joked and talked with us about what had been going on in their worlds of work, fast food, and friends. The tales they spun were funny and shocking and life at its best. I laughed and voiced my opinions in places where I thought it needed to be placed. I hugged them and loved them, and out of the corner of his eye, Tom watched me, watched us.

I placed my fork on my empty plate and sighed in contentment, "What are your plans for the evening?"

"I plan on hogging the couch and fighting Lily for the remote," chimed Shelly. She popped the last tator tot into her mouth and grinned.

With a shoulder bump, Lily argued, "Um, I believe as the oldest I should get the couch and the remote."

"Nope!"

My girls bolted to the living room laughing and pushing to claim their spots. They were staying home with us tonight. Maybe I could squeeze onto the couch with them. My heart twisted a little bit as Tom and I cleared the table.

"We got some good ones right there," he said with pride as he watched our girls wrestle on the couch. Before I could agree the doorbell rang, and Lily shoved Shelly off the couch to go answer it. Lily stretched out and officially claimed her spot.

I heard Shelly's voice declare, "Yea, she's in the kitchen," she then ran across the room and dove on Lily. I listened to them laugh and smiled until Alyssa rounded the corner. I saw Tom stiffen beside me.

"Alyssa, what's up?" My protector asked.

"Tom, need a minute with Olivia," she stated then looked to me and asked if we could talk.

"Outside," I pointed toward the kitchen door. I placed my hand on Tom's arm and looked to him to steady my nerves. I gave him a tight smile and turned toward the door. Alyssa was settling into a deck chair as I came out. Just as the door was shutting I heard Tom yell for the girls to help him clean up the kitchen. Wow, he made the bed and cleaned the kitchen all in the same day.

"What?"

"What, what?" asked Alyssa.

"What do you want?"

"I want to talk about what's been going on and find out what the fuck you said to Neil."

I leaned back in my chair and rested my head. "What's been going on? Well, our friend was abused and put in the hospital, and you believed the fault lay with Tom and me..."

"But wa..." I threw up my hand to stop her from talking.

"You asked two questions, and I am going to answer them. Then you can leave." She huffed. I continued. "As I was saying, you in your stupidity believed we had something to do with her being beaten. As for Dr. Matthews, he told me the reason you and I weren't talking was because of him. Why would he think it was because of him, Alyssa? Answer that for me." I raised my head to look her in the face.

"Why else would you stop talking to me?"

"Because you are a fucking idiot and believed the line of shit Trish fed you. That is why I want nothing to do with you." I took a breath and threw my hand up again to stop her from opening her mouth. "Does it bother me that you are fucking my fantasy? Yes, because I know your history, Alyssa. You play with them like a cat with a mouse. Men are entertainment, remember?" I leaned my tired body against the table. "Dr. Matthews was someone none of you had touched, or tarnished. Now, I could care less about any of you." I pushed myself back into the cushions of the chair and laid my head back again. I looked up at the darkening sky and could still see the clouds had covered the day.

"Tarnished? So I tarnished Neil."

"No, you tarnished my fantasy. Pay attention like you do when Trish talks."

"I told you what she told me."

"Yes, you did. You also said it wouldn't have happened if Tom and I had stayed out of it, remember?" I lifted my head and waited.

"If you hadn't pissed Richard off it wouldn't have happened."

The chair tipped over behind me as I jerked upright. "Get out!" I screamed and pointed to the door. "Go!" The door was jerked open and Tom was standing next to me within moments. I could see Shelly and Lily's faces pressed to the window. "I don't need your shit right now. Just go, Alyssa. When you quit wearing your ass as a hat maybe we can talk, but not now."

"What's going on?" Tom demanded.

"I wanted to know why she's pissed at me."

Tom encircled me with his arms to barricade me from everything outside of the bubble he created. "Because you believed a lie about her, you believed someone who has been lying a long time to cover the shit Richard had been doing to her. You were wrong," he explained. "You should really think about all of it, Alyssa: Trish wearing long sleeves in the summer, too much make-up, not wanting to go out or see people. I'm not very close to her, but even I saw it." Alyssa stood and stared at him. There it was. Dots being connected, a picture was starting to form.

"Leave," I whispered from the crook of Tom's neck. "Make her leave."

"You need to go, now."

The screen door opened and Lily eyed Alyssa. "Mom and dad said to go." Lily held the door demanding she leave.

"I'll get the front door," Michelle yelled as she ran to open it.

I buried my face further into Tom's shoulder and clung to him for support. I heard footsteps and doors closing and felt more arms, four more to be exact.

Michelle wiggled in closer and whispered, loudly, "Screw her. Let's make popcorn and *watch Finding Nemo!*" We all erupted into laughter and decided that was an awesome idea.

"I get the couch," I screamed as I yanked the door open and made a run for it. The girls followed and we somehow found a way to wrap ourselves around each other comfortably.

"Fine, I'll make the popcorn, set up the movie, and sit alone," whined Tom.

"Okay," we sang in unison and giggled as we nestled ourselves down into the couch. My heart twisted a bit more. I wanted this to last forever.

As the credits started to roll Shelly called it quits and Tom kissed me good night. I sat curled up on the couch with Lily. "How is everything? You know, with Darren."

"We're done. I found out he had been screwing around for a while and was only using me to get rides and the money to do shit," she hissed. "He was the one who talked me into going places and doing shit so I would pay for it. But, he would piss moan if I wanted to do something. God, I feel stupid."

I pulled Lily into my arms and explained she was very lucky to have friends who loved her enough to tell her. Those people are rare and she needed to keep them close. Not everyone would stand by her. We talked for a while before she called it a night and went off to bed. I sat in silence for a while, but I wasn't alone. Oliver had joined me on the couch. He curled up in my lap demanding a good scratching. I ran the memories of the evening through my head.

Tom holding me under the covers, making dinner with my family, Alyssa's interruption, and curling up on the couch with the girls like we did when they were little. Moments with my family were the ones I needed to stock up on. I needed to build more memories like that for them and me. I scooped up Oliver and carried his fat, orange butt up to bed with me. I slipped under the covers and decided to hold Tom the way he held me…and sleep.

Well, that didn't work. A few hours later I found myself stalking people on Facebook. I had some boring ass friends. Boring enough I yawned, so I lay down on the couch and hoped the sandman would bash me on the head with a bag of magic sleepy-time dust. I woke later to the gurgling of the coffee pot. I wished they made cologne that smelled like coffee. I would have been all over Tom if he wore it. The same would have been true for bacon. Who ever invented the automatic timer on the coffee pot needed a medal. He/she was a true hero in my eyes. I went in search of a mug big enough to start the process of waking up. That would have been a swimming pool, but we didn't have one of those. It was zero dark thirty and I was hugging a mug of lovingly prepared coffee when Tom shuffled his way into the kitchen. I slid a mug to him, "I heard you coming."

"Thanks. Why didn't you come to bed last night?"

"I did, but woke up really early, so I Facebook stalked for a while, then dozed on the couch until I smelled coffee." I had to admit Tom was still pretty hot for a dude in his forties. The V that women dream about running their tongues along isn't as pronounced but you can still make it out and the light dusting of gray only made his blonde hair shine. Those blue eyes were still so full of life and adventure. I wanted to be a part of those adventures.

"What?" he asked with a quizzical grin.

"What, what?"

"You were staring."

"Can you blame me? You're hot!" Good cover! I laughed and let my eyebrows bounce to enhance my reply.

"Really, you wanna take that thought upstairs, or should I dishonor you right here in the kitchen?" He sidled closer to me but neither of us let go of our coffee.

"And sacrifice coffee time? I think not, but you can kiss me," I proffered my lips and waited.

"Then a kiss I shall give, and I will set my coffee down to do it," he smiled and gave the sweetest closed mouthed kiss, because we both had major morning breath laced with coffee.

Gross!

"Mmmm...thanks," I praised, "but I don't regret not giving up coffee time," I smirked up at him as I raised my mug to my lips.

"I understand," he replied while he refilled his mug. "I gotta go get ready for work."

I followed him back up the stairs where he showered and dressed, and I made the bed and gathered the laundry to stuff down the laundry chute. I could feel his eyes on me, watching me do the simplest of chores. Was he thinking the same things I was? Would I be doing these things a year from now? Would I be here a year from now? Of course I would, where the heck was I going to go? I ignored his eyes and continued on with my chores. I gathered my clean clothes for my shower and laid them on the bed.

"It's about that time, babe. Work calls," Tom declared as he put his arms around my waist. "How about we go to lunch and then head to the doctor's office, sound good?"

"Sounds good," I rose up on my toes and kissed him stupid.

That's how you send your man off to work.

He slipped from my hands and left me to my morning. I had hours to *kill*. Hours. I had an idea. I threw on my clothes without a shower and grabbed my purse, keys, and cell and made my way to Lowes. Flowers! I was going to add more flowers and what-nots to my garden. If I was going to be stuck in my own head thinking about unpleasant things, I was going to be surrounded by beauty and lovely smells. Along the way I stopped off at the gas station, got a cup of Pumpkin Spice coffee, and filled the tank in my little car. I loved Pumpkin Spice. I couldn't believe they still carried it because it was advertised as a seasonal flavor. I wasn't gonna bitch about it, that's for sure. It was still quite early, and everyone was on the road heading to a job or school, and I was going to buy flowers. There were a few cars at Lowes when I got there, but I thought they probably belonged to the workers. With my purse hanging from my shoulder and my wonderful coffee in my hand, I walked in to the garden center and felt peace. A calm settled over my brain as I looked out over the rows and rows of color. Day lilys, asters, bleeding hearts, chrysanthemums, and forget-me-nots called out to me. I got a cart, without a wobbly wheel, and slipped from row to row picking through the rainbow before me. I filled my cart with decorative pots, flats of flowers, an orange metal cat that looked like Oliver, and a new garden hose holder.

Once home, I backed my car down the drive and unloaded my treasures onto the deck. I plotted my garden by placing the flowers around the yard, looking for the perfect spot for each one. I dug and chopped and fertilized. I arranged and rearranged and planted. I watered and watered and watered. I planted bleeding hearts and forget-me-nots in beautiful pots and left them on the deck. Appropriate? I hoped not. I looked out at my hard work and smiled. I made a point to choose perennials, so that they would come back each year to say 'hello' and 'remember.' I sat on the deck and finished my iced tea before I headed to the shower. I was muddy and sweaty and at peace, for now. I laid out my outfit and turned on the music player on my phone. In the shower I rubbed away the dirt and wanted so badly to rub away the things that had left a stain on my life. In only a week I had lost two friends and gained two lumps. I had cried tears for them and for me. I had feared for one and for me. I was angry at them and at me. But, I had to choose me for the moment. I had to get my shit together and deal with my issues before I attempted to wallow in any of theirs. I let Blue October sing to me about overcoming fear and tried to heed the words. It was time to step up and stand strong no matter what was to happen. Right, I was shaking in my skin. I dried myself off and dressed in jeans and a t-shirt. A little heavy for the day, but it seemed fitting. I dried my hair in less than a minute, added a few swipes of mascara, and Chap-Stick. Ahhh...masterpiece. Nope, just me.

Tom came home at 11:30 and showered and changed into clean clothes. I sat in the living room and ran my hand threw Oliver's fur while staring at the wall.

"You look like you're watching paint dry."

"Huh? Oh…if it's still wet after three years then we have a problem."

Tom pointed at my leg and smirked, "Do you want the lint brush or did you plan on taking Oliver with us?"

I looked down to find I was covered in bright orange hair. "Crap." I stood and attempted to brush away the hair when Tom approached with the lint brush. He ran the wand down my leg and laughed at the amount of hair he extracted.

"Look at that. There's enough hair to grow another cat."

"Grow a cat? Puts another spin on 'cat tails.'"

"Speaking of growing, I saw the yard," his eyes resting on my face. "It's nice." He stepped closer and kissed my temple, "Anywhere special you want to eat?"

"Not really, I have no preference. I'm probably gonna eat light. I'm on edge and don't want to get sick." He knew what I was trying to say and took my hand.

"Okay then. I want Subway. 'k?" I agreed with a nod. Tom led me to the back door toward the garage. "Let's take Sweet Caroline. She needs some fresh air."

"Don't I feel special," I clutched my chest, "I feel honored to be able to join you."

"Just get in the car, woman," he instructed with a smack to my ass.

"Ouch, that hurt," I barked as I rubbed my back side. "What was that for?"

"Disrespecting the '57 Chevy," he sneered but I could see he was trying to suppress a chuckle. We slid onto the soft leather and he leaned over and placed a kiss on my cheek. "Buckle up!" We were off.

We sat in Subway and ate our lunches. We talked about his morning and my flower explosion in the back yard. We talked about the weather and the news and anything but the appointment that was less than an hour away. I wasn't up to eating much, so I got half a sub and a small drink, but couldn't bring myself to finish it. The closer the clock ticked to 1:30 the worse my stomach responded. But could time move quickly, no, it had to creep. I picked at my lunch as Tom wolfed his down.

"You gonna eat that," he asked while pointing to the remains of my sandwich.

"No, you can have it." He was pushing it into his mouth before I finished my response. "Hungry, were ya?"

"Mmhmm," he mumbled with a full mouth, "starved." I watched him finish my lunch in no time. It was 1:05, twenty-five minutes, twenty-five very long minutes to go. "You ready?" Tom asked as he wiped his mouth.

"No," I whispered with my face in my hand. I ran my fingers back and forth along my forehead and let out a sigh, "but what choice do I have." I ran my hand down my face and looked into his concerned eyes. "Let's do this."

"Let's do this."

We were back in Caroline in less than a minute. The drive to the doctor's office was less than five minutes, which still gave me around twenty minutes to wait. I went to check in with the desk while Tom claimed us a few seats in the waiting room.

"Mrs. Carpenter, Nurse Nancy will take you right back," stated the voice behind the bubbled glass.

"Ah, okay." Nurse Nancy appeared seconds later at the door.

"Mrs. Carpenter, are you ready?"

"Can my husband come with me?"

"Of course," she looked out into the waiting room as I waved Tom over.

I took his arm. "They are ready for me now."

"This way, please," instructed our tour guide. We wondered the halls and turned a few times. I was lost. Nurse Nancy stopped near an open door and ushered us in, directing us to two chairs. "Dr. Khudiadadzai will be right with you." She gave me a slight nod and a soft smile as she closed the door. We were in an office, not an examination room. There were no blood pressure cuffs hanging from the wall or distasteful posters. Those were replaced with framed certificates, diplomas, and a few personal items. This was *Dr. -Carmel* Bliss's- office. We sat in the two chairs available in front of Dr. K's modest desk.

"What's his name?" Tom asked with a confused look on his face as he squinted his eyes in an attempt to read the name that appeared inside a frame.

"Dr. Khudiadadzai."

"If you say so," he accepted with a shrug.

We sat quietly for what seemed like forever, but only a few minutes had passed when we heard the light knock and the door open, enter *Dr. -Chocolate Dipped Fantasy-.*

He was fine. Truly a beautiful man, sigh...

"Hello, again Mrs. Carpenter, and you must be Mr. Carpenter," Dr. K smiled while extending his hand to Tom. "I'm Dr. Khudiadadzai or Dr. K."

"Tom," offered my husband as he shook my doctor's hand.

"And please call me Olivia," I offered as we all settled in. Dr. K took his seat on the other side of the desk and laid a chart out in front of him. I saw what appeared to be x-rays. Those must have been my MRI images.

"I received your images yesterday and took some time to review them," as he spoke he began to slide the images out in front of Tom and me so we could see what he was talking about. I looked at image after image and felt my heart drop. I could see something. "As you can see, right here and here," he pointed with the tip of his pen, "there is a small mass in your right breast, but a substantially larger one in your left. Olivia," I tore my eyes from the horror show before me to look into his soulful eyes, "I told you I would not tell if it was something until I knew. This is something."

"What is it?" asked Tom as he slid an image closer to get a better look.

"I won't say until we have a chance to test it."

"You mean a biopsy," I choked. I hadn't taken my eyes off of him.

"Yes, we need to do a biopsy to see exactly what we are dealing with." Dr. K sat back in his chair, "We can do it as soon as tomorrow. We are able to do what is called an ultrasound guided

169

core-needle biopsy here in one of the exam rooms. We would only biopsy the left breast at this point, since the mass is larger in that one. There appears to be what we call Pectoral muscle invasion. Simply put, it appears the mass has invaded the chest wall," he pointed to invisible lines on several of the MRI images spread out on his desk to show where this had occurred.

I saw fuzz.

Tom stiffened a bit, "That fast? What does that entail?" I stiffened. A lot.

*Dr. -Car*amellow- pulled a pamphlet from inside his desk and laid it out for us to review. "What would happen is we would locate the mass with the ultrasound, you would receive a local anesthetic in the breast tissue near where the needle would penetrate," as he explained the procedure he showed pictures of the process. "A very small incision would be made so that the needle will pass through the tissue easier."

"I wouldn't have to stay the night or anything, right?" I asked through the hand I had clamped over my mouth.

"No, Olivia. You would be able to go home right after."

"How painful is it?" Tom asked as he continued to flip through the pages of the pamphlet. I could feel the panic start to rise.

"It can be painful," he stated clearly while looking right at me. "Even with the local. You may bruise from it too. You may have a small amount of bleeding, but it can be done quickly, and you will be free to go home and rest in a place where you are comfortable. The discomfort can be easily managed with Tylenol, no prescriptions would be required. The biopsy would be sent to pathology for testing, and as soon as I receive the results you would be notified." He explained the entire process to me a second time, photo by photo, to be sure I was fully aware and able to make an informed decision.

"Let's do it," declared Tom with his matter-of-fact voice.

"I'm sorry Mr. Carpenter, Mrs. Carpenter has to make that call."

I looked at Tom as he reached for my hand. He threaded his fingers with mine and brought our hands to his lips. He whispered 'I love you' against the skin on the back of my hand and looked for my answer in my eyes. I chewed on my lower lip as a few arrogant tears rolled down my cheeks. "Let's do it, tomorrow," I decided with my eyes still locked with Tom's. "Can Tom be there?"

"Mr. Car...," he started, but shifted gears, "Tom is welcome to come. During the procedure, however, he will have to wait in the waiting room. The moment we are finished, we will allow him back in to be with you."

"Okay."

The next few minutes were spent scheduling the biopsy for nine the next morning. I was given instruction to not wear perfume, deodorant, or lotions. I was told I could eat beforehand, but to make it a light meal. Like I was going to be able to eat, who were they kidding? I was glad Tom was with me because there was no way I would have remembered half of the things I was told. Dr. K shook our hands and held mine for a few extra seconds. With a tight smile he wished us well and he left the office. Nurse Nancy came for us and guided us back out to the waiting area. She must have been part blood hound because I was as lost coming as I was going. I don't recall much of what happened after I said 'let's do it.' I think I shut down after that.

I left Tom standing in the waiting area as I went to the ladies room. I clambered to get into a stall before the dam broke and I made a fool of myself in front of the two women who were washing their hands. I sat on the toilet with my purse on my lap and shoved the straps into my mouth. I bit down hard to stop the sob from escaping. I heard the door open and close and prayed the other ladies had left and no one had entered. I needed to pull myself together, so I could walk out of the ladies room with my head up. Why? Who the fuck cared if I was a snotty mess anyway? Tom? I was pretty sure he was in the waiting room rubbing his hairline bald. I needed to get home and think. No, wallow. I pulled a long stream of sand paper from the toilet tissue dispenser and tried to mop myself up without ripping off skin. I went to the sink to wash my hands when I caught sight of myself. Mascara was a bad idea because it was oozing down my cheeks with the tears. I dug through my bag for some make-up wipes, and did what I could to pull myself together. I washed my hands again and tossed the paper towel in the trash on my way out. Tom was leaning against the wall outside the ladies room. He had been staring at his shoes when he heard the door open. Straightening he held his hand out, and I slipped mine into his.

"I think we need ice cream. What do you think?" he asked with a smile that made me want to cry, again.

"I could go for a peanut butter cup blizzard."

We walked hand in hand toward the car, "With whipped cream?" he asked.

"Nope, chocolate syrup."

"Done."

*****

Tom and I sat on the back deck admiring my newly planted garden while enjoying our ice cream. We remained silent. Silence was okay. We both had a lot to think about, a lot to ponder and absorb. We needed to find peace within ourselves to find peace with each other. I thought about what the next day would hold and prayed I could handle the pain that may come with it. I thought about the 'what if's' and 'what next's' to the process. I wondered and I pondered and I came up short of an answer. I looked over at Tom who was looking at me. "What?"

"Just thinkin'. You?" he asked as he shoved another spoon full of peanut butter cup ice cream into his mouth.

"I thought I smelled something burning. Does it hurt?" I can be a snarky bitch, but it made him chuckle, and we needed that right now.

"Wow, that was original. Did you come up with that all by your lonesome?"

"Yup. I be so smartly." I sent him a raspberry on the wind. He gave a simple smile. It had an edge of sadness to it I couldn't bear to see. "Hey," he met my eyes, "it's nothing 'til it's something, and right now it's nothing."

"Nothing." I don't think he believed the word he spoke. It hung there with an unnatural bite to it. Nothing – yet. "So, show me this wonderful garden you planted. What's the orange thing over there in the corner?"

172

"Oliver's twin! I found this cool metal cat painted to look just like the Lolly Monster," I giggled as I went in search of Oliver in the house. I came out moments later hindered by an animal who desperately needed to go on a diet. "Let's see what he thinks." I carried him over to where Oliver 2 sat and put him down in front of it. He looked at it, walked around it, batted at it, then peed on it. "I guess he doesn't care."

"He's a cat. How much was he supposed to care?"

"Oh well, I guess he'll learn to like it better when he understands that when he dies I'm burying him and putting Oliver 2 right on top of his grave."

"You have a twisted mind, my dear, a twisted mind indeed."

"You love me and you know it." I was caught off balance when I was yanked into Tom's arms. He held me tightly around my waist and gave me a deep peanut butter flavored kiss.

Scooping me up in his embrace, he dared me with his words, "Let me show you how much."

Hey now, put your tongue back in your mouth. There are things a lady will not share. We all know I'm no lady, but I don't kiss and tell either.

Chapter Thirteen

Apparently he loved me a lot, but it didn't take too long to show. Well, part of it at least. We lay in our too-small bed with my ear over his heart. We lay there talking about the garage and his work, my garden and what more I wanted to plant, the girls and how proud we were of them. We talked about everything other than what was going to happen the next day.

"Wanna grab Chinese take-out tonight? I'm thinkin' sushi," Tom questioned. "I can swing by Wasabi Joe's and grab some food."

"Crab Rangoon! Sign me up."

He placed a kiss on the crown of my head. "You have to let me up, so I can put some clothes on. They might have a problem with me walking in in all my awesomeness."

"Right," I shifted out of his arms, so he could exit our bed. It felt colder somehow. Vacant without his arms around me, "You should text the girls to see if they are coming home and if they want anything," I suggested as I pulled the covers up to my chin to try to chase away the chill he left behind.

"Can do. Are you gonna stay in bed, or will you be getting up?" He wondered aloud as he slipped his leg into his abused jeans.

I smirked and gave him the one eye-brow salute, "I'm up. I'm already dressed and combing my hair. Can't you see it?"

Tom walked to my side of the bed and caged my body to the mattress with his outstretched arms. His lips met mine, briefly. "If you want to stay in bed, I'm good with that."

I reached up and held his head steady as my lips reached for his. "I'm getting up," I whispered and kissed him stupid. "Now, go get me some food," I demanded when we came up for air.

"You can stay in bed, and I can get back in there with you and we could have round two?" His eyebrows danced on his forehead and I laughed. "Fine, get your fine ass up, and I will go get food." He gave my back side a swat as I rolled to get out of bed. "See you in a bit."

Tom left carrying his boots in one hand and pushing his other arm into his favorite *Monty Python* t-shirt. I sat on the edge of the bed and hugged the covers to my chest. Thoughts drifted through my mind, but nothing seemed to stick. Words floated in front of my eyes, words I didn't understand. Words like pectoral muscle invasion, ultrasound guided biopsy, scalpel incision, core needle... I couldn't draw that picture in my mind. I had nothing to draw from. I slid off the bed and threw on some clothes. I went to the bathroom to get cleaned up. I ran a comb over my short mop. I went through the motions and I stood in front of the mirror looking at the source of my situation. It was funny to think other women had been jealous of my *boobs*. *'You have great breasts,' 'I wish mine were that big,' 'Are they* real?' Oh, they were real, all right, a real pain in the ass. I had worn a bra every day since I was eleven years old. I hated bras then and I detested them now. "Fucking things," I spat as I tossed the comb back into its drawer and left the bathroom.

I was setting the table for yummy food when I was blessed with both of my beauties. "Hi guys! Did your dad text you about sushi?"

"Why do ya think I'm home," Shelly declared as she stuck her head in the fridge. "Who wants what to drink?" she asked as she grabbed a soda.

Lily was spreading out the silverware and napkins, "I'll take a soda, too."

"I've got iced tea, but grab a soda for your dad." We finished setting the table and sat to wait for Tom to get home. "So how's life with my girlies? How's work going, Shelly?" I asked as I sipped my tea.

Shelly slurped down half the soda she held, *"Ahhh, burp!"*

"Shelly! Gross!" Lily blurted with a look of absolute disgust etched on her face.

"Better out than in," Shelly explained as she set the offending drink on the table. "Work's been okay. I saw Darren during lunch today," her eyes drifted up to Lily's, "he looked pissed. What's up sis?"

"How would I know? I haven't seen him since we broke up the other night," Lily objected with mock innocence. The look on her face was clear. She knew something about Darren's anger.

"What did you do, Lil?" I asked with real interest in her answer.

"I just made it clear, to everyone, the kind of person he is. He's a cheater, liar, mooch, lazy, selfish, and can't kiss to save his life."

"And how did you share thi*s with* everyone?" I asked crossing my arms over my chest, bracing myself for the response.

"Facebook, twitter, mass text, billboards."

"Billboards?" I squeaked.

"No, but I thought about it. It cost too much."

With a straight face, Shelly replied, "That's okay cuz I asked the guys to spit in his burger and drop his fries on the floor, a lot."

"Oh My God, Shelly that is just…" just what… "Revoltingly awesome." I may have been an adult and a mom, but that's what you get for fucking with one of my girls. They stand up for each other. They fight with each other, but fight *harder* for each other. I was, almost, proud. No, I was proud. I shook my head as they laughed at Shelly's revenge toward the douche-bag who screwed over her sister.

Yup, he was definitely a douche pickle.

Lily rounded the table and took hold of Shelly and hugged her fiercely. "That's my sister, right there. I love you." Just as they were sitting back down, the kitchen door swung open with a bang.

"Who wants food?" Tom bellowed while holding the bags as if he had conquered and killed our supper. Me caveman, you cook...insert grunts here. He sauntered to the table and dropped the bags. He placed his fists on his spread hips and adopted the best Superman stance possible, "That's right. Who da man? That's right, I da man."

"Our hero," cooed Lily as she brought her clasped hands to her cheek and batted her lashes at her daddy.

My family was a bunch of odd balls. We found the funny where ever we could. Even in moments where funny was hiding, we managed to pull it out by its feet and hold it down while we laughed as it struggled. Joy is precious. Laughter is rare. We learned to hang on to it, tickle it, and make it ours. I watched the three most important people to me spread out the feast and share their love with each other. I listened to them talk and laugh. My heart beat a little faster with the thought I might not be there for moments like those. I shook the image from my head and reached for the sushi before they ate it all. Priorities, people. You gotta have priorities.

Sushi, people, sushi!

We ate, we talked, we laughed when I put too much wasabi on a piece of California roll, and from time to time, my eyes would lock with Tom's. We didn't say anything to Lil and Shelly about what was coming. We hadn't even talked to each other about talking to anyone else. Did he understand now why I didn't tell him earlier? There was nothing to tell until there was something to tell, right? I would keep telling myself that until it started to make sense. Maybe I would learn keeping people in the dark was what was best for...them...me? It was better for somebody, it had to be, right? I wasn't sure who. I was gonna eat my sushi and enjoy my evening until the world made since. That was going to be a very long dinner and a shit ton of raw fish, and I was getting full.

We enjoyed our dinner, and in the end, I got to do the clean-up. Lucky me. Michelle hit the showers to hose off the stench of greasy cheese burgers, and Lily was making plans for her evening. My Tom had disappeared into the office and was riveted by whatever it was he was doing, so once I finished in the kitchen I escaped to our room. It was a beautiful night for a walk, so that was what I was gonna do. I changed into comfy clothes and walking shoes. I let Tom know where I was going and got a wave as his response. I wondered what he was doing, but not enough to question him. Lil was coming down the stairs as I was heading out the door.

"Where ya goin'?

"Walk, it's pretty and not too hot so I'm gonna take a spin around the park," I explained as I dug through my purse for my head phones. "Wanna come?"

"Thanks, but I'm going to the movies with some friends. There is nothing better than movie theatre popcorn with enough butter to cause a coronary."

"True, very true," I kissed my awesome daughter and told her to have a handful for me and then made my escape.

I let my feet lead me to the park. Prince was playing in my ears, or was it the artist formerly known as Prince? I was sporting a pair of dark shades. The darker the better to people watch. I can see them, but they have no clue I'm watching. I had the need to see life, other people's lives, in full motion. I went with the intention of clearing my mind of all the shit crammed into every corner. It felt like I was mucking a stall. Let's see, Trish was out of the hospital. Good or bad, she was out. Alyssa was pissed about me talking to Dr. -You're screwing my friend-, because I made him question the crap she was telling him. I get to have a needle shoved into my boob tomorrow because I have shit growing in there that shouldn't be growing in there. I knew I had a green thumb, but I don't think that was what I wanted to be growing, ever. Did I miss anything? Oh, and a douche-bag broke my daughter's heart. I wasn't too worried about him, between Lil and Shelly, he was toast. I could think all I wanted about each of these things, but thinking wouldn't change them in the least. I couldn't help Trish as much as I wanted to. Until she reached out, I had to stay out of it. It killed me a little every day to know what she was going through, but could do nothing about it. Alyssa, she had to learn to be honest with the people in her life. Over the time I had known her, I learned to take things she said with a grain of salt. Dr. Matthews seemed to actually care when he talked to me about her the other day. All I could do was hope she saw the error of her ways before it was too late.

I walked and watched. I watched kids play. I watched parents root for their kid's ball team. I watched an older couple walking their dog while holding hands. I stopped by the skateboard park and watched the kids challenge fate with twists and jumps. I cringed and was in awe all at the same time. I watched squirrels, and I watched dogs watch squirrels. I watched moms pushing strollers, and guys checking out girls. I watched life happen all around me and felt sad. That was the moment when my own mortality became obvious. I wasn't going to live forever. Time was now a factor in my world. Time, a four letter word, how fitting. I made my way to my favorite place in the park to find it occupied. A young man sat with his arm around an equally young lady. Her head lay on his shoulder, and they spoke in whispers, words they only wanted to share with each other. I walked away and hoped they found the right words, words that would last as long as they did. I walked on. Had I said the right words to Tom? Had I said the right words to my babies? What about friends and family? Of course I didn't. I had much to say and, possibly, a limited time to say them.

This is the moment I decided I needed to start writing it all down. I needed to make you all see how much I loved you. I needed to show you.

If it turned out I was healthy, fingers and toes crossed, I wanted to make a change. I wanted to become the person I should have been all along. I never wanted anyone in my life to ever doubt my feelings for them. I never wanted them to ever question their value in my eyes. I wanted to be the B.I.T.C.H. I always claimed to be, Brave, Intelligent, Tenacious, Caring, and Hopeful. It was time to start.

*****

I heard the shower when I got home and assumed it was Tom since the girls left. I slipped out of my sweaty clothes and stepped into the steam filled room. "I hope my husband is in here somewhere. I can't see you."

"Then use your hands and feel your way," he chuckled.

"Subtle, very subtle," I quipped. "Wanna share the soap?"

"I was about to get out, but I'm game to wash your back."

I slid my hand around Tom's waist and rested my head between his shoulder blades. "I love you, you know that right?" I murmured against his skin.

He turned in my arms so we were facing one another. He held me tighter. His lips rested against the crown of my head. "I love you more."

"Not possible."

He spun us so my back was to the water letting the heat engulf me. "You were gone a while. Did you walk to Zimbabwe?" He asked as he leaned back so he could look at me.

"No, just wandered around the park for a while. It was nice out there. I do wish I had used some bug spray though."

"Well, I'll get out so you can get washed up," his arms dropped away from my body and I gave a faint whine. "I'll be between the sheets when you get out. Just sayin'."

"Oh really, and this is important?"

"Very."

Tom stepped out of the shower and wrapped a towel around his waist, buffed his head with another. I was reaching for the shampoo when he reminded me, "Remember the doc said no perfumey stuff. Maybe you shouldn't use body wash."

"Yeah, you might be right." I washed my hair and used a bar of soap to clean the rest of me. It didn't smell nearly as good, but Tom was right. I made quick work of it. I turned off the water and grabbed a fluffy towel to wipe away the wet. I wrapped one around me and another for my head.

"No lotion!" I heard coming from the other room, "or deodorant!"

"Got it," geesh, did he think I forgot. Clearly he did. I donned my robe that hung on a hook on the back of the door. I hung my towels on the rack and left the steamy room. Tom was where he said he would be, tucked beneath the sheets. My bedside lamp was the only light on in the room which was plenty to find my night gown and make my way to the bed without stubbing a toe. Tom's eyes were closed and his right arm was thrown over his head. His left arm lay across his chest and rose and fell with each breath he took. I took my place beside him. I settled down into the too small bed and reached up and released the room from any light. I couldn't see anything, but could hear a pin drop.

"Night, Babe," Tom grumbled as he turned to face away from me.

"Night."

And I laid there willing sleep to come.

It was 7:30 when Tom came to wake me. I don't know when I finally fell asleep, but I can tell you that 7:30 was way too early. I wanted to become intimate with my pillow, but Tom was blocking the attempt.

"Ya gotta get moving. I brought you some coffee," he said as he jostled me some more. "The doc said you could eat, so I figured coffee would be okay." He started to bounce up and down on the bed trying to dislodge me from my comfort.

"I'm up! Stop!" I rolled over and faced the man I wanted to kill. "Was that necessary?"

He tipped his head to give my question some thought, "No, but it was fun."

"Jerk."

"Maybe so, but someone has to get you up. Come on," he reached his hand out to me, "you have a big day and need to get moving."

I took his hand and resigned myself to the fact I had to get up. I took another shower, more for a wake up than anything else. I decided on simple, comfortable clothes, nothing tight or difficult to put on. I figured a sports bra was a good idea. I caught myself before I put on my deodorant, then tossed it back in the drawer. No lotion. No perfume. I was gonna stink.

I met Tom in the kitchen. His elbows were resting on the counter, and he was rolling his coffee mug between his hands.

"Is there any more coffee?" His eyes met mine. What was that look? Fear? Concern? "Yes, but are you sure you want another one before we go?" he asked. "I don't want you getting sick."

"Half a cup? I have time."

His head shook, but what was he going to do? Then I remembered my walk the night before. "You're right. I'll have water instead," I walked to the sink and rinsed out my mug. "Thanks for watching out for me," I added as I got a bottle of water from the fridge. The look on his face was priceless. You would have thought I told him we won the lottery, shock and awe.

"Someone has to," he snorted. "Depending on how you feel after, I'll make you something to eat. 'k?"

"Sounds good," I smiled at him. I took my bottle of water to the living room and rummaged through my purse to make sure I had what I needed. I took my cell off the charger and found I had a message from *Charlotte*.

Hello Chickie! I heard tell your man was home with you. Keep the screaming to a low rumble. Wouldn't want the coppers called for disturbing the peace. Lol

I wish. There might be some screaming today, but not for anything *fun*.

I'll keep that in mind. Lol We need to do lunch/movie again. It was fun, and I like hanging out with you. :)

Tell them how you feel. Tell them they have value. Tell them they are worth your *time*.

Too right that. Let's plan!

"You ready, babe?"

"Ready as I'll ever be," I sputtered as I slung my purse over my shoulder. "Let's do this." I really wasn't ready, but what choice did I have?

*****

We sat in the hard plastic chairs in the waiting room after checking in. Waiting. Waiting. Waiting, and getting more and more nervous. I was so glad I didn't have that second cup of coffee.

"Mrs. Carpenter," Nurse Nancy called from the door, "Come on back."

Tom and I stood and prepared for what felt like my walk to the gallows. Time to be brave. My stomach twisted, but was thankfully empty. Tom took my hand and led me down the hall. Nurse Nancy showed us into a larger room with massive equipment.

"Mrs. Carpenter," I gave Nancy a raised eyebrow at her mistake, "Olivia," she smiled. "Okay, Dr. K needs you to remove everything from the waist up. There is a gown on the table. Put it on so the tie is in the front." She flipped through my chart and made a few notes, "Did you eat anything this morning?"

"No, just a cup of coffee and water."

"You remembered no perfume, deodorant, or lotion?"

"None of the above."

"Good, okay. Go ahead and get changed and Dr. Khudiadadzai will be in shortly. Mr. Carpenter, you will be able to stay with Mrs...Olivia until the procedure starts. I will take you back to the waiting room until they are finished. Any questions?"

I looked to Tom and shook my head, "No, we're good, thanks."

"I'll leave you to it then," she nodded as she pulled the door shut behind her.

I moved to the table and prepared myself. I removed my top, bra, and sandals. I hopped up and sat on the table...and waited. Tom took my clothes and purse and slipped them under the chair near the door, then came and took my hand in his. He ran his rough thumb over the back of my hand.

"Are you okay," he worried.

"I won't be okay until I am home watching TV and eating mint chocolate chip cookies."

"Is that what you want? Mint chocolate chip cookies? I can pick some up at the bakery after I get you home." His thumb continued its journey over my hand. "You name it, and I'll get it."

"Just a hug for now, please," his arms came around me, and I rested my head on his shoulder. The shoulder that has always been there for me to lean on, he was there while I was picking up the jagged pieces of my childhood and the aftermath of a violent break-up. These shoulders carried our children in play. They bore the brunt of labor. These shoulders carried my world, and today, they held me up. "I love you. Thanks for coming with me."

Tipping his lips to my ear, "I love you too." His hold tightened a bit more. Just enough. Just right.

Our moment was interrupted by a knock and the door swinging open. Dr. K joined us along with Nurse Nancy and one other. "Good morning Mr. and Mrs. Carpenter."

"Good Morning Dr. K," I croaked. I was still swallowing down the tears which had been forming while safely swallowed up in my husband's arms.

Dr. Khudiadadzai took the next few minutes to explain the procedure again to ensure we were fully aware and had no lingering questions. Tom planted a kiss on my forehead and said he would be back as soon as it was over. Nurse Nancy showed him back to the waiting room and I was left in the hands of the good doctor.

"Are you ready?"

"If I said yes you would know I was lying."

Dr. K gave a soft chuckle, "You are right. Shall we get started then?" I gave a curt nod. "You will have to remove the gown," I pulled the tie and let the gown fall away and shifted to lay on the table. "Roll to your right side...good. Now take your left arm and raise it over your head... like that." The other tech busied himself with preparing the ultrasound and gathering instruments. Dr. K moved out of sight, but I could hear him at the sink washing his hands and donning gloves. I heard him moving back in my direction. "Okay, I am going to put some gel on your skin, then using the ultrasound I will locate the area I want to biopsy. Okay?" I nod. "Then I will inject a local into the area to minimize your discomfort. Remember I said it may not stop all the pain, but should help?"

184

"I remember."

"Good," he squeezed the cool gel onto my left breast and used the ultrasound wand to smear it around. "Let's find the spot."

The screen in front of me made no sense. I saw black, white, and gray fuzzy stuff. Nothing more and nothing less. I could see the tissue move on the screen as the wand passed over my skin. As Dr. K made a few passes he began to focus the wand's movements in a specific area. "Hold the wand steady right here," he ordered the tech. "Olivia, I am preparing to give you the local. Take a deep breath and let it out slowly. Ready?"

"Yes."

"Now," I inhaled and as I slowly let it escape my lips I felt the needle break the skin. I crushed my eyes shut and my breath came out as a hiss. "You're doing great. Steady. I am going to move the needle around a bit to inject the local around the biopsy area." I kept my breathing shallow. Small whimpers escaped me and tears ran from my eyes. It fucking hurt! If that was only the local, what the hell was the biopsy going to feel like? "Okay, I'm removing the needle...and...it's out. Now we need to wait a few minutes to allow it to take effect. You did great, Olivia."

"Doctors always say that, have you ever had anyone not 'do great'?" I pointed out.

"I have had a few that were pretty testy," he chortled. "Not the kind of patients you say 'doing great' to, ever." I could feel some pressure around my breast, "Can you feel that?"

"Not really."

"Good, it's taking effect," he took the wand from the tech and started sliding it over my breast again in search of his perfect spot. "Hold it here," he gestured for the tech to take hold of the wand. "Olivia, I am going to make a small incision, you shouldn't feel it, okay."

"K," I whispered. I closed my eyes and breathed.

"Can you feel it?"

"No."

"Good, okay. I am going to insert the core needle and gather some of the mass," I felt the pressure of the needle passing through my breast and was handling it fine until I wasn't handling it well at all. I gasped and stiffened under Dr. K's hand. "Olivia? Are you feeling this?"

"Oh yeah…"

"Remain calm and stay as still as possible. I know it hurts. It will be over quickly," he moved the needle around and jabbed at the mass, then moved it again and jabbed more. "You really are doing great. One more pass and I'm done. Good…and done. I am removing the needle now," he removed the needle and moved out of my line of sight.

"Ma'am, I'm going to clean you up and put a bandage on the incision, okay," the tech explained.

I opened my eyes and looked at the stranger's face, "okay."

I heard a beep, "Bring Mr. Carpenter back to the ultrasound room."

"Yes, doctor," a disembodied voice responded.

"Your husband will be with us in a moment," said Dr. K as he assisted me in getting up and pulling the gown around me. Nurse Nancy showed Tom back in to the exam room. He quickly moved to me and looked at me for any indication of how I was. I hugged the gown to me and gave him a stiff smile. "Olivia did great," Dr. K gave me a knowing smile, "she did have a good deal of pain during the procedure. I would like her to rest and not do any lifting at least for the rest of the day. Tylenol should be enough to control any pain, but if it doesn't seem to be working call us, and I can call in a prescription to the pharmacy. Do you have any questions?"

"Do I need to do anything special for the incision? Can it get wet?"

"Nothing special, you can shower. Change the bandage if needed," he made a few more notes in my chart. "As soon as pathology has a chance to review the slides, we will contact you and set up another appointment to go over the findings," he gave me a sweet smile. "You really did do a great job."

"I do what I can," I chuckled.

"Get dressed and when you are done one of the nurses will show you back to the front."

Tom looked to Dr. K, "I know the way. Can we go then?"

"Of course. Olivia, get some rest and we will talk soon."

"She will," stated Tom as he gave *me the "you-will-do-as-you-are-told"* look.

*Dr. -I'm craving a ca*ndy bar- left the room on the heels of the tech leaving Tom and me alone.

"Do you need some help getting dressed?" asked Tom as he gathered my things from under the chair.

"Probably," between the two of us we managed to get my bra and top back on with minimal discomfort.

"Not nearly as much fun putting your clothes on as it is taking them off," I gawked at him for a moment and tried to sling my purse over my shoulder when Tom stopped me, "He said to limit your lifting and that thing weights a ton."

"Right, so are you going to carry it?"

"I'm secure with my manhood," He smirked as he slid one arm around me and grabbed my purse with the other. "Ready?"

"Where is a camera when you need one?" I laughed, but stopped quickly when I felt the tape from my bandage pull at my skin. Best not do that again. Ouch.

"Let's get you home."

My hero.

*****

Tom tucked me in on the couch with my favorite pillow, which I hugged to my sore chest. He went to the kitchen to get me a drink and some Tylenol for my discomfort. A girl could get used to treatment like that...minus the huge needle hole and incision that was in my poor boob and the frickin' pain. Setting the glass of juice on the coffee table, Tom sat on the edge of the table and looked down at me, "Do you need anything else?" he asked while brushing the hair away from my face.

"No, I think I may try to take a nap. I really didn't get much sleep last night," I replied in a drowsy mumble.

"Good. You sleep and I am gonna give Wayne a call and see how things are at the shop. Okay?"

"Mmmm...'k."

I jerked awake to the sound of thunder. How long was I asleep? I didn't know it was gonna storm. The banging came again making me recognize it wasn't thunder, but someone thrashing my door. Tom was nowhere in sight, so I shifted gently off the couch to see who it was. Clutching my pillow to my chest I pulled open the door only to be standing face-to-face with Dick Head himself. Grabbing me by my arms he screamed in my face, "Where the fuck is that worthless cunt?"

Wincing in pain, I tried to pull away from the vice grip he had on my biceps, but I had no strength to fight. So, I screamed. "Let go of me!" I kept screaming, and he kept jerking and spitting vile words in my face.

"Get your fucking hands off my wife, NOW!" growled Tom from behind me. A hand reached past me and latched onto Richard's neck and squeezed. "You touch my fucking wife again and I swear they will never find your body!"

I was released from Richard's grip and tossed aside like I was no heavier than the pillow lying on the floor. I stood in my doorway and watched as all hell broke loose in my front yard. Tom shoved Richard until they both thumped to the unforgiving concrete of the front walk. A swarm of fists and elbows landed with muted thuds. Tom was on top...no, Richard...no, Tom...they rolled and swung and screamed and I stood frozen to the spot. People were pouring out onto the street to see what was going on and to refuel the rumor mill. I don't know how long I was unmoving when the sirens over took the grunts emanating from the grass. Tom was on his feet kicking Richard as he was trying to right himself. Once steady, Richard charged Tom, grabbing him around his waist. He took him down hard onto the driveway. Sirens wailed, two cop cars rumbled to a stop at the curb, kicking up dust. The doors flew open as four officers bolted toward the melee playing out for the entire neighborhood. Tom was being pulled in one direction as Richard was dragged in another, both still spitting anger. I didn't know what to do. Tom was bloody and being handcuffed. The officer settled him down onto a step on the porch and went to help hog tie Dick Head.

"Are you okay?" Tom asked looking up into my petrified face.

"Am I okay? Are you okay?" I asked as I stooped down and sat on the step next to him.

"I'm good. Did he hurt you? Are you bleeding or anything?" His eyes scanned my arms for marks and looked for blood on my t-shirt.

"No, I'm okay, really," I whispered and leaned into him.

"Ma'am, I'm gonna need you to step over here so I can ask you some questions about what happened," demanded one of the quartet of cops. I slowly stood and stepped a few feet away from my husband who remained seated. His head hung lower, a huff of air passed from him and his eyes closed. I stood where I still had Tom in a clear line of sight. My arms were wrapped loosely around my chest as I looked up at the cop. "Ma'am, can you tell me what happened?" I filled my lungs and started to replay the events of the last...what...ten minutes or so? Wow, it seemed longer. I informed the officer of my earlier procedure so he could get a better idea of why Tom reacted the way he did.

"Okay, well, we are going to have to take both men in."

Tom looked up from the stoop, "You better call Wayne and tell him what happened. I don't want you driving, so have him come get you and then come get me." The officer was helping him to the patrol car when he pulled away to kiss me. "Do not drive," he demanded as the officer moved him toward the car. "Call your doctor, too!" he blurted out. The officer placed his hand on Tom's head and guided him into the back seat of the cruiser. I turned and immediately went in search of my phone.

Chapter Fourteen

Wayne and Molly were at my house in less than twenty minutes. When I called Wayne as Tom asked, he told me to grab all the documents of the procedure I had that morning so the police could better understand Tom's reaction to Richard's attack on me. I didn't know how it would help, but I did what he said. I was sitting on the front step with my arms wrapped around my aching boob when they pulled up. I had taken Tylenol earlier but not since waking to Dick Head's invasion. It would have to wait. I ran to the car and scurried into the back seat.

"Do you have everything?" asked Wayne.

"I have everything you told me to get," I said, a little breathless, while trying to fasten the seatbelt in a way that wouldn't hurt. Damn shoulder harness.

His eyes met mine in the rear view mirror, "What happened, exactly?"

I spent the few minutes' drive rehashing the events that put my husband in the back of a police cruiser. I felt guilty enough, but having Wayne eyeballing me made it worse.

"So, he was defending you, right?"

"Well, yeah," I reasoned. "I didn't have the strength to fight him off. It hurt like hell." I looked down at my arms where Richard had taken hold and squeezed. Bruises had already started to form. They were gonna be nasty by morning. At least I would have proof to show the cops. Molly's hand reached out to me.

"We'll have him home in no time," she reassured while patting my hand. "He was defending you."

I nodded and looked out the window as Wayne was pulling into the police station. The following hour was a blur of uniforms and questions and photos of the bruises that were forming on my arms. Molly sat with me through it all. Wayne handled as much as he could short of explaining actual events. That's where I came in. I answered more questions, drank bad coffee, really bad coffee, filled out more paperwork, offered photo copies of my medical papers, and more paperwork, and finally... Tom. His eyes were frantic as he scanned the room looking for me. Our eyes locked and so did his trajectory. I had barely made it to my feet when he was on me.

"Are you okay? Did you call the doctor?"

"I'll do that when we get you home," I whispered as I slid my arms around him. "Let's just get you home, okay?"

Tom looked to Wayne and then the officer behind the desk. "What do I have to do?"

"Mr. Carpenter, I have some paperwork for you to fill out here," the officer gestured to the chair for Tom to sit. "I don't see you having any issues. It's clear that Mr. James is at fault."

"Ya think," Tom snapped while signing his name to another form. "Look at my wife's arms."

The officer glanced at me and gave me a gentle smile, "You should have those looked at, especially after what you had done earlier today."

"I will."

"Yes, she will. Is that all? Am I free to go?"

"Yes, sir, you are free to go. You will be hearing from us soon in regards to Mr. James' charges," the officer explained as he gave Tom copies of the papers he had filled out.

Tom nodded, took the papers, placed his arm around my waist and escorted me from the building. "Thanks, man. I appreciate you coming to help," he began. "I'm sorry you had to, but glad you did."

"That's what brothers are for. Besides, I can now say I am the only brother who hasn't been in jail," Wayne offered with a chuckle. "Come on, I'm starving. Let's go get something to eat."

"Can we stop at the medical center first? I want them to take a quick look at Liv."

"You got it," Wayne declared as he held the car door for Molly.

Tom held my hand as I slid into the back seat. As good as his word, Wayne went straight to the medical center and I was seen rather quickly. Dr. K looked concerned, more about the bruises than the incision site. He said to watch the incision. If it opened up I was to come back in for a stitch or two, but he didn't expect anything to happen.

Wayne and Molly were waiting for us when I slipped into the restroom to wash my hands and take some Tylenol. I stepped out in time to run right into Alyssa. I yelped in pain as we collided.

"Oh my God, I'm sorry," she stammered. Realizing who she ran into caused her to change her stance, "oh, well, sorry. I wasn't looking where I was going."

"It's fine," was all I had in me.

Giving me a quick scan, Alyssa's eyes fell to my arms, "Wait, what happened to your arms?"

"Oh, these," I held my arms out so she could get a better look at Dick Head's handy work. "These were given to me earlier today by Richard. You know, Trish's non-abusive husband," I smeared more distain on the rest of my answer, *"The guy you defended."*

"What did you do to piss him off?"

"What did I do?" I screeched. Tom came flying around the corner at the sound of my voice.

"What's going on? You okay, babe?" His eyes swept over me and settled on Alyssa. "What do you want?"

I placed a hand on his arm and explained she wanted to know what I did to cause Dick Head to attack me. "You really are stupid. Liv did nothing to that piece of shit other than open our front door he was trying to bust down. He came looking for Trish," Tom spat at Alyssa. "Come on, babe. You need to eat." Tom wrapped an arm around my shoulder and turned us to leave.

A voice I knew asked, "Is everything all right?"

"Dr. Matthews," I acknowledged, "everything's fine. We're leaving."

"What happened? Are you all right?" He asked as he looked at the deep purple marks that were wrapped around my arms. I really needed to change into a long sleeved shirt like Trish use to wear.

Tom eyed Alyssa, "Why don't you ask her? Maybe explaining it to you will open her closed eyes." Dr. Matthews looked to Alyssa as Tom guided me out the door, Molly and Wayne hot on our heels.

"Molly, do you have a sweater or long sleeved top I can slip on? I really don't want the world asking me what happened," I asked.

"I think I might have something in my bag in the trunk."

"Thanks."

Molly didn't have anything in the trunk, but Wayne did, so we sat in a restaurant with me swimming in one of his sweat shirts. If I had a belt it could have been a dress. Either way, I was thankful for it because it came down well pass my fingertips, effectively hiding the storm of color spreading across my biceps. It felt like it hid me, hid me from the prying eyes of the world. It didn't hurt that Tom had me slide into the booth, putting me between the wall and him. He put himself between me and everything else, like he put himself between me and Richard. Between me and an attack...but he couldn't block them all. The worst ones are the ones that come from the inside.

I sat and listened to the conversation happening around me. I spoke when needed, but offered nothing of my own. I was tired. I hurt. I wanted the solace of home. Was it still a place of comfort after today? Hmm...maybe my peace wasn't from the walls, but the lives within them. I picked at my Pollo Feliz which was sad because I loved that stuff. Grilled chicken covered in cheese and shrimp, lust on a plate. My appetite was M.I.A. I wanted my tight fitting bed. I wanted to give myself over to the warmth of my comforter and a fat orange cat.

Stating the obvious, Tom pointed out, "You look beat. No pun intended."

"Yeah, I am."

With the bill paid and tip on the table we made our way to the car. I couldn't get home soon enough. In the grand scheme of things, it was still very early, the sun was still up, but all I wanted to do was go to bed.

You know how the sun is. It stays up all day. Get it? No?

Home, there it was in its entire splendor. Wayne pulled into the driveway and we all stepped from the car. I quickly said thank you and goodbye. I chose not to hug them for fear it would hurt more, so I went to unlock the door while Tom said his piece.

"Wayne, thanks again, man. I owe you one," Tom clasped his hand with his brother's.

"Just tell me you're gonna be at the shop tomorrow. We still have a shit ton to get out."

"Bright and early, dude, I'll be there. I'll even bring donuts." With one last wave, Tom climbed the steps of the porch. "Let's get you to bed."

"No arguments here. I'm gonna take a shower first." I looked at Tom, really looked, for the first time since the fight. He looked better than I thought he would, but it was still quite evident he had been in a fight. His lower lip was split and puffy, there was a bruise and scrape on the side of his forehead and some redness around his left eye. I took his face in my hands and kissed each spot and thanked him for saving me from Dick Head. "I'm so sorry this happened to you."

"Hey," he took hold of my hands and laid them on his chest, "I would do anything for you, babe. You know that."

I petted his chest, running my hand over the softly worn t-shirt, "I know."

"Go on. Get up there and take a shower and get to bed. I'll bring you some Tylenol."

I gave him a stiff salute and crawled up the stairs. I turned on the water so it would be good and hot when I climbed in. Getting undressed was much harder than it was earlier at the doctor's office. Thank God my sports bra was really stretchy cuz I worked it down over my hips versus trying to get it over my head. The bandage over the incisions sat on the far left side of my left breast. It was almost under my arm. It had a good seal on it and I didn't see any signs of blood. Just to add to the collection that Dick Head gave me, a bruise was forming around the area. This one was not nearly as dark as the ones on my arms, but it was there none the less. I shimmied out of my shorts and kicked off my sandals. I was very ready for my shower. I greeted the warmth with a sigh. I dropped my shoulders and let the water try to wash away the stains of the day. My stiff muscles started to loosen, allowing me enough flexibility to wash away the stench of the day. It felt like my shoulders had been hugging my ears for the last few hours. The tension in my jaw was making my teeth hurt. I used my lavender soap in hopes of relaxing. I squeezed the gel into my hands and worked it into a lather. I brought the bubbles to my nose and inhaled deeply and rolled my head in a circle in hopes of working out the kinks. I let the aroma do its best as I ran the lather all over my body.

Tom found me standing in the steam and holding my hand over the bandage. "Is it coming loose?"

"No, I'm trying to keep some of the water off of it."

"Your fingers are pruny. You gonna get out soon, or do you plan on becoming a fish?" He jested as he pulled fresh towels from the linen closet. "Come on, let's get you dry and into bed," he held up the towel as an open invitation. "I put the heating pad in the bed to get it warm for you."

I turned off the water and felt the chill instantly without the liquid heat running down my body. "That was sweet of you. Who are you? Are you a pod person?" I looked at him with skepticism. "Either way, I like this Tom. Can he stay?" I asked as I stepped into the waiting Tom.

"Nah, he's only visiting," he said as he patted me dry, "When you're better, he's outta here."

When you're better... that was a loaded statement.

"Darn, I like this one. Can he visit from time to time?" I tried to ignore his demand. "You can call on him when you are trying to be romantical." I gave him a cheesy grin and handed him my night gown. I was clearly going to need some help getting into it.

He shook his head at the gown, "Here," he said as he picked up a folded shirt off the toilet seat, "I brought you one of my button-down pajama shirts. It should be easier for you to put on." He held out the hideous plaid thing, but I accepted the option. He held it out for me to slip my hands in and worked it up to my shoulders. It was so much easier than trying to pull a tube over my head. Tom turned me gently by my shoulders and began closing the buttons. "Do you need anything before you go to bed?"

"Just some more Tylenol and water."

"Already waiting for you on the bedside table," he smiled with satisfaction. "Into bed, let's go."

"Aye, aye, Captain."

"Wrong branch, baby," he chuckled as he helped me get settled. Tom took my hands and pushed up the sleeves of the shirt to examine the bruised fingerprints forming on my arms. He brushed his fingers over them gently as the fury started to grow in his eyes.

"Hey, it's over. I'm okay. They are a few bruises that will go away before we know it," I took his hands and leaned in to press my lips to his. He ended it far too fast as he pulled back from my embrace and walked with me into the bedroom.

"You need to sleep. Take these," he demanded as he handed me the two tiny pills. He watched me as I popped them into my mouth and swallowed them down with a good swig of water. "Okay, sleep...now." He held up the comforter as I settled into the bed. He tucked me in like I was a child and placed a stern kiss on my forehead, "Night, babe."

"G'night back," I whispered as the light went out. He lingered in the doorway for a moment, back lit by the hall light. I watched as his head dropped and he turned away and slowly closed the door behind him. It had been a rough day for both of us. We both were bloodied and bruised from our battles which neither of us won. I curled up around myself and closed my eyes and prayed sleep would be easy, be safe, and be *quick*.

I was shaking as I hid under the kitchen table. I hoped I was far enough back she couldn't reach me. She was in rare form tonight. She came back from the bar with a fire lit in her, and I was the target, again.

"Where are you? You fucking little bitch! When I get my hands on you, I swear you will regret hidin'!" Mother screamed as she threw open doors in the hunt for me. "There you are! Come 'er, NOW!" I crawled out from my sad hiding spot into the grasp of pure evil. All I could do was brace myself for impact and hope it ended quickly. It never ended quickly.

"Liv, Liv, baby, wake up! You're having a nightmare. Hey," Tom's urgent voice overtook my dream. "Hey, there you are." My eyes opened as Tom shook me awake, causing pain to shoot through my battered body.

"Argh...shit."

"You okay? You were thrashing around pretty good."

"Hmm...fine...tired," I was so sleepy, sore, scared, but awake. I rolled to see what time it was, 4:22 a.m., too early to get up. "Sorry I woke you, go back to sleep."

"I'm going in to get some work done," he yawned as he bent to tie his boots.

"It's too early, babe. Come back to bed, please."

"As much as I want to, I need to get caught up on some of the jobs I let slip yesterday," he turned and leaned across the bed and hovered over me. "Go back to sleep. You need your rest to face Lil and Shelly this morning. They heard what happened and came home just as you went to sleep. I wouldn't let them get you up, so I'm sure they will be on you like a rash when they get up."

"Great, I can hardly wait," I mumbled as I closed my eyes, wanting it all to go away. Reality hit and they sprang open as I sat up in a panic, wincing as I went, "Did you tell them about the doctor's appointment?!" I asked with a little too much alarm.

"Shhh..." he brushed his knuckles down my cheek, "No, I thought we should have that conversation together. They heard about the fight, that's all."

I slumped in relief, "Okay, good. Yeah, we need to figure out what and when we will talk to them," I approved as I leaned my back to the head board. Tom was still sitting on the edge of the bed looking at me with...what was that look in his eyes? It was gone as fast as it appeared.

"All right, well, I have donuts to buy," he leaned over to me and placed a simple peck on my lips. "Don't do anything too strenuous, and I would feel better if you stayed home today," he added as he pushed himself back up to his feet.

"I have no plans," I stated as I looked up at him. He tucked in his t-shirt and tugged on his logoed work shirt. "Thought about working in the garden, but I think I will stay out of the neighbors' line of sight for a while," I gave a slanted smile as I held up my arms.

"Good idea. Gots ta get a move on. Love you, see you later."

"Love you, too."...and he was gone. He had left the door open. I saw movement. The flicking of a bright orange tail. Oliver jumped up on the bed and slipped into the spot Tom had vacated moments ago. "Hi, Lolly, how are you this morning?" I asked as he rolled to offer me his tummy. Tummy scratches were his favorite. I settled back down into my warm bed and gave him belly rubs. I slid the monster cat closer to me and loved on him. His purr seemed to settle my mind and permitted me to relax and to once again find sleep.

*****

"Shhh...can you see? I can't see. Oliver's in the way."

"Shoo him off the bed."

"Are you two done?" I asked with closed eyes. "What are you trying to see and why is Oliver a problem?" I inquired as I rolled to my back. I had been curled around the cat, and quite comfortable.

My girls clambered onto the bed. Lily scooped up Oliver and claimed his spot while settling him on her lap and Michelle lay on her side at the foot of the bed holding her head up in her palm. "So let's see 'em?" Shelly growled. "Let's see what that piece of shit did."

"Vulgar, much. Geesh, Shelly," Lily quipped before turning her deep brown eyes to me. "Are you okay?"

"I'm okay. Here," I said as I slid up the sleeve of Tom's sleep shirt and offered up my arms for them to scrutinize. I saw horror on the faces of my girls. Lily gasped and threw her hand over her mouth, and I could see rage forming in the blue glint of Shelly's eyes. "I'm okay. They are just bruises, they will go away. Nothing to get worked up over," I tried to reassure them, but it was evident no matter what I said, they weren't gonna be sold.

Shelly snarled the obvious, "Dad is pissed. He wants that jerk to bleed."

"That would explain his face," Lily muttered. "Everyone was talking about the cops coming here. Some asshole said dad hit you and the cops were taking him away. Stupid fuckers!"

"Well, at least you know that isn't true. Your dad would never hurt me, ever."

Lily tipped so her head rested on my shoulder, "We know. So, where is the piece of crap who hurt you?" she asked pointing to my arms.

"I guess, in jail. He was in jail for what he did to Trish. I'm guessing fighting with your dad put him back in there."

"I hope he becomes some huge guy's bitch!" boomed Shelly, "see how he likes being tossed around, the little prick."

"That's a lovely thought," I couldn't help but chuckle, "I'm glad you're on my side, Shelly, cuz you scare me some times."

"And you wonder why you don't have a boyfriend," snickered Lily, only to be greeted with a flying throw pillow.

"As fun as this is, I need to take some more Tylenol and get something in my belly. I be hungry."

"Wanna go get breakfast?" asked Shelly with hope in her eyes.

"To be honest, I don't want to be seen at the moment," I explained by lifting my arms, "ya know what I mean?"

"Right, we could go get something?" offered Lil.

"Sounds good, now move it so I can get up and dressed," I said as I shooed them from my bed. Oliver joined the girls in exiting my room. I got up and closed the door. I leaned my back to the door. How are we going to tell them the rest of the story?

*****

I was pouring myself a lovely cup of coffee when the whirl-wind that were my daughters blast through the front door. They were talking a million miles a minute to a third voice. Who the hell did they bring home? I quickly adjusted the sleeves on my cardigan to hide the evidence of what happened yesterday. I didn't need some gawker coming around to sniff out info for the rest of the rumor hogs.

"Look who we found in the bakery claiming to be buying donuts to bring to you," said Shelly with a side long glance at Charlotte.

With a look of shock on her face, "Now hear this missy, I'll have you know that was what I was there for. See for yourself." Charlotte held up a large box of pastries and the girls attacked it. Charlotte laughed at the sight then scanned me. "I hear tell your man was brawlin' in the front yard," she moved through the kitchen, claiming a mug and pouring herself some coffee. She added the sweet and took a sip, "What's the story, girlie?"

The four of us sat down at the table and served up donuts, milk, and coffee as I doled out the story of Tom and Dick Head. I had to modify it because no one knew about the doctor's appointment or the biopsy. I regaled them with the blow-by-blow of fisticuffs that brought the entire neighborhood out to scrutinize the event. The girls informed me the rumor mill was in full swing, and the story was dad caught me in bed with some guy and was beating the crap out of The Dude for it.

Um...gross. Really people? Does it always have to lead back to a bed?

"I'm sorry you guys have to hear that about me and your dad," I sighed dropping my head into my waiting hands. I rested my elbows on the table and looked up at my innocent daughters, "It's not fair to you that people can't tell the truth."

Shelly laughed with a mouth full of chocolate donut, "The story will be different by the time I get to work later. It's kinda funny to hear what they come up with," she snorted and took another bite of her donut.

"God, people are stupid," added Lily.

We joked and chatted for a good while before the girls' lives interrupted, taking them away from me.

"Things to see and people to do! Later," bellowed Shelly from the door as she made her exit. Lily followed a few minutes later with her purse and an envelope. She said a quick goodbye and slipped out before I could ask what was up. I hope she didn't manage to scrape together enough money to put up that billboard.

"Now that yer girlies are gone, yer not tellin' all," said Charlotte as she crossed are arms over her ample breasts.

With my eyebrows trying to touch, I feigned innocence, "What do you mean? I told you what happened."

"Ye told me what were safe. I know yer holdin' somethin' back. I'm guessin' it's somethin' ye don't want yer girlies to know. Am I right?"

I sat on my nervous hands and looked at the grain of wood on my table and gave a single nod. Charlotte leaned on the table, placing her elbows in front of her to support her. "Tell it."

"I haven't told anyone, except Tom, of course."

"And now me."

I slid out of my chair and went to pour another cup of coffee, or maybe to put some space between Charlotte and me. I was trying to pick just the right words when someone knocked on the front door. I jumped. A flash of yesterday's event slammed to the forefront of my mind. It wasn't him, but the look on Charlotte's face was questioning me. I pulled my shoulders back and strode across the dining room, heading for the front door. Charlotte wasn't far behind. I couldn't see who it was from the window at the top of the door so I opened the door with caution. Molly stood in all her pristineness waiting to be asked in. This should be interesting.

"Oh, well I was wondering whose car was out there," Molly noted as she dropped her purse on the table by the door. "Charlotte, isn't it?" she asked as she turned to look at the woman she offended a week ago.

"Ya know it is," snarled Charlotte with her arms back over her chest.

Great! Like I didn't have enough crap to deal with right now.

"Okay, look, we are gonna sort this crap out now," I asserted as I led them both back to the kitchen in search of my coffee. I was gonna need it. "Sit," I commanded, "all right then. Charlotte, Molly is my sister-in-law. Family. Therefore she will always be a part of my life." I turned my eyes to Molly, "Molly, Charlotte is my friend, one of the truest I have and therefore will, also, be a part of my life." I looked back and forth between them. "Last weekend needs to be forgotten because I am gonna need both of you right now." Molly jumped from her seat and came to me...and hugged me. Weird.

"What's goin' on?" asked Charlotte with concern and confusion running across her plump face. "What happened?"

Molly and I made our way back to the table where I sat between them and played with my coffee mug.

"Are you going to tell her, Olivia?" uttered Molly as she reached for one of my hands.

"I was about to when you got here."

"Tell Me What!?" Charlotte demanded as she threw her hands up in the air, "Quit acting the maggot and get on with it."

"Acting the maggot? What?" asked Molly, "What language are you speaking?"

"Quit messin' with my mind already," Charlotte clarified looking to Molly. "What's goin' on, Olivia?" That look was so harsh it burned.

I prepared myself with a deep breath and let the words fall where they may. "I had an appointment yesterday morning for a biopsy of a mass that is in my left breast. So when the asshole showed up and manhandled me, Tom went a little crazy." I looked up at my friend, then to Molly. Molly was calm because she already knew, Charlotte, not so much.

She opened her mouth and searched for words that didn't come. Charlotte tried again but all she had was, "What? Biopsy?"

"Yeah."

"An' you knew about all this?" Charlotte asked Molly.

"We ran into each other at the doctor's office where Olivia had no choice but to tell me. She was a hot mess and needed my help."

"Hot mess? And you wonder about my words."

Molly huffed at Charlotte, "She was lost and confused and alone." Molly shot daggers at me with that last word. Alone, yes I was alone.

"Yes, I was alone. God, Molly. I wasn't ready to tell anyone at that point. There still isn't anything to tell. Not till the pathology report comes back at least," I conceded and snatched a napkin from the holder next to the box of remaining donuts. I could feel the tears fighting with my eyeballs for release. "I didn't want anyone to worry for no reason." And the ugly cry started, you know the one where your face contorts into whatever monster you were supposed to be before you were born human. I w*as the Creature from the Black Lagoon*. Turned out I needed more than one napkin, and by the time I croaked out the whole story to Molly and Charlotte, we were fighting over the few napkins that were left. We then moved on to paper towels.

"I'm not tryin' to be a shit, but yer face looks like it be meltin'," chuckled Charlotte as she pointed to Molly. "All yer make-up ran for da hills, girlie."

I looked up at Molly and had to drop my head back down and roll my lips into my mouth to prevent the laughter from bursting out. I looked up through my eyelashes and could feel the giggles vibrating up from my body, begging to get out. Charlotte couldn't hold it any longer and let the laughter go.

Molly straightened her spine and dead-eyed Charlotte, "It can't be that bad." She excused herself from the table and went to the bathroom to inspect the clown chaos that was now her face. From the bathroom we heard, "Oh my Lord!" and Charlotte and I both just lost any semblance of control, howling in laughter.

"Do ye think she fell in? She's been in there fer a bit."

"No, I didn't fall in. What a disgusting idea," stated Molly as she moved across the room to reclaim her seat. "It took a bit longer to get the mascara off, is all. Olivia, you really should have wipes available in your bathroom for this kind of thing."

"I'll keep that in mind the next time the circus passes through." The laughter came again and eventually Molly joined in. We poked fun at each other, Molly taking *c*are not to pick on Charlotte, after the things she said last weekend it would have been in bad taste.

"Have you told Lily and Michelle yet?" asked Molly during a break in our little chuckle-fest. That was one way to pull us out of the fun and throw us into the fire.

"Not yet, but Tom and I plan on doing it together."

*****

It was nice having people here who cared about me, even if I was waiting for them to jump across the table and have a death match on my dining room floor. Molly was coming around to being human and Charlotte didn't try to kill her for the things she said. Thank God! However, it was also nice to be alone. They left and I settled into a quiet state of mind until the phone rang. I didn't recognize the number, but with everything going on I wasn't going to ignore it.

"Hello?"

"Olivia?"

"This is she."

The male voice replied, "This is Neil, Neil Matthews."

A little shocked I asked, "Dr. Matthews? What can I do for you?" Why was he calling me?

"Olivia, I'm calling because I'm worried about Alyssa. She's really upset about what's been happening between the two of you."

"Really? Then why didn't she call me?"

"To be honest," he said clearing his throat, "she didn't think you would take her call."

I huffed, "She's probably right, but that doesn't give you the right to get involved."

"I understand, but she said you told her to talk to me about the issues with your other friend, Trish. I agree with you, Olivia. Alyssa was wrong in her stance. She feels bad now that I explained it all to her."

"So..." I was getting pissed. I had to learn to control my anger. Maybe later, "What you're saying is she believed you, but not me. I have known her longer than you, I know things about her I am sure you don't, we have shared events and moments together, but because you said it, it must be true. Is that right?"

He stammered a bit before he spit it out, "Look, she was getting information from Trish and from you and didn't know who to believe. She didn't want it to be true that Trish's husband would do that to her. She wanted it to be what Trish told her, simply an accident."

"Do you see how ridiculous that sounds? She wanted something to be true that clearly wasn't. What more did she need, a friggin' billboard to see what he was doing to her? A giant sign with his face on it which said, 'I'm a wife beater'?" I heard muffled noises coming from his end of the call, "Is that her? Why won't she talk to me?"

"No, I'm at the office, one second," he requested.

I listened to his muffled voice remembering how I use to love listening to him, looking at him. Now, I could barely stand to talk to him.

"Sorry, I'm back. I can't speak for Alyssa abou-"

"But you are speaking for her! You called me to defend what she said and accused me of. Did she tell you she blamed me and my husband for what happened to Trish?"

"How were you responsible? I don't understand?"

"It seems she still didn't tell you everything. She told me it was our fault because we hid Trish. But if it was an accident, what did it matter if we pissed him off?" I was snarling mad now. I had to get off that call, "Sounds like you need to talk to Alyssa a bit more. Makes you wonder what else she hasn't told you." I heard a harsh intake of air and a low rumble. I think I struck a nerve. "Dr. Matthews, it was nice of you to call, but I think this conversation is over."

"Yes, it seems so."

"Bye," I hung up before I heard a response. I had been pacing throughout the call and realized I was winded. I went to the living room and tossed myself down on the couch. Bad idea. That kinda hurt. Dumbass! I hugged a throw pillow to my chest and curled up my body to protect myself from the onslaught of thoughts that were fighting for space in my brain. It had been a rough day and it was only mid-day. I had several more hours to go before I could officially call this day done. Screw that, I decided, I could sleep a few of those hours away. So I did.

Chapter Fifteen

I lay on the couch and channel surfed for the remainder of the day. Tom came home with no pomp or circumstance. We sat quietly in the living room saying nothing and doing less. What was there to say? It's not like I got a call from the doctor or anything. It was Saturday after all. It's not like they were in the office working on my pathology report, right? They weren't gonna spend their personal time worrying about me while I worried about me. Why the hell not!? Why aren't they focused on me, damn it! I hated waiting.

And that didn't change throughout this whole process, hurry-up and wait.

The monotony of all that nothing was interrupted by something, my phone notified me of a text message from *Lily*.

Don't go anywhere! I'm bringing home pizza and I need to talk to you guys. No, I'm not in trouble ;-)Yet.

Not in trouble. That was good to know. I typed out a quick message:

K...c u soon.

"That was Lily, she's bringing home pizza and said she wants to talk to us."

Tom turned his head so I could see the stress stretched across his face, "Why? Is everything okay?"

"She said she's not in any kind of trouble. Just wants to talk," I shrugged and decided I should get up and get things together for the meal Lily was bringing home. I was so thankful for it since I hadn't thought of preparing anything. "How was the shop? Busy?" I asked to fill some of the silence.

"It's getting better. We still have eight cars waiting for repairs, but nothing too bad. Just hail dents," he mumbled as he lifted his tired body out of the recliner. "I'm gonna go take a shower before dinner, 'k?"

"Yeah, okay," I shuffled to the kitchen to find paper plates and set the table for dinner. I was up on my tippy toes trying to reach a stack of plates when Shelly breezed in through the kitchen door.

"I got it," she said as she reached up and grabbed the plates that had avoided my fingers.

"Thanks, Lily texted and said she was bringing pizza home. Are you staying for a while?"

"For pizza, I would eat with a pack of hyenas."

"That's a bit...drastic...but, okay. Can you put the ranch dressing on the table and some napkins," I requested as I pulled glasses from the cabinet. "What do you want to drink?"

"Do we have iced tea? Or whatever we have."

"We have tea," I moved to the fridge and handed her the drinks to set out on the table.

"Where's dad?"

"Shower."

"Thank God. He always smells like sweat, oil, and funk after work," she giggled.

"Comes with the job, sweetie. I kinda like the smell. It's how I know him."

"Gross, what, like it's his cologne or something? That's nasty, mom!" She shivered with a touch of disgust.

I smiled. One day she would see, or smell, that one thing that triggered memories of someone.

Like the smell of a garage reminded me of Tom.

Flowers on a breeze brought Lily to my thoughts.

The Beatles sang Michelle into my mind's eye.

Someday my girls would have these reminders. Maybe they did then, but didn't quite understand what they were, or how important they were. I knew. I cherished them as much as I cherished the people they represented. We continued to chit-chat about nothing and everything, about nothing important and things that someday would be. We created a memory, a simple moment in time we shared. It may not have been a profound, life altering moment, but it was important to me and maybe someday it would be of equal value to Michelle. I turned on the stereo to be greeted by Duncan Sheik singing about not being able to find air. I felt that way a lot lately. I felt the pressures of the events of the last week squeezing my chest. I really needed to chill out.

"There she is! My favorite sister in the whole world! The bringer of pizza," Shelly bowed as Lily walked through the kitchen to the dining room carrying the pizza as if it were a divine offering.

"Don't say I never gave you anything. Eat, peasants, eat!"

Tom stopped in the entryway to the dining room, "Peasants, who you callin' a peasant?" he asked with mock anger. "If I'm a peasant, what does that make you?"

"The Over Lord, muhahahaha," Lily said with a flourish. Okay, it was a sad attempt at an evil laugh but it gave us all a good chuckle.

Shell was already at the table stacking slices onto her plate. Looking up at the rest of us she stuffed a point into her mouth and with a mouth full of cheese and raised eyebrow, asked, "What?" We all looked at her like she had two heads, or at least was rude enough to start eating without us. "It's pizza, did you think I was gonna wait for you guys? Come on."

We sat and began to snag slices from the box, "Why would we think anything less of you, Shell?" I answered. "We still love you though."

"Speak for yourself! I barely like her sometimes," joked Lily, "She is a pain in the ass"

"And you're not," mumbled Tom through a mouthful of food, "I think you are both pains in the ass."

"Ahhh, feel the love," sighed Shelly. "I feel so wanted."

Dinner continued that way for the duration, at least until all the pizza was gone. "So, what did you want to talk to us about, Lil?" asked Tom as he wiped grease from his hand on a wad of napkins.

"Hang on," she said as she slid from her chair and went and got her purse. She slipped back into her seat and pulled an envelope from the inside pocket. "Okay, so I decided to do something today, something that will affect my *future.*"

Please say you filled out college applications, please say you filled out college applications, please say you filled out college applications...

"I joined the Air Force."

"You what!" Tom shrieked, my jaw hit the table, and Shelly's eyes nearly popped out of her head. "What? When the fuck did you do this? Why? I..." he was at a loss for words, so was I.

Lily calmed herself and pushed the paper plate away from her space. She laid the envelope in its vacated spot, putting her hands up to either surrender or quiet us. "Let me explain," she asked as she looked around the table at each of us. "This is what I wanted. Mom, you want me to go to college, and I can in the Air Force. Dad, you want me to be strong. The Air Force can teach me how. Shelly, you want my room," she smirked, "You can't have it! So put that idea right outta your head." We all chuckled at her attempt to make light of the situation.

"Tell me this isn't about that douche bag ex-boyfriend," I begged.

"God, no! One of the reasons he cheated, I think, is because I talked to him about it a few weeks ago. He didn't want me to do it. He actually *told me I couldn't do it*, like I was too weak to do it, or something."

"Sweetie, we know you can, we just don't understand w-why," I stammered. Why would my Lily want to do this? She never mentioned wanting to do this before, ever. Tom sat with his arms crossed over his chest staring at his little girl, waiting for an answer.

"I want you guys to know I did this for me, not because of Darren, or school, or anything like that. I did this because I want to go to school," she looked at me, "my way. I want to know I can do this on my own," her eyes left mine and found her dad's. "I want to prove to you guys I am strong, like you. I want to start my life on my own terms. Besides, I get to travel!" She grinned.

"Oh, they told you that you would travel. They told me the same thing when I joined the Army. I didn't. They didn't send me overseas. They moved me around, here, in the states," Tom grumbled.

"Who cares, even if I never leave the state, this is what I want. Can you understand?"

I dropped my head and stared at the now empty pizza box, "Yeah, we can understand. It is a hell of a surprise, ya know," I conceded, "You have to let us wrap our brains around it."

Shelly bumped shoulders with her big sister, "I think it's kinda cool. My sister joined the military," she smiled, "and that means I can come visit you when you are someplace really cool."

With a bump back, Lily smiled at her sister, "You would find a way to make this benefit you, ya pain."

Tom reached for Lily's hand, "I'm proud of you, kiddo."

"Me too, how long do we have before you leave?"

"Two and a half weeks, I asked for a little time before I had to go."

I hissed with an intake of air, "That fast? Wow. Okay, so what do we need to do before you go?"

And the discussion began. We looked over the paperwork Lily had in the envelope she placed on the table. Contracts, lists, requirements, tests...when did she do all of that? The answer was when I was too focused on me to pay attention to anyone else. Our beautiful daughter had made a decision. An important decision and I was so proud of her. Would I miss her? More than mere words could ever describe, but I would honor the choices she made because they were good ones. The four of us sat together joking, talking, trying to sing the Air Force song, and made more memories. Later that night, I found myself standing in Lily's bedroom doorway watching her sleep. I quietly slipped in and climbed into bed with her like I did so many times over the years. I hugged her and whispered my pride and love into her sleeping ear. I remembered nightmares of Boogie Men, tummy aches, fevers, and story time. I remember making shadow puppets, sharing the day's adventures, and making plans for the future. That was the future, that very moment as I held my adult daughter, who made adult choices and adult decisions. The future was staring me in the face and I didn't like it, not one bit. I wanted a rewind button. I wanted a chance to revisit and change events. No, I wouldn't change anything. Each and every event I had lived through created who I was at that moment. They built the beautiful girl who lay snoring next to me. No, I wouldn't change a thing, well, maybe two little things. I looked at the history decorating her bedroom walls. Pictures of friends, family, moments in time which could be captured on film, school banners, newspaper clippings, posters of boy bands, and piles of stuffed animals that no longer held a place on her bed, all chronicling Lily's growth. Lily shifted in her bed and turned toward me. I could feel her warm breath against my shoulder as she curled into me as she did so many times when she was small. I would miss this. Tom appeared next to Lily's bed and held out his hand to me. I slipped away from Lily's sleeping form and took Tom's proffered hand. We sneaked out of her room as quietly as we went in. Tom wrapped his arm around my shoulders and placed a kiss on my temple.

He whispered, "Come on, let's go to bed." I nodded my agreement and let him lead me to our room. In silence we took our places in our puny bed, but I clambered closer to him seeking out his comfort and warmth.

"She's a smart girl," he whispered. "I'm impressed."

"Yeah, she's something," I choked.

"She will be okay, Liv. You'll see."

"I know. All I see is my little girl, not some grown woman who is ready to leave home, ya know?"

"Yeah, I know what you mean," he agreed and tightened his hold on me. We both fell silent. I resumed thinking about Lily's fate and her future, but Tom was thinking about something else.

"We need to tell the girls about what's going on with you, babe," he spoke so low that if it had not been completely silent in the room, I doubted I would have heard him.

I felt a ball forming in my throat. The ball of feelings that had a strangle hold on me for weeks, "I know," I croaked, "When?"

"Tomorrow," he said as he nuzzled his cheek against my head, "Lily needs to know what's going on before she leaves."

"Okay, tomorrow."

Tom turned his body towards me and pulled me in closer, wrapped his arms around me and kissed me gently behind the ear. "I love you, babe."

"I love you too."

Neither of us slept very well. I don't remember dreaming, just flashes of Lily growing up and leaving home. I heard Tom grumble in his sleep a few times during the *night... "Don't go, you promised,"... "You can't go."* Poor guy took it harder than I thought he would.

I woke to a cold spot on Tom's side of the bed. It was Sunday. The garage was closed on Sundays. He slept in with me on Sundays. I was confused and my brain was in a lack-of-sleep fog. I worked my way up and sat on my side of our bed with my feet dangling down toward the floor. It was 8:13 and my snuggle-buddy wasn't there. I stuffed my feet into some slippers and pulled on my favorite, beat to hell, sweater and went to the bathroom in search of rejuvenation. Nope, not there, but there was coffee in the kitchen. I did what I needed to do in the bathroom and went in search of a cup of wake-the-hell-up. That was when I got the shock of my life. T*om, Lily, and Michelle were making breakfast together.* Holy Shit! I quickly pulled my phone off the charger and turned on the camera app. They hadn't noticed me yet, so I stood behind the wall that separated the living room from the dining room and stooped down as low as I could. I poked the phone out around the wall and pushed the capture button at least twenty times. I quickly pulled it back out of sight and scanned through the pictures I took. The first eight were of them working together in the kitchen and joking around. *The last dozen were of them after* they noticed the camera sticking out from behind the wall. Crossed eyes, guppy lips, nose picking, and general goofy faces appeared on the screen…and that was what Tom had done! I burst out laughing, blowing my already blown cover.

Shelly poked her head around the corner and asked, "Would you like to join us or would you rather practice your P.I. skills, cuz they be lackin'?"

"Smartass."

"Yup, better than being a dumb-ass, right?"

Tom came around the wall and held out his hand to me to help my old feeble ass climb back up the wall. Argh.

"I know you want coffee, but what do you want for breakfast."

I smirked at him, "Anything I don't have to make."

We enjoyed a wonderful breakfast that I didn't have to make or clean up after. It was…odd. The girls were talking and joking, not arguing or nagging one another. Tom was attentive to Lily too. I guess knowing she was leaving changed their outlooks on things. I watched them move around each other, loading dishes into the dishwasher and wiping the counters. I watched as Tom turned the sink sprayer on the girls, and laughed as they shrieked and tried to get away. It was as if they were eight and ten all over again, before being cool and hanging out with their friends became more important than family time.

Shelly took my cup from me and I whimpered, "I'm getting you more…geesh."

"Oh, well in that case, thanks."

Lily and Tom came back to the table and took their seats. Shelly joined us a minute later carrying my fresh cup of coffee.

"Okay, so I told the girls we had something to talk to them about," explained Tom as he reached for my hand.

"Now!?"

With a single nod, "Yes, now," he rubbed my hand and looked at me with a demand in his eyes.

"Okay, you're freaking me out over here," chuckled Shelly, but I could hear a little apprehension mixed in. "You're not splitting up, right?" She asked with terror in her eyes.

"No," Tom barked and tried to smooth it over, "I'm still hot for your mom," he said with bouncing eyebrows and a slanted smirk.

213

"Um...gross. I don't need that picture in my head," gagged Lily as a slight shiver ran through her body and Tom laughed. "So what's going on?"

Tom looked at me and waited for me to speak. I opened my mouth, but nothing fell from my lips. I tried again, nothing. With a squeeze and another nod I began.

"You guys know that a few weeks ago I had a doctor's appointment," they nodded, "well, I had to see another doctor because of what the first doctor found." I looked up into their faces. I didn't want to tell them. I had to tell them. "Two lumps were felt, so I had to see a specialist, Dr. Khudiadadzai, and have a MRI." I looked at their faces again. I started to see a reaction. "So, on Friday morning I had to have a...biopsy..."

"Wha...a...biopsy? What does this mean, mom?" gasped Lily.

"We don't know yet. We have to wait for the tests to be run and the report to come back."

Shelly began waving her arms around, "Wait, wait, wait...Friday? Friday is when that douche-pickle attacked you!" she slammed her hands down onto the table causing the pepper shaker to fall over. "Did he hurt you worse? You know, because of the biopsy?"

Tom reached across the table for Michelle, "No, she's okay. I took her back to see the doctor after I got out of the police station. The doc was more worried about your mom's arms."

Lily was twisting her fingers and picking at her nails. She wouldn't look at me. "Where are the lumps, Mom?"

I put my elbows on the table and held my face in my hands. I sighed in resignation, "One in each breast. The left is larger. That's the one Dr. K did the biopsy of." I raked my fingers through my hair as the room fell into a very uncomfortable silence. I could see questions bouncing around in their minds, but none escaped their lips.

"If you don't ask the questions, I can't answer them."

They stared at me for a few more minutes.

"Is it cancer?" muscled out Lily. I could see it hurt her to even release the idea into the room.

"That's what the biopsy was for, to see if it is or isn't."

"What if it is?" prompted Shelly.

"I don't know. I guess I would work with the doctor and figure out what I would have to do," I shrugged because I didn't know. 'What if's' are the worse questions to answer. "We'll cross that bridge when we come to it, I guess."

Lily inhaled with a jerk, her head lifted to look at me in a panic, "I'm leaving in a few weeks. What do I do? Will they let me cancel or go later? Oh my God, what did I do?" She started to go into a full-on panic. Tom moved over to her and took her in his arms and rocked with her for a minute.

"We can go and talk with your recruiter, but what's done is done, sweetie," he answered, "The military won't keep you away from family if something happens." Turning her in his arms, Tom held her at arm's length and made her look him square in the eyes, "But nothing is going to happen." They both began to nod together.

Shelly sat silent. If you knew her the way we did, you would know that was not a good thing. When Shelly withdrew into her head, it wasn't good at all.

"Hey, Shell. What's going on in that beautiful head of yours?" I prodded hoping to get her out of the blackhole she was building. "Talk to me."

Her eyes were glazed over with unshed tears, and her bottom lip gave a slight quiver, "Nothing, I'm good."

"You really are a terrible liar," I remarked as I got up and stepped around the table and sat on her lap. That got her attention. "Talk to me."

Her shock at my move started to fade into something else. She wrapped her arms around my middle and rested her head against my elbow. "Why?" she whispered, "Why you?"

"Why not me?" I asked and wiggled on her lap to make her look up at me, "Sweetie, this can happen to anyone, anywhere, anytime. It just happened to be me," I leaned my forehead to hers, "It's not like I volunteered. Either way, we will survive this. Right?"

"Right."

We sat huddled against one another. The four of us took turns hugging and talking more about things we didn't know or understand. We asked questions that at the moment had no answers. I tried to avoid the 'what if's.' I didn't want to answer things I prayed would never come to pass.

"Okay, that's enough. We have no reason to wig out until there is one. What are we all doing today?" I asked to make them all move beyond what just transpired.

Shelly whined, "I've gotta work. Ugh, can you write me a note so I can stay home?"

"Would you stay home?"

"No, I would be hanging out with the besties," she responded with a 'Duh' expression.

"Then...no."

Tom sat shaking his head, "I thought you had a better work ethic than that."

"Nope, if I could get outta work I would," she gave her dad a cheesy grin, "But you still love me."

"I guess."

Lily took off to spend some time with her friends and Shelly exited to go to her non-fun job, leaving Tom and me to do as we wished. I was exhausted, emotionally and physically. Having a conversation like that with the ones you love can be hell. Can be? Correction, it is hell. No doubt about it. I had to get my mind off that topic. What better way to do that than...housework. So Tom and I went about our lives. We were not going to let the unknown touch us any more than necessary. He went out to mow the lawn, and I went to do the laundry. I would have been happy to trade.

*****

I was lugging the last load up the stairs from the basement when I heard my cell ringing. I slid the basket onto the dining room table and went to get the call before they hung up...too late. Just missed it. I slid my finger over the phone to see who it was. Alyssa. Did I call her back? Did I let her suffer a bit more? Did I care? She was only gonna keep calling. I needed to deal with it. I was about to call back when my phone indicated I had a voicemail. I slid my finger across the button, so the voicemail would *play*.

"Okay, um, I get you don't wanna talk to me, um, but...I wanted to tell you I was wrong. Neil and I talked about Trish and, um, stuff.

So I kinda get it now. Can you just call me back so we can talk? Okay, well, bye."

I couldn't tell if she felt bad or just annoyed. I decided not to call, but to send a *text.*

Me: U available?

Alyssa: For what?

Me: Meet me @ the park in 30 & we can talk.

Alyssa: K

I went out back with a cold glass of tea for Tom to let him know what I was doing.

"Hey, babe!" I hollered over the mower. I could see the sweat making indiscriminate shapes on his t-shirt. I raised the iced tea glass a little higher, so he understood I brought it for him, along with a few wet paper towels to cool off with.

With an exhale of air Tom came over to the deck. He used his forearm to try to wipe the sweat from his brow. It didn't work so well so I tossed him the wet towels.

"You rock! Thanks," he said as he wiped the towels over his face and neck, "God, I love you."

"What's not to love?" I joked and handed him his tea. "I'm about to head to the park. Alyssa called again, and I think I need to get this shit settled with her. We are gonna meet there. At least that way, I can leave whenever I want, ya know?"

Gasping for air after chugging the entire glass Tom shrugged, "If you think that's best," he patted his back pocket, "Call me if you need me, or want a ride home."

I knit my brows together and tilted my head, "Okay," I wondered. Why would I need a ride? I walked to the park all the time. With confusion lingering, I spun in my spot and went in search of my walking shoes.

*****

I was listening to Michael Martin Murphey sing about a girl running after her pony in a blizzard. It was sad and almost spoke to me of prophecy. I really needed to get out of my own head some times. I walked to my favorite spot near the fountain. The shade was good and it had a bit of privacy. I sat on the bench that she and

Matilda found me lying on before. I lay my arms along the back of the bench and extended my legs out in front of me with my ankles crossed. I tipped my head back and watched the sunlight move through the branches and leaves. I watched squirrels play tag and birds find seclusion among the branches.

"Hey."

I lifted my head to see Matilda drooling inches from my leg and Alyssa standing farther back.

"Hey," I replied as I tugged my earbuds out of my ears. I righted myself on the bench, giving her room to sit if she so chose. "Before we get into this I wanna make something clear. If you accuse me of anything, I'm outta here. Got it?"

"Yeah, got it," she agreed and pointed to the space beside me. I gave her the go-ahead to settle into the spot. "Neil and I talked about the whole Trish debacle and he showed me how wrong I was."

"I know. He told me."

"He told you? When?"

"The other day. He called and tried to plead your case for you," I leaned forward and placed my elbows on my knees and turned my face in her direction, "I wasn't impressed."

"I didn't know he did that, I swear. I didn't put him up to it."

"So I gather."

Alyssa fidgeted and wove Matilda's leash between her fingers. The massive dog had found a cool spot in the dirt to plop herself down. "I know what I said was wrong. I know you and Tom didn't do anything to cause Richard to hurt Trish. I'm sorry?"

I shook my head and looked down between my knees and watched the ants carry pieces of leaves along the sidewalk. "What I don't understand is how you could understand it when Neil explained it, but looked at me like I was an alien life form when I told you what happened?"

"Well, he's a doctor and knows the signs and stuff."

I shifted onto one elbow and turned my torso toward her, "Did he see Trish?"

"No, he's not her doctor."

"But he was able to know the signs without seeing her?"

"Yeah..."

I turned back to my original position and shook my head again, "Whatever."

"What?"

I sat up and put my back to the bench, "He knew the signs, but hadn't laid eyes on her. Is that what you're sayin'?" she nodded, "Doesn't that seem a little off to you?"

"Why would it?"

"For fucks sake, Alyssa! Are you blind?" I put my hands up to stop her response. "It doesn't matter. You finally see what I was saying about Trish and that fucking Dick Head. That's all that matters at the moment."

"Have you heard from her?"

"Why would I hear from her? You said she didn't want to see me, so I haven't been around."

"She's gone. Looks like she packed up her stuff and the boys and took off."

"Good for her. She's finally thinking," I said as I crossed my arms over my chest and winced. Thankfully she didn't notice. I loosened the pressure. "That explains why Dick Head came by the house Friday. He was looking for Trish."

"Why would he think she was at your place?"

"Because she came there the last time."

She nodded her head in understanding and continued to play with the leash. "Are we gonna be okay, Olivia?" she asked as she finally turned her head to look at me.

"I guess. It's gonna take some time for me to forget, but I can forgive you now. You really hurt me when you accused me of making...well you know what you said."

"Yeah, I know."

Matilda's attention was captured by the squirrels that were scurrying around the trees above and she was ready to play too. She gave the leash a tug and Alyssa nearly dropped it.

"Shit! Matilda!"

"Looks like she's done sitting and wants to run," I noticed. There was a small dog park on the other side of the grounds where you can safely take your dog off their leads.

"Wanna walk over to the dog park with us?" asked Alyssa as she got a better grip on the leash.

"No, I think I am just gonna go home. I don't need all those old busy bodies whispering about the bruises. You know, wondering if Tom did it?"

"I get it. I better get Matty over there before she drags me."

"Have fun."

"I'll call you, and we can get lunch or something," Alyssa offered with a touch of question on her face.

"Yeah, sure, lunch."

We both stood awkwardly for a moment. Normally we would have given each other a hug, but I wasn't ready, and I think she sensed it. I stepped in the direction of home, and she followed my lead by stepping in the other direction.

"Okay, well, I'll talk to you soon," she threw out with a small wave.

"'k."

I made the trip back home in silence. No Prince, or Blue October, no Casting Crowns, just me, my mind, and the sounds the universe wanted me to hear. I waved at the few neighbors who tested fate by acknowledging me after the incident the other day. Amazingly enough, none of them asked me any questions. It was funny how we had lived here for years but didn't have any real friends on the block. Our friends were from other areas of our lives. Was that weird? Was it weird we didn't have block parties or BBQs with our neighbors?

I thought about some odd stuff back then. Get over it.

I made it home no worse for wear. Alyssa and I didn't completely mend fences, but at least I didn't have the urge to shake her. I didn't know if our friendship would ever be where it had been, but tomorrow was another day.

I found Tom coming down the steps from a shower when I stepped through the front door.

"How'd it go?" he asked as he stopped on the bottom step.

"We aren't gonna be besties any time soon, but we can at least share a bench without me choking her," I explained as I took off my shoes. "I'm gonna go take a quick shower. Figure out what we can do for dinner." I trotted up the steps and into a much-needed shower.

When I came down a half an hour later I found Tom pulling tacos out of a sack. It looked like we were having tacos for dinner.

"Dinner?" I chuckled.

"Yes, would Madame like a soda or a beer?"

"A soda, dear sir."

"Very good," he bowed and then went to the fridge for our cold drinks. He brought them back and said, "I rented a couple movies from Red Box, we can have 'taco movie night.' What do ya think?"

"Sounds like a plan, babe."

We settled in for the night. We enjoyed spicy goodness and absolute stupidity on a DVD. We cuddled up on the couch together and stayed that way for the remainder of the night. He roared his laughter in my ear and held me as I chuckled along with him. It was awesome. I had to remember the next time I felt blah to have Tom select the movies. I knew they would be silly enough to bring me out of whatever funk I was in. Just another reason why I loved him.

Chapter Sixteen

Get up. Live through the day. Go to bed… Get up. Live through the day. Go to bed…

Get up. Live through the day…Argh!! It's been five fucking days! Okay, so maybe I shouldn't have counted the weekend, but fuck, it's been five days. I was ready to rip out all my hair. Should I have called them to see if the results had come in? No, they would have called if they had. They would have, right? Maybe they don't care. I knew they didn't care as much as I did. How could they? It wasn't their body on the line. Those selfish bastards don't give a fu-

My inner rampage was interrupted by, yup…the phone. I looked at the caller ID and felt my heart rate increase. I felt my cheeks redden and my hands shake. It was them.

"Hello," I said with a nervous quiver in my voice.

"May I speak with Olivia Carpenter, please," requested the now familiar voice of Nurse Nancy.

"That's me."

"Mrs. Carpenter, this is Nancy from Dr. Khudiadadzai's office."

"Hi Nancy," I tried to make light of this unwanted, but much needed call, "How are you?"

"I'm fine. Um, Dr. K asked I call and tell you, um, your test results have come back from pathology."

"Okay." Shit. Shit. Shit. That was what I had been piss moaning about not minutes earlier. *Pull it together*, I chanted.

"He would like to see you, so he can discuss the findings. Are you available at 4:30 this afternoon?"

Why did he need to see me so fast? What did they find? Do I want to know what they found? Of course I want to know. Don't I?

"Um, I can make it then. Should I bring my husband or no?"

"Yes, you should bring him with you. We will see you this afternoon, 4:30," clarified Nancy.

"I'll be there. Thanks for calling."

When did I get in the car? I found myself parked at 3C's (Carpenter's Car Care). I sat staring at my fingers wrapped around the steering wheel. They were white from my grip and shaking from my nerves. It was barely noon when I pushed open the car door and stood on weak knees. I grabbed at the roof of my car for support. I lifted my eyes to the open garage doors. Miguel, Charlotte's husband, was running his hand and eyes along the fender of a classic Mustang. I assumed it was to see if he had fixed any damage. Either that or he liked rubbing cars. That was an odd thought. I let my eyes scan the garage for him, my support, my shoulder, my other half. I found him standing in the doorway talking to a woman, explaining some paperwork he was holding. She was standing way to close for my liking and she put her hand on his *arm*.

Oh, I don't think so!

I pushed away from my car and slammed the door a little too hard. I heard the windows rattle in my little Versa. Tom would have been pissed if he had noticed. How could he notice? *Little Miss -Let me rub my tits all over your arm-* had his attention. I marched across the lot and into the garage. I stopped short of where they stood.

"Oh, well, if you think that's best Tommy. You are the expert at smoothing out the problems," *Ms. -Look at me-* cooed.

"Right, it's gonna be a...at least five days before we can get your car back to you. We, um, have to order a part and there are a few cars in front of you," stuttered Tom.

She ran a witchy finger along Tom's, or should I say Tommy's, forearm and pouted up at him, "Are you sure there's nothing I can do to get my car back a little quicker?"

"No. He told you there are customers in front of you," I thundered behind them causing Tom to spin, and her to lean around his shoulder to see me.

"Excuse me, but I was talking to Tommy. Not you," she sneered.

My eyebrows jumped as I looked to Tommy who was giving me a pleading look. "Tommy? Well, well..." I repeated. I stood with one hip jutted out and my arms crossed over my ample chest. I was running my index finger over my chin and reviewing what I had seen and heard. "Do you prefer being called Tommy?" I asked.

"I prefer being called whatever it is you want to call me," he muttered as he dropped his head slightly. Good answer. I smiled.

"I thought you were gonna..." she whined.

"Gonna what, sweetie?" I asked with honey dripping from each syllable, "Did you think he was gonna take you out, or maybe take you out back to the office and work out a payment plan? That's very sad, sweetie."

"Who the fu-" Tom spun before *Miss -I'm pretty, so I get what I want-* could finish what she was about to say.

"She is my wife, so be careful what you say," he shoved the papers in her direction, "You will be called when your car is ready."

"Yeah, call me when you're ready," she leered and gave a sexy little twist of her hips.

"I will not be calling or doing the work, it will be assigned to someone else. It will get done as soon as possible," Tom stated plainly. "Have a nice day." Tom spun back toward me leaving the tart to sputter and turn a nasty shade of red as she stormed out of the garage.

"Hey, babe," he whispered as he extended his arms to me which I did not accept. "Do you honestly think I was gonna do anything with that piece of work?" he asked as he dropped his arms back to his sides.

"No, but you shouldn't have let it get that far. You made her think she was gonna get somewhere with you."

"Not a shot in hell, babe," he raised his arms again and that time I stepped toward him. "To what do I owe this visit?"

Fuck. My green-eyed-monster stepped all over the reason I had come by. I rested my forehead on his sternum and whispered, "They called." I felt his body jerk and stiffen all at once.

"Come on," he gritted out as he took me by my waist and led me to the back offices. I saw Wayne at his desk with his face glowing from the computer screen in front of him. We walked further still. Tom's office was on the other side of Wayne's. It wasn't nearly as neat and smelled of grease and gasoline. It smelled like him. Tom cleaned off the chair that sat in front of his desk and motioned for me to sit. He turned and shut the door. I heard him release a breath he seemed to have been holding, "What did they say?" he asked as he came back to me, knelt down in front of me, and took my hand in his. He didn't take the seat on the other side of the desk and I was glad. It would have put him too far away, and I needed him close.

"They want to see me, er, us, at 4:30. Can you go with me?" I whimpered as I looked into the pools of concern looking back at me.

"Of course I'll go." I nodded and looked down at my hands that were safely engulfed by his. "Did they tell you anything?"

"Not really, but Nurse Nancy seemed, I don't know...off," I quirked my head to the side, "Ya know what I mean?"

"Yeah, I know." He was sitting back on the heels of his boots when he shifted to stand. "I'm gonna go tell Wayne I need to go, okay?" he asked as he released my hand.

"Now? It's only 12:30. Shouldn't you stay longer?" I asked out of concern for the shop. As the words fell from my lips we both jumped from the bang that ripped through his door. We both jerked our heads, but didn't see anyone. We did however hear more thumping. "Let him in," I said with a touch of a smile.

Tom smiled and twisted the knob, trying to control how hard and fast the door flew open. Homer was on me in a mere second, and his tongue was just as fast. Homer was the shop dog. Of course everyone else called him 'Horror' because he wasn't, well, he wasn't attractive in any way, shape, or form. I loved him in spite of it. Miguel found Homer when he was a pup. He had been dumped in a box and tossed behind the dumpsters at 3C's. He was a hot mess when they found him. A couple days at the vet medical center and an eight-hundred-dollar bill later, he had a home. They took him in and the rest was history. It wasn't unusual to walk into the garage and see two jean covered legs and a furry wagging tail sticking out from under a car. Homer, 'Horror,' loves the guys and the guys love him. I wanted to take him home, but Oliver would not have tolerated him. I sat scratching his head and squishing his face. I loved a dog with jowls. He had 'em. The vet said he was part pit bull and part boxer, but he was all ugly.

"Horror! Dude! Down!"

"Don't yell at him. He's fine," I giggled as Homer wagged his tail and demanded my affection. "He misses me. Right, boy?" I coaxed. "Do you have any t-r-e-a-t-s?" I spelled out. If you ever needed proof dogs understood the words you say, just say the word 'treats' and see what happens.

"Top shelf behind my desk. I had to move 'em up. He kept finding 'em and eating the whole damn box," Tom pointed to the box I was in search of. "I'm gonna go talk to Wayne. I'll be right back," he said as he walked out the door.

Homer kept me company while Tom spoke with Wayne about leaving for the rest of the day. I felt bad. They were so busy lately. It meant more work for Miguel and less time for him with Charlotte.

"Who are you?" demanded a gnarly voice.

I looked up to see a rather distasteful looking man leaning in Tom's doorway. "I'm Olivia, Tom's wife. And you are?" I asked while keeping Homer between me *and Mr. -Nasty-*.

"Wife, huh, didn't know he had one. I'm Randy, the new guy."

"Nice to meet you, New Guy," I fake smiled and focused my attention back to the dog.

"What do ya need, Randy?" I heard Tom ask from down the hall.

"Just lettin' you know I was gonna go grab a burger. Is that cool?"

"Yeah," I heard his voice getting closer, "Hey, are you up for a few extra hours today? I have to leave, but we still have the Donovan job to get out," Tom asked as he came back into view.

"Sure, okay. I can always use the extra cash."

"Cool. Miguel will be here with you. I told him you guys can cut out around 6:30."

"Can do. I'm gonna go grab that burger then," they nodded at each other and Randy gave me a very uncomfortable sideways glance. Um, eew!

Tom reached in the doorway and took hold of the doorknob, "You ready, babe?"

"Yeah."

"Horror! Out!" barked Tom as I walked towards the doorway. Homer scurried by me and out of Tom's office. He trotted down the hall and threw himself down on his bed outside of Wayne's closed office door. Wayne looked up from his computer screen as we passed by and gave a head jerk to acknowledge our leaving. Tom did the same. I waved. I guess I wasn't cool like them.

Tom took my hand and led me back through the garage. We stopped briefly and talked to Miguel about the overtime for Randy and the plan for the next day. We said our goodbyes and walked toward the lot. I told Tom I would see him at home and went to my car.

*****

"Tuna," was Tom's response to what he wanted for lunch.

"Can do."

Tom sat on the steps and untied his boots, "I'm gonna go get cleaned up," he said as he gathered up his rancid boots and took the stairs up to our room. I made my exit to the kitchen to make us both some lunch. I wasn't hungry, but I knew I needed to eat something. I hadn't really eaten a whole lot since my biopsy. I did my best around the girls, but I'm sure they could tell the difference. It didn't matter much now since I would have some answers in a few hours. Or would I have more questions? It sucked, either way you looked at it. It could still have been nothing, right? It could just be a fibroid, a mass of tangle tissues, or an annoyance, nothing more. I kept trying to make it all nothing while I made lunch. Lunch was ready, but the issues I was trying to talk away were still there. Hanging right in front of me, literally.

We sat quietly and ate. I cleaned up the mess, and Tom took his place in front of the 60 inch flat-screen he was so proud of. I

227

scurried up the stairs to get cleaned up and change my clothes. I smelled like the garage, and that ain't a purdy smell on anyone. I did my thing and we still had time to kill. I decided to waste some time checking my email and Facebook. That's a sufficient waste of time. I started with my email. I deleted the junk and skimmed through the rest. There was an email address I didn't recognize, but the subject line got my attention: *Trish*. I clicked it and began to read.

Dear Olivia,

I know I am probably the last person you want to hear from, but I needed to say I am sorry for everything. You were trying to help. I know now. I didn't know what to do. I was scared and unprepared. One of the cops you talked to came back and saw me again before I was released from the hospital and gave me the contact info for a shelter that would take me and the boys until we could find a safe place. I took him up on it and he got me the help I needed. I stayed at the shelter for a few days until my brother could get out there to help us leave before Richard found us.

I heard about what Richard did to you. I am so sorry all my shit had to come back on you. I wish I could turn back time, but we know that can't happen. All I can do now is try to live like you have, strong, smart, and independent. It's gonna take time, but it's something I want.

I love you, friend. Thank you for making me see what I wanted to be blind to. Just know I am safe and in the care of family. I am surrounded by love and so are the boys.

Thank you for being there for me.

Trish

I wiped the tears from my eyes and called Tom to the office so he could read the email.

"Good for her," he said with emotion hugging his words. "I'm glad she got the hell away from him."

"Yeah, she did it," I said in awe, "She did it sooner than I thought she would. I'm so proud of her." I hugged myself and looked up at Tom's kind face. "You're a good guy, ya know that?"

He looked down with a confused look, "Why are you telling me something I already know?" I swung my arm out and connected with the leg that was closest to the chair I sat in.

"You're a jerk too. Did ya know that?" I asked and stuck out my tongue.

"Um, yup."

"Go away and let me check the rest of my email." Tom chuckled and left me alone with the laptop.

I sat there trying to figure out what to write back. What do you say? You go girl? Good for you? Proud of you? I knew how hard it was to pick yourself up from that situation and try to start over. You had to learn to trust all over again. That was the hardest for me. You had to be willing to step out of the norm and rebuild a life. I didn't have children and it was hard. I couldn't imagine how hard it would be for Trish with two boys.

Dear Trish,

I want to say it will be easy, but it won't be. At least you have family there with you to help. I am sorry if I said things that hurt you, but at the time, I thought you needed to hear them. I love you to pieces and want nothing but peace and happiness for you and those wonderful boys. Take the time to learn how to trust. That was the hardest thing for me. Trust. Have faith in yourself.

Give those boys a squeeze from me and if you need anything, I'm here.

Love you bunches,

Liv

I wanted to know if she had reached out to Alyssa, but it was more out of jealousy than interest. She let her come around when she shut the door to me. In the grand plan, it didn't really matter, but to my ego, it did.

I scanned through the rest of my emails, then moved on to Facebook. I scrolled and scrolled, paused from time to time on people's posts, but left none of my own. I watched a few videos and chuckled at some e-cards. I had no wisdoms of my own to offer, nor did I care to post something silly. I glanced at the clock on the screen and saw I still had three quarters of an hour to go. Ugh. It wasn't fair time flew when you were having fun, but was as slow as molasses in the winter when you had to wait for something important. There seemed to be more seconds in a minute the more you wanted time to pass. I shut down the laptop and pushed away from the desk. I went to the bathroom and did my thing. I double checked my appearance. Yup, I looked like the world had crashed down on to my shoulders. I went to the kitchen for a glass of water and an Advil. A dull headache was creeping up from my neck. I tried to roll my head around to relieve the tension which had a strangle hold on my neck. It...didn't work. I found Tom in the recliner with his eyes closed and the TV on some hunting show. He didn't hunt.

"Psst...Tom."

"Hmmm..."

"We need to get ready to go. It's five after."

"Hmm...okay. I'm up," he said as he released the leg rest on the chair. "Are you ready?"

"Ready as I'll ever be."

"Just give me a second to wake up and we can go."

*****

We sat in the waiting room. I saw her again, Tracy Parish. She was sitting on the other side of the room with a bag with knitting needles sticking out. She had on a very colorful sock hat with a big pink pom-pom on top and a breast cancer awareness ribbon pinned to it. When her name was called she followed the nurse and disappeared through the same door she did the last time. Where did you go, Tracy?

"Mrs. Carpenter."

My eyes caught Nurse Nancy's as I got up from my seat. She didn't have the same smile on her face. It was more aware.

"This way," she motioned for us to follow her. We took the journey to Dr. K's office instead of an exam room. "He will be right with you," she assured us, and pulled the door closed behind her.

Tom and I looked at each other at the same time. Neither of us smiled. I was teetering on the balance beam between panic and … nope, I was standing at the precipice of panic. One faulty step and I was going over. We heard him before we saw him. The tell-tale tap on the door to indicate that he was coming in was our only preparation. The door swept open and there he stood, holding a green folder.

"Good afternoon," he started with a smile which did not reach his chocolate eyes, "I'm glad you were able to come in on such short notice."

"No problem," grumbled Tom.

Dr. K took his seat behind his desk and laid the folder out in front of him, "I hate my job sometimes, and this is one of those times," he looked up at me, then back to the folder which he opened, "Olivia, you have cancer."

I reached out to brace myself with the edge of his desk. He didn't say anything I wasn't preparing myself for, but hearing it from him made it real. I had cancer. I had the big "C."

Tom was holding my hand, but I could barely feel the contact. I was swimming in my mind, trying to find solid ground.

"What does that mean?" I whispered.

Shifting through the papers in the file, Dr. K began, "I could show you these test results and MRI images, but it would only confuse you, so I am just going to give you the answers you are looking for." He pulled his arms up and placed his elbows on his desk and clenched his fists in front of his face, "You have Stage IV Invasive Ductal Carcinoma, simply, you have a severe form of breast cancer."

"Severe? What do you mean by severe? Like a hell of a fight or...?" Tom's questions were as 'severe' as the diagnosis.

"Mr. Carpenter, Olivia," Dr. K hesitated as if he were trying to find the softest words possible. "Severe means it's a worst case scenario. The MRI shows the cancer has metastasized, meaning it has spread beyond the breast. It appears to be in your chest muscles as well."

"So, I'm terminal?" I asked.

"Yes."

"What do I do now?" I demanded. "What do I do to live?"

Dr. Khudiadadzai sifted through his papers again and slid a piece of paper out for us to look at as he spoke, "This is a treatment plan. First, you need to have a mastectomy. You may want to consider a double mastectomy since there is mass in the right breast as well. During the surgery, I recommend the lymph nodes under your arms be removed."

"Why? Is the one in the other breast cancer too?" asked Tom.

"It may or may not be. We didn't test it. I felt them while examining Olivia while completing the biopsy and found them questionable. We don't want to find they are cancerous later and have to do another surgery. Also, it's not possible to remove the lymph nodes after a mastectomy is done. In cases of large areas of Ductal Carcinoma, there tends to be a higher chance of hidden areas of cancer. It is best to remove as much of the areas of invasion as possible." I could hear the tremor in his voice. He was afraid. Afraid for me.

"Okay, so I need to have a double mastectomy and then what?" I was still holding on to the edge of his desk for support, "What else? Is there a cure or treatment?"

Dr. K pulled his arms closer to his body and stared down at my death sentence written on the papers spread out on his desk. "Chemotherapy and radiation can slow the growth, prolonging your life."

Tom's hand moved to my shoulder and he pulled me closer, "Prolong, but... not cure?"

"Yes," he confirmed and turned his eyes from ours.

I couldn't stop the tears. I held my face in my hands and let my body mourn. I curled into Tom's chest and let the storm over take me. He rocked me and whispered words I couldn't hear over the downpour of fear and sadness. He rode out the shock waves with me, never letting go.

"How long?" choked Tom.

"Months." Dr. K released with a staggered breath, "Treatment can give more time."

Tom reached over and pulled my chair closer to him and held me tighter. "How soon do we need to start? Like, when will she need the surgery?"

"Nurse Mayor has already called the surgical unit to fast track an appointment for Olivia. She was able to get you an appointment for next Tuesday. Once you meet with the surgeon, a treatment plan will be put in place and a surgical date can be set."

"What about my insurance? Does it cover all this?"

"With your permission, we can begin the process of getting the authorization numbers, clearing everything with your insurance provider."

My tears became the shakes. The rains stopped, but the thunder remained.

*****

We spent the next forty-plus minutes talking about a treatment plan. I had to decide on the doing or not doing the double mastectomy. Did I want to do reconstruction at the same time? Who the hell cared if I had tits? I was dying!

"She'll do the double mastectomy."

"Mr. Carpen-"

"Just call me Tom."

"All right, Tom, that is up to Olivia to decide. As much as you want to help, it's still her body," Dr. K explained.

Tom looked to me, "Tell him you'll do it."

I sat slack jawed at his insistence, "What? You act like it's a given. I haven't wrapped my brain around any of this," I snarled and grabbed my chest, "and you are demanding I just lay them out on a table and volunteer to have them chopped off." I threw my elbows down on the edge of Dr. K's desk and held my head in my hands. My fingers worked their way into my short locks and were scratching at my scalp.

"Olivia, you don't have to decide right this second," soothed Dr. K, "You have until you meet with the surgeon to decide what you want to do. Take this time to think about what is best for you. I have plenty of information to give you that you can do some research on your own." He reached across his desk and touched my arm, "If you have any questions, you can call me any time."

*****

I sat in the car with a stack of pamphlets on my lap. I hadn't looked at any of them because it wasn't real. This was a nightmare and I was gonna wake up and be peachy keen. All would be right with the world. All I had to do was wake up. Come on, *wake up! Wake Up!*

"Are you okay?"

"Well, ain't that the dumbest question you've ever asked," I snickered, "No, I'm apparently dying."

The rest of the trip home was quiet. Not comfortably silent, just silent. When we finally got home I made a bee line for the door. I dropped everything on the table by the front door and went right up to our room. I needed to be alone. I needed to crawl into bed and hide from the Boogie Man who was out to steal my life. But, the Boogie Man got to crawl under the covers with me. He got to go where ever I went because he was killing me from the inside. I stripped out of my clothes and dove under the comforter looking for solace. All I got were cold sheets. I pulled the comforter up over my head and I curled up into the fetal position and held onto myself for dear life. He had to be wrong. Those had to be someone else's results. My boobs are bigger. The ones in the images didn't look as big as mine so they can't be my results. I lay under the cover of darkness staring at the nothingness that was wrapped around me. I crushed my eyes shut, all I saw were the images the doctor had on his desk. Words flashed behind my eyes, cancer, mastectomy, MRI, metastatic, chemotherapy... NO! I was fine. They were wrong.

Chapter Seventeen

I must have fallen asleep because when I woke it was evening. I was alone. It was so quiet in our room without Tom's breathing next to me. The alarm clock read 8:17. I needed to get up but really didn't want to. I was lonely but didn't want to get up. I would remain alone. No sooner had I thought that when my door pushed open a bit. I didn't see anyone, but knew instantly I was no longer alone. I was in good company. Oliver had come to my rescue. My large, orange, roly-poly cat had come to show me I wasn't alone after all. He jumped onto the bed and went in search of my face, which he proceeded to rub with his head. His sandpaper tongue made contact with my nose, and I reached for him to pull him under the comforter with me. He lay on my chest, kneading at my skin, kneading at the knots I wanted to rip from my body. He kneaded the Boogie Man. I hugged him to me and listened to him purr and hide his head under my chin.

"Mom?" I heard Lily whisper, "Are you asleep?"

"Yup, I'm asleep. I'm sleep talking."

I felt the bed give as she sat on the edge. "Dad made dinner. Are you hungry?"

"What'd he make? Anything worth getting out of bed for?"

"I don't know. How do you feel about whiskey and cigars with a side of motor oil?" Lily alluded to her disgust while her nose wrinkled at the thought of each of those items.

I bolted upright, letting the comforter and Oliver fall away from my chest. "What do you mean? Is he drinking?"

"Well, duh. That's why I said whiskey," she jested, "Wanna tell me what's up? Did you guys get in a fight? That's the only time he does that."

I looked down at the rumple of blankets at my waist and ran my fingers through the folds, "No, we didn't get in a fight," I sighed. I pushed the comforter away as I slid my legs to the other side of the bed. "I better go talk to him." I sat for a moment on the side of the bed and rubbed my eyes.

"What's going on then? If you aren't ticked at him for something stupid then, what's up?"

"We'll talk about it later," I dodged. I pushed from the bed, grabbed a robe, and left the room. Lily was on my heels as I got to the stairs.

"I can tell something's wrong. I swear I'm smarter than you give me credit for."

I turned to face Lily at the bottom of the steps, "Why would you say that? I have never treated you like you were stupid."

With her eyes not missing a trick and her hand on her hip, "Keeping us in the dark is just as bad, ya know."

I couldn't argue with that, so I turned away and went out to the garage to see Tom. I found him sitting on a stool at his work bench. His back was to the door when I came in. His head hung low, he was spinning a short thick glass in his right hand and held half a cigar in the fingers of his left.

"Hey you," I whispered as I approached him. "You okay?"

"Nope. You?"

"Nope," I mimicked, "What do we do now?"

236

"I don't know about 'we,' but I'm getting drunk," he declared as he downed the rest of the amber liquid in the glass. He reached for the bottle a few feet away and refilled the hollow glass.

"What about the girls? Lily knows something is up."

"And?"

"And? What? I guess I will tell them on my own. You sit here and get cozy with that bottle, and I will go tell them they are going to lose their mother," I turned on my heel and stormed out of the garage. Before I made it to the back door I heard glass shatter and Tom scream at the top of his lungs. I paused for a moment to see if he would appear at the door but... he didn't. I yanked the screen door open and left him to his anger.

"Was that dad?" gawked Lily.

I nodded my head and looked at the floor. "He's upset."

"No kidding. So are you gonna tell me now?"

I looked up into her concerned eyes, "Is Shelly here?"

"She'll get off from work in about ten minutes. Why?"

"Because I will tell you both at the same time," I explained and escaped into the bathroom. I supported myself with my hands on the vanity and stared at myself in the mirror. I was going to have to explain this...this fucked up situation to my babies. Alone. I turned on the water and splashed some on my face to try to focus on what I had to do. I could have waited until Tom was in a better state of mind. No, I needed to do this as soon as possible. Waiting wouldn't help anyone. I patted my face dry and wiped my hands. "You can do this. You have to do this." I pulled open the door and returned to the kitchen. Lily was sitting at the breakfast bar holding a soda can in her hands. She watched me walk by her to go into the kitchen. "Do you want me to make you anything? Have you eaten?" I asked as I went to get myself a soda.

"Nope, I'm good," she answered without taking her eyes off me. "It's bad isn't it?"

"What's bad?" I asked as I took the seat across from her and opened my soda.

"You know what I mean."

I took a sip of my drink to give me a moment to think, "Yes, but I will explain everything when Shelly gets home. I don't want to do this twice," I explained as I shook my head and turned my eyes away from hers.

"It's that bad?"

I sat in silence. I clasped my hands together and held them in front of my mouth. I found my teeth sinking into the knuckle of my thumb. I was stopping myself from talking by drawing out my own pain in blood. I could taste the metallic tang on my tongue before I realized what I was doing. I moved away from Lily quickly and disappeared into the bathroom again, this time to clean up my stupid act. I washed my hand and searched the medicine cabinet for a Band-Aid. I had to get it together. I had to be strong for Lily and Michelle. I had to breathe. I opened the door and could hear Lily's voice. I rounded the corner to see the girls sitting at the breakfast bar talking quietly. Michelle saw me first, and I could tell from her expression Lily had said something to her to get her upset.

"What's going on, Mom?" she begged.

I retrieved my seat and focused on the condensation on my can, "I have to talk to you guys about the appointment I had this afternoon."

"What appointment? I didn't know you had an appointment?" plead Shelly.

"Well, I didn't have one set. They called me to come in."

"Why?" sought Lily.

I took a sip of my drink and searched my mind for the right way to tell them I was going to die. Sooner than we all expected.

By the way, there are no RIGHT words to do that.

"They called me, so they could talk to us about the test results."

"Us? So dad went with you?" probed Lily.

"Yes, your dad went with me."

Lily's mouth hung open, and her eyes grew larger.

"What? What's going on? What the hell am I missing here? Where's dad?" machine-gunned Shelly.

"Dad's drunk in the garage and it's because of whatever they were told at the doctor's office. Am I right?" surmised Lily.

"Yes," I hesitated, "the news wasn't what we were expecting." I looked up into the stricken faces of my beautiful daughters. I hadn't told them I had been given an expiration date, but I could see on their faces they knew. "They gave us some disturbing news, which is why your dad is in the garage drinking."

"Just tell us," demanded Lily.

I reached out my hands to take one of each of theirs, "I have cancer," I gave their hands a gentle squeeze and added, "Terminal cancer." I could feel both of them jerk at my declaration. Both of their hands started to shake along with their bodies as they began to weep.

"No, they're wrong, you're not...No!" demanded Shelly as the tears raced to the edge of her chin and dropped away. Lily sat silent and let the tears fall uninterrupted down her cheeks. My girls were beautiful, even with sorrow and tears etched on their faces. I held fast to their hands. Shelly's wet lips lowered to my hand as she kissed my knuckle and laid her cheek to my warm skin. "No, no, no, no..." she whispered as she sobbed against my hand. Lily sat stoic. Unmoving. Unresponsive. Unprepared.

"Hey, hey, hey, shhhhh," I soothed, "We will get through this."

Lily searched my face for the answer to her question before she asked it, *"We? We will get through this? You won't be here to get through it with us. You will be gone."* I dropped my face. She was right. Here I was making promises I knew I would not be able to keep. I wouldn't be here to ensure they would, indeed, make it through this twisted situation. I was declaring my death sentence to these young girls and telling them it would all be roses and sunshine in the end. They would be without a mother, and I would be without a life. How fucked up was that?

"I'm sorry," I murmured, "You're right."

"How long?" croaked Shelly between sobs.

Could I tell them? Should I tell them? "I'm not really sure. Dr. K said treatment can give me more time."

"How much time did he say?" demanded Lily, "How much?"

Shelly raised her head to see the answer escape my lips. I looked from Shelly to Lily and back, "Months," leaked from my dry mouth.

They gasped in unison. I watched their jaws hang and a flood of tears fall from their eyes to the counter below. Shelly jerked her hand from mine and came around the counter to fall into my arms and claim a shoulder to weep on. Moments later, Lily found the other. I held my babies in my arms as they cried for me. They cried for me. I was making my babies cry. No mother, in her right mind, ever wanted to make her children cry for her. No mother, who loved her children, ever wished pain on her children. I wanted to take back the words that caused this pain. It wasn't words that caused it. It was something beyond my control. It was something unwanted. It was deadly, and it was mine.

"What's goin' on?" grumbled Tom as he shoved the back door open. He was trashed.

"Talking to the girls."

"'d you tell 'em?" he slurred with an accusation lingering on his lips, "Without me?!" I didn't respond. I just looked at him like he was a three-headed monster storming through the door.

Lily looked at her father and pointed out the obvious, "You were too smashed to be a part of this conversation. It is hard enough to hear it, but I didn't want to hear it from my drunken father." Tom staggered back a bit at the verbal bite taken out of his pride. Lily and Michelle were standing between me and Tom, like a protective wall. He was angry, but I knew it was at the situation, not me.

I patted my girls on their shoulders, "It's okay, guys. He's upset about all of it." I stepped beyond their intended protection and wrapped my arms around their dad. "I know how you feel, babe. I really do," I whispered. I could smell the whiskey with each breath he released. He engulfed me in his arms and released the bottle in his hand. It clanged and bounced, but did not break. Like us. We could be knocked around, but would survive the trauma. This time, only three would survive. It hurt to know I would be absent from family portraits, from special occasions, from their futures. I tightened my hold on Tom and cried. I felt four more arms wrap around us and felt the warmth of my beautiful girls radiating through me. We stood together, cried together, mourned together, loved...together.

It was hard to pull apart, but we couldn't spend the rest of my life huddled together crying. I had living to do, and plans to make. We broke apart and sent Tom to shower. I met him in our room with two Advil and a glass of water, "Take these." He sat on the edge of the bed and did as I said. "You should go to bed. You're gonna have one hell of a headache tomorrow."

"Don't wanna sleep. Need to figure things out."

"You can't figure anything out in a drunken stupor. Come on, lay down," I begged as I pushed him down to his pillow. He went without a fight and passed out cold in a matter of moments. I left the bathroom light on, the toilet seat up, and a towel on the edge of the sink...just in case the whiskey decided to make an encore performance. Yuck! His snores informed me I would need to sleep elsewhere. I slipped into my comfy pajama pants and a loose tee. I stuffed my feet into my fuzzy slippers and grabbed my ratty old sweater. I left his sleeping form as quietly as I could, but in reality, I could have had the high school marching band parade through and it wouldn't have made him flinch. He was gonna be one hurtin' unit come morning.

As I was moving toward the stairs to go to the kitchen I heard Shelly's voice. It was sad and filled with tears.

"What are we gonna do?" she plead. "I don't want Mom to ..."

"I know, Shelly, but what can we do?" demanded Lily. "It's not like we got a vote. The cancer didn't ask if it was okay to kill our mom." Shelly burst into tears. I could hear Lily try to soothe her baby sister, but how could you make this all better?

I stepped into Shelly's doorway, "Mind if I come in?" They both looked at me with tears streaking from their eyes. Lily patted the spot on the bed next to her. They were huddled together and I squeezed my way in. "Hey," I said as I lay my hand on Shelly's wet cheek, "I'm here right now. We still have lots of memories to make, okay?" She knotted the fingers of her delicate hands and gave a slight nod. "And you," I said as I looked into my Lily's sad eyes, "It is not your job to make it all better. You, my little flower, are a victim in this mess, too."

"What about you? Who's gonna make it better for you?" she demanded, "Dad? He got drunk the moment you guys found out."

"He got drunk because when we got home I went and hid under the covers. I hid and he didn't know what to do." I pulled them down on the bed and slid between them. We curled around each other like we did when it was bed time and I would read to them about adventures and little boys with lightning scars and field journals with information on hidden worlds. When did we stop doing that? When did they get too big for me to hold them like this? Time was cruel. It took, but never gave. It passed, but never slowed or stopped. Time, I didn't have enough of, and I couldn't convince time to slow for me.

We talked for hours and held on for dear life. We remembered moments in time that meant a lot to each of us. I told them the tales of the days they were born, sharing in detail the events of their emerging into this world, and how they were the most beautiful babies born anywhere, ever, in all of time. They were the smartest, most alert, sweetest babies anyone had ever seen. At least, that was how I remembered them. We talked about boyfriends, best friends, school, work, and the future. Their futures. Lily was scared about the decision she had made, and I did my best to soothe her. I was proud of her, and I told her so. I thought what she decided was brave and selfless. I told her she would do wonderful things and see faraway lands, not to mention, hot guys in uniform. Shelly shared her fears of never having a boyfriend, of friends making stupid choices, and her junior year coming up fast. We talked about what was next, more appointments, surgery, treatments, time. We petted Oliver, who found his way to us at a very late hour. Finally, they slept, and I held them as I did when they were small. I watched them sleep and kissed their eyelids and wished them happy dreams, as I did all those years ago. I pulled the blankets up over us and lay between them and drifted into an unwanted sleep. Sleep was wasting time. Time I didn't have to waste.

I woke some time later to moaning. The girls were safe and sound next to me so it could only be one other person. I found Tom praying to the porcelain gods. His head was propped up on his forearm as his face dangled below the rim of the toilet. I wet a wash cloth and wiped his forehead and neck. I ran my hand up and down along his spine and told him it was better out than in and not to fight it down. With a deep intake of air he heaved again and rid his body of the poison he had tried to drown his emotion in. I stayed with him as he suffered from his ridiculous choice. I wiped his face and soothed his back until the heaving stopped and he finally pushed away from the cold porcelain fixture. I got up from the floor, where I sat holding him, and rooted in the medicine cabinet for more Advil. I gave him the little tablets and a glass of water to wash them down. He climbed up to the sink and rinsed out his mouth and turned toward me and pulled me into his arms, "I'm sorry I did that."

With a light chuckle, "I'm sure you are and it ain't over yet, big guy."

"That's not what I mean," he pushed me away slightly so he could look at my face. "I shouldn't have gotten drunk and left you to talk to Lily and Shelly alone."

My stomach tightened. "True, but what's done is done. We can't worry about the things we can't change. We have to focus on the rest," I shared as I pulled him back into my arms. I rested my head over his heart and listened to the steady rhythm. "Let's go to bed. You should text Wayne and tell him you won't be in tomorrow." We went to the bedroom and climbed into our very small bed.

"We are too busy for me to call off. I guess I'll have to suck it up," he moaned as he laid his head on his pillow.

"You're gonna be a mess at work and that won't be safe for anyone, especially you."

"Uh huh…"

And…he was asleep. He would see soon enough how bad he was going to feel. I almost chuckled about it, but then I remembered why he had drunk himself into this mess to begin with. I had cancer…terminal cancer.

Sleep avoided me for a while. It would come within my grasp only to flit away when a thought slammed into my head. I finally gave up and made my way to the kitchen. It wasn't as early as I thought. The coffee pot clicked on as I walked into the kitchen, 5:00. I must have lain there longer than I thought. I didn't wait for the coffee to finish brewing before I stole a cup. I went to the office and started up the machine on our desk and waited for the screen to wake. I spied some mail from the last few days we had neglected to open. I sorted through the stack making piles for bills and trash. Geesh, didn't people ever write letters anymore? I couldn't remember the last time I had opened a letter. I guess, if it counted, it was Christmas and they were cards filled with *those let me brag about my year letters*. If I cared, I would have known about all those events long before they sent out the Christmas cards. They weren't fooling anyone with those puffed up versions of the truth, but if it made them feel better, what did it matter? I finished sorting through the stack, threw away what was trash and set the rest *in the 'to be paid'* drawer of the desk. I hated that drawer. We didn't have *the 'let's be frivolous and spend this on fun shit' drawer*. Oh well, life goes on...for some. I shook the thought from my head, swigged some coffee and logged into my email. Trash, trash, spam, spam, read later, spam, sales ads (keep), trash...and no response from Trish. Maybe that was a good thing. Maybe she was focusing on today and not what happened. Good for her. I moved on to Facebook to read the classic literature that was the inner thoughts and turmoil of the masses. Nope, just wanted to read some of those e-cards, they were funny and could say so much with just a few words. I skimmed my time line to see if there was anything going on when I noticed my name tagged in a post.

Nadine Winters: What's up with Olivia Carpenter? Is it true that her hubby beat her? Wonder what she did?

That was proof of how stupid my neighbors were. *Should I respond? Yes.*

Olivia Carpenter: Well, it would have been in better taste to ask ME what was going on instead of posting it here, but if you want to look ridiculous on fb then who am I to stop you. Tom has NEVER beat me. I, my dear neighbor, was attacked by someone else. Next time you don't know the truth, don't make up your own version of it. If you have questions and you want the TRUTH then ask me.

Now that would start a shit storm on Facebook. I would have to check it regularly to see what came of it. Tom wouldn't like it, but there was no way I was going to let our neighbors see him in such a bad light. He was a good man and didn't deserve people making crap up, not with everything that was going on. Screw them!

"What are you doing up?"

I jerked my eyes from the screen to see Tom standing in the doorway to the office holding a mug. "I was sorting the mail and wasting time on stupid people on Facebook," I explained as I lowered the laptop and snapped it shut. "How're you feelin' this morning?"

"Like crap on a stick."

I gave him a soft smile, "You want me to call Wayne?"

"No, I need to go in. We have a lot to do."

"You mean like little -Look at Me's- car?" I asked with a sneer.

"Yes, her car and a few others. Her money is just as important as anyone else's, but I will not be working on her car or dealing with her," he soothed as he moved through the room to where I was sitting. He rested against the desk beside me and tipped my head up with a gentle finger at my chin. "I promise. You are the only one who matters to me," he sealed his statement with a coffee flavored kiss.

I sighed, "I know. Sorry."

"You have nothing to be sorry for."

I pushed back from the desk and got up. I threw my arms up over his head and gave him a soft kiss and whispered, "I better get you some Advil, cuz you have to have a nasty headache." He moaned in response and I left him to get the tablets. I found Tom standing in the kitchen pouring a glass of orange juice to wash down the pills I was bringing him. He held out his hand, and then popped them into his mouth followed by the cool juice. "Thanks, babe."

"You're welcome. Do you want me to fix you something to eat? It might help your stomach?"

"I'll hit a drive through and grab something on my way in," he said as he took me in his arms, "Are you gonna be okay? I mean by yourself?"

"I guess. Are you gonna tell Wayne?"

He hesitated, "I think I should. I mean, they already know something is up, and I may need him to cover for me, ya know."

I hugged him closer, "Yeah, I know. I guess I will call Molly and let her know too." We stood in each other's arms for a few

245

moments. I absorbed his warmth and his scent, soap and a hint of whiskey.

"I gotta get movin', babe," he whimpered then kissed me gently on the forehead. "You call me if you need anything. Anything," he demanded as he held me at arm's length.

"Got it."

He pressed a demanding kiss to my lips, but retreated before I could fully respond. That was so unfair.

"See you later. Love you," he offered as an apology for leaving me.

"I love you too. Bye."

I hated when people said 'love you.' It seemed empty. It felt like an incomplete emotion. Was putting 'I' in the statement difficult? Did it mean something else if the 'I' wasn't in it? Was their love less than? Was I reading way too much into something so small? No, if you were going to profess your love for me, the least you could do was put the 'I' in there. I would have to tell him how I felt about that.

I turned on the radio in the kitchen, poured myself another cup of java, and went in search of breakfast for Lily and Michelle. I worried about how they would be after the talk we had. Shelly was quick to share her feelings, but Lily tended to hang on to her emotions with a death grip. She had already had an emotional shakeup with the douche bag ex-boyfriend, and we just added to her load of shit to deal with. She always wanted to be so strong. She wanted to be seen as a tuff cookie. But, she had a soft center. Shelly was the polar opposite, quick to cry and even quicker to anger. She would stand up to a charging bull and win if it pissed her off, but then cry if she hurt it in any way.

I settled on making monkey bread because I knew it was a favorite of both girls. As I was rolling the chopped-up biscuit dough in the cinnamon sugar mix, I caught movement in the dining room. I jerked my head to see Shelly sitting at the table watching my every move.

"Hey, when did you come down?"

"Few minutes ago."

I held my hands up for her to see, "Wanna help me make monkey bread?" She slid from her chair and came into the kitchen. Instead of taking over the rolling she grabbed me in a very tight hug. Her head rested on my right shoulder and I tipped mine to lie on hers. "Hey, what's going on?" I murmured in her ear. "Are you feelin' okay?"

"No. I don't think I will ever feel okay again," she croaked through the tears she was trying so hard to hang onto.

"What do you mean?"

She sniffed and pulled away from my hold, "You're leaving me."

"Leaving?" I gasped, "Baby, I'm not leaving. Leaving means I have a choice and I would never choose to leave." She turned away from me as I went on, "Hey, look at me...look at me," she turned back, but refused to catch my eyes with her baby blues, "I plan on fighting every step of the way. Telling me I'm terminal means nothing to me, I will live as long as I am meant to. If that is six months, six years, or six decades I will make the most of every second." I reached out to her again and held her close, still trying not to get the gooey mess of my hands all over her. "Now, are you gonna help me or not?" I asked as she pulled back. I wiggled my fingers in her face, "Or am I gonna make you wear breakfast."

A gasp came from the other room, "You wouldn't dare ruin monkey bread on her," Lily chuckled. "That would be wrong on so many levels." She gave me a protected smile. It didn't reach all the corners of her face, it only kissed her lips. I would take it.

"I would never ruin monkey bread! Do you know how hard it is to get good monkey bits?" I shrieked, "My dealer can't get me anymore for a while." Lily came into the kitchen and pressed a kiss to my cheek and assumed the position next to me. Both girls rolled dough and plopped it into the loaf pan and joked about monkey bits and when they were in season. I smiled and built a memory.

*****

Monkey bread consumed and cleaned up, the girls went about their business. Shelly had a shift at one and Lily had things to get done and a list of things to buy before her enlistment started. I had phone calls to make. I needed to tell Molly and I decided to tell Charlotte too. Maybe I could tell them *together.*

247

Me: Molly and Charlotte- I need to talk to both of you. Can you come over today? I can make lunch?

I tapped send button and waited. Charlotte was the first to respond.

Charlotte: You got it, chickie. Just say when.

Me: I'll let you know when I hear from Molly. You cool with coming with her here?

Charlotte: I'm cool if she is.

Thank God. I didn't think I could handle them together if all hell was gonna break loose.

Molly: I'm getting my nails done at noon, but I can come by after.

Me: We'll see you then.

I sent a quick message to Charlotte to pass on the time and went to the kitchen to pull something together for lunch.

I was channel surfing when I heard a car pull in the drive. I popped my head up from the couch just in time to see bright red hair bouncing by the front window. I hollered 'come in' before she even had a chance to knock.

"Hey, Chikie!" Charlotte squealed, "Haven't laid eyes on ya in a few days. What's the story?"

I smiled at my friend. You couldn't help but smile, "The story will have to wait until Molly gets here. It's not something I want to tell twice," I grimaced, "Do you want something to drink?"

Charlotte looked at me in assessment. It felt like she was trying to see what I wasn't speaking of, not yet at least. "Whatcha got?" she asked in a way that could have meant more than the drink selection.

"Um, I have iced tea, coffee, lemonade, water, milk, and soda," I listed as I opened the refrigerator and stuck my head in to avoid her questioning stare.

"Lemonade sounds nice. I think I'll go with tha'," she chose as she laid claim to a seat at the table. I was pouring her lemonade when I heard a knock at the door. I set the pitcher down and went to answer it. Molly swept in like she was a duchess and I the lowly maid servant.

"I am parched. What do you have to drink?" she demanded as she dropped her purse onto a dining room chair, "Charlotte, nice to see you again." Charlotte gave a slight nod in recognition but said nothing. I rambled off the list of drink options as I finished pouring Charlotte's lemonade. "Lemonade will do," sighed Molly. I poured our drinks and took them to the table. I had laid out a garden salad with dressings, and fruit salad with yogurt for lunch before the ladies arrived.

"Please, dig in. Let's eat," I suggested. We ate and shared the casual conversation that comes with a meal. Nothing too heavy as to upset the stomach or cause upset. Nope, I would save that until after we had consumed a meal. Molly talked about the manicurist and how inept she was and how the prenatal vitamins tasted horrid, then having to back track to clarify she was indeed pregnant for Charlotte's sake. It wasn't like they were close friends. How the heck was Charlotte to know? I could feel Charlotte's agitation setting in, especially since she and Miguel have had some issues with having children. "It's a blessing for Molly and Wayne," I tried to explain. "They have been trying for some time to have a baby. Isn't that right, Molly?" I wanted Charlotte to see she wasn't alone in her struggles.

"A few years, nothing we couldn't handle."

Charlotte slapped a smile on her tight lips, "Well, congratulations."

"Thank you."

"So, Olivia," Charlotte quizzed, "when do you plan on telling us why we are here?"

"Um, are you both finished with your lunches? Did you want anything else?" I avoided answering by stacking dishes and putting things away.

"Olivia, you invited Charlotte and me over here to talk to us, now talk," demanded Molly as she wiped the table in front of her with her napkin.

"What's the story, Olivia?"

I sat in my seat and looked from Molly to Charlotte and back again. Charlotte took my hand in her itty bitty fingers and waited for my words. "Um...er...I ...I have cancer." A collective gasp lifted into the air. "Tom and I went to see the doctor yesterday to see some test results," I looked to Molly who knew more than Charlotte, "The MRI images had shown masses on both breasts and we did a biopsy last week. Um...he said I have Stage IV Invasive Ductal Carcinoma."

Molly grabbed my other hand, "Stage IV? Are you sure it's Stage IV?"

"That's what the pathology report said."

"Wait, wha' does 'Stage IV' mean?" asked Charlotte with confusion and concern leaving slices along her brow.

Molly looked at me to see if I would be able to say the words. "I know what it means, Liv." She nodded to me and continued, "It means the cancer is terminal." With the final word Molly looked up into Charlotte's face and waited for it to sink in. Charlotte's jaw became slack and a tear slid down her plump ruby cheek.

"You're...you're...wait, no. Wh... if they are wrong?" pleaded Charlotte, "They could be wrong, right?"

"They could be wrong, but it's not likely," I explained, "They did the biopsy Friday morning and I had the MRI a few days before that. Molly was there when I did the MRI," she nodded in agreement. "The tests and images show... I have terminal cancer," I wiped a tear from my cheek, "As much as I want to believe they are all wrong, I saw the images. It's in both breasts and it's bigger in the left and has spread."

Chapter Eighteen

"It has metastasized?" gasped Molly. How did she know what that meant?

I nodded in confirmation, "Dr. K showed us the MRI images, and it showed the mass has moved into the muscle behind my left breast." Molly still had my hand in hers, but was now squeezing it a bit harder than I was comfortable with. I tried to pull it from her grasp, she let go when she realized what she was doing.

"Sorry."

"'s okay." Charlotte was sitting quietly letting this information settle over her. It was kind of scary. I had never seen her so quiet, this introspective. "Charlotte? You okay?"

She shook her head a bit, "What? Did you just ask me if I'm okay?" she asked in horror, "Of course I'm okay. You, you are the one that needs us, love."

"No, it's no sweat. I think they are wrong. I think once they go after the little bastards they'll figure out it's a fibroid or one of those things where I ate a twin in utero and it's in my boob," I lightly added, "you know, the ones with teeth and hair." Charlotte's jaw sat on the table in front of her and Molly looked completely disgusted. Joke failed. Oops!

"That...ew...was disgusting," gagged Molly, "How could you think that way, Olivia. Do you think this is some kind of joke?"

"Look, I'm not sure what I think. Doctors can be wrong. Tests can be wrong. I don't want to settle for this expiration date they have stamped on my forehead. I'm stronger than that." I shoved away from the table and stomped into the kitchen. I poured myself some water and tried to calm down.

I felt a small hand slide over my shoulder, "No one said anythin' about givin' up, chickie, but you can't be playin' with what the doctor said. They don't toss those words out lightly, ya know," cautioned Charlotte, "We want you to be all righ'. But you have to listen to what they be sayin'."

"She's right, Olivia. Between the images and the biopsy result, you have to see the doctor is right. You have to trust he knows what is best for you."

I felt crowded now that both women had me cornered at the sink. I had nowhere to go, nowhere to run. No way to escape the Boogie Man, so I smashed the glass in the sink instead. I jerked around to look into the faces of the women I thought gave a shit about me. "So, I'm to toss in the towel. I'm to give up. Is that what you're sayin'. Curl up and die, Olivia!"

Molly stepped closer and took my shoulders in hand, "You know damn well we would never say that. You still have a life to live, and we want you to be strong for it. You have to wake up and see this isn't a mistake," with a stiff shake, "Listen to me! I lost my older brother to cancer when we were just kids. This isn't something to play with." With another quick shake of my shoulders, "Do you hear me? It's time to fight, not play some stupid game." She shoved me away and turned away from me. How did I not know about her brother? I didn't even know she had a brother. I leaned back against the counter with my hands on either side of me, gripping the edge. I looked down at my feet like I would find some magical answer to the worst cosmic joke ever played on me.

"Come on, Liv. Come back and sit down," Charlotte coaxed as she took my hand and started to lead me back to the dining room.

"I'm gonna clean up the glass before anyone gets hurt." She guided me to my seat and went to clean up my tantrum.

"I want them to be wrong. Why can't they be wrong?" I asked no one.

"We learned, with my brother, the doctors don't want the diagnosis any more than you do. They don't want to tell you you're sick. They don't want to tell you you're on a time line," insisted Molly, "It's just as shocking and personal to them. Your doctor didn't want to have to tell you that you have cancer. He wanted to tell you that you had the hairy tooth thing you were talking about." I choked out a laugh. It sounded even funnier coming out of her mouth than it did coming from mine. I looked up into my sister-in-law's eyes and saw someone who had suffered at one time and someone who cared now.

I took her hand and gave it a gentle squeeze, "Thanks. I didn't mean to yell at you guys." I looked to Charlotte who had dumped the last of the glass in the trash, "I don't know...I don't...I don't understand. What did I do? Did I not eat enough green stuff? What?" I asked as the tears started to slip from my eyes again. I asked questions that made no sense and no one could answer. There were no answers to give. I had cancer because I had cancer and that was that. I excused myself from the table and went to clean myself up from my childish outburst. I blew my nose, splashed water on my face, and washed my hands. I had to pull myself together. I stood supporting myself with my hands on the edge of the vanity. I could do this. I was stronger than this. I was going to be fine. Right? I left the bathroom and made my way back to Molly and Charlotte.

"...Love you , too. Bye." I caught the tail end of a phone conversation Molly was having. She slipped the phone back into her purse.

Before I could ask her about the call, "Feel a wee bit better?" asked Charlotte with caution screaming across her face.

"Yeah, I'm good. I need to keep myself in check."

"No, you don't. You need to feel what you're feeling when you feel it. Holding it in will only make matters worse," corrected Molly, "Understand?"

"So, I'm to pop a cork whenever I feel like popping a cork? How the hell is that beneficial to anyone?"

Molly shook her head, "Not for anyone, for you. If you keep things bottled up it will only make you feel worse. You have to be strong mentally, physically, and emotionally to fight this." Charlotte nodded her agreement and gave me a sweet smile. I couldn't argue with them at the moment. I didn't have it in me.

We sat quietly for a few minutes. "Do you guys want more to drink or eat?" I asked when the silence got to intense.

"I'll get it," declared Charlotte as she got up, "Do ya think I'm gonna let you anywhere near another glass," She chortled, "What'll it be, ladies? More lemonade?" Molly and I accepted the offer and Charlotte poured us each a fresh glass. She was closing the refrigerator when the back door opened and Tom stepped through. The sun was at his back which caused him to be a dark shadow standing in the doorway. Almost like it wasn't him. As he moved to shut the door I could see his face and I was right, it wasn't him. The man I loved with everything I had wasn't standing there. It was a shadow of him. A darker version of him. Sadder.

"Well, that tells me it is time to go. Charlotte are you ready?" insisted Molly.

"Er… I'll put our glasses in the kitchen, and we can go."

They scurried about gathering their things and saying hello and goodbye to both Tom and me. They were gone in a whirlwind, and I was left sitting staring at my husband who shouldn't be home yet. "You're home early."

"Yeah, Wayne told me to go home and be with you. Said I wasn't in any shape to be there today," he mumbled as he took a seat next to me. "Molly called and told him about…you know."

"Cancer. It's called cancer, and it's a word you need to learn to say."

He crossed his arms on the table and slid them out far enough so he could lay his forehead on them. "I know the word. I wish I didn't," he said causing his voice to echo away from the table near his lips. "I wish."

I placed my hand on his head and stroked the short blonde fuzz, "I know. Me, too." We sat quietly, letting our neglected wishes hang in the air. "Hey, how's the hangover? Are you okay?"

"It's nothing I didn't earn. Where are the pain killers?"

"I'll get 'em."

Tom grabbed my arm before I could leave my seat, "I can get them. Where are they?"

"Medicine cabinet in the bathroom," I responded with a purse of my lips and a question etched across my forehead.

He released my arm, "I'm gonna go take a shower. 'k?"

"'k," and off he went in search of relief.

*****

"Have you had any lunch?" I asked as Tom stepped off the last stair.

"No, I'm not really hungry and my stomach is still fucked up."

"I can't imagine why," I smiled. He looked like hell. Was it the bender last night or the reason for the bender that had him looking like ten miles of bad road? "Come sit with me and we can melt away brain cells watching daytime TV," I reached out my hand from my perch on the couch, "Come on," I coaxed. He took my fingers in his as he sat down next to me. I curled into his side and let him hold me close. That was where I was supposed to be…forever. I pulled out of his grasp and stood next to him, "Lie down." He didn't argue because I knew he was tired. He didn't exactly get a good night's sleep. I pulled the throw off the back of the couch, and settled next to him. I spread the blanket over us and turned on my side into him. I draped my arm over his stomach and wrapped a leg around his, "Let's take a nap. We haven't done that in a long time."

Tom wrapped his arm around my shoulders and pulled me closer, "Sounds like a plan." With my head pressed to his chest, I listened to his breathing even out and the steady thump of his heart. It didn't take long before he had drifted off to sleep. It took longer for my mind to slow enough to rest. I waited while listening to the thumping of his heart. When was the last time we curled up like this? It had to be a while. I remembered when the four of us would find a way to cuddle together on that very couch and watch Disney movies. We would make a big bowl of popcorn, gather up our pillows and blankets, and cuddle up tight to watch genies or princesses dance on the screen. Even Tom would join in. He was twelve after all. I smiled at the memories. So many wonderful memories. Christmas trees, sleepovers, surprise birthday parties, Halloween decorations, long talks, tickle fights all took place right there. My world had been held within these walls. Within these arms.

"Hey...hey. Wake up peoples!"

"Wha...Shelly? What's wrong," groaned Tom rubbing his eyes with the heel of his hand. I leaned back to try and get a better look at the reason I was awake.

"Nada, let's go out to dinner," she smiled as she waved cash in front of our faces, "My treat. Well, as long as it's not, like, lobster or filet mignon. I don't have the cash flow for that shit." She was already out of her work uniform and showered. "I'm a starvin' Marvin and I do not want crap. Get my meaning?"

I tried to get up gracefully, but ended up slipping backward right off the couch. I was wedged between the couch and the coffee table and was howling in laughter. What normally would have had Tom and Michelle in stitches had them looking at me in terror.

"Oh my God! Are you okay? Does anything hurt?" shrieked Shelly as she dropped to the floor to assess for injuries.

I slapped at her hands, "I'm fine. How many times have I done this? Any other time you would be rolling on the floor laughing with me." I righted myself and straightened my shirt, which had somehow gotten twisted in the struggle.

"Yeah, well, you weren't... just wanted to make sure you were alive," Shelly squeaked, "Geesh."

"I'm good. So where are we going to eat?" I asked to get the conversation moving away from me, "and is Lily going?"

"Is Lil home?" mumbled Tom as he swung his legs off the couch to sit upright. "I'll pay for dinner, just figure out where you wanna go," he added while scratching his head. He stretched and pushed up from the cushions.

"I dunno... Lily!!!" Shelly screamed.

"What?!!!" Lily screamed back.

"She's home."

I shook my head, "Thanks, Shell."

Thunder rumbled from the stairs from Lily's hurried feet, "Sup? What did ya need?"

"Shelly offered to take us to dinner. Didn't think you'd wanna miss out on your sister buyin'," explained Tom as he slid by Lily to go clean up a bit.

Excitement spread across Lil's face, "Oooo...I want...lobster!"

I chuckled and shook my head, "Sorry, she already took that and filet mignon off the menu."

"I don't want a burger, ya cheapskate!" hollered Lily.

"Me neither ya mooch! Ya know you don't have to come at all."

"And miss out? I don't think so," smirked Lily. Her phone chirped from her back pocket. She pulled it out, scanned the cryptic words, tapped out a response, and shoved it back into her pocket.

"Do you have other plans? I asked, "You don't have to come with us if you have something going on."

"Nothing that can't wait. I would rather have dinner with the family tonight," she smiled, "Besides, it's not like Shelly buys dinner all the time." Her grin creeped from ear to ear as she rubbed her hands together, "I'm gonna make it all worth it."

"Dad said he would pay," Shelly retorted in her best 'nah-nah-nah-nah-boo-boo' voice and stuck out her tongue.

And so the evening went...we went to dinner at a nice Italian establishment that served vats of food, not plates. We ate too much and laughed even more. Through each chuckle or smile I could see the hint of a shadow. The levity never quite made it to their eyes and they thought I didn't know, thought I couldn't see. I could see the Boogie Man lurking in the shadows. The Boogie Man was always near. We were playing pretend. We were pretending all was right with the world, that we had the world by the ass, that life couldn't be better. We were full of shit. Who cared? We were together and at that moment, it was enough to shove the Boogie Man out of the way.

It was still early when we left the restaurant. There was at least another hour of daylight left to enjoy. "What's everyone doing tonight?" I asked as I buckled my seat belt.

"I got people to see and 'laters' to say," announced Lil.

"I'm not gonna be doin' that, but I will be hangin' with my peeps and maybe catch a movie since Dad paid for dinner," cheesed Shelly. "Thanks, dad."

Smiling at Shelly in the rearview mirror Tom said, "No problem. It was nice of you to offer, but keep your cash, kiddo."

I rubbed my very stuffed belly and announced, "I think I'm gonna try to walk off some of this pasta. I can barely breathe I'm so full."

"Just unbutton your jeans like dad does," Shelly snickered.

"Hey, don't judge. It gives me more room."

"To eat more?"

We all laughed and chuckled the rest of the way home. Once home, we all went our separate ways, but before the girls left to do their own thing they sought me out to give me a kiss and hug. It was nice. Odd, but nice. I knew why they were doing it, and I hated it, but there was nothing I could do or say to make it okay.

"Have fun and be safe!" I hollered after each as she went out the door.

"You still going for a walk?" asked Tom.

I dropped my walking shoes in front of me and sat on the bottom step to put them on, "Yup, do you want to come? It's not like I power walk or anything. I just...meander along."

"Meander? Did you say 'meander'?"

"Got a problem with that, do ya?" I teased as I stood up in front of him.

"Nope, I was clarifying you are old enough to use the word 'meander.'"

I was shocked and my jaw dangled loosely from the bottom of my face. "Old! Who ya calling old? You're older than me."

"I know," he smirked, "Are we going for this walk or not?"

I harrumphed and pushed past him to open the front door, "Come on, old man. Try to keep up."

We took our time and enjoyed the cooling evening air. Tom entwined his fingers with mine and kissed my knuckles as we walked down our canopied road. I pointed out things I thought were beautiful or interesting. We talked in circles avoiding the ugly at our center. I showed him my favorite spot, and we sat for a while. We walked toward the ball fields to watch the children play. We smiled and commented on other couples we saw walking around the park.

Some were young in their relationship. You could tell by the way they touched and tilted their heads towards each other and smiled as they talked. Older couples were happy to walk in silence, enjoying the world around them with the person who was attached to them by their hand, and hopefully their hearts. Then there was us. What did people see when they saw us? I saw a man whom I was so blessed to hold hands with, a man who would drop everything for me. He was a man whom I loved in the purest way possible, my other half. He was the man I would be leaving soon. That thought caused a lump to form in my throat and a tear to sting the corner of my eye. I turned my gaze away from him so he wouldn't see my weakness.

"Hey, what's wrong?"

"Nothing."

"It's not nothing," he stopped our trek and wiped that blasted tear from my cheek. "This," he held up the finger that cradled the tear, "tells me it's not nothing."

I flicked the tear from his finger, "It's nothing. Let's head home before it gets dark, okay?"

"Sure."

Sleep avoided me again. My mind ran a marathon around memories, worries, and unanswered questions. I found myself in front of my computer seeking solace scanning the normal lives of friends on Facebook. Friends? I wondered how Trish was and if I should reach out to her and what about Alyssa? Should I tell her? Would she care? Could we ever rebuild the foundation of our friendship? What did I have to lose?

I clicked on messages and typed out one to *Alyssa:*

Alyssa,

I know things are tense between us and I have no idea how to fix it except to face it. I would like to talk and I don't think a lunch break would give us enough time to do it. Are you available after work sometime this week? Let me know what would work for you. We could talk at my place or where ever. Let me know.

Liv

The ball was in her court.

I returned to Facebook to see if anyone had commented on the stupidity that was Ms. Nadine Winters. A few comments were there and they sided with me, basically telling Ms. Nadine to mind her fucking business. Nadine, on the other hand, made a feeble attempt to save face.

Nadine Winters: Well, Olivia Carpenter, it's not like you ever talk to any of your neighbors.

How are we to know if things are safe in your house?

Olivia Carpenter: Did you ever think I don't talk to you because you are nosy and like to spread gossip? It doesn't matter if it's true or not. You'd make it juicy no matter what. I surround myself with people I can trust. Have a lovely day,

Nadine.

Well, that would do…absolutely nothing to deter her from poking her nose in to other people's business. Oh well, I felt better for saying my piece. What would she do? Unfriend me? Whoop dee doo! I had more pressing matters to deal with than her, like sleep. I needed to sleep! I gave up on the nothingness of social media, took a night time sleep aid, and went on a journey to find the elusive Sandman.

Chapter Nineteen

Days seemed to fade into one another. I drifted through in a fog. I didn't want to think. I didn't want to feel. I didn't want to believe any of it. I went through life as if all were right with the world and as far as I was concerned, it was. I dug more holes in my garden and planted pretty things. I drank iced tea on the deck and watched the birds. I walked to the park every day and found things to be amazed by. You'd have thought I wouldn't be amazed by things, but I swear I had never noticed some of this stuff before. I even waved at Nadine on one of my many walks. She didn't wave back. Go figure. I went to the gym. Why not? I did days before I … they were wrong. Move on.

I was up bright and early. Actually it was dark and early. It was dark outside and within me. I was angry, but I wasn't sure at who or what. Alyssa hadn't responded to my message yet. Maybe she hadn't seen it. Maybe she had and doesn't want to see me. Maybe she fell off the planet and no one had seen her in days. Maybe. I talked with Molly on the phone every day. Who would have thought she could actually be human? Color me surprised. Charlotte doesn't do phones. If she wanted to chat she would pop over and do it face to face. It was a good thing I liked her face because she liked to chat.

Besides, it cracked me up to see Oliver stalk her, and her freak out over the cat from hell. I swear he knew what he was doing every time he snuck up on her.

Once again, I found myself sipping coffee watching Oliver stalk birds when my phone chirped to let me know that I had a text.

Alyssa: Just saw your message on fb. Sorry I didn't get it sooner. Are you available today?

Why not? It was Sunday and I had no other plans. Why not ruin my day with old crap?

Me: Sure. I guess. When, where?

Alyssa: Park? We can walk Matilda and talk. How about in an hour?

Me: K, c u then.

Tom joined my fun as I hit the send button.

"Mornin' beautiful."

"Back at cha, hot stuff."

"What's the plan for the day?"

I snorted, "I have plans in an hour. Not fun plans, but plans none the less."

"Not fun plans? Why not fun?"

"I am meeting Alyssa in the park to hash over all the crap that has been going on. I'm not looking forward to it, but I hope we can move past it."

Tom sat back in his chair and sipped from his "World's Greatest Dude" mug. He seemed to be in deep contemplation when he nodded his head and offered, "'k."

"'k?" I probed, "Is all you got? 'k?"

"What do you want me to say? You guys have shit to hash over and the only way it's gonna happen is to make it happen," he shrugged. "At least it's gonna be in public. You're less likely to go ape shit on her."

"Less likely, but not out of the question," I added with a smirk and a raise of my coffee cup, "Cheers! I gotta get dressed."

"Go get 'em…er…her. You got this."

Shoes tied, ear buds in, I headed out the door to…to what? Confront Alyssa about the things she said? Try to make nice? Hell, I had no idea what was about to happen, so I just walked to the park. I made my way to my spot so she could find me easily. I sat at the edge of the fountain and tossed a coin in and made a wish. What should I wish for? World peace, lottery numbers, false test results…that's the one. I wished for false test results. I wouldn't even be mad if they called me to tell me the tests were wrong. Cuz they are wrong.

"Whatcha wishin' for?"

I turned to see Alyssa walking toward me, "World peace." I helped close the distance and reached out for the pony on the other end of the leash, "Hi, Matilda. Who's a good puppy?" I rubbed her head, avoiding the drool hanging from her lips. Gross! "Let's walk your pony," I say as I led the Great Dane along one of the paths.

"So, how's it going? Neil said he saw you at the office last week. You okay?" she quizzed.

Great, we get to start with pleasantries. "I'm fine. So, um…we need to talk about what's been going on."

"Yeah, I know."

I ran my hand along Matilda's back as she lumbered along between us. "Some of the stuff you said was wrong."

Alyssa quirked up an eyebrow, "What did I say that was so wrong, Olivia? I really don't know what I did?"

I jerked my head to look at her, "You honestly have no clue as to where you fucked up, do you?" she shook her head. "You blamed me for what happened to Trish and apparently still do. I didn't make Dick Head do anything he wouldn't have done any other day."

"She said you guys pissed him off and that's why he lost it on her," she started, "Look, Neil explained Richard is an abusive prick, and he would use any excuse to hurt Trish. I get it now. I was wrong, and then to see what he did to you…" she fell silent for a moment. "Is that why you were at the medical center? To have your arms looked at?"

"When I ran into you?"

"Yeah."

"Yeah, that's why I was there." That's why I was there then, but earlier was a whole other matter.

"But you didn't see Neil. You saw *Dr. -What-cha-ma-call-it- guy.*" Ha! Another candy bar name, it made me smile, just a little smile, but still a smile.

"What does it matter? I needed to have my arms looked at. Who cares who I saw?"

Alyssa stopped short, "Why do you have a problem with me dating Neil?"

Standing beside her, I turned to face her, "I don't have a problem with you seeing him. It bugged me at first, but now I don't give a shit. The problem I have with you has been the whole Trish thing, not Dr. Matthews."

"His name is Neil," she snipped.

"To you," I pointed at her, "but not to me. He was my doctor, not my friend."

"Was your doctor? Why isn't he still your doctor? Are you holding our fight against him? What the fuck, Liv?"

I shook my head in disbelief, "He is a fucking gynecologist. It's not like I need to see him more than once a year. He isn't a general practitioner. The reason I didn't see him about my arms is because my arms aren't connected to my uterus." I was exasperated. She was so frustrating sometimes.

She finally connected the dots, "Right. I didn't even think of that. I just thought..."

"You thought I was upset you were bangin' the good doctor."

"Why do you have to put it that way, Liv? I like the guy."

I started walking again. I needed to move. I was agitated, "Alyssa, I don't know how many tales of tiny dicks I have listened to from you. How many," I held up my index fingers with a minimal amount of space between the, "those guys didn't 'measure up' and now, all of a sudden, you are seeing my gyno. I'm sorry if I was worried you were gonna fuck him over too, because that's what you do," I huffed the last bit out and kept powering forward. Matilda was panting and leaving a trail of drool in our wake.

"Slow down!" Alyssa barked in a pant, "Matilda can't move fast anymore."

I looked down at the poor animal between us, "Sorry Matilda." I slowed to a more comfortable pace for the old lumbering lady. I bet Alyssa was having trouble keeping up, too.

"I know my dating history. I know why I did the things I did. But, people can change, ya know."

"So are you saying you have changed?"

"Yeah, I have."

"Then why was Dr. Matthews under the wrong impression about our argument?"

She paused to let Matilda sniff around in the grass, "How was he wrong?"

"You told him I was upset because you were dating him, not because you blamed Tom and me for Trish being in the hospital. He seemed surprised. That's why he talked to you, by the way. It was because I told him about the things you said." I crossed my arms over my chest and stuck my tongue out at her in my mind.

"That was because of you," she snarled, "He was pissed! He accused me of lying to him."

"Didn't you? You didn't tell him the real reason."

"Screw you, Olivia. You think you are helping, but you're not. You stick your nose in and make things worse," she stepped closer and poked my chest, "You caused one hell of a fight between Neil and me, because you can't stay out of shit."

I leaned in closer, "He called me, remember. Or didn't he tell you," I looked down and smiled, "You need to learn to clean up your own shit, Alyssa, cuz the pile you're standing in is pretty deep and it stinks."

"Damn it Matilda!" was all I heard as I turned and walked away. It looked like the foundation of our friendship took a lethal hit. I didn't know if we would survive it.

I found myself wondering around the park with no true path. I didn't understand how I got to this point. I was down two friends and up two friends. I lost Alyssa and Trish, but gained Molly and Charlotte. I missed Trish and Alyssa. I missed *'dip and drinks'* night and the history we shared. I missed being able to walk into the middle of a conversation and know what they were talking about. I missed inside jokes and touchy subjects. I missed my old life. Old life? It was only a few weeks ago. In a few weeks' time everything changed and in a few weeks more, who knew? I dug my ear buds out of my pocket. I had stuffed them in there when I was talking to Alyssa. I stuffed them back into my ears and cranked some Aerosmith and walked...faster than Matilda could handle. Ha! That song always made me think of *Mrs. Doubtfire.* I came around the corner to my favorite spot and found Tom sitting on the bench.

"What are you doin' here?" I panted and tugged the ear buds out, again.

"You've been gone a while and I wanted to make sure you were okay," he explained while lounging back on my bench. "This spot is nice. Plenty of shade."

I walked over to where he sat and plopped down next to him, "I know, that's why I like it." I lounged back like him and kicked out my feet. "So what do you wanna do for the rest of the day?" I asked.

"First, I want you to tell me what happened and then, who knows?" He crossed his hands behind his head and waited for me to talk.

"She says she doesn't think we had anything to do with Trish's hospitalization, but then she lied to her boyfriend about why we were arguing to begin with. She told him it was because they were dating."

"Why would it bother you if they were dating?"

"It is kinda weird, he's my gynecologist. He's seen me naked," I shivered at the thought.

"So."

"So...and she tends to use guys and toss them out like take-out containers. I didn't want her to do that to Dr. Matthews."

Tom sat up and leaned forward putting his elbows on his knees, "Why does it matter if she tosses him? That's between them."

"I know," I sighed as I sat up. "I'm good. It doesn't affect me. It's the Trish shit that still has me ticked. She can bang the fire department for all I care, but don't blame us for shit we didn't do."

We walked back home, both waving at Nadine as we passed her house, and decided to take Caroline out for a drive. We took her top down and went... with no destination and no time constraints. We drove until we found trees, fields, blue skies, and houses that weren't sitting on top of one another. We found a tiny little diner with only a dozen tables in the entire place. It had the best sweet tea and an even better cheese burger. We spoke very little on our journey, but when you have been together as long as we had, silence didn't mean we weren't communicating. It meant we were listening to the unspoken words. I heard Tom smile as he tipped his head to the sun. I heard him humming along to the radio. I heard him thinking about things I refused to think about. I heard worry covered by the peace of the moment. I heard a talk coming, but I wanted to avoid it for as long as possible.

Hours later, we pulled Caroline into the cover of the garage. "What do you want for dinner?" I asked as I slid my arm into the bend of his elbow.

"Um...wanna grill? I haven't burned meat in a while."

"No you haven't. What would you like to burn?" I inquired as I pushed open the back door.

Tom walked passed me to the freezer, "Let's see what we have." As he scanned the meat selection I poured us some tea.

"Whatcha lookin' for?" Shelly asked as she came into view.

"Food."

"What kind of food?" she looked up into the face of her father.

With bouncing eyebrows, "I need to burn some meat. Any ideas?"

"Armadillo tails? Mom could make some giraffe spot stir fry with skunk juice?"

Tom looked at her like her brain had oozed out her ear, "What?"

I laughed. That had been a game I played with the girls when they we younger. Whenever they would ask me what was for dinner, we would try to come up with some of the craziest menus we could. Sometimes we would even gross each other out.

"We could have hyena jowls boiled in drool," I added.

Tom gagged, "That is sick."

Shelly and I laughed, "Mom wins!"

"Sorry, babe, how about we burn some dogs? Quick and painless."

"Dogs it is."

We went through the motions of making dinner and chatted with Shelly before she went out to roam the streets with her friends. Time seemed to move faster than I remembered. Were dinners always so quick?

"I'll be back later," Shelly said as she squeezed the air out of my lungs, "I love you."

"I love you, sweetie. Have fun."

Tom and I cleared the table and went about the chore of loading the dishwasher. The monotony of life, "I think we should talk about your doctor's appointment on Tuesday." Crushed by one statement.

"What's there to talk about?" I lightly asked, not wanting to have this conversation.

"We need to decide what to do, you know, surgery." I finished loading the dish washer as he stood back waiting for an answer. "Well, what do you think?" he pushed.

"About what, Tom? What do I think about what?"

"Dr. K said we had to make some decisions about doing the mastectomy or double mastectomy."

"I know what he said." If I kept it light, then maybe he would leave it alone.

He grabbed the ketchup from the counter and put it back in the refrigerator, "I think we should do it, the double mastectomy. Let's do it."

I dropped the dish washer soap and gaped at him, "Let's do it? Let's do it? No talking about options, just do it? Just cut 'em off? They aren't yours to decide to cut off. You don't care how I feel about it or how I will look after. Are you really that fucking heartless?"

"Heartless! How am I fucking heartless? I want my wife to be with me as long as possible and if that means getting rid of the problems," he stated while motioning to my breasts, "then so be it."

I closed my hands over the offending masses, "They are attached to my body. They are a part of me. What will I look like without them? Christ Tom, you always said you liked my tits."

"But I don't love you because of them. They were nice, and I enjoyed them, but now, they have to go. I want you, not your tits! Can't you see that?" He looked at me with fear in his eyes. "I want my wife." He picked up the soap container from the floor, filled the dispenser, and started the machine. He took both glasses of tea to the living room and set them on the table and came back for me. Taking me by the hand, he led me back to the couch, snagging a box of tissues along the way. "Sit," he instructed as he sat down, "We have to talk about this. We have to be on the same page when we go in there."

"But..."

"No buts, we have to do this," he said as he shifted sideways. He brought his knee up and threw his right arm up along the back of the couch. He took my hand with his left, "We need to do this."

"I don't want to," I whined and tipped my head to rest it on the back of the couch.

Scooting closer and reaching for my other hand with his right, "Babe, I don't want to do this either," He shook his head, "I never wanted to do this, but we have no choice. We have to deal with this, now."

I stared at my lap where our hands were entwined. I noticed our wedding bands. His was banged up from work and mine shone like new. I told him many times to take his off when he went to work. He told me that ring was right where it belonged. Banged up and scratched, it meant more to him than any other possession, even Caroline. I ran my fingers over his band and marveled at its strength. It was like each scratch or ding made it stronger, made us stronger. "Okay, let's do it."

"What? Do what, babe?" He searched my face for some clue.

I turned my eyes to his, "We'll do the double mastectomy."

He pulled me into his arms and lay back on the couch pulling me down on to his chest. He ran his hands along my spine as I cried, again. "It's for the best, babe. I love you for a million reasons, but your tits aren't anywhere near the top of the list."

"See, you do love my boobs," I mumbled into his chest.

"I love Little Debbies, too, but if I never had them again I wouldn't care."

I pushed up from his chest, "Even Nutty Bars?" I asked with shock on my face.

He smiled, "Even Nutty Bars," he whispered as he pulled me back down to his chest. I felt his lips make contact with my head. "I'd miss them," he chuckled.

"Good to know."

We lay there talking for what seemed like hours. Turned out, it was hours.

Lily strolled through the door, "And what are you two doing? No, wait! Do I want to know what you are doin'?"

"We're talking," Tom grumbled, "You know, what adults do with their clothes on."

"We could do it with our clothes off," I added.

"Um...ew! Please, don't," she gagged. Strolling over to the recliner she asked, "Whatcha talkin' about? What you are gonna get me as a going away present? Go with...cash. Yup, right color, right size, fits in the pocket nicely." She gave the cheesiest grin ever and sagged down into the chair.

"Sorry, we weren't discussing that, but we already decided on luggage as your gift," Tom jested as I pushed up to climb off the couch. "Hey, where ya goin'?" he asked while gripping my arm.

"Got to pee."

"Oh, okay." I scooted off to the bathroom to take care of business. When I returned to the living room, my very adult husband and barely adult daughter were engaged in an intense pillow fight. I had no way of knowing who was winning, but does anyone really win or lose a pillow fight? I picked up my throw pillows as I made my way into the room, dodging attempts at attack.

"Mom! Save me from your Neanderthal husband!" screeched Lily, "He's trying to take my head off!"

Lobbing another pillow at Lil's head, Tom laughed, "You started it, ya brat."

"Hey...hey...HEY! Cool it before you guys break something," I scolded and sat on Lily to control the next pillow attack.

"Okay," they replied in unison.

"She's no fun," grumbled Tom.

"I know, right?" agreed Lil.

"Yup, someone has to be the responsible one," I defended. I tossed my arm over Lily's head and wrapped it around her shoulders, "Besides, I think you won."

"She did not!"

"I beg to differ, dear. She clearly won."

Lily smirked and stuck out her tongue. Yup, we were a bunch of children and loved every minute of it.

"So, what were you guys talking about when I came in?"

Tom and I looked at each other. I shrugged my shoulders as if to say "should we?" Tom nodded. "We were talking about my treatment options."

The smile that was once on Lil's face went into hiding, "What options?"

I moved from Lily's lap to the couch to join Tom. He sat up like an adult to have an adult conversation, "We were talking about your mom having a double mastectomy. We meet with the doctor on Tuesday and wanted to have a game plan when we got there."

Lily pulled her legs up to her chest and rocked the recliner, "Will that get it all?"

"No, sweetie," I stated, "It won't."

She solemnly nodded her head in understanding, "It won't get it, but you have to do it?"

I nodded back, "It's recommended so I have more...," I looked down at my fingers that worried the fabric of my shirt, "Time. Time is all I want," I looked up to watch the first of many tears stream down her face, "More time."

"Well, ain't this a buzz kill," declared Tom as he got up, "Who wants a soda? I need a soda."

Lil's hand jerked up, "Me, I'll take one."

"I'm good, babe. Thanks," I let my eyes make their way back to Lily, "Do you have any questions? I might not have the answers, but I can find out when we talk to the doctors again."

She remained quiet for a minute, thinking, "No, it's fine. I guess we'll find out when you guys do. Can you promise me something?" she asked as her dad handed her a can of soda.

"What?" he asked.

"Promise to tell us the truth and not keep us in the dark," she fiddled with the tab on the can, "I'm not gonna be here for everything, and I don't want you to keep secrets from me."

"Lil," Tom laid his hand on her head, "I promise to keep you informed every step of the way, but you have to understand there will be nothing you can do when you're gone."

"I know."

"Okay," I blurted out, "Enough of this. Let's make popcorn and watch a stupid movie. I don't want to think about this for the rest of the night."

"Cool, can I pick the movie?" begged Tom.

I rolled my eyes at him. I did say a stupid movie and he was quite talented at picking just that. "I'm going to regret this, but fine." By the end of the movie, I felt as if my IQ dropped at least 10 points. Bear in mind, I didn't have any to spare. But, we laughed. We left the funk of our earlier conversation behind and enjoyed the idiocy of Tom's choice of movies.

He has horrible taste in movies, then and now. Ugh! ;-)

Chapter Twenty

Monday passed by quietly. All that meant was no one wanted to talk about the impending doom of the next day. If we didn't talk about it, then it wouldn't happen. Out of sight, out of mind, like when you were a child and pulled the covers up over your head to protect you from the darkness and whatever was hiding there. You never thought that whatever it was that was scaring you could pull the blankets back and get to you. You always felt safe under the covers of your own bed. That was us, pulling the blanket over our heads to hide from the Boogie Man. The Boogie Man was already there, no matter where I went, he went with me. I was wrapped in his shadow and didn't know how or if I could shake him off.

The hours were filled with laundry, cleaning, short chats on the phone with Molly and Charlotte, and two hovering children. I wanted to say it was a pleasant day, but it was far from it. The stress of the unknown can be debilitating. I was merely going through the motions. When prying eyes left me, I slipped away to my computer and begged Google for answers, or at least a list of questions to ask. It was funny, each time I searched 'terminal' it led me to sites on the five stages of dying, denial (yup), anger (most definitely), bargaining (what could I trade?), depression (probably), and acceptance (nope). That was when I learned how much I hated the internet. There was so much information, yet no clear cut, in your face, answers to anything I actually wanted to know. I had more questions than answers. I slammed the laptop shut and stormed from the office.

I folded laundry, vacuumed floors, planned dinner, and avoided the office with a vengeance. When I couldn't find anything else to preoccupy my overactive imagination, I picked up the remote and surfed. I flipped from Lifetime to OWN and back. I found something to watch, but nothing to pay attention to. I needed something to numb my brain, and so went my day and night.

Morning found me early. It shook me awake like Christmas did for children, minus the joy of surprises to come. I wasn't joyful in any way, shape, or form. I wanted to pull the blankets up and hide from the day. Instead, I kicked away the covers, stuffed my feet into my slippers, and went on a mission for coffee. I sat at the breakfast bar sipping from my cup, staring at the digital readout on the microwave, and wishing time away.

"Morning, beautiful," croaked Tom with the first spoken word of the day.

I nearly jumped out of my skin, spilling part of my mug, "Shit! I didn't hear you come down," I lunged from my seat to snag a handful of napkins to stop the spread of heavily creamed coffee.

"Sorry, babe," he offered as he refilled my cup and poured himself the first of many today. "What time do we have to be there?"

"Ten, you can go to work for a few hours then come get me and we can go together," I said lifting my mug, "or you don't have to go at all," I murmured.

He sat on the stool on the other side of the bar and stirred the ton of sugar he poured in his coffee, "Why wouldn't I want to come? I don't want you to go through this by yourself."

"I can handle it, ya know. I'm not a child."

"Never said you were, but you are my wife, and I'm going." With that clear declaration, Tom picked up his mug and left me to stare at the now empty space he vacated. "I'm taking a shower." He was telling me, but not inviting me as he usually would.

That was fine, because I really wasn't interested in being naked in front of anyone today. I felt ripped open and exposed enough these last few days. Oliver scratched at the kitchen door to be let out for his morning romp, so I joined him on the deck. I took a seat and slid another chair closer to put my feet on. I hugged the mug close to my chin and slouched down into the dew-covered cushion. Couldn't I stay there, surrounded by the beauty I planted and the fuzzy cat stalking the bird feeder? I felt safe, comfortable, and at peace, but no answers lay within the for-get-me-nots or bleeding hearts. The snap dragons had no words of wisdom and the sunflowers had yet to show their faces. So be it. I had to go out into the world and learn of my fate.

I climbed the stairs in enough time to hear Tom on the phone, with Wayne, I assumed. "Right...Depends on what we find out...I know...Yeah, I'll talk to you later, man."

"Wayne?"

"Yeah, I was letting him know I won't be in and may not be there later," He explained while threading a belt through his jeans. "He's ticked, but he'll get over it."

"I told you..."

"I'm going."

I sighed, "Fine, but I'm not the only one who needs you around," I grumble while shoving things around in my drawers looking for something to wear, but seeing only wads of color. Tom stood before me freshly showered and dressed in a light blue polo, jeans, and his favorite shit kickers, and I was sporting pajama pants with giant pink hearts, an old tee, and my much loved, but ratty, sweater. Quite a pair we made.

"Let's get breakfast."

"Okay. Let me shower and make myself presentable."

He wrapped me in a hug and kissed my forehead, "Okay, you are looking pretty rough." I slapped at him and looked at him with a dumb founded expression, he laughed, "You always look good to me, babe."

"You're a jerk," I harrumphed and extricated myself from his grasp. I made a bee line for the bathroom, but graced him with a full moon just before the door slammed shut. I could hear him laugh over the spray of the water.

A half hour later I was cleaning up the mascara on my face after poking myself in the eye, again, when Tom poked his head in the bathroom, "You rea...what the hell did you do to your eye?"

"Poked it with this," I groaned as I waved the mascara wand over my head.

"Well, try not to poke out the other eye before we go," He jested, "I'll meet you down stairs."

"I'll be down in a few minutes." I gaped my mouth, leaned in to the mirror, and applied black tar successfully to my other eye.

It was a quarter to nine when I slid across the bench seat of a booth at Maria's Diner. We scanned the menus for our morning's gastrointestinal adventure when Alice approached with two glasses of ice water, "What can I get you's to drink?"

"Coffee," we sang in unison.

"I'll give you's a few minutes to figure out what you want."

You's? Yup, she said you's. Wouldn't kid you's. Lol

I chose my meal, sipped my coffee, and stared at Tom. He stared back. We said nothing for what seemed like an eternity. The crickets were interrupted by Alice delivering our breakfast, "Can I get you's anything else?"

I shook my head, "No, this is great, thanks." We ate in silence, not a good silence. The time was coming. The plan would have to be voiced and put into play. But, I was still hoping they were wrong. Alice skittered by every few minutes to mess up our coffees by pouring in more. She asked repeatedly if we needed anything else, and we responded with shakes of our heads. We ate slowly with our heads down. There was no more staring into each other's eyes. I glanced up at the clock, just over half an hour to go. I left Tom at the table and went to the restroom to take a few deep breaths and to wash up. I popped a mint into my mouth, straightened my top, stood up straight, and demanded I pull my shit together. Tom was paying the bill when I made it back to the dining room. He tossed a wad of ones on the table, "You ready to go?"

"Nope, but it's not like I have a choice, right?"

"Nope," he smiled.

We checked in at the medical center about fifteen minutes later, and it took at least fifteen minutes to fill out the paperwork. Didn't doctors' offices share information on shared patients? Geesh, it would have saved a tree from all the paperwork. It was a new waiting room with unknown staff. There was only one other person in the room with us, and he seemed to be more interested in the morning talk show than the strangers who had invaded his solitude. The door swung open across the room and a woman walked out and straight to the desk. The gentleman unfolded himself from the chair he occupied and met her at the window. I guessed that meant I was next. The door swung open again...

"Mrs. Carpenter."

I gathered my purse and my courage to face the hall that waited. Tom and I walked to the nurse holding a chart. She looked every bit a nurse, all the way down to the old-fashioned white Velcro shoes.

"I'm sorry, but Dr. Fraiser will want to see you alone first. Then we will be more than happy to bring him back," Nurse *−Velcro−* stated.

Tom patted my shoulder, "I'll be right here." I simply nodded my head and allowed Nurse -*V*- to lead the way.

We only went a few doors before she stopped and reached for the handle, "Please, have a seat. Dr. Fraiser will be with you in a moment." She was gone in a flash, and I was left in an office staring at plastic models of breasts lining a shelf behind a large desk. This guy must have really enjoyed his job. He got to look at boobs all day. I was startled when the door opened without a courtesy knock.

"Good morning, Mrs. Carpenter. I'm Dr. Fraiser," I accepted the outstretched hand that was thrust in my face.

I hesitated as I allowed my eyes to adjust to the *woman* who stood before me, "Um, Good morning, call me Olivia, please."

"All right, Olivia," she corrected, "First, I want to explain why I wanted to see you alone first. That's your husband in the waiting room, correct?"

"Yes."

"Good, I'm glad he's supportive. Now, back to what I was saying. I wanted to see you because I have found that spouses tend to push their ideas off on my patients, not allowing them to decide their own treatment plan. Do you understand?"

I chuckled a bit, "I understand."

Dr. Fraiser smiled at me, "He does that, doesn't he?" I nodded, "Okay, so let's talk about you." She ran through the same results Dr. -*Chocolate Dipped*- explained to me not a week ago. Then she began rattling off letters and numbers, *HER2 negative, T4N2M1, I agree with your doctor's prognosis*...What? She might as well have chanted C3PO or R2D2. She looked up from the sheets in front of her, "I can see I have confused you somewhere along the way."

"Yeah, um, I understand the stuff Dr. Khudiadadzai explained last week, but what are HERSXYZ and the other numbers and letters *mean?*"

"HER2 is a test to see if your body is producing too much of the HER2 protein. This protein causes rapid cell growth which is a bad thing in your situation. You luckily have tested negative for the protein. As for the other letters, T means tumor and the number, 4, is the stage or size, understand?"

"Okay."

"N is for nodes, or lymph nodes and the number represents spreading, and M means metastasized and the 1 lets us know it has. Does that help?"

I gulped down air and turned my eyes away from her. I willed the tears not to fall and stiffened my spine, "Yes, I understand," I faced her and the future head on. "There's no chance this is all a really big mistake." I accepted it.

"No, Olivia. I wish I could tell you it is, but...we need to face what is in front of us and make a plan."

I agreed, "A double mastectomy, removal of the lymph nodes, and chemo."

"So you have already looked at your options," she acknowledged, "I agree. We will also be inserting the port for your chemotherapy treatments. It is easier for you if it is all done at the same time. It is easier to recover from one surgery versus two, agree?"

"True, will I have chemo right after surgery?" I squeaked.

"No," she reached across the desk to pat my hand, "Typically, chemo starts in about three weeks. The delay is to ensure you are recovering well from the surgery, make sure there is no sign of infection, and to do a cardiac test to be sure your heart is strong enough to move forward."

I leaned back in my chair and dropped my hands in my lap. I rubbed my damp palms along my legs and hesitated, but forced out the words, "Do you agree with Dr. K about the end result? Only having months?"

Dr. Fraiser sat quietly staring at me for the longest fifteen seconds of my life, "Yes, I agree with his prognosis," She straightened up in her chair and crossed her arms in front of her on the desk, "Olivia, this is about giving you as much time as possible. I can't promise forever, but I can promise a little more time."

One single aggressive tear made a break for it and ran as fast as it could down my cheek and hid at the corner of my lips, "Okay, then reconstruction is pointless," I snorted to myself, "Can Tom come in now, please?"

She gave me a soft smile, "I wouldn't have recommended it anyway," she picked up the office phone, "Can you bring Mr. Carpenter back, thank you," she dropped the receiver into its cradle, "He'll be here in a minute."

Dr. Fraiser produced a box of tissues and offered them to me, "Thank you."

A gentle tap turned our eyes to the doorway. Tom stepped through and immediately knelt next to my chair and took my hand, "What's goin' on? You okay?"

I patted the chair next to me, "Here, sit down, and Dr. Fraiser can explain," I waved my hand over her desk and the piles of papers, "all this."

Before he sat, Dr. Fraiser introduced herself and shook his hand, "Tom, call me Tom."

"Okay, Tom, here's what we have decided..."

Sometime later Dr. Fraiser had answered every question that popped into our heads. Surgery was scheduled, six days from today. Laden down with every pamphlet, lab request form, and instruction sheet within a ten mile radius, we exited the building.

"I think we should have a party," I decided.

Tom skidded to a stop and stared at me with disgust on his face, "You want to what? Are you out of your fucking mind? So we can celebrate what, having your tits lopped off, maybe the fact you're dying."

"Exactly," I started walking toward the truck, "I want to have a farewell party. Besides, we should do something for Lily, too. She leaves in," I counted on my fingers, "nine days," I gasped. "Wow, that fast." That settled it, I was going to throw a party to bid farewell to parts of my body and to a huge chunk of my heart.

We climbed into the truck and sat while Tom tried to wrap the idea around his brain, "You're serious? A party?'

"Yeah, we'll celebrate Lily leaving for basic training and then later we can...I don't know, burn my bras or something."

"You know that's pretty demented, right?"

I turned sideways in my bucket seat, hiking my knee up into the seat to face him fully. I took his hand, "Babe, I'm running on a clock here. I want to run screaming. I want to pound on something," I shook with the anger I had been hiding from everyone, including myself, "But nothing will give me more time. Nothing! So," I calmed myself, "let's celebrate what we do have. Let's have a stupid party," I almost begged.

He shook his head at the absurd idea, "Okay, if that's what you want then that's what we'll do."

I texted Lily and told her not to make plans for Friday. We swung by 3C's, so Tom could talk to Wayne. While they were huddled in Wayne's office, I went to search for two friends. Homer found me before I found him. He greeted me with a wagging tail and ready tongue. I petted him and squished his face in my hands. I praised him for being a good boy, and we went in search of Miguel.

"Hey, Tom's wife."

I jerked my head to find Randy leaning on the vending machine, "Oh, hi...Randy, right?"

"Yup," he smiled, I shuddered.

"Where's Miguel?" He pointed to one of the bays. I spotted Miguel's back end sticking out from under a hood, "Thanks," I threw over my shoulder as I headed towards the bay. Randy said something behind me, but I was too focused on where I was going. "Hey, Miguel," I called as my body cleared the doorway.

He slid out from under the hood and picked up a rag to wipe off his hands, "Olivia, what're you doing here?" I motioned to hug him, but thought better of it when I saw the grease. "Don't wanna do that. You would have to throw away your clothes if you did," he chuckled.

"Got it. Hey, do you and Charlotte have plans for Friday night?"

"I wouldn't know. You'd have to ask her. I'm a good boy. I do what she says," we laughed. I could see she was a power house and clearly, he agreed.

"Well, would you want to come to our place and bar-be-que? Have a beer or two or six," I smiled.

Still wiping his hands on the rag, "Sure, sounds like fun. If Char's up for it and if so, count me in."

"Yea! It'll be...interesting," I toss out with a smirk. "I hope to see you then," I waved and turned back toward the offices with Homer still on my heels. I rounded the corner and nearly bumped into Randy.

He reached out his hands to steady me, "Easy, lady. Wouldn't want you getting messy," he oozed, "So, you're having a party, huh. Celebrating anything important?"

I brushed my hands down my arms where his hands had touched, "Our oldest daughter joined the Air Force and, um, we wanted everyone she knows to come and wish her well."

"Too bad I don't know her."

I quirked my head to the side and pursed my lips, "Um, I think you are too old to be messing with an eighteen year old girl, don't you?"

He gave me a sleazy smile and slid by me. He gave me the creeps. "Come on, Homer," I whispered, "Let's get outta here." Tom and Wayne were still sitting where I left them going over the schedule of upcoming jobs. "Hi, Wayne."

"Liv, I hear we're having a party."

I looked at Tom who still didn't seem to be fully on board with the idea, "That's right. I want to have a party and that's that," I poked Tom on the shoulder, "Okay?"

He rubbed his shoulder like I hurt him, "Got it." I smiled at his childish behavior.

"I invited Miguel, and I'll call Charlotte when we get home," I looked over at Wayne who had is fingers entwined, cupping the back of his head as he leaned back in his chair, "Should I call Molly too?"

"Wouldn't hurt, I've been known to forget to tell her stuff."

Tom burst out laughing, "You? No? Never, Mr. Forgetful over here," he jabbed his thumb in Wayne's direction, "When's her birthday again?"

"Shut up."

*****

I made all the calls and invited the people I wanted around me when all hell was breaking loose in my life. I let the girls know what I wanted to do and when. Lily would be there and Shelly would come straight home after work. So, the guest list was complete, now I needed to make a grocery list for food and booze. Definitely booze, lots of booze. I was gonna need booze.

I shopped, cleaned, and cooked over the following days. I ordered an Air Force themed cake for Lily and a boob cake for me. It was an odd order to place, to say the least. I left the liquor store with boxes of spirits and intoxicants. My plan was to not remember what the party was for. I guess that would be the denial stage of the five steps of dying. Did I skip anger? Oh. Hell. No. I was pissed at my traitorous body. It was kind of hard to do anything about it. What was I gonna do, beat my own ass? Anger seemed pointless, and I didn't want to waste the time I had left piss moaning about shit I couldn't change.

I picked up the cakes on Friday morning. I cracked up when I opened the pristine white bakery box to find two nipples staring at me. Lily's cake was beautiful. I choked up from pride for my little girl's choices. Little girl, she wasn't so little any more. She was a woman making adult choices and I was going to miss her so much. I got my purchases home and got everything ready for the festivities. Tom and the guys were gonna cut out early, leaving the closing to

Randy. Our shindig would be in full swing by six o'clock, and I hoped to be well on my way to three sheets to the wind by 6:15.

"Need any help?"

"Hey, kiddo, can you get the paper plates and stuff together so we can get the grill going as soon as everyone gets here?"

"Can do."

Lily and I skittered around the deck getting everything ready and trying to keep Oliver out of the food. By quarter to six, Tom was pulling in the drive.

He waved, "Hey, babe, I'm gonna go jump in the shower. I'll be down to help in a few."

"Cool."

Tom was back in what seemed like 8.2 seconds. I wished I could get ready that fast. No sooner had he appeared, than everyone else started showing up. The party started, and I poured the first of many drinks. We ate. We drank. We laughed. We avoided my little problem and focused on Lily instead. She enjoyed the love and attention, but I think she liked the gifts even more. She was showered with gifts of cash which were, as she said, the right color, and the perfect size. The evening progressed with drinks, cake, more drinks, a bonfire, another drink, boob cake...and another drink. I was beyond the pale. I drank more than would be acceptable any other time, but tonight, I didn't care.

The ladies and I huddled around the bonfire and joked and laughed. Molly was the only sober one among us which made it even funnier.

"You are going to have a terrible hangover tomorrow. You know that, right?"

"Yes, I am aware," I stammered and giggled, "Hey, grab that bag over there by the door, would ya?" Molly eyed the grocery bag that sat on the deck by the door. I had collected all my bras. The pile included lacey, colorful, sexy, not so sexy, athletic, and expensive.

Molly dropped the bag next to my chair, "What are all those for?"

"All what? What ya got in the bag, girlie?" slurred Charlotte.

Lily and Shelly pulled up a few lawn chairs next to us, "You ready mom? I have a few to donate to the cause," smiled Lily.

"Donate to what? What are we donating?" asked Molly.

I pulled a black lacy number from the bag then passed the bag around, "Take one and I'll show you what these are for." Everyone pulled out a bra. I held the bag up, "Do you guys want in on this?" I hollered asking the guys if they wanted to grab a bra.

"Nah, babe, I think we're good over here," yelled Tom. Wayne and Miguel leaned in to ask Tom a question. He pointed in our direction, crossed his arms over his chest and leaned against the railing to watch the events about to occur.

I stood cradling the bra in my hands, "Okay, we all know I have breast cancer. We all know I'm…terminal. Cuz of that I'm not gonna get fake boobs. No boobs means I don't need these," I say wiggling the bra over the flames of the bonfire. "I say we have our own little bra burnin'. Let's say goodbye to my tatas with a good ol' fashion burnin'." I dropped the lace into the flames and watched it twist and shrivel and melt away.

Holding my bra in her hands, Charlotte checked the tag, "Damn it! If they were my size I'd be stealin' 'em, but, they're not." With a wince she tossed the straps, cups, and discomfort into the pit. We each took a turn tossing a bra in and watching it disappear like my tits would in a few short days. I watched the fire lick away at the material of each piece of cotton, lace, and silky bra. I hadn't noticed Charlotte had slipped away until she returned.

"Here," she announced as she tossed a wad of fabric into the fire.

"What the hell is that," Shelly asked while trying to distinguish the article, "It's not a bra," she said, poking it with a stick.

"It's ma thong."

"That is nasty!" squealed Lily, "Why would you throw that in there?"

Charlotte took a good long drink of her beer, she lowered the bottle and looked at Lily, "because, my dear, that lil' fucker was ridin' where it didn't belong. Them damn yokes are a pain in the ass."

I burst out laughing at the spectacle of her panties sparking up in the fire. "Wow, I suppose them little bead things don't like the fire much."

"I'd say not," chimed Molly, "Just so you all are aware, I have no intention of throwing my panties or bra into the bonfire."

"Good to know," I clucked.

"Sorry 'bout the panties," Charlotte mused, "They was hurtin' ma crack."

We all burst out laughing and continued to burn the contraptions meant to house things I would no longer have. I looked over at the men to find Tom watching the antics. He raised his beer to me in salute to what I had chosen to do. I raised my glass to him and turned my attention back to the flames.

"Ya know," Charlotte began, "You could go do one of those amateur night things at the strip club. Ya know, show 'em off before...well, before..."

My blurred gaze slid over to her sweet face, "Are you fuckin' crazy?"

"Hey!" croaked Shelly, "That's my mom you're talking about. That's wrong."

Throwing her hands up in surrender, "It was just an idea. Don't get yer panties in a twist." She chuckled at her own statement, "I can't get mine in a twist cuz they're smoke," she laughed while poking at the hot embers.

"Those were pretty toxic," Shelly stated in all seriousness, "That is an image I will never be able to scrub from my brain. Thanks." The laughter started out as a few giggles but built into full on roars.

It was exactly what I needed.

Chapter Twenty One

Hangover? That was an understatement. My mouth tasted like I had licked the floor in a bar on the questionable end of town. My head thumped like it was keeping time to any '80s heavy metal *abomination*.

Shoot me.

I forced one eye open. I was overjoyed to find Tom had pulled the curtains tightly and left me a glass of orange juice and Advil. I loved him so much. I, however, didn't want to move...ever. If I hurt that bad lying there then movement meant my head would explode, but not before I vomited up a lung. I promised everything holy or other worldly I would never drink alcohol *again* if I survived this one poorly planned event.

Do you know how I knew Tom was the most amazing person ever? He put a straw in the juice glass. A straw. The answer to my problem. I popped two tablets in my mouth and slurped down the juice with minimal movement. *Oh, thank you, thank you, thank you...Tom was my hero*...again. I lay there long enough to allow the pills to work their magic and then gingerly made my way to the bathroom to make myself human. Well, closer to human than I currently was.

I found my family sitting around the breakfast bar eating. It smelled vile. It looked worse, but I was sure it was the hangover screaming at me. Tom handed me a glass and nodded for me to drink, *hair of the dog.* Gross! But I drank the bitter liquid and prayed it stayed down.

"Nasty," I gagged. I stuck my tongue out and mocked wiping it off on my hand.

"No worse than what you were drinkin' last night. I'm amazed you crawled out of bed at all."

The girls snorted at the comment and agreed whole-heartedly. They proceeded to regale me with the events of the previous night and I was glad to find out I wasn't the only one who cracked them up with acts of stupidity. Apparently, Charlotte is quite amusing. I laughed along with them, even though it hurt more than drill bits being shoved up my nose. *I will never drink again. I will never drink again. I will never...drink that much again.*

Tom decided to go into the garage for a while to catch up on work, and I decided to take the girls shopping. Lily needed things for basic training, and I needed to spend time with them. As much time as I could.

"So, you can't take regular clothes with you? What are you supposed to wear?" asked Shell in shock at finding out Lily couldn't bring her closet with her to Basic Training.

"The recruiter said I should bring a couple days' worth of clothes, but to make sure they wouldn't draw attention to me."

With a devious smile, Shell clucked, "I guess I get to have whatever you can't take then."

"I think not, young lady," I snipped. "I will mail her things to her once she gets to wherever she is going." I tapped Lily on her thigh and gave her a soft smile, "Right?"

"Right."

Shell crossed her arms over her chest in a huff, "Well, that sucks."

"I'm sure there are things I won't want to take at all. We can go through my closet later, okay?"

287

"Cool beans!" Shell squealed.

"Argh! Hangover here," I winced.

We chatted and chuckled in the car to the mall. We joked, scavenged sales racks, tried on things we would never buy, even if we had the cash. We window shopped, hit the makeup counter at *Macy's* and let them transform us into super models, and hit the food court. I was dragged into stores I would never have gone into and will never go into again. I watched my girls and noticed they weren't girls anymore. They were women, young women, but women. When did I let them grow up? Why did I let them? We didn't go into the *Disney* store or *Build-a-Bear*. They didn't ride the dolphin on the carousel. They didn't hold my hand. I found a bench outside of *Hot Topic* and told them to go in and have fun. I faked a headache. Well, it wasn't completely false. I watched them laugh and smile. I watched them hold things up to each other wondering what the other's opinion was. I watched. I cried inside.

"Hey, Olivia." I turned my head to find Alyssa and Dr. -*Douche Bag*- standing next to the bench.

"Hey."

"Um...what are you doing?"

With a smirk I said, "Tap dancing, and what are you doing here at the *mall*?"

"What the fuck..." but before she could spit out the rest of her jab Dr. Matthews interrupted.

"We were looking for swim suits. I want to take Alyssa to the beach next weekend."

"Ain't that nice," I rolled my eyes and looked back into the store window.

He cleared his throat and asked, "How are you, Olivia?"

What the fuck? What was he thinking? "Fine," I sneered, "why do you ask?" Answer that one mother fucker, doctor/ patient confidentiality, dumb-ass.

"Oh, no reason," he tipped his head and looked at me like I should know what it was he was trying to get me to say.

I smiled and turned back to the show behind the store window. Alyssa had stepped away to gather herself when Dr. -*Mind Your*

*Own B*usiness- sat next to me. "I think you should tell her what's going on."

"What's going on?"

"You know I know."

"I am well aware of what you know, Dr. Matthews."

"Neil, my name is Neil."

I turned my face in his direction and sought out his eyes, "I call my friends by their first names, Dr. Matthews."

"I see. Well, Alyssa is your friend. Maybe you could reach out to her."

"After what happened? I don't trust her," I shook my head at him, "She would probably say I deserve this for causing Dick Head to beat Trish to a pulp." I stood and regarded him on the bench, "I don't need that kind of stress in my life. What's left of it at least," I turned and started for *Hot Topic's* entrance.

"Liv, wait."

I stopped, but didn't turn toward her, "What?"

"What can I say?" Alyssa wavered, "what can I do to fix this?"

Looking at her reflection in the door in front of me, I slowly shook my head, "Nothing." I pushed the door open and went in search of family. I watched through the window as Neil approached Alyssa and wrapped his arm around her, pulling her close. I saw the shimmer of tears on her cheek. It broke my heart, but forgiveness wasn't in me. He led her away, and I put the moment behind me. I wandered around the store seeing nothing and ignoring the *"Can I help you find some*thing?" inquiries. I moved around racks of t-shirts and shelves of hoodies.

"Mom, what do you think?"

I blinked away my blindness to see Shelly sporting a white spike-covered belt and suspenders. "Um...it's a look."

"Is it bad ass or bad choice?"

"I think it's just...bad."

Lily burst out laughing as she approached from behind me, "I told her it was ridiculous."

"I like the belt and I like the suspenders. I don't like them together," I back-pedaled. If Shell liked it then I wasn't gonna rain on her parade.

Michelle smiled at me, "See! Mom likes it, well, pieces of it."

Lily knew what I did, and I think she even understood why, "I guess it's not too awful."

Shelly bounced on her toes and clapped her hands in excitement. Her grin ran across her face like the *Cheshire Cat*. Fitting, since the outfit choice looked like it belonged to the *Mad Hatter*.

We zipped in and out of stores, and I kept a look out for Alyssa and Dr. *-Dumb-ass-*. I only saw them once during the remainder of our mall visit. I kept my distance while Neil passed judgment on me by shaking his head at me as if I were an errant child. He could go pound coal for all I cared. I had better things to do than worry about him, or her for that matter.

"Did you get everything on your list?" I asked as I maneuvered through traffic.

"I think I have it covered. I had some of the stuff at home and all you guys got me luggage, so I'm good to go," confirmed Lily.

"Cool, so what are you and your friends gonna do before you leave?"

"Oooo...have a party and invite your awesomely amazing little sister!" bellowed Shell from the backseat.

"Um...no. No party. No nothing."

I pulled into the parking lot at our chosen destination for dinner, "Why not? You can have your friends over and have a sleepover or whatever."

Lily looked at me with a tear teetering on the edge of falling, "I figured I would be at the hospital with you."

"Oh." Yup, I'm an idiot. I hadn't thought it out, but she was right. I would be in the hospital in just over a day. "I'm sorry."

Lily shook her head as a way to remove the conversation from her mind, "Come on, I'm hungry. Let's get a table."

End of conversation.

*****

After greeting Tom and handing off a warm to-go box of food, the girls and I disappeared into Lily's closet. We searched for items and pushed away others. She gave Shelly a few things to keep her from whining. Lily packed her suit case, and I packed boxes to be mailed once she made it to her first duty station. I hoped it was far, far, away and thrilling. A place where she could be surrounded by beauty every day and a place where her sister could visit that held no bad memories, only possibilities.

It was well into the wee hours of Sunday morning when Tom coaxed me from Lily's room to our bed. "I missed you," he whispered in my ear as he pulled me closer under the covers. He raked his teeth across my earlobe and I was done. I was awake, alert, and *ready*.

Anything you want. Yes, to every demand. Salute!

Ahhhh...the evening ended well and I slept like a baby...well, better than I had in weeks.

*****

Morning arrived with a countdown ticking in my head, this many hours, so many minutes until I wore a gown with no back and even less style. I lay with my back to Tom as I looked outside through the small gap between the curtains in search of magical rays of light. All I saw were clouds and sparkling beads of rain rolling down the window pane, my favorite kind of day. It was earlier than I thought, so I slipped from our bed quickly and quietly. I stood for a moment at the foot of the bed and watched the way his chest rose and fell with each breath. I was in awe of the strength he wore even in sleep. I knew his strength, but I was given a back-stage pass to the sweet man he tucked tightly behind the muscles, grease, and attitude. I caught my hand mid-air. I must have been reaching out to touch him. No, he needed to sleep and I needed to feel the rain.

*****

The rain fell softly against my hoodie as I walked around the back yard. It always smelled clean after a good down-pour and the flowers always seemed so happy. Their heads were held higher, and their colors danced in the rain droplets. The stains that built up over time seemed to wash away and leave everything with a clean slate. No tarnish or cloud of dirt, only the new. I knew then I had to do that for the people in my life. I needed to give them the clean slate they deserved after my departure. I needed to give them a reason to raise their heads high and search for the sun. I needed to write letters to them all. I needed to tell them what they have meant to me and what I hoped for them in the future. I needed to start. Now.

I escaped to the office and became intimate with my laptop. I spilled out thoughts and hopes, absolution, and begged for it in return. I reached out to people I wouldn't have if my end weren't looming, casting a shadow over everything I had done from that moment until there were no more moments. Some of these letters wouldn't reach their destinations until after I had gone. Just because I wished them well, didn't mean I wished to see them in my remaining time. I could grant forgiveness while being faceless. I huddled behind the screen and hid my emotions on the pixilated page. Letters and thoughts danced across the page in a twisted dance of death and regret. *Dear Mother...*

*****

"Hey, babe. Whatcha doin' locked up in here alone?"

I lifted my weary head to see Tom leaning against the door jamb. His arms were crossed casually over his chest, but his eyes were telling a different story. They spoke of concern, fear, and doubt. They showed his insides, while his outsides tried to contradict the truth.

"Writing down some thoughts. What are you up to?"

"Molly called. They want to come over and spend some time with us today," he shifted his stance in an asking manner, "does that sound okay to you?"

"Sure," I allowed the response to fall out of my mouth without intending to. "Why don't you see if Charlotte and Miguel want to sit and do a death watch too?" Oops...I didn't intend to say that. Shit!

Tom shook his head at me in disgust, "Is that what you think? That my brother and Molly want to," and with his fingers making quote signs, "see you one last time?"

"I..."

"No. Is that what you think? Because I can tell them not to bother, I can tell them my wife thinks they are being fake?"

292

"You're kidding, right? Up until this," I grabbed my breasts to draw a picture, "Molly had nothing to do with me, and Wayne only knew me as his brother's wife. So, fake? Yes." I pushed back from the desk and walked around to where he stood, "Does it mean what they are doing now is fake, no. But I don't feel like it's for me. It feels like it is to be supportive toward you and the girls and for that I am thankful." I placed my hand on his chest over his heart. He was coming down from a burst of anger, and I could feel it pulsing through my hand. His breathing was calming along with his heart.

"Did you ever think maybe you kept them at arm's length? You don't trust easily, and you doubt peoples' intentions," he placed his hand over mine and laced his fingers with mine. He held our connected hands over his heart and let me feel his truth.

I dropped my forehead to his chest and admitted, "You're probably right. Trust is a hard thing to grant, and I have been bitten on the ass one too many times to give it easily."

Tom ran his hand through my short hair and rested his chin on my head, "I know, babe. I know," he whispered.

With an attempt at lightening the mood, "Are we cooking, or are they?"

"Do you really want Molly to cook?" he chuckled.

"She's gonna be a momma," I looked up into his eyes, "she needs to learn."

"True enough."

"Maybe..." I hesitated.

"What?"

"Maybe, I could kinda teach her. You know, how to cook some stuff. Maybe give her some of my recipes or something."

The smile he held on his lips was reflected in his eyes, "That would be great. I think Wayne would appreciate it too," we chuckled at the thought of Wayne getting meals that weren't black and set off the smoke detectors two rooms over.

So, that's what I would do for Molly in my remaining time. I would teach her to cook and write down recipes and maybe...let her in. Maybe.

*****

We sat around the patio table and chatted and joked. Molly called Charlotte and invited them over for an evening of fun. More like an evening of keep *Olivia's mind off tomorrow*. I must say, it worked. Don't get me wrong, the idea of the following morning was never far from thought, but the people sharing this table were standing in front of me holding the Boogie Man off, at least for now. I was surrounded by family I was learning loved me and friends I loved like family. An idea popped into my head, and I scurried away as quickly as possible. I heard Tom yelling after me in concern, but I kept moving. I was coming out of the office holding a small canvas bag when Tom found me.

"Hey, what's going on? Are you okay?" he asked while holding me in front of him looking for a physical reason for my cut and run.

"I'm fine. I just wanted to get this," I held up the bag and saw recognition in his eyes.

He smiled and returned to the office for a piece I forgot. We made our way back to our guests and were greeted with concerned looks. I held up the bag and said, "I want pictures." Tom began setting up the tripod as I got everyone into place for a large group photo. As I mounted the camera, I looked over at the group assembled for me. Tom, my love, Lily, my precious flower, Michelle, the music in my world, Wayne and Molly, the family I never knew I needed, Charlotte and Miguel, the family I chose… and Oliver, who made his way to the center of the table and plopped down and waited for his close up. I was one lucky terminal bitch.

"Okay, guys," I squealed as I made my way to my designated seat, "and ten, nine, eight…smile!" We all cheesed and wrapped our arms around the person on either side of us and took the first of many photos of the night. But that photo, that photo…would hang in each of our homes as a reminder of a love filled night…and in memory of my boobs.

I didn't drink because of surgery in the morning and Molly didn't because she was carrying my niece, or nephew but the rest had enough to keep us all in stitches. Charlotte taught everyone Irish pub songs and spun tales of foreign lands. Miguel had to interpret a few times when she rambled so far into her accent we had no clue what she was saying. We found the funny in many moments that night. We found the joy in each other. We found and built upon a connection that would hold us together through the hell waiting on the other side of sunrise. But for now, hell would have to wait.

The evening was called to a close fairly early. The following day was Monday, after all, and people had to go to work and some (one) had to get parts cut off, and others had to wait in waiting rooms while said person gets things cut off. Yet another reason to hate Mondays. I hugged everyone and wished them a safe journey and watched them leave my orbit. I was left wishing my gravity was strong enough to hold them...a little while longer.

"Whatcha wanna do now?" asked Shell as she dropped down onto the loveseat, "Wanna watch a movie?"

I looked around the room at the three most important people in my life, "Yeah, I wanna watch a movie," I smiled, "but in our bed. I think it's a 'family bed night.'" Family bed started when the girls were small enough to fit between Tom and me. We would curl up and watch Saturday morning cartoons or watch Disney movies late into the night. It was an excuse for the girls to sleep in our bed and an excuse for me to hold them all night long. I watched as the girls bolted to their rooms to get ready for bed, and Tom and I walked hand in hand to ours. I had just slipped under the covers when the girls came skidding through the doorway holding pillows, blankets, and a stack of DVDs to fight over.

"I get the middle," they screamed in unison.

"No, I do!"

"No, I do!"

"Neither of you does," clarified Tom, "Your Mom goes in the middle and I get the right side, Oliver," he pointed to the orange fuzz-ball, licking places he shouldn't, lying on my left, "gets to stay where he is and you two get the bottom."

"But..." started Lily.

"But nothin'. It's decided. Now, which movie do you want to watch?" Tom asked me.

I sifted through the DVDs the girls chose. I was shocked to see all kids' movies. No shoot-em-ups, space ships, car chases, or sparkly vamps. I smiled and chose *Monsters Inc.* It was one of their favorites and I knew there wouldn't be any dispute in my choice. I slid to the middle of the bed and leaned my head on Tom's shoulder. I shifted my legs slightly apart to allow Michelle room. She placed her pillow on my lap and curled up in the space I made for her. Lily made her space in the gap between my leg and Tom's. Both of their heads were in reach of my hands and I ran my fingers through their hair as we settled in to watch bright colors dance across the screen.

It was 12:57 am and I was staring at the frozen screen looping on the television. Tom's head rested on my shoulder and my babies were sprawled across the lower half of the bed. Oliver sat near my elbow and seemed to watch me. We stared at each other for a moment when I asked him if he thought I would come home. He responded by walking up onto my chest and lying down. His head rested on my left shoulder and he purred in my ear. "You're no help," I whispered and leaned my head a bit closer to the other man in my life.

I pushed play on the DVD player and allowed the movie to play again to try to push thoughts from my head. It didn't work. About an hour later I pried myself out from under the mass of bodies in our bed. Oliver was the only one to fight my escape until I placed him on the warm pillow I left behind.

I had things to do and time was a precious commodity. I had things to write to people I didn't want to write to and to people I didn't want to leave. I woke the computer from its rest, and forced it to listen to me admit fault and forgive others. I shared my tears with the click of the keys…until my alarm went off reminding me, I had to get ready for…who was I kidding, I wasn't ready and never would be.

I wasn't ready. No one was ready.

Chapter Twenty Two

I was starving! I hadn't eaten since seven p.m. *yesterday* and it was now 7:45 the next morning. I sat on a bed in a very unattractive ass-baring gown, which I was blessed to wear backwards, waiting for my life to change. The nurse would be in shortly to put in the I.V. and give me something to relax. Me, relax? That's easy. Tell me it was all a bad joke. We will all have a good laugh, and I will go home intact. No? Then I will stay tense. Shell and Lily sat at the foot of the bed trying to make me smile, and Tom stood at my side holding my hand in his. His thumb ran a nervous path back and forth over my knuckles, and I picked at the ugly gown I was forced to wear. They told us they only allowed two people in the preoperative holding area. I told them it was a good thing I allowed three into my pre-op area. What were they gonna do? Kick me out? It's not like I brought in feral sextuplets.

Can you tell I was a bit pissy that morning?

They let us be. We stayed quiet and out of the way. No harm, no foul. The nurse came in a few minutes later and proceeded to put in the I.V. Had I mentioned yet I hate needles? No, really? I hated them. A lot. This was no exception. After a brutal jab and some wiggling around the nurse was taping down the needle and tubing to my arm.

"How was that?" Nurse -*I will jab you till it's in*- asked.

"Better than a root canal," I responded with a roll of my eyes.

Tom rubbed my shoulder and leaned over to kiss me on the head, "Be nice," he whispered and I laughed.

"I was being nice." I watched the clear liquid drip through the tubing which led to my arm. It was warmer than I thought it would be.

A loud tapping caught my attention as Dr. Fraiser poked her head in the door. "Good morning, Olivia. Olivia's fan club," she smiled as she nodded to the girls and Tom who was still gripping my hand. "I'm sorry, but I need you all to step outside for a few minutes while I play connect the dots on your mom," she held up a blue felt-tipped marker. "You can come back in to smother her in kisses before we take her to the surgical suite." Dr. Fraiser smiled as she held the door for my clan to slip out of sight. She turned toward me and tipped her head, "So, how are you doing?"

I held up my arm and pointed at the needle, "According to the nurse, I'm relaxing."

"Are you?"

"Um...nope. The important question is how are you? Are you in a good mood? Did you sleep well last night? No late night partying before surgery, right?"

Dr. Fraiser gave a girly giggle, "No, I assure you, the party ended early enough to allow me a few hours' sleep."

Yup, I liked her. "Good to know."

"Well, let's get our little party started. Sit up for me and open your gown." She took the next few minutes drawing the equivalent of bad stick figures all over my chest and underarms. She would never have made it as an artist. She explained what she was marking and why. I didn't want to know, but I had to know.

I was back in the horizontal position when Tom and the girls came back in to kiss me goodbye. How depressing. I may have been relaxed due to the 'la-la-land' liquid dripping into my arm, but even

I realized how depressing it was to hear goodbye as I was being wheeled down the hall to be hacked up. I watched the ceiling tiles and bright lights flash by me as I was wheeled away. Would that be the last thing I would see outside of the operating room? Well, that would have sucked beyond words.

It was so fucking cold in that room. It felt like a meat locker. I started to shiver.

"It's normal. It is rather cool in here," a nurse with the most beautiful eyes I had ever seen sympathized as she tossed a warmed blanket over my goose-pimpled flesh. "Don't worry, you will be kept warm throughout the procedure."

"Th..th..thank y..you," I chattered. She gave me a soft smile and moved away to do whatever it was she did. I saw the door swing open and a grape walked in. It held its hands up and away from any surface. Nurse -*Beautiful Eyes*- assisted it with gloves and walked with it to where I laid.

"Hello again, Olivia," greeted Dr. Fraiser, "how are you doing?"

"C..cold."

"You'll warm up, I promise. Last thing I want to do is turn you into a Popsicle," she joked. "Are you ready? Do you have any questions?" I shook my head and waited for what was to come.

I felt a hand touch my shoulder as a voice addressed me from behind my head, "Olivia, I'm Dr. Dean, your anesthesiologist. I am going to place this mask," he explained holding the mask up for me to see, "over your nose and mouth. I want you to breathe normally, okay?"

"'k."

"All right, here we go." He placed the mask over my face.

I saw Dr. Fraiser move up next to me and I could feel her hand on my arm, "See you in a few hours, Olivia."

"Ahhh...ummm."

*****

"Sir, she may not wake up for a while. You really should go home. We will call you if anything happens."

"She will see me when she wakes up," he murmured, "I want her to know I didn't leave her. I would never leave her."

"But, sir…"

"No, I'm staying."

"Go…go home," I croaked, "I see you."

Tom sat upright in his chair and reached for my hand, "Hey, you. How ya feelin'?"

"Tired. Go."

"I'll stay with you."

I opened my heavy eyelids, "Go home, please. I'm okay. Need sleep." I let my lids slam shut and begged him to go home before sleep over took me once again. I felt his lips on my forehead.

"I will be here first thing in the morning. I promise."

*****

"Mrs. Carpenter, I need to take your vitals, okay?"

"Argh…'k."

*****

"Mrs. Carpenter, I need to take your vitals, okay?"

"Wha'?"

*****

"Mrs. Carpenter, I need to take your vitals, okay?"

"Again?"

All night! All night they woke me up to take my temperature, blood pressure in my leg, pulse. All I wanted to do was sleep. Why wouldn't they let me SLEEP? For the love of all that was holy…I just wanted sleep.

*****

"Hey, beautiful," I heard as my eyes started to flicker open, "I missed you." Tom whispered in my ear. He kissed me on that one sensitive spot just below my ear.

"I remember," I croaked.

"Remember what, babe?"

"Last night. You. Here."

"Good," he sighed, "I didn't want you to think we left you all alone."

"No."

I heard a light tapping on the door, "Mrs. Carpenter, I need to take your vitals, okay?" Oh for God's sake! Again? I grumbled as Tom slid out of the nurse's way. "Dr. Fraiser will be in for rounds in a little while," the nurse said as she finished up with her charting.

"Thanks," I said without meaning it.

I avoided looking down. I avoided the pressure I felt. I avoided the unavoidable. I looked at Tom, who kept his eyes glued to my face. They never slipped beyond. They never drifted further. The blanket was pulled all the way up to my shoulders. My hands stuck out on either side but my chest was not visible. I was sore, but not in pain, and I was pretty sure that was due to the liquid still dripping into my left arm. I rolled my neck a bit and tried to shrug my shoulders. I was feeling a little stiff and a lot antsy. I moved my arms to make sure they worked and found they did and could reach the top of the blanket. I let my fingers rest on the top edge of the sterile cover. I was still looking at Tom. I begged him with my eyes to pull the blanket down, but I had to do it. I knew he wouldn't do that to me. He wouldn't. He gave me the slightest nod in acceptance. He told me to do it without words. We didn't need words.

I slowly hooked my fingers around the rough edge of the blanket and slowly pulled it down. Our eyes stayed locked on each other's. Tom held my other hand and absentmindedly rubbed his rough thumb over my knuckles. As the blanket dropped away I could smell some kind of antiseptic. It invaded my nose like a skunk on the side of the road. I unlocked my eyes from Tom's and forced them to travel across the bandages that banded my chest. They ran flat across my chest. Flat. Level. Smooth. I let my hand skim lightly across the bandage. There was nothing there. Blank. I sought out Tom's acceptance and found it crystal clear in his eyes. His eyes shimmered with tears I knew he would never let me see, but I knew they would fall. He reached his hand up and wiped away the tears I didn't realize were sliding down my cheeks.

"You are beautiful," he whispered. "I love you, so much."

I gave a *'you are full of shit'* chuckle to the beautiful comment, but finished with, "I love you more with every breath." We were interrupted by a tap at the door.

"Good morning, Olivia," Dr. Fraiser greeted us with a smile, "Hi, Tom. How are we feeling this morning?"

I gave a snort to disguise my sadness, "Lighter. I think I lost some weight yesterday." Tom squeezed my hand in his and smiled down at me.

"Maybe a little," Dr. Fraiser agreed while holding her thumb and forefinger a short distance apart. She let a smile settle over her face, but I couldn't tell if it was real or the face she showed her patients, "I would like to examine you and see how you are doing this morning, and then I want to show you a few exercises you need to do to keep your neck, shoulders, and arms from getting stiff, okay?"

"Not like I'm gonna say no."

"Do you want Tom to leave?" she asked in the most casual way.

I looked to Tom for his answer, "It's up to you, babe," I said. He looked stricken. He looked as if had I asked him to identify a dead body as a member of the family. "It's okay," I said squeezing his hand, "why don't you go get some coffee." He looked so sorry. "It's okay, go," I released his hand and smiled. He hesitated until I shooed him away, "go." He nodded his head at me then lowered it, turned and walked out the door.

"Okay, so let's take a look…"

Dr. Fraiser only removed a few bandages to evaluate my incisions. She explained the tubes that were running out of my body from four different places. They were there to allow built up liquid and blood to drain from my body. It was collected in little bulbs that provided suction. They were attached to a little elastic-looking belt around my waist. Because I had both breasts and the lymph nodes from under each arm removed, I had a tube coming from each incision. She showed me the port put in place during the surgery as well. That was how I would be receiving my chemo treatments in a few weeks. As she progressed with my exam she said the coloring of my skin looked good and the drainage appeared minimal. All in all, I was doing well…that's what she said, anyway. My opinion was on the other end of the spectrum. A nurse came in and assisted with replacing the bandages which covered the places where my breasts used to be. They showed me the exercises she mentioned and asked if I had questions. What was I gonna ask about? What did you do with my boobs? Stick 'em in a glass jar? Send them off to a medical school to be studied?

"Your breakfast will be here shortly," the nurse informed me, "would you like to sit up?"

"Yeah, please." She raised the back of the bed to a more upright position and helped me get situated. "We will be removing your catheter a little later. We want you to get out of bed at some point today."

"Do I get a voice in the matter?"

She gave me a bright smile, "Nope."

"Woohoo!" I mimicked joy...not very well, mind you.

Breakfast came and I picked at it. Tom demanded I eat. I demanded he eat it for me. He didn't and I ate more than I wanted to make him happy. Sleep sneaked up on me and dragged me under its cloak of darkness.

*****

Tom had slipped away during my nap. I hoped he had gone home and gotten some rest. I fiddled with the blanket that lay over my chest. The pain was bearable, the loss, not so much. I was lost in my misery when I heard her...

"Look at ya!" squealed Charlotte, "Ya look like," she stood back a bit and evaluated my form laying there, "shit. I'm goin' with shit."

I mocked shock and hurt, "Well, tell me what you really think. Don't hold back."

"Ya know I won't lie to ya, sweets."

"I know and that's one reason I love you."

"There are more? Do tell," she smiled so brightly she could compete with a Christmas tree. Charlotte scanned my sad little hospital room, "Ooo...flowers. Who'd ya get these purties from?" she asked before shoving her face into a bouquet of roses. With her face still buried in the very large bouquet, she carried them to the bedside table.

"I hate cut flowers," I declared as I ran my thumb over the velvet petals.

"Why ever not? They are quite lovely, don't cha know."

"They're dead. From the moment someone hacked them from their roots, they were dead," I stated as my fingers roamed through the petals. "They get shoved into a glass jar and given to people in declarations of love or gestures to say get well, but what they gave was dead. What I got was a front row seat to the rot and decay of what were once beautiful and alive."

"Well isn't that a disturbing thought. Aren't you lil' Mary Sunshine today," sniggered Charlotte.

I looked at my friend who was still admiring the flowers, "It's what you are doing, ya know. You're sitting front row to watch my rot and decay."

Spinning around with a swirl of fire-engine red curls, Charlotte placed her hands on her ample hips and whipped out her attitude, "Shut up, you. That's enough talk like that."

"Stating the facts, friend," I said. I looked to the roses again, "I don't understand it, if you wanted to say 'I love you,' or 'I've been thinking of you,' or even 'get well soon,' wouldn't you want it to last longer than seven short days? Why wouldn't you just buy a plant?" I asked in all sincerity. "Shit, for what they paid for the bouquet they could have planted a row of rose bushes in my garden. You know, something I could admire, water, and take care of, something that would remind me of the person who gave them to me, a gift I wouldn't toss in the trash when the petals started falling out like my hair will."

"For Christ sake, Livie, it was a gesture of kindness. They wanted ya to know they were thinking of you today. Isn't that something?" argued Charlotte.

"It would have meant more if they were from someone who didn't know how I feel about flowers. They're from Alyssa and Neil. She knows, or should have remembered, how I feel about flowers. What this tells me is I was an afterthought." I swallowed past the tightening in my throat and demanded the tears not fall. "She sent flowers, but hasn't bothered stopping by." I decided I would have those dead sticks delivered to Dr. -*Douche Bag's*- office, card and all. I don't have time to waste on false friends and fake sentiments. I knew very well my friendship with Alyssa was on thin ice. Then, I felt it crack. "I guess a vase of dead shit is all I'm worth now." Our friendship had suffered a few blows. Maybe it was too late.

Dismissing the uncomfortable vinyl chair, Charlotte scooted up onto the bed and took my hand. "Now you listen to me, sweetie. I'm here, Molly is bringing yer lovely girlies soon and yer man is bringing us coffee. Correction…good coffee. That be a whole lotta love coming yer way. Who needs the chancer and her lick-able boyfriend? Hell, ya got lots of us who will buy you all the damn plants you want and then some."

"So, I have a garden full of friends…is that what you're trying to say, ya goof-ball?" I smirked. "Which ones are the pricks?"

"They're the cut flowers."

I burst out laughing only to clutch my chest in pain. There was nothing to clutch, nothing to hold on to. They were gone. The terrible *two* were…were what? Being dissected and studied? Tossed in an incinerator? Turned into coin purses? Hell, I don't know. What I do know is they were no longer where they were supposed to be, and I wasn't sure how I felt.

Charlotte sat with me through a lovely lunch of soup, tea, and Jell-O. Jell-O is and will always be wrong. It is unnatural and weird. I dislike Jell-O immensely. Charlotte, on the other hand, loved Jell-O, and I was all about sharing. We were eating and discussing whether or not I could be president of the itty bitty titty committee when Molly and my lovely girls walked in. I pulled the cover a bit tighter around me to shield them from seeing…seeing nothing. There was nothing to see.

"There they are," I reached out my hand to them as they rounded the bed on the opposite side as Charlotte.

"We got you something," gasped Lily.

"You're gonna love it," declared Shell. They set a gift bag on the bed next to me and tried to suppress giggles by covering their mouths tightly with their hands.

"What did you two do?" I asked reaching for the bag. I looked over to Molly for any clue as to what may pop out of the bag. She raised an eyebrow and shrugged to say she had no idea. I tucked my hand down into the bag and shifted the tissue paper around so I could grab whatever put the sparkle in my girls' eyes. I lifted a white teddy bear from the depths of the bag. It had a bright pink mask and a dress with "Super Mom" stitched across the chest.

"She's a super hero," blurted Shell, "She's your super hero."

Lily reached over and took the skirt in between her fingers and began to raise it, "Look under her skirt."

"What? Why?" I asked puzzled. Once I saw what they wanted me to see, I laughed. No fake *'oh how cute'* laughed but full out ugly laughed. It hurt but was worth it. Tucked under the layers of my super hero's skirt was a bright white pin that read *"I'm not wearing any underwear"* in hot pink letters.

Molly leaned over to see what was so funny and smiled, "You should put that on. It wouldn't be false." I didn't know which was more comical, the pin, or the fact Molly made a funny. We chuckled and clucked for a few minutes about the awesome gift my babies brought me. Our revelry was interrupted by a nurse holding a fresh gown and pushing a cart.

"Sorry ladies, but I need a moment with Mrs. Carpenter, please," she gestured to me, "we will only be a few minutes, and maybe you can convince her to walk down the hall and back." They all looked at me and agreed to wait outside until the nurse was finished. She closed the door, "Let's get your catheter out and get you dressed for a stroll with your cheer team out there."

"What? You mean I will have to actually get up and go into the bathroom to pee? Bummer, I was kinda liking the idea of never having to get up in the middle of the night to pee ever again." She laughed along with me and shifted the rolling table away from the bed. "Hey," I remembered, "you'll get a kick outta that," I point to the bear. "Lift up the skirt."

She eyed me like I was a perv but lifted the skirt anyway, "Bahahahaha...OMG! That is perfect!" She enjoyed our twisted sense of humor as much as I did. "Well, let's get some panties on you so we can prove the button wrong."

"Sounds like a plan to me." The catheter came out quickly and with little discomfort. Embarrassing as hell, but what was I gonna do?

I had packed a small bag of clothes and toiletries she pulled from a locker in the corner, "I'm going to help you to the bathroom, and you can brush your teeth and get cleaned up, then I will help you get dressed, okay?"

"Sounds good."

I asked her name, and she pointed to a white board on the wall which indicated who my nurse was that day. My nurse was Deana. Deana helped me out of bed and walked with me to the bathroom. I supported myself on the edge of the vanity while she gathered my toothbrush and paste. She laid out my items and exited to offer me some privacy. I brushed the fuzz from my teeth and washed my face, neck and other areas that needed attention. I gently and slowly lowered myself down onto the lid of the toilet and attempted to dress myself. I looked like a two-year-old trying to put on a turtleneck. It wasn't working out very well for me. Deana knocked on the bathroom door at the perfect moment.

"Come in, please. I can't pull my shorts up."

Deana pushed open the door and knelt before me, "I can help." She slipped my shorts over my feet and shimmied them up to my thighs, "You have to stand to get them the rest of the way up, but let's get these gowns around you first."

I had a gown on the right way and one on backwards as a mock robe and my shorts had been set right and pulled up. I was standing in the doorway of the bathroom in hospital issued slippers when Deana allowed my clan back in. "Mrs. Carpenter, why don't you try to walk a bit, and while you are gone, I will strip your bed and put on some fresh sheets."

"Okay...so which of you lovely ladies wants to hold me up?" Lily and Michelle took a side and held me gently as we did a promenade along the hall. I could see the girls were concerned, but they never said a word, so I did. "I'm okay, you know that, right?" They nodded their heads, but said nothing. "Ask?"

Lily looked at me with a question mark etched in her forehead, "Ask what?"

"Anything. Everything. But don't brush it under the rug like it doesn't matter. Ask me anything."

Shelly's mouth opened and closed and opened again. I stopped our slow movement along the wall and turned to my baby girl, "What? What do you want to know?"

"Um...well...where do...," she scratched her head in search of the words, then raised her eyes to lock on mine, "Mom, where do babies come from?"

That's my girl. :-)

Chapter Twenty Three

Tom was in my hospital room when the girls and I made our trip back. He was sitting on the edge of my freshly made bed talking with Charlotte and Molly. His head was low, but his voice was much lower. His fingers fiddled with the lid on his paper coffee cup, "Got one of those for me?" I asked while shuffling toward the bed. I was happy to see him but the bed missed me. That little trip wore my ass out.

He looked hurt. He pressed his hand over his heart, "Do you doubt I would bring you a cup? That hurts, Liv. Right here," he patted his hand over his heart.

"Forgive me," I winced as I tried to shift back into bed. Tom moved to try to help me get into place.

"You okay?" he asked in almost a whisper, "Do you need me to call a nurse?"

"I'm good. Just need a minute." He sat next to me holding my hand. I breathed through the pain and tried to relax. I turned to look at his worried face, "Babe?"

"I'm right here. What can I do?"

"Hand me my coffee."

He chuckled and reached over and pulled the rolling table over the bed, "I got you raspberry," he said, leaned down and gave me a very sweet kiss. You know the kind you give your ailing grandma.

What the hell was that?!

"Thanks. Now would you like to give me a real kiss?"

Shell gave a gag, "Gross."

"Get over it," Tom growled and gave me a real kiss, one that showed me he still wanted me sans boobage.

I gasped for air when he released me, "Now, that's what I'm talkin' 'bout!"

"I do what I can. Anything else I can do for you?"

"Not with an audience."

Molly cleared her throat, "Um…other people here. Maybe you didn't notice." They all gave Tom and me the eye.

"Okay, okay," Tom surrendered, throwing his hands up in defense. Tom moved to the chair. Molly and Charlotte sat on either side of the bed, and Lily went in search of more chairs. We sat and talked a bit about me. I wanted to talk about anything but. I tossed questions to Molly about her pregnancy and how she was feeling. She had miscarried in the past and was fearful, but hopeful because she had made it to thirteen weeks.

"Do you guys want to know what you're having, or do you want it to be a surprise?" Lily asked.

Molly smoothed her top over her non-existent belly, "Both. We want to know, but at the same time we want it to be a surprise."

"How will that work?" asked Tom.

"I have no idea," Molly giggled.

Charlotte lit up! I swear I could see the light bulb flash over her head, "Oh! I know! I know what you can do," she was giggling and bouncing on her toes.

"Do you plan on telling or should we guess?" asked Molly.

"All right, well, you could take someone to the appointment, not Wayne, but a friend. Then have the doctor scribble down what yer havin' and give it to the other person ya brought with ya. Then we have a party and the friend surprises ya with what ya be havin'. You know with balloons or something in the right color."

Silence. You could hear the wheels turning in everyone's heads.

"I like it!" squealed Molly.

And so...the planning began. About a half hour in Tom called it quits. It was not a conversation he had any interest in, "Babe, I'm gonna let you ladies figure all this out. But, not too long," he looked to the women surrounding me, "she needs to get some rest." Lily shot him a salute and he smiled. "I'll come back later and have dinner with you."

"That would be perfect," I sighed. He leaned in for a quick kiss and left me in the hands of four amazing ladies.

I pushed for Charlotte to be the one who went to the appointment with Molly. It was her idea ...and I hoped their budding friendship would grow stronger. Molly's appointment wasn't for a couple of weeks, and by then I would have started chemotherapy. Molly agreed and Charlotte beamed. Ideas were tossed around and jotted down, and I grew more and more tired.

"All right ladies, it looks like Liv is barely hanging on. Let's scoot so she can get some sleep," offered Molly.

I reached out and touched her hand, "Thanks." It was for more than the announcement to exit and I think she understood, thanks for opening up to my friend, thanks for coming, thanks for being family. She tendered me a smile. We said our "laters" and kisses were passed around. Then...sleep. It slipped in as the door slowly closed, and it glided a veil over my eyes, whisking me away.

I woke some time later to find Dr. Matthews sitting beside my bed. He wore jeans and a very well-fitting t-shirt...okay, it was drool worthy, but I wasn't interested, much. "What are you doing here?" I mumbled in my haze. I reached my hand up to my face to wipe away the sleep that hung there and any drool, in case I had been drooling in my sleep... or at him.

"I wanted to see how you were doing and ask why you had the flowers I sent dropped off at my office?"

"I hate cut flowers and Alyssa knows that."

"I see. Alyssa didn't know I was sending them."

I raised the head of the bed so I was in a more upright position to drop the hammer on this ass clown, "Then why the fuck did you put her name on them? If she had nothing to do with them, then her name shouldn't have been on the damn card."

He sat there staring at me like I was bonkers. Maybe I was, but that wasn't for him to judge. "I thought it would be a nice gesture and technically, it wasn't my place to tell her what was going on with you. She still doesn't know, Olivia."

I stiffened and winced, I sucked in air through clenched teeth, "And she shouldn't because I didn't tell her."

"She is still upset about your argument the other day," he leaned closer to the bed, "what will it take to fix this?"

"I don't know," I lay my head back on the bed, "I don't know if it can be."

Neil glanced around the room and then out the door. It was as if he were looking for something, answers to everything that went wrong. I followed his gaze to see what or who he was looking at. Alyssa. She stood stock still with her mouth agape.

"What the fuck is she doing here?" I hissed.

"I asked her to meet me at the nurse's station so I could take her to lunch," he feigned innocence.

"And the fact you have to pass this room to get to the nurses station happened to slip your mind?"

"No, actually it hadn't," he looked me in the eyes, "I hoped she would see me in here talking to you."

"You really are an asshole. I'm glad you will no longer be my doctor," I spit.

"Why?"

"Because I'm terminal, and you know it." I didn't know if he actually knew or not, but I assumed. He could have easily found out, right?

"Well, are you going to invite her in?"

"It's a public space and besides, I didn't invite her, you did."

Neil raised his hand and waved Alyssa in. She seemed to hesitate, each step had a hint of reservation attached to it. "What happened to you? Did Richard get out of jail and come after you again?" she asked as panic sliced across her face. She stood there clutching her purse to her chest and breathing hard.

"No."

Neil touched my arm and I jerked it away, regretting it the moment the shot of pain screamed up my arm, "You should tell her."

"Why don't you do it doc? You set this whole thing up," I growled from anger, or was it the pain?

A knock interrupted the haze of discomfort in the room, "Mrs. Carpenter, I'm here to check your I.V." Deana explained as she crossed the room to the I.V. stand. "Hello, Dr. Matthews, nice to see you."

"Deana, always a pleasure." I watched Alyssa's eyes scan Deana then move to Neil and lock. What the hell was that, and did I even care? Maybe...a little.

"We will be disconnecting the I.V. later, once we are comfortable you can take pain meds by mouth. Maybe after dinner," Deana explained as she wrote a few notes on my chart.

"Okay." She slipped from the room as quickly as she had come in.

Alyssa's eyes never left Neil's, "What's going on?" I got the feeling the question covered more than what was going on with me.

"Ally, Olivia had surgery yesterday," he looked to me for permission to continue and I gave it, "She had a double mastectomy. Olivia has cancer, baby." He was so gentle in how he explained it to her, why had no one been that gentle with me?

Alyssa's eyes jumped to mine, "Why didn't you tell me?"

"Why would I? We haven't had a conversation in the past few weeks that didn't lead to a fight," I shrugged. "Besides, I didn't want to take the chance you would call me a liar." I dropped that little dig and watched it bore a hole in her. Her jaw hung lax, and I watched as her eyes filled until the tears started to fall.

Neil got up and went to her side to brush the tears away, "How long have you known?" she asked him.

He looked over at me, then down at the floor, "I found the lumps."

313

"Why didn't you tell me?"

"He couldn't, doctor/ patient confidentiality," I bit out. "Sorry it is such an inconvenience to you."

"Fuck, Olivia! You know I would have been here through all this," she said as she acknowledged the room with a wave of her hand.

"I have enough shit to deal with. I didn't need to add you to the pile."

"You are such a bitch."

"Alyssa," snapped Neil.

"Well, she is."

"Yup, I'm a bitch and," I add, "I'm dying."

She looked to Neil in total disbelief, "Yes," he said, "she is."

"Oh my God..." she gasped with her hand over her lips.

"What are you doing here?" barked Tom, "You okay, babe?" he asked as he strode through the room to my side. "I asked you already, why are you here?"

"I wanted to see how Olivia was doing," Neil turned and took Alyssa's hand, "We should go." Alyssa stared at some mystical point in front of her and gave no response. "Take care, Olivia."

I spent the next thirty minutes filling Tom in on the ambush I awoke to.

God, I needed another nap after that crap storm. So I took one and I think I'm gonna take one now.

*****

It was well past visiting hours, and I lay alone in my room staring at the wall. The TV was on, but I hadn't even looked at the screen. So much had happened, and I was trying to get it all straight in my head. The world pushed my little problem to the side to make room for Molly's baby, Alyssa's set-up by Neil, my Lily leaving in two days, fucking flowers, Charlotte helping Molly, super hero teddy bears, Shelly's funny ass question, and Tom's kisses.

"Mrs. Carpenter, I'm Cade, your night nurse."

Holy Mother of God! He was amaze-balls!

314

"Hi, call me Olivia, please."

His magazine cover smile snaked across his pristine face to only be interrupted by the most perfect dimples, "Okay, Olivia. I am going to check your vitals, give you your pain medication, and anything else you may need."

That is a loaded offer if I ever heard one.

"Okay." I offered up my leg for the blood pressure cuff and opened my mouth for the thermometer. We went through the motions and were done in no time at all. I took the little white paper cup and tossed back the chalky tablets and washed them down with the water Cade offered.

"Is there anything else I can get you?"

"Actually, could you help me up? I would like to go to the restroom before I settle in for the night."

"Absolutely," Cade offered me his arm and provided the help I needed to maneuver out of the bed. He helped steady me as I made my way to the bathroom. "I will wait out here. If you need help just call my name."

If you need… yes, I …no I didn't.

"Thanks, I'll be right out." I did what I had to do. I brushed my teeth, washed my face and hands, then shuffled to the bathroom door. He was right there as he had said he would be, "Can I try to make it on my own to the bed? I need to start moving around on my own, right?"

"Sure, I will just follow you in case you need a hand." I managed the short trip by myself. Cade helped me climb back under the covers and settle in for the night. "The meds should be kicking in shortly. Sleep well," he wished and wrapped the call button cable around the railing near my hand. "Call if you need anything."

"Thanks…" I mumbled as I started to drift off to sleep.

I was watching as Michelle walked down the aisle at her wedding. She was beautiful, and Lily was her matron of honor. But why was I so far away? Shouldn't I be in the front row watching my baby girl get married? I saw Tom hand Shell off to a young man and take his seat in the front. I made my way through friends and family to where Tom sat…holding another woman's hand. He smiled as he watched our daughter say her vows, and he looked at this woman at his side and placed a gentle kiss on her lips. No...no...no...those were my kisses. He smiled at me that way. Not her. I yelled at him to stop, but no sound came out. I reached for him to push him away from that strange woman, but my hands landed on nothing. The scene disappeared only to be replaced by another.

"She's beautiful, Lil," cooed Tom as he looked down in his arms where he held a baby. "She looks just like..."

"Mom," Lily smiled, "I know."

I wanted to see. I wanted to see my granddaughter, but I couldn't get close enough. Something held me back.

"Here ya go, honey," said a woman handing a glass to Lily, "Now scoot, Tom, I wanna see my grandbaby."

No! No! That's my granddaughter, not yours! Why couldn't they hear me, see me? I want to see the baby, let me see her!

"It's so sweet you named her after your mother," that woman stated, "She would have been so proud of you."

I am proud. I have always been proud of her and Shelly. What's going on? I reached out to touch the bundle in that woman's arms only for it to disappear. No!

I was standing on a beach with two sets of footsteps in the sand before me. I followed them with my eyes to see an older couple walking hand in hand. I walked closer and closer, my heart in my throat with each step.

"I love you, babe," he whispered as he kissed her cheek.

"Oh, Tom, I love you too."

I sunk to my knees and screamed. No one heard me. My life had been taken by another woman. Where was I? Why wasn't I here with him? I slammed my fists against the sand as it turned into grass, thick, green, warm grass. It was warm and I could feel the sun caressing my face. I could smell flowers, lots and lots of flowers. I got to my feet and looked out around me...rows and rows of headstones. Oh God! Who died? I looked down at the stone that lay at my feet to see my name in weathered letters etched into the gray granite. I dropped back down to my knees and cried. I lay there weeping when I heard footsteps coming closer to where I was curled up. The sound stopped at my feet.

"Oh, Liv, I miss you so." I looked up to see an old man standing there holding a potted tulip. *"We should have been together forever, but fate had other plans. I did find someone to share my life with. I have been happy like you said I would be, but you were always my love, my Liv."*

"Grandpa, are you ready to go yet?" whined a young girl. She had my eyes.

"Olivia Grace, don't talk to your grandfather like that," scolded Lily. *"Whenever you're ready, dad."*

"I'm ready," Tom leaned over and placed the tulip next to the headstone. He stroked his hand along the cold stone that held my name, *"Love you, babe. See you soon."*

No...No...No!

"Olivia...Olivia...Mrs. Carpenter?"

I jerked awake and felt the pain radiate through my heart. It wasn't physical pain that ripped through me but the pain of loss.

"Mrs. Carpenter? Are you alright?" Cade asked as he took my pulse.

"Huh, what?"

"It looked like you were having a nightmare. Are you okay?"

I blinked my eyes to clear the fog that hung like a curtain, "Yeah, it was a dream." I scrubbed at my face with my hands to try to erase the visions. I pulled my hands away to find them wet with tears I had shed in my sleep.

"Here," Cade offered me a small box of sandpaper disguised as tissues to wipe away the dream. "Are you sure you're okay?"

"Yeah, it was just a dream," I smiled, "I'm fine, thanks."

"Okay...call if you need anything. Even if it's to talk, okay?

"Yeah, thanks." Cade slipped from sight and the dream replayed itself from memory and I cried. What did it mean? The wedding, a baby, that woman, the beach...my grave? Life would and must go on without me. Was that it? Me realizing they, all of them, would move on? My babies would get married and have children of their own, and my Tom would find someone else? I cried some more. I was going to be wiped away. I wasn't going to be there for any of those moments. I wasn't going to plan weddings or hold grandbabies. I wasn't going to grow old with Tom. I was going to die, soon. I cried and cried until I fell back to sleep, a very dark, very lonely sleep.

Time was running out...my time was running out.

Tick tock, fast went my clock.

Chapter Twenty-four

"We'll get you out of here today," smiled Dr. Fraiser. "I'll have your nurse come in and explain how to care for your incisions and the drainage lines. I will remove the tubes and bulbs at your follow-up appointment."

"Thank God, I am so ready to get outta here," I sighed in relief, "I want a bath and my bed."

"Talk to the nurse about how to bathe safely. You have to stick to sponge baths for the time being."

"Sponge bath, milk bath, Turkish bath, I don't much care what you call it as long as I can remove the stench of hospital, I'll take it."

Dr. Fraiser and I talked about the nightmare. "I was informed that you had a nightmare last night." I chose not to respond. What was the point? She was already informed that I did. "It's not unusual to have nightmares on certain types of medication. Maybe we should reevaluate the prescriptions."

"I don't think it was the meds."

"Oh, what do you think caused it?"

I looked down at myself and waved a hand to indicate all of me, "Reality."

"You may be right." She said it was normal. My mind was finally starting to see what lay ahead...or what didn't lay ahead for me. I had to start coming to grips with what will be. Treatment could only buy me time, not forever. I had to be wise with the time I had left. I had to make a plan. I had things I wanted and needed to do.

Deana was my nurse again that day, and she ran through how to do a proper sponge bath and what to watch for. Infection was my biggest battle to fight at this point. I did a practice run on my own before Tom came to bring me home. Deana helped me dress in yoga pants and t-shirt. It was the first time in decades I put on a top without a bra. No bra...I almost felt naked. It was a strange sensation to not feel that band hug my chest and the straps digging into my shoulders. I looked down...straight down to the slippers on my feet. Nothing blocked my view. Weird.

I settled back in my bed and decided to make a plan. I wanted to be a part of the future even though I knew I wouldn't be there, physically. I would find a way to have a voice in the tomorrows I wouldn't see. I scribbled down thoughts and ideas, tossed around plans and hopes. I decided on things and tossed others. I had things I needed to do now, but instead I killed time. I popped in my ear buds and let music take me to another place. I let the joy, anger, love, and loss of others carry me away willingly. I let the theme of *The Breakfast Club* make my demand. I wasn't going to allow myself to be easily forgotten.

I opened my eyes sometime later to the voices of my family converging on me. I tossed my phone and ear buds aside to enjoy the music that was their voices. It was late afternoon which caused the discussion of what drive-through to visit on the way home.

"No," bitched Shell, "I work there. Why would I want to eat there?"

With a confused look Lily asked, "The question is why wouldn't you? Like ya said, you work there."

"Because I know what really happens in the kitchen and if they knew it was me placing an order...let's just say we wouldn't want to eat the food."

"That's kinda scary," I chirped. "Don't I get a say in where we eat?"

"Of course you do," clarified Tom, "They just want to influence your choice."

"Shelly sure as hell did. We won't be eating there...ever."

We discussed the merits of each fast food place in the area and decided on pizza. I liked pizza. I won. All we had to do was wait for the paperwork that said I was released. The girls skirted around the room collecting my things and stuffing them haphazardly into my bag. When all was crammed in, the girls flopped onto the bed with me and waited for Deana.

"Excited to leave are we?" chuckled Deana as she came in with a stack of papers.

"I'm starving, and we can't go eat until you spring our mom from this medicated prison," clucked Shell as she hung her head back off the edge of the bed.

"That's what I am here to do." I signed my name a half a dozen times and listened as Deana re-introduced me to the aftercare instructions and "what to look for" sheet. My follow-up appointment card was amongst the pile as well, next Thursday. Eight days of sponge baths. I needed a bigger sponge. "Okay, it looks like you are all set to go. Mr. Carpenter, if you want to bring your car around to the exit on this side of the building, I will wheel Olivia out to you."

Tom shoved his hand in his pocket and extracted his keys, "On it."

Lily smiled, and grabbed my bag, and jogged to catch up with her dad, she looped her arm threw the crook of his elbow and sang, "We're outta here."

Deana brought the wheelchair to where I sat on the bed, "Do I really have to ride out in that?"

"We like to take our customers out in style," Deana stated in her best snotty concierge voice.

"Well, in that case, by all means," I claimed my stylish seat and allowed Deana to parade me down the hall to the exit where Tom waited.

*****

Shell sent out a text from my phone letting everyone know I was home safe but wanted some much needed family time before Lily left the next day. With interruptions put at bay, we settled in and spent time together. Lily didn't have to be at the Military Entrance Processing Station (MEPS) hotel until five p.m. the next day. I had a little over 24 hours, and I was going to use every minute. Lily got me settled onto the couch with pillows and blankets, much to Tom's dismay, "You should be in bed, not down here." I agreed, but explained we needed the room to spread out and spend time being us. "Fine, but I am laying right there," he pointed to the space between the couch and coffee table, the space right below me. No argument came from my lips.

Once blankets and pillows were stacked and piled, we ordered pizzas and laid out a buffet on the coffee table. I fought taking my pain meds in fear they would put me to sleep, but the pain won out and so did sleep. Sadly I lost two precious hours of time with my amazing girl. When my eyes opened, I found her sitting at the end of the couch with my feet in her lap. She was laughing at something her sister had said. I lay silent and watched two of the most important people in my life share memories and build new ones. Tom sat across the room from me in his recliner. His eyes were on me. I gave him a soft smile. "Welcome back, babe. Are you hungry?" he asked moving in my direction.

"Yeah, I am. Did you guys save me anything?

"Pepperoni, extra cheese, black olives and spinach waiting for you, Madre," said Shell as she piled pizza onto a paper plate. "What do ya want to drink?"

"Water's good," I said trying to get up from the couch.

Lily stood to stop my rise, "Hey, hey now, where do ya think you're goin'?"

"To pee," I grinned.

"In that case," she helped steady me, "do you need help?"

"Um...I think I can pee fine without you, but thanks for the offer."

"Gross, and I meant do you need help getting there, duh."

We both laughed at the idea of Lily assisting me in the bathroom, "No, I can make it on my own," I was still chuckling as I shuffled off to the bathroom.

Once I was settled back on the couch and chewing on a piece of cold pizza, the TV lit up with home movies. I sat in awe of how they had grown and how Tom and I had aged. I laughed and cried and wished and wished and wished for more of everything. Those hours were filled with remember when's, and I remembered them all, and I was so happy they all did too. We watched Lily's favorite movies and criticized her choice in films, "God, you get your lack of good movie choices from your dad. You two just love B rated movies," I whined, "Must we watch *Tank Girl*...again?"

Lil grinned and slid the DVD in and pushed play, "Yup, and don't you think it's fitting since I'm leaving for the Air Force tomorrow?"

"No, considering there aren't any genetically engineered kangaroos waiting for you in basic," I mocked.

"That you know of," she tossed back. I couldn't argue with the unknown, which was for sure. I bowed my head signaling she won the argument and was proud she did. Tom did not get to sleep where he wanted. Instead, as the evening inched by Lily came and sat on the floor near my shoulder and laid her head next to mine on the pillow. We whispered and talked beyond the ability of Tom and Michelle to stay awake.

At some point we fell asleep. I woke in the early hours of morning needing help with my discomfort. I reached out to get my pills when I heard, "Let me get that," from the gruff freshly woken voice of Tom, "Can you sit up?"

I shifted my body to push myself upright, "I'd like to sit outside for a bit," I got to my feet and moved toward the back door and my favorite place.

Tom met me at the patio table with water, two tablets, and a blanket he draped over my body, "Are you feeling okay?" he asked, his words heavy with concern.

"I'm fine. I haven't been outside in days and needed to feel the night sky on my skin, ya know," I lay my head back and looked up at the star-filled sky and watched as the colors changed over time and became dawn. I looked and saw Tom had fallen back asleep in the chair next to me. His feet were propped up on another chair, his arms crossed over his chest, and his head sloped to one side. I watched the rise and fall as his chest expanded and deflated with each breath. He was beautiful. Not in a "pretty boy" kind of way, I could never be with a guy who spent more time in front of the bathroom mirror fixing his hair than I did. I wanted a man who was without a doubt a man, and I got him. There had been many times over the years I needed the man he was to hold me up, to give me strength. I leached off his strength and he let me. He offered it up without hesitation. He gave me his shoulder and held out his hand to me, he wrapped me in his love and protection without concern for himself. He loved me and I him.

I sat and watched him as the sun rose in the sky. I thought about the nightmare I had and came to see it wasn't a nightmare at all. It was the foretelling of the future, the future my family deserved once I left them forever. I loved him so much I wanted nothing more than for Tom to find happiness once I could no longer give it myself. The plan started to build in my head and my heart. It was the right thing to do and I would do just that. I was jolted from my thoughts by the luscious smell of coffee and the smiling face of my Lily. She placed the mug in front of me and cradled one of her own, "Morning," she whispered looking at her father sleeping inches from me.

"Good morning to you. Why are you up? It's very early."

"It is, and you disappeared. I wanted to make sure you were okay."

"Your dad hasn't left my side," I smiled, "I bet he would even offer to help me in the bathroom." We both chuckled.

"Would you let me if I offered?" yawned Tom.

"Doubtful."

"You're no fun. Hey, where's my coffee?" he whined.

Lily raised her cup to her lips and smirked, "In the pot."

He pushed away from the table and got to his feet. With a deep stretch he pointed at Lily, "Did ya hear that? She left my coffee alone in the pot," he shook his head. "That's just wrong, so wrong." He yawned again and went in search of his abandoned coffee.

"Shell still snoring in there?" I asked.

"God, I am so glad we have separate rooms, cuz that buzz saw would drive me nuts."

"You're no peach to sleep with either. You are a serious bed hog."

"So, it's not like I'm sharing my bed with anyone."

"True, but still," I mumbled reaching for my cooling mug, "you would come in at night when you were little, and before morning, your dad would be on the couch and your feet would be in my face." We laughed at the image of her toes stuffed up my nose. I wouldn't have traded it for anything. Nothing.

"What would you ladies like to do for breakfast?" asked Tom from inside the screened door.

I thought for a moment and smiled, "I could make you French toast. How does that sound?"

"Can you? I mean, are you okay to do it?" Lily asked a little concerned.

I shrugged, "Why not? It's not like I'm gonna run a marathon and I have you to help me."

"Sounds like we're having French toast," declared Tom from the kitchen.

It was a perfect opportunity to teach them how to make the French toast they loved so much. Maybe I should make a little cookbook for them and Molly? God knows Molly needs it.

"Okay, so now you have cracked the eggs into the bowl, add a teaspoon of vanilla, a half a teaspoon of sugar and half a teaspoon of cinnamon...good, now whisk the hell out of it."

"Why are we doing this and not you?" asked Shell as she watched her sister beat the crap out of a half dozen eggs.

I shrugged, "My arms hurt, and I don't think I have the strength to do it alone."

Lily eyed me with doubt, "Is that the only reason?"

I looked down at my hands and picked at my nails before answering, "No," and that was the close of that questioning. "Texas toast bread works great or sliced French bread. It's all about what you like. I think we have some Texas toast in the fridge." I continued the lesson without a drop of the hat. Teaching them how to cook bacon was a lesson all in itself. Eek! They were more afraid of bacon grease pops than a swarm of snakes. Yelps and squeals could be heard down the block. Through it all Tom recorded the event in pictures. It was fun and heart wrenching at the same time. I wondered if they felt the same way.

"Great job, ladies," praised Tom as he leaned back in his chair patting his full belly, "I must say, I never thought burnt French toast could taste so good." A collection of napkins flew across the table at him in protest to his snarky comment. "What? I was serious. It was good," he defended, poorly.

I did what I could to help clean up, then slowly climbed the stairs. I was in need of a sponge bath. I followed the instruction, but still needed Tom's help trying to wash my hair. That was a hot mess. Live and learn right? Well, in my case live as much as possible and learn as I went. I was determined to stay awake and spend my time wisely with Lily. She was my priority that day, not me.

Once I was clean and dressed Tom helped me back down the stairs to the couch, "You should take your pain pills, babe."

"No, maybe a couple Advil will take the edge off, but I don't want to chance falling asleep." He shook his head, but went and got the bottle and a glass of water.

"Mom, if you are in pain take the meds. I don't want you to suffer to stay awake," Lily persisted.

"I would suffer more if I fell asleep and missed time with you," I explained with a tear stuck in my throat, "I want to be with you, not dream about being with you, okay?"

"Yeah, I get it," she smiled and took my hand and gave it a quick squeeze, "I'm gonna hit the shower before Shell uses all the hot water. I'll be right back."

Michelle slid into the room like she was sliding across a Broadway stage, or at least a scene out of *Risky Business*. "What are we doing today, parental peoples?"

"Spending it with your sister," said Tom taking her by the hand and pulling her along the floor in her socked feet like he did when she was small. Memories of when she would pretend the floor was ice and slide across it with very little grace flooded my mind. Even now, there was no grace involved. It made me smile, but made my heart constrict tightly in my chest. I watched as Oliver walked across the floor and stop to stare at the ridiculous sight playing out in the living room. It almost seemed like he shook his head at them, then turned and hopped up on the couch with me. He didn't climb on me like he usually would. He sat next to me and laid his head on my thigh. I scratched his head and petted him gently, "They're silly, aren't they, Oliver?"

"Puurrr..." That was good enough for me.

The day progressed too rapidly for me. Wayne and Molly came by to see Lily before she went off on her whirlwind adventure. Wayne poked fun at her for being a puny girl going into the military. He didn't mean it, it was just in fun. Molly still couldn't understand why she would want to wear the same outfit every day and look like everyone else. Where was the fun in that? Through all the joking and fun everyone seemed to keep a close eye on me. I wished I didn't take the focus off my Lily. I wished I could take back a lot of things over the years. Wishes in one hand, shit in the other...which fills faster? If nothing else, Lily got to see how much she was loved by friends and family. There was a constant stream of knocks at the door and texts blowing up her phone wishing her well and a safe journey. Her girlfriends wanted pictures of hot guys in uniform. I think one or two of her guy friends asked the same. God help us if Shell asked too. We took pictures and poked fun and cried and loaded up the car. Then we argued...

"I am perfectly fine to go for a car ride."

"You haven't taken any pain meds all day, and I can tell you are hurting. You need to rest," demanded Tom.

"Telling me I have to rest doesn't mean I will, and if you make me stay home while my baby leaves for basic training, I can guarantee I will NOT rest."

"Fine," he spit in frustration, "but when we get home, you take your meds and go to bed, understand?"

"Jawohl," I barked with a German salute. Such a dictator.

"Come on, ya smartass. Let me help you to the car."

"Are we taking Caroline?"

"Only the best for my soldier," Tom smiled, but sadness remained around his eyes.

The trip took less time than I had hoped. She didn't have to be there to check in until five but we showed up a half hour early. I refused to let her go until I absolutely had too. I wanted to give her a real hard hug, but I couldn't without pain radiating through my body.

"I'm sorry I can't hug you properly. It sucks," I whined.

Lily took hold of my hands, "I know you love me. How could you not? I'm half of you and half of the guy you married. So, I'm whole awesome." We laughed and leaned our foreheads together.

"I am so very proud of you, sweetie. I know you can do this. It won't be a cake walk, but you are strong and so smart. Be proud of yourself, okay? It takes balls to do this."

"I can do this, because strength runs in the family. You'll see," she whispered. I nodded my head and watched her hug her little sister and be engulfed by her dad. Hugs and kisses were passed around, and around, and...well you get the picture. By the time Lily walked to the check-in desk, she only had a few minutes to spare. She checked in, turned, waved, and disappeared down a hall.

Ozzy serenaded us with *Mama, I'm Coming Home* on our journey back home. I knew Lil was going to be gone for a while, but I would hear those words from her, "Mom, I'm coming home." I just had to be patient and strong. I had so much to do to prepare for the end. I had gifts to leave and letters to write, and I needed to start, now.

Tom did everything short of carry me up the stairs to our bed. He helped me change into some comfy pj's and settled me in for the night. I took the pills he thrust in front of me with little argument. I was in need of them, and I knew I would be asleep in no time at all. Tom kissed me soundly, ordered me to sleep, then slipped from the room. I settled my head down as my cuddle-buddy sauntered his way up the bed. Oliver lay tightly against my right side but did not search out space on my chest as he would any other time. Did he know something wasn't right? Could he tell? Hmm...I stared at the ceiling wondering what Lily was doing so I sent her a quick text before my eyes slammed shut.

I love you and am proud of the choices you have made for yourself. You are strong, smart, beautiful, and full of Carpenter spirit. You can do anything you put your mind to.

I reached my left hand over and scratched Oliver's fuzzy head, "She's an amazing kid, ya know that right? Night, buddy."

I will always be proud of my girls.

I embraced sleep as I would a gentle lover and prayed the nightmares would be kept at bay, allowing me peace.

Chapter Twenty-five

I woke with a chuckle. I had a dream Bill Murray was Lily's drill sergeant. It was like a replay of St*ripes*… *"That's the fact jack."* I knew Lily's adventures would be nothing like that but I found it amusing and it was a much needed break from the dreams I had been having. The fact I was sleeping soundly was a blessing as well. It had been eleven days since my surgery and seven since Lily marched off into her future. The pathology reports had come back to confirm the diagnosis and prognosis. That spurred on more nightmares, but it also forced me to plan the last chapter of my life in spite of them. The dark dreams still visited, but once I thought them through, they weren't so scary, just sad realities of what lay ahead.

The only thing that truly ticked me off over the last week was the neighbors. They had caught wind of what was going on behind our front door. I received text messages, phone calls, Facebook postings, and even visits. Thankfully none were from Nadine. Most of them were to confirm the rumors spread by Nadine, and were short lived. Others were from people who actually gave a shit about what was going on and wanted to help. Help? How exactly were they gonna do that? Were they gonna volunteer to do chemo or maybe I would do chemo and their hair would fall out. Maybe I would have the poisonous chemicals pumped into my body but they get to vomit for days on end...so, how were they going to help me?

Oh well, life went on and would with or without me. To prove the point I worked on planning my participation in my family's future even when I was merely a ghost. With Molly and Charlotte's help, I had been able to get a few of the things to start the process. I had been working on letters and cards to be given on days I should have been there for: birthdays, graduations, weddings, grandbabies. I wrote and cried. I poured love into the ink and spread it across the pages so my family would feel my love for them in the times to come. I tried to focus on the things I could do versus the things I would never do. I could write, I could leave words, wishes, and love for those around me.

When I could no longer rip my own heart out, I helped Charlotte plan the gender party for Molly. She showed me ideas she had scoured the internet for hours to gather. She had an entire binder full of plans. Pinterest had become her new best friend. We had created a monster. An intervention was in the works. Molly's doctor appointment wasn't for another two and a half weeks, but it was clear Charlotte was excited, maybe more than Molly was. I was happy to see they had started to form a real friendship over the last few weeks. It was good to see and sad to know it was my diagnosis that pushed them together. What difference did it make? They were friends now and that was all that mattered.

"You up?"

I rolled to see Tom standing in the door way, "Nope."

"I guess I get to drink this warm, milky, sweet cup of coffee I made for Olivia, but since she's still asleep," he raised the mug to his lips when I reached my hands out for it.

"Gimme," I whined and puffed out my lower lip in a pout.

He remained standing, "Only when you actually get out of bed. Come on, you can do it," he coaxed, "That's it, come on." I unfolded myself from the comfort and warmth of our bed and resigned myself to the fact I had to get out of bed anyway, my follow-up appointment was today. "Just think, you may actually be able to take a shower after this appointment," he wiggled his eyebrows and handed me my coffee, "I could even wash your back."

I took a long sip of my morning elixir, "I'm not so sure you're gonna wanna see all this," I waved my hand down the front of my body, "This old gray mare, she ain't what she used to be."

"Enough," he growled, "I am fucking sick of hearing you cut yourself down about this," he gestured to my less than ample cleavage, "I don't give a fuck about your tits, or not having tits. I love you. You have got to stop wallowing in this self-pity bull-shit. It's time to put on your big girl pants and get in this fucking fight," he spit, "It's time to bring out the bitch you have chained up in there somewhere. You are stronger than this," he took the cup I was hugging to my bandaged chest and set it on the dresser to pull me into his arms. "You have to fight," he whispered in my ear, "Fight for more."

"More?" I whimpered into his shoulder.

"More time, more life, more us."

"More," I let the word roll around in my mouth and sit on my tongue. Yes, I wanted more, but I knew I wouldn't get what I wanted, at least as much as I wanted. He was right though. It was time to bring out the bitch. I had a lot of ugly coming my way and I had to be strong enough to handle it.

Tom pushed away slightly and took my face in his hands, "Get cleaned up and dressed and I will make you a fresh cup of coffee, okay?" I nodded. "Good," he rested his lips to my forehead and whispered, "I love you," then spun and walked out of the room.

I stared at where he once stood, wondering how to be as strong as he believed I could be. I had to fight for so much in my life but I had never had to fight for my life – well, fight for some more time in the life I had. This was a losing battle after all. Screw that, this game wasn't over yet. It was time to bring out the fight, release the B.I.T.C.H. and fight for what's mine.

Two completely different people in two completely different lives could be dealt an identical hand of cards. How is it that one wins while the other loses? Desire? Fortitude? Skill or is it the B.I.T.C.H. factor? The strength needed to survive. I had to call on it several times in my life to continue breathing through an abusive childhood, mom's "friends," a boyfriend who liked to hit, lay-offs, empty wallets, and figuring out how to feed four people with nothing more than a package of ramen noodles, a chunk of polish sausage, and leftover vegetables. Yeah, I had the B.I.T.C.H. factor...in spades. All I had to do was figure out if it would help me out at all in that situation.

I sipped coffee from the travel mug Tom gave me as we drove to the medical center. I wanted to get things moving. I had a lot to get done and not a lot of time to do it. "What comes after this appointment?" asked Tom.

"What do you mean? Like, later today, or next procedure?"

"The second one."

I really wasn't sure, "I think I have to have my heart checked to see if it is strong enough to handle chemo." Tom nodded his head slowly and swallowed another gulp of his coffee.

We had barely settled into the waiting room when my name was called. Tom stayed put and I followed the aide in periwinkle blue scrubs down the hall. She was moving rather quickly.

"Dr. Fraiser will need you to remove everything from the waist up. Here's a gown for you to put on. She will be in shortly," and off she went. It appeared she was having a bad day or really needed to pee. I was leaning toward "peeing," just cuz it was funny. I let the smile hang on my lips while I shuffled out of my loose t-shirt and slid on the thin gown. I sat on the examination table and waited for the good doctor. She tapped on the door only moments later.

"Morning, Olivia. How are you feeling?" she asked while claiming a seat in a rolling stool.

Why do they ask ridiculous questions like that? It made no sense to me, she knew how I was – light two boobs. "I have nothing to compare it to, but I seem to be doing fine."

"Good. Let's take a look and see if we can remove these drainage tubes." She carefully removed the bandages and thoroughly examined each incision for signs of infection, "It all looks good," she offered as she began searching the cabinets for the medieval tools needed to extract the hoses dangling from my body.

"Is this gonna hurt?"

"Yes, but not horribly. These," she indicated the tubes, "have been in your body for a week and a half so it will be uncomfortable taking them out."

"Well, it's this or I get to have these bulb thingies banging around my hips for the remainder of my life. Um…no."

Dr. Fraiser called for assistance. Thankfully it was not periwinkle scrubs. Doc was right…it fucking hurt. But, it wasn't as bad as everything I had already gone through or what I would be going through soon enough. The silver lining was I could go home and take a much needed shower. I was sore but ready for some soap and water. I wanted to kiss Dr. Fraiser.

"There are a few openings in the schedule for cardiac testing tomorrow," Dr. Fraiser informed me while she was placing small bandages on the four holes left by the vacated tubes. Unfortunately, the tube hanging out of my chest would have to remain until…the end.

"Okay, should I talk to them at the desk?"

"Yes, they already know what the next step is for you, so just make the appointment out there."

"Can do. Am I good to go?"

She removed the latex gloves and tossed them into the biohazard can by the door, "You are good to go. Get dressed and I will have someone take you to the front desk."

"Thanks."

I found myself back in the truck sipping on the cold coffee in my travel mug. "My appointment is at 11:30 tomorrow. I can see if Molly or Charlotte can go with me. I know things are getting backed up at the garage."

"You don't mind? I'll go if you want."

"No, it's fine. It's a few tests, nothing major, right," I took another sip, "So are you gonna go in after you drop me off at home?"

Tom looked over at me, "Why would I do that?"

"Why wouldn't you? I'm gonna take a much needed shower and putter around the house. Go if you want to go, I'll be fine."

"What if I want to wash your back?" he smiled.

"Why woul-"

"Don't."

"Don't what?"

Tom turned into the driveway, cut the ignition and turned to face me, "Don't start talking bullshit about how you look. Don't assume I am any less attracted to you than I was two weeks ago. Just don't."

Well, ain't that peachy? I pissed him off, "I didn't."

"You were going to." I couldn't argue with that.

I stood in the bathroom no longer stunned by what I saw. Angry scars in place of the indicators that signaled to others I was a woman. They were a beacon. A giant arrow pointing out I was a girl. Not anymore.

"You're beautiful."

"How can you say that?" I argued.

"Because you are breathing."

I huffed, but not at him. I huffed because of him. He saw me, not the scars. He loved me, not my breasts. I was an idiot. "Come on, let's take a shower and maybe I'll let you wash my back." I took Tom's hand and led him to the water.

I can't explain how much better I felt after that shower. My hair was clean, my skin squeaked, and I smelt sooo much better. I no longer offended everyone. Hell, I offended myself. I lay in our bed and relaxed. Tom had washed my back and other areas of need, then carried me to our room and "washed" me some more.

What?! I ain't dead yet. ;)

I felt loved. I felt blessed. I felt tired. I shooed Tom back to the garage to spend time with his friends and to catch up on work and I took a nap.

I was pulled from sleep by the shift of the mattress. I opened one eye and saw Shell's body lying next to me. She was facing away from me so I curled my arm around her sun-warmed form and nudged her to move closer. She intertwined our fingers together, "I'm sorry if I woke you up."

"It's okay. I needed to get up anyway," I squeezed her as best I could, "What have you been up to today?"

"Work."

"And now what? You going out?"

"Nah, I think I'll hang out here for a while. I need to do some laundry. The sniff test failed a few times."

"Failed?"

"Yup, I can only wear things so many times before they reek and I have to wash them."

I smiled, "You are one sick puppy and you smell like one, too." We lay quietly for a little while. I listened to her breathe. I laid my ear to her back and listened to her heart beat. She was so strong, so energetic, and so alive. I wanted nothing more than to be there...always. "Okay, chuckles, let's get your laundry going so you don't scare people away with your stench."

"Meh."

I gave her a shove and laughed at her lazy attitude, "Come on. I'll even help. Maybe," I held my hand out as a sign to help me up.

Shell sat down next to me and sighed, "You don't have to help me mom. Do you need me to do any of your stuff?"

"I need you to help me up," I smiled, "Laundry sucks so why not get some help with it." Not only does it suck but it takes forever which meant I would get to spend time with my little girl. I interrogated her about her life and dreams. I questioned her about boys and gave advice. I answered questions and wiped tears.

"Baby, we're all terminal. From the moment we are born, we are terminal. The only difference is I have a general idea of when my expiration date is."

"How can you be so fucking calm about it? You're gonna die."

I wrapped Michelle in my weak arms and held her to me, "Calm? No, I'm not calm about it. I just realized it was a waste of time, and much needed energy, to fight anything other than the cancer itself. I want the time I have left to be filled with you, your dad, and sister," I held her at arm's length and looked into her glistening eyes, "I want to laugh and love and build memories. I want to watch the flowers bloom and see them grow. I want peace." Her tears came in a steady stream, her breathing picked up and she began to sob. "Cry, it's okay. I cry. I cry, but I will not allow this crap storm to stop me from loving and living every day I have left."

"But I don't want you to die."

"Me neither, but we didn't get a vote. All we can do is live strong until then." I held her close again and let her tears fall on my shoulder. I cradled each one and allowed them to take root in my heart.

*****

I found myself sitting in front of my laptop for the first time with a goal. I began to share the events as they happened with no lies to soften the blows, no smiles to hide the tears. I had a plan. I knew what I wanted to say and I needed to get down to it before time ran out.

"Hey, woman, whatcha doin'?"

I looked up to see the love of my life leaning in the doorframe. He looked amazing standing there with a smile on his face just for me. He shone like a star to decorate my sky. He loved me and I was blessed. He had to know, so I told him, "I love you."

"I love you too," he stated in a matter of fact tone, "and to what do I owe this declaration of love?" He crossed the room to where I sat. He leaned back against the edge of the desk and ran his hand down my arm, "Are you okay? Did something happen?"

"I'm fine. I want everyone I love to know it without a doubt," I choked, looking up into his eyes.

"We do. We do." He closed his eyes and lowered his head, "You have never failed at showing us...ever." He opened his eyes and they glistened with unshed tears. He straightened away from the desk and shook the emotion from his head, "Have you eaten since this morning?"

"Um...no."

He held his hand out to me, "Let's go raid the fridge and see what the neighbors have dropped off for us."

I closed out the document I had been working on and shut the laptop, "I really hate and, kinda love that everyone is doing this. It's kinda creepy but I get to be lazy for a little while longer."

We wondered down to the kitchen and Tom started pulling bowls and platters out of the refrigerator, "Let's see what was dropped off for our consumption today."

"Food, I love food," announced Shell coming into the kitchen with an arm full of clean dish towels.

"Looks like we have meatloaf," he stuck his tongue out mimicking a gag, "potatoes of some sort, hmmm...what's this," he mumbled as he pulled foil off another bowl, "I have no clue what this is but if it tastes like it smells we will all be hospitalized before nightfall." He slid the bowl closer to the trash and continued his search for eatable items.

"I could always make grilled cheese?"

"Sold," cheered Shell, "I'll get the stuff out."

With Shell's help I whipped up some grilled cheese sandwiches and tomato soup. I knew it was summer but grilled cheese and soup had always been my comfort food. There was nothing better on a rainy day than to curl up with a good book, a soft blanket and comfort food. I needed comfort and so did Tom and Michelle. It was moments like this that I missed Lily most. We needed each other but were missing a piece of our whole. I sent out a whisper of love to our soldier girl and fed the few who remained.

"Hey, dad, what kind of stuff did you eat when you were in basic for the Army?"

"To be honest, I ate whatever was fast and would get me out of the chow hall faster. You never wanted to draw attention to yourself."

"Did you tell Lily?" I asked with a mouth full of cheesy heaven.

Tom wiped his mouth on the back of his hand, "Yeah, I let her know," I handed him a napkin and gave him a smirk, "Thanks, I told her to be fast and silent. You don't want them to know your name. If they don't know your name, they can't scream it from across the barracks." We chuckled but no humor filled the noise. What had my baby gotten herself into? Tom took my hand and kissed the knuckles, "She'll be okay. You have to have faith in her."

"I do. I wish I knew what was going on," as if on cue, my phone rang. "Hello?"

"Mom, how are you feeling? Are you okay? What did the doctor say?"

"I'm fine, baby. How are you? Wait, let me put you on speaker so we all can talk," I slid my cell on to the table, "Okay, you're on speaker. The doc said I was healing fine. We were just talking about you."

"Yeah, cool, I'm doing okay. I was freaked out the first couple days, but now that we got our uniforms I feel better."

"I bet you look like a dork," laughed Shell, "Green never was your best color."

"Shut up, I look like everyone else and I'm cool with it. Okay, so, I only have a few minutes cuz we are all trying to call home. I love you guys and miss you tons."

"We love you too, kiddo. Keep your head down and don't let them learn your name," advised Tom.

"I know, dad."

We chatted back and forth for a few more minutes about what she was doing and how proud we were of her before Lily had to hand the phone over to another scared girl who desperately wanted to talk to loved ones. We shared our love, good wishes, and farewells. I had comfort food and comfort from my family. It was a good day.

I learned quickly to embrace the good days and manage the bad.

Chapter Twenty Six

I convinced Tom that he should go to work. He insisted he take me to my cardiac testing but I made a deal that if Charlotte came later to bring me home he would go to work.

"Fine, but I'm not happy about it," Tom grumbled.

"Babe, it is going to take nearly two hours between blood work and the echo...echo...what the hell is it again?"

"Echocardiogram, it's like an ultra sound, like you had when you were pregnant."

"Right, that thing. I told Charlotte to come around quarter to one."

Tom pulled up to the front of the medical center to drop me off closer to the door, "I still don't like you being alone. I should go with you."

"I love you too. I can manage. I don't need you sitting in a waiting room for hours getting annoyed." I closed the truck door and leaned into the window, "Go, I will call you if I need you." He simply nodded and pulled away. I sent a quick text reminding Charlotte of the time to come get me and then went to check in.

It was an absolute whirlwind of boring. The most exciting thing was the drive to the medical center. They took blood for testing, a lot of blood. A chest x-ray to check I had lungs, I think, and I got to lay on a table for over an hour while some guy ran a gooey wand along my chest over my heart. He wasn't much of a conversationalist and I didn't really have much to say.

At least my boobs weren't in the way. Not funny? I thought it was.

I was informed my results would be forwarded to my doctor and I was dismissed with little fanfare and no "after care" sheets. Thank God. It was simple, painless, boring as hell, but required I do nothing afterwards. I liked doing nothing. It was one of my favorites.

Charlotte was front row center when I came down the hallway. She waved at me as though I couldn't possibly see that strawberry red head bobbing around. She had tamed the mass in a long rope braid that lay over her shoulder and rested on her chest. I wished I had hair like hers. Mine was short and dark and would soon enough be non-existent, along with my eyebrows, lashes...I wondered if all my hair would fall out, you know, down there? I decided I would have to Google that. Was I gonna look like a naked mole rat? Um, gross.

Turned out... I did lose all my hair. Meh, it was only hair.

"Wow, you look good," noted Charlotte with a touch of wonder.

With a quirk of an eyebrow and confusion I responded with a questioning, "Okay?"

"I mean for havin' ta workout yer heart an all."

"Workout? I just had to lie on a table."

Her eyebrow mimicked mine from moments ago, "Oh, I thought they was gonna be testin' yer heart."

"They did, but I didn't have to run a marathon to do it. They used this sonogram thingy to get pictures of my heart beating, that's all."

"Good, because I wouldn't want to take ya to lunch if ya reeked," Charlotte chuckled, "Let's get sushi." An Irish woman, married to a Mexican who loved sushi, she was one of a kind.

"Mmm, yes, please."

We slid into a pristine little table that held chopsticks, forks for the lame, dipping dishes, and a beautiful tea pot. I tried sushi for the first time a few months ago. I was curious so I dragged Tom to The Red Dragon for date night. We shared yet another first in our lives together. I guess we were sharing a first at that time as well. I mean, neither of us had ever dealt with cancer before, right? It was a first, not a good first, but still a first. How many first was I going to miss out on? First college graduation. First wedding of a child. First grandchild. There was a lifetime of firsts I would not share with Tom or my daughters, but I was going to make sure they knew, beyond a doubt, I was there celebrating with them...somehow.

Flicking my nose, "Earth to Olivia."

"Ouch, what the hell was that for?"

Charlotte crossed her arms over her chest, "I was talkin' to ya and you were off driftin' in space."

"Sorry. Was thinking."

"Did it hurt?"

I quickly ordered a cold green tea, "Did what hurt? The test?"

"No, da thinkin' part." We shared a much needed laugh. It was like I had to get out of one mind set and grab on to another. I was tired of everything being about me and what I was dealing with. I wanted to fall to the wayside and enjoy the moments of other people. I wanted to feel their joy. "I found more ideas for the party on Pinterest."

I laughed again at her excitement, "Let's see what you got." Little did I know she had an entire binder stuffed with ideas crammed in her shoulder bag. We looked at cakes, cupcakes, food, games, and idea after idea as to how to reveal what the baby will be. I sneaked bites of food while Charlotte rambled on in awe of the ideas so many people shared on line. I could only hope someday soon a party like that would be planned for her. Would I be there? Doubtful.

"So, what do you think?"

"Huh, oh, um...you have some great ideas."

Slamming the binder shut, Charlotte huffed, "Were you even listening?"

"I was, really. It's a lot of ideas and you only have a couple of weeks to get it all together, ya know?"

"I know," she sighed, "I don't know what I like more."

"I like that you asked everyone to wear white, that way, when the color is revealed, it will stand out. I like the bow tie or hair bow idea too. You just have to settle on things."

"I know. I can't talk to Molly about it. I want it to be a total surprise for them."

I took her hand in mine, "I know and I think what you are doing is beyond wonderful. You are a truly good person, Charlotte. I love you."

"What?"

"What, what? Hasn't a friend ever told you they love you?"

"Why would they?"

"So you know. So you never doubt how someone feels about you. I want the people I love to know without a doubt I do. What better way than to tell them. I love ya, Charlotte." I squeezed her hand then reached for my chopsticks to stuff another piece of spicy tuna roll in my face.

Wasabi, good. Ginger, bad. Just my opinion.

I think I stunned her into absolute silence. We finished our delicious raw fish with little more than yummy noises coming from either of us. I snagged a piece from her plate and offered up one from mine. What better way to figure out what to get next. It looked like the California roll was next on my list to try. There were so many things I had always wanted to try and not just raw fish.

"Charlotte, what's on your bucket list?"

She sputtered and choked down the piece of crab Rangoon she had taken a bite out of, "Bucket list, why do I know those words?"

"It's the list of things you want to do before you die."

"Liv, you're not gonna die."

"Yes, I am," I stated matter of factly, "You know that. I know I am on borrowed time." What could she say? She knew the truth, but didn't want to face it any more than I did, but I had to. I watched her eyes look everywhere but at me. If you don't look death in the face did that mean it couldn't take you? If I kept my eyes closed, would death not stop at my door? Nope. Death would come and I knew it. "Charlotte, I don't mean to sound, well, I don't know how I sound, but we know the prognosis. I'm not saying anything we don't already know. I want to do things I always thought I had time to do," I shook my head at the thought, "...later."

"I always wanted to ride a roller coaster."

I could work with that, "I'll ride one with you. I love roller coasters. I hate Ferris wheels though, so don't even ask." We talked about things we were chicken of and others we wanted to try for no other reason than we wanted to.

Charlotte dropped me at home after our emotional roller coaster. I gathered the mail and kicked the cooler that *another* concerned neighbor placed on our porch. They didn't seem too concerned with the idea they might be giving us food poisoning by leaving food on the front porch for hours. I have thrown away more food in the last few days than I had in months. It had to stop.

After I tossed my stuff on the front room table I headed to my laptop and a much-needed visit with Facebook.

Olivia Carpenter: *To all my wonderful neighbors who have taken time and effort to make meals for me and my family, we thank you for your kindness and show of love and support. I am feeling stronger and am able to cook for my family again. Thank you for the blessings you shared with us. Stop by and collect your dishes and say* "Hi."

Post

I went to the kitchen and gathered up all the plates, bowls, baking dishes, and Tupperware at our door. Some had their names on them while others were without claim. I chuckled at the thought they didn't want us to know who made what. That way we couldn't put a name on the less than eatable ones. I was carrying the dishes out to the dining room table when my doorbell rang. I still approached my door with caution after Dick Head's visit a few weeks back. I rose up on my toes to eye whoever it was that poked the bell. Of course, it was Nadine, our resident queen of gossip and slander. I released a sigh of distaste then opened the door.

"Nadine. I'm assuming you saw my Facebook post."

"Yes, of course I did. May I come in?" Did I really have a choice?

I held the door further open, "Of course, can I get you anything?"

"Goodness, no, I know you have gone through quite a bit lately. I can get us something from the kitchen." Oh, hell no you nosey bitch.

"Nadine, I am quite capable of tending to guests. Would you like lemonade or iced tea?"

Her face puckered like she had already sucked on a few lemons, "Tea, please."

Being the good hostess, not, I offered her a seat and went to pour two glasses of tea. "Here ya go. Are you here to claim some of these dishes," I waved to the array of items on the table.

"I may have one or two over there," she sipped her tea and gave it a look as if it were lacking. "I also stopped by to see how you and your family are doing."

"We are fine, thank you."

Nadine scanned the room and eyed the family portraits scattered about, "When I lost my Henry a few years back, it was quite difficult, lonely, even. I wanted to let you know I am here if Tom," a touch of a smile licked her lips, "or your lovely girls need someone to talk with."

Really? Did I look that stupid...don't answer that. "I understand your feelings of loss, but Henry didn't die, Nadine, he left you. I will, however, make sure to pass on the warning, I mean word, Nadine, but, I wouldn't hold my breath if I were you."

"What do you mean?"

"Well," I leaned closer, "I may be dying but I'm not dead yet. This isn't some *Lifetime* movie, Nadine. I'm not looking for my husband's next wife or my children's new mommy, but if I were it sure as hell wouldn't be you."

Her jaw hung slack for a moment before she realized how transparent she was, "I never said any–"

"You didn't have to," I interrupted. "I am far from stupid and I can read you like a book. I will pass on the word to Tom you're interested. It should give us both a good laugh later and I may even use it in the future when I need a laugh the most. Thanks." I stood and my intent was clear, she had to go, now. "Leave the glass on the table and take your dishes with you. Future visits won't be necessary." Nadine gave a huff and set the glass down with a thud. I could hear the "Well, I never!" in the hiss of breath she released. I escorted her back to the door. Just as she stepped through the screen door I saw her body spin. She turned in the attempt at giving me one last word or subtle gesture that was greeted with the resounding slam of the front door. That was the second time I was attacked following the ringing of my doorbell. I was beginning to hate the sound of the damn thing. Why the fuck was I dying when there was plenty of nasty-ass people like Nadine who could have taken my place? Why me? Who did I piss off in my life that awarded me that fucking honor? It wasn't fair. I reveled in my anger and came up with quite a list of people who should be in my place instead of me, a list that made no difference. It wasn't like I could magically switch places with any one of them. The anger sapped what little energy I had, forcing me to seek the welcoming embrace of my too small bed, the bed that held me closer to Tom. I felt a hot river flow from my closed eyes and pool on the pillow which cradled my troubled head. Sleep came, but it was filled with random thoughts and emotion ran rampant. I saw glimpses of Nadine's face too close to Tom's. Her hand brushing against his cheek and...

"Shhh...,"I heard his whisper, "go back to sleep, baby."

"No, no," I shook my head to clear it like an etch-a-sketch. I had to get that image out of my mind before it ate a hole through my sanity. "I'm awake. I'm up. I'm up."

Tom lay on his side next to me, looking at me with caution, "You okay? It didn't seem like a good dream was playing behind your eyelids."

I could feel the pooling of tears and if I blinked they would spill, "It was a terrible dream, horrible," I croaked.

"Tell me about it."

"I don't wanna talk about it."

"I don't care if you want to talk about it. I want you to tell me anyway."

I searched for an excuse to not tell him. I waited for divine intervention (which we know never came). I gave up and told him about the dream and Nadine's visit earlier in the day.

"Do you think I would ever go to her for...anything?"

"No, but someday you will seek out someone. Someday you will need someone."

"Nope, never."

I smiled a sad smile, "You will and you have to be okay with it. I know it will happen, babe. Shit, the women are lining up waiting for me to make my grand exit. You are handsome, kind, sweet, and might I add, well trained. You are a catch and at some point someone else will be blessed to have you."

Tom wrapped his warm arms around me and pulled me closer. I rested my head on his chest and listened to the constant rhythm of his heart, "No one will ever replace you. Ever."

"That's very sweet, but unrealistic. I agree, I am irreplaceable," I chuckled, "but that doesn't mean you won't find someone you want to spend time with." I sat up and leaned against the headboard, "We have to talk about this. I love you so much," I sighed, "and it kills me to ever think of you in another woman's arms, but I won't be here and you shouldn't have to be alone." Tom hugged my legs to him and put his head in my lap. I ran my hand over his short wiry blonde hair and I felt the silky prickle against my fingertips, "I want to know you will find happiness again, that you will find love." He held on tighter as I spoke of him moving on, moving forward...without me.

"I will never love anyone the way I love you," he whispered.

"You better not. I am one of a kind, mister. Do me one favor."

"Anything," he said, then righted himself and sat next to me in bed. He interlaced his fingers with mine, "You name it."

I rolled my head along the edge of the headboard to look at him, "Don't marry too soon, 'k?"

"I love you and that isn't gonna stop, ever. Besides, I don't think our children would be too happy about me 'moving on,'" he hooked his fingers in air quotes. We both laughed because we both knew how true that statement was. "I think Lily would kick my ass and Shell would go after any woman who even tried to get my attention."

"Better start setting aside bail money cuz women try to get your attention now. It's only gonna get worse when I'm not here."

"You will always be here," he whispered and placed our linked hands over his heart. I curled in tighter to his body and held on. I didn't know how many more times I would get to feel his warmth against me, so I was going to take every opportunity I could until I couldn't.

We both held on. We scooted our bodies back down onto the bed and wrapped each other in the security of our arms and legs. I held on like there was no tomorrow and he held on like there was. It was as if we could make a future happen by sheer will alone. I kissed him, hard. I tried to get so close I would become a part of him, live within him, be consumed by him. And I was.

Chapter Twenty Seven

Days passed without my permission. Why didn't I have a say in where the time went and how fast it chose to get there? I had things I wanted, no, needed to do and time was fighting me every step of the way. It felt like my life was in a hurry and I wasn't keeping up. One minute felt like a second, a weekend felt like a day, I didn't want to sleep because it felt like I was wasting what little time I had left. I wanted time. More. Fucking. Time.

My cardiac results came back. I was strong enough, physically, to handle the stress of chemotherapy. WooHoo! Fuck. "We have you scheduled for Monday at ten. Eat normally and take any medications you have been prescribed. Don't come in with the idea you will get sick. Some do, but some don't. You need to stay strong. Do you have any questions?"

The nurse was so matter of fact about it all, how could I have any questions? "No, not at this time."

"Well, if you ever do, ask. We are here to make this as comfortable for you as we can."

I didn't think that could be possible, at all, "Thanks, I'll see you Monday." I ended the call before the receptionist, or was she a nurse, could respond. Some people got sick but some didn't. The thought rambled around in my gray matter. How di*d s*ome not get sick from chemo? Was there some magic trick to it? Time to Google it. When did Google become a verb? Another question that would never be answered in my life time, not a shock considering my life span was dwindling with each passing second...but wasn't that true for everyone?

Google search: How do you prevent vomiting with chemotherapy?

Holy crap-tastic Batman. Pages and pages of "suggestions" and "reasons" for sickness and preventing. Question was, what was real and what was a load of bullshit? Some sites claimed you may be more vulnerable to vomiting if one or more of the following applied:

What chemotherapy drugs will be used...*the poisonous ones*.

You're a woman...*duh*.

You're younger than 50...did it count if I felt older than dirt?

Likely to vomit when sick...wasn't that what "sick" meant? *Geesh*.

History of high level of anxiety...*only about this*.

Morning sickness during pregnancy...*only every second of every day*.

Not a drinker...really? If I was a lush I would handle chemo better? Was it too late to start?

My favorite was...dru*m roll...if you got it into your head you would get sick then you probabl*y will. Awesome, so it could all be in my head. Well, shit balls. How the hell was I supposed to get it out of my head? *Don't vomit, don't vomit, don't vomit, don't vomit...all that made me think of was vomiting. I'm fucked.*

I poked the little red "x" to close out the screen and opened the document I had been working on. I had more to write, more to catch up on, more words of wisdom, okay, maybe not wisdom...all right, my words were wisdom. I surrounded myself with memories and poured them out onto that electronic page. I cried and chuckled. I found anger below a thin layer of skin and fear below that. I tried to justify it and will it away. I tried to make you see and to un-see. I tried to give you a piece of me to hold on to. To hold onto when I wasn't there to hold you back, when my arms wouldn't reach from the other side of life. I wanted my words to be able to hold you and make it...what a load of crap. I couldn't make it better. I couldn't take away the pain. I couldn't stop the sadness, but I could be there. If only through my words, I could still be there.

I continued to spin tales of what was and what I hoped would be. I thought of you with the words I chose. I thought of you as I shared my loves and fears. I thought of you with each page collected. I had to show you I would love you forever and always, to the moon and back a hundred bazillion times. I would always be as long as you thought of me, loved me.

My fingers faltered on the keys when my cell vibrated on the desk next to me, "Hello?"

"Mom? Hi."

"Oh, Lily, how are you, baby girl? What's going on?"

She gave a soft sigh, "I'm good. How are you? Have the test results come back yet?"

I wished she didn't have to worry about me while she was going through so much, "The results came back fine. I am good to go, but what's going on out there? Have you shot a gun yet?" I didn't really care but I had to get her to focus on something other than me.

"Not yet. I think we are still a few weeks out from doing that. It's weird. I am doing stuff I never thought I could do or ever dreamed I would want to. Did you know they don't call you 'woman' or 'girl?' They call us 'female.' It's bizarre."

"Female? Why on earth do they call you that?"

"I have no clue but it is better than 'split tail,' gross."

"Um, yeah," I shivered at the idea of some guy calling my amazing girl that, "I guess 'female' isn't so bad after all."

She laughed, I missed that laugh, "I guess. How's dad and Shell?"

"We are all good. We miss you bunches and tons and are so proud of you," I shared updates of what was going on at home. I told her a few of her friends stopped by from time to time to see if we had heard from her. I told her that her ex-boy toy got dumped by the girl he cheated with. Maybe I shouldn't have told her. I hoped it didn't make her miss his sorry ass, but it was nice to share in his public humiliation. Once again, time went by in a blur and I was left saying goodbye. "Do you need me to send you anything, a care package or something?"

"Cookies, I miss cookies. Make enough for me to share with the rest of the girls, oops, I mean 'females,'" she said in an authoritative voice followed by a snort.

"You got it, baby girl. I will get right on it."

"I love you mom."

"I love you more.

"Bye," she whispered.

"Bye." The call ended but I held the phone in my fingers wishing I could see her face. I missed my Lily. I missed her smile and quickness to hug. I ran my finger over the phone and tapped symbols on the screen until folders of pictures dotted the screen. I skimmed through the memories. Moments in time captured for future enjoyment...and another idea formed. I plugged my phone into the laptop and downloaded every photo on my phone to my computer and began another project to touch the future.

"Whatcha doin'?"

I jerked my head up to see Shell in the doorway of the office munching on fries, "Playing on the internet," I responded as my fingers swiftly saved my work and closed out the screen. "What are you eating?"

"Fries, want some?" she held out the greasy package to me to take my fill.

"Those look good. I might as well enjoy all the bad food I can before I can't keep it down?" I stretched my lips into a straight line to show sheer horror, "Eek."

"Gross, mom. Why would you say that while I'm eating?" she tossed the fry package on the desk in disgust.

"So I could eat the rest of your fries."

"That's just wrong."

I stuffed another fry into my mouth, "I know," I smiled with a fry covering my teeth in a crispy grin, "but you still love me," I mumbled through the mess in my mouth.

Michelle shook her head in mock horror, "I do. I don't know why I do, but I do." She dropped into the chair across from the desk, "We doin' anything tonight?"

I picked around the fries to find the crunchy ones, "Not that I know of. Did you have plans?" *Crunch, crunch.*

"I don't know. I haven't hung with any of my friends since..."

"Since the boob fairy came and took back what she gave me decades ago?"

She flopped her legs over one arm of the chair and rested her head on the other, "You know you're weird, right? I think they make meds for that," she grinned.

"You love me just the way I am. So, you gonna go hang with the girls then or...is there a guy?" she smiled...no, she was grinning. "Hmmm...what's this? Does my Shell like a boy?"

"Mom, God. He's...he...he's just a guy I met at work. He comes by all the time and we..."

"We? We what?"

"Talk, just talk, okay? Geesh."

I smiled at my red faced daughter. She likes a boy. "Are you guys going out?"

"Nah, we are kinda talkin' for now. We don't know each other yet and I'm not gonna say he's my boyfriend if I don't know anything about him, ya know?" she picked at the dried fast food gunk on the front of her shirt, "My friends call guys their boyfriends before they even know how old the guy is. It's kinda sad."

"You are one smart cookie. Oooo, cookies, Lily called."

"How do cookies and Lily go together?"

"She wants 'em. She wants us to make and send her cookies. You game?"

She turned her glorious face towards me, "Not tonight, I have a date," she finished with a grin. "Can we do it tomorrow?"

"You, me, and cookie dough? Sounds like a plan."

"Cool," she unfolded herself from the chair and came around the desk and placed a kiss on top of my head, "I gots ta shower. Wouldn't want to offend The Dude."

"Does The Dude have a name?"

"Kyle, but I'm diggin' 'Dude.'"

"The Dude, how does he feel about it?"

"I don't know. It's not like I've asked him," she chuckled as she spun on her heel and strode from the room with a purpose. I hoped it was to hose off the stink of greasy burgers and fries. I sat and rocked in the comfy desk chair. How was I supposed to concentrate and get things done when that chair made me want to take a nap?

"Hey, hot stuff, what're you up to?"

I jerked so hard I nearly fell out of said chair. I snapped around to find Tom walking towards me with a cold beer in his large hand, "What are you doing home so early?" I squeaked.

"Early? Babe, it's after six."

"Oh shit, I must have lost track of time," not something you should do in my position.

"What did you do all day?" he asked as his butt met the seat Shell had vacated only minutes before.

"Not much. Lily called and begged for cookies and Shell is upstairs showering for a date," I smirked at the last word.

Tom's eyebrows jumped up, "Date? Do tell. Who is the little punk?" his eyes narrowed and he chugged from the beer can he held a bit tighter.

I smiled at his physical display of concern, "A guy she met at work."

"Does he work there? That's not a good idea. You know, to date someone you work with."

"No, he's a customer. She said they have talked a bit and just want to get to know each other a little better."

"I know what the little punk wants and it ain't to get to know her better."

I snickered at him, "Give your daughter some credit there, big guy. You don't have to clean your gun just *yet*."

"Yet being the key word." We talked about Shell's impending date and the care package that Lily requested. I asked about his day and he about mine. It was the normal stuff, the everyday, nothings new, no looming doom, kind of questions every couple asks. We decided on dinner, cooked, wished Shell a good (safe, sex free) date, and settled in front of the boob tube. Boob tube? Ha, how fitting…Boob. I had issues pushing forward from the back of my mind. I needed to say my piece before I rested in peace.

"Babe?"

"Hmmm," he mumbled.

I shoved the words out before they could hide under my tongue, "I want to talk to you about some…some plans I've made. You know…about when I'm…gone."

His head dropped a fraction and I could see his chest rise and fall a bit faster than before, "If this is about me re-marrying…"

"No, it's not. It's about what I want done with…me. What I want done with my body."

"What? What you want done?" he sat up right in his recliner and supported his head in his hands. Leaning forward, he placed his elbows on his knees and sighed, "What do you want done with…you?"

"I thought about donating my body to science, you know, like medical schools, or maybe a tree urn. What do you think?"

"You can't guarantee your body would end up in a medical school. You could be sent to some local community college where a bunch of idiots would make bets to get each other to look under the sheet. No, no donating," he looked over at me, "What's this tree thing?"

I jumped up from my usual seat on the couch, "Hold on, I printed some stuff off about it," I scurried away to the office to grab the stack of papers. "Here, take a look and tell me what you think," I said and handed him the forms. Tom read through the short stack and as he got to the last page I interrupted, "You wouldn't have to put me here," I waved toward the back yard, "We could see if I could be donated to the park or if I could be planted in the…"

"Planted? Plant you? You want me to plant you? What the fuck?"

"Babe, I want to live and I can. As a tree," I went to him and sat on his knee, "I don't want you to visit a rock in a yard full of rocks. I don't want to be mistaken for an ash tray on some mantle somewhere. I want my grandchildren to climb me and lay in my shade. I want lovers to carve their names in me to hold forever," I swiped a tear that hung from my lower lashes. "I want to live on. I want to be a solid, touchable thing." Tom pulled me further onto his lap. I curled up in the love he offered, not from his form but from his heart. I tilted my head so I could look up into his face and was met with his tears, "Oh, babe, I'm sorry. I didn't mean to upset you," I tried to right myself so I could wipe away the evidence of the hurt I caused but he wouldn't allow it. I tucked my head under his chin, "We can look into something else. Other ideas if that's what you want?"

"I don't want to visit a rock either," he croaked, "I don't want ashes or stupid kids looking at you under a sheet…I don't want any of it," he scrubbed at the tears. "I just want you, alive."

"Me, too, this was the only way I could think of."

He rocked us in the recliner, saying nothing. He held me and caressed my back with his rough hand. He placed kisses on my head and inhaled my scent. He whispered his love into my ear and cried with me. "It's a beautiful idea. You will make a beautiful tree."

"I want to be a pine tree, a Jerusalem Pine. It sounds so majestic, and it stays green all year. Alive all year." I took him by his hand and led him to the office where we looked at tree options. "I think we need to order it now."

"Now? Why?"

"I'm not planning on going anywhere right away but I wouldn't want you to have to do this when I am at my worst," I explained, "This way it is done and is one last thing to weigh you down at a time when all hell is breaking loose." How could I make this easier? Was there a way to make my death softer for those around me? "I know this sucks, but…"

"There is no *'but'* that could make this less suck-worthy." Tom filled out the order form online, punched in his credit card number and pushed "purchase." My forever home had been ordered. I was going to be a pine tree.

Tom took me in his arms again and pulled me back onto his lap, "Where would you like to spend eternity?"

"I really don't know. I thought about here but if and when you have another woman in your life, would it be weird for her?"

"Not that it would matter, but if she cared enough, she would understand. See, that would be a deal breaker." He looked in my eyes and smiled, "You are my deal breaker. Besides, I think the kids should get a vote, don't you?"

"Did you plan on living here forever? I think you all would be happier if I was in a park or out in the woods somewhere. God, it's weird to refer to myself as a tree," I commented as a sad smile slid into place. It seemed to spend a lot of time on my face as of late.

"I want you close," he whispered, "I want to be able to be near you at the drop of a hat. I need that."

I took Tom's face in both of my hands and kissed him gently, "As long as I am in your heart, I am close."

"If we planted you in the woods I'd be afraid someone would cut you down for a Christmas tree or something."

"But, wouldn't I look pretty covered in twinkling lights?"

"You would." He scooped me up into his arms and carried me away to our room. No wife toss. I kind of missed wife toss. He used to toss me up in the air and let me land in a sprawl across our bed. He didn't do that anymore. I was placed not tossed. It was gentle, soft, and tender. He honored me. He said goodbye with every touch, every kiss. It was as if our love had come full circle. In the early days it was about proving our love. We showed it in gentle touches, precious moments, and kisses that made me cry. Over time it became games and laughter only to twist back to the softer times. I missed the chase up the stairs, the laughter and tickling, the wife toss and making love without a care. I missed us as we were. I missed what was, but I held on with all I had to what we shared at that moment.

"I love you, Liv, with all my heart."

"I love you more."

Chapter Twenty Eight

I opened messages on my phone and tapped out a *text*.

To: Charlotte Quiles, Molly Carpenter

Hey Ladies! Lily called and asked for cookies. U up for some baking today?

Send

What kind of cookies should we make my lil' soldier girl? I wondered. The memories of little girls pressing out sugar cookie dough and cutting out shapes drifted into my stress-addled mind.

"Mommy, are you a baker?" asked Lily.

"No, Mommy is a mommy. Right?" Shell squeaked in that annoying little sister way.

"She can be a mommy and a baker cuz daddy is a daddy and a machanick."

"You mean a mechanic," I corrected my little flower.

"I know. Dat's wha I said."

With flour dusted across her delicate nose, Michelle poked at the dough, "Mommy, do you machanick like daddy?"

"Nope. I am your mommy and that's enough for me." I kissed the flour-dusted cheeks of my babies then slid a tray of wonky shaped sugar cookies into the oven.

Beep...Beep

Two text messages wiped clean the memory of baking with my girls.

Molly Carpenter: *I guess I can. I don't have any other plans as of yet.*

Well, la de da...sometimes I wondered if she knew how she came off to people? Did she know she was snobbish or was she blind to her own words?

Me: Great! I'm looking forward to visiting.

Charlotte Quiles: *Can we make oatmeal cookies? I love oatmeal.*

Me: Lol...I think we can do that. C U soon.

My friends were coming to spend time with me doing something for my girl. I was blessed to have these people in my life, even if Molly needed to take her attitude down a notch or a dozen. None of us were perfect. We all had our flaws, but loving someone meant you were to embrace the good as well as the bad.

I heard the telltale thud of a teenaged girl falling out of bed. I waited patiently for her to shuffle down to the kitchen. "Morning, sunshine."

"Grrr."

"Well, ain't we Miss Perky this morning."

"Meh."

"It is always a pleasure talkin' to you. Are you gonna help make cookies for Lil today? Your Aunt Molly and Charlotte are coming to help," I shared as I pulled out the fruit salad from the fridge, "Here, eat something."

"What, no donuts?" she grumbled as she scooped some cantaloupe into a bowl.

"Nope, I need to eat healthy, so you get to eat healthy with me. Ain't you lucky," I gave her a wide grin and topped her fruit with a scoop of Cool-whip. I read the perfect saying somewhere when the girls were little that fit that very moment... *I give you milk because it's good for you. I add chocolate because I love you. "Cool-whip, to prove my love."*

"Thanks, when are we doing cookies?" she mumbled through a mouthful of white fluff.

"When your Aunt and Charlotte get here," I said while going through cabinets and pulling out flour, sugar and other items we would need. "Do you have any ideas what kind of cookies to make?"

"Let me think...no-bake, chocolate chip, peanut butter, sugar, snicker whatchamacallits, gingersnaps...shall I continue?"

I laughed with each added name, "No, I think I got it. What are snicker whatchamacallits? All the other cookies are good cookies."

"Snicker somethings... I don't know what they're called."

I searched the pantry until I found what I was looking for and placed the container on the counter across from Shell, "They are called snicker doodles and I noticed you didn't mention this kind of cookie."

She gave a sour face, "Why? Who the heck eats oatmeal cookies anyway?"

"Charlotte." Our private chuckles were interrupted by the doorbell, "Speak of the devil."

My friends came armed with supplies for cookies and other fun items to stuff into the box. "My mother would put popcorn in boxes to help keep her Christmas cookies from becoming stale. She did a lot of baking during the holidays," explained Molly as I looked at the bag of popcorn with concern.

"Oh, okay. I've never heard of that before but if nothing else, they can eat the popcorn too." We made cookies, lots and lots of cookies. Too. Many. Cookies. Not as many as Michelle suggested but there were dozens of cookies cooling all over the place. "Please, tell me you guys are gonna take some of these home with you. There is no way I can mail all of these to Lily without the box exploding or sending all those girls into diabetic shock."

Charlotte's arm shot up in the air, "Sign me up fer some of the oatmeal."

"I'm sure Wayne would love some. I need to watch what I eat."

Charlotte and I both looked at her as if she farted, "What?" we screeched in unison.

"Why ya watchin' what ya eat, girly?" Charlotte pried, "You barely cast a shadow as is."

Molly placed her well-manicured motherly hand over the tiny bump that was forming, "I need to stay healthy for him or her."

I understood her fear. I remembered the call telling us she had lost her last pregnancy, "No cookies for you," I barked in my best Soup Nazi accent, "I will eat your share while I can," I declared and stuffed a peanut butter cookie into my mouth and chugged some milk. "*Ahhhh...*burp."

"I thought you guys were the adults here?" snorted Shell. "This sounds more like the cooking class at school, where the guys are there only to eat the food."

Molly gave a soft laugh and regaled us with a tale of her school days and how she caught the school kitchen on fire, "...and that is why you never spray non-stick cooking spray over the open flame of a gas stove." I couldn't control the laughter that burst from me. I thought I was gonna pee myself and Charlotte was snorting with each attempt at catching her breath which only made me laugh harder. Molly joined in and Shell stared at us like we had lost what little sanity we had left. We shared silly stories of our childhoods, of cooking mishaps, and charred remains of eyebrows. I told of the many adventures of Lily and Michelle even as Shell begged me not to. I warned Molly of the craziness that would befall her once her little one was able to balance on two feet. There was joy to be had that day and I grabbed hold with both hands and went along for the ride...laughing all the way.

"Have you and Uncle Wayne picked names yet?" Shell asked Molly upon her return from one of her multiple trips to the bathroom.

"Not really, we've got a few ideas but are going to wait until we know what this little one is," she explained while rubbing her belly and looking at it with the purest face of love. "I want a little boy, a little Wayne or we may name a boy after my brother, Michael."

"Or ya could name him Wayne Michael, we'll see soon enough. Actually, I will know before ye," grinned Charlotte, "is it weird I'm excited about finding out what yer havin'?"

"Yes," we all chimed in, only to be followed by loads of laughter. The only thing that could have made that moment better would have been finding out Charlotte was pregnant too, or some crazy miracle happened and I was gonna live forever...like a vampire. I always wanted to be a vampire.

*****

"Please tell me we aren't having cookies for dinner," Tom begged when he saw the amount of baked goods lining the dining room table.

I was packing the box destined to carry all that sugar when I smiled at the sound of his voice, "You don't want chocolate chip cookies for dinner? What's wrong with you?" I joked while loading in the packages of cookies.

"Popcorn, what's that for?" he asked while filling his cupped hand with the popped kernels.

"To keep the cookies fresh."

"If you say so. What are we havin' for dinner?" he probed, downed the rest of the popcorn in his hand and rubbed his nearly empty stomach.

I closed the box to Lily with a few strips of packing tape, "How does grilled salmon sound? With steamed rice and fresh green beans?"

"That's what I'm talking about. Where is it?" he asked looking around at the tornado of cookie crap.

With a wink and a smile I walked to the refrigerator, "Right here," I smirked as I pulled the raw fish from the fridge. "If you get the grill going, I'll cook."

"Done."

*****

"That was damn good, babe. Hit the spot," Tom sighed and rubbed his bloated belly.

I poked at the bulging mass, "You look about as far along as Molly. Whatcha got in there, a baby elephant?"

"Ha ha, very funny. Do you want to see the trunk?"

"Perv."

"You love me anyway."

I did.

I do.

I nodded my head in agreement, "I do. I really do. Now," I stood and started to gather the dishes from the table, "help me with the dishes and let's go for a short walk in the park. I need to work off the massive amount of dough I ate."

"Your wish is my command."

"In that case, you do the dishes," I taunted.

"I say your wish is my command and all you want is me doing the dishes? That's sad, babe, really sad," Tom snorted, "I could think of better things to command me to do, if you know what I mean."

"I know, which is why I chose dishes," I giggled as I ducked and dodged his attempts to scoop me up. "Come on, I'll help so we can walk before it gets too dark."

The park was packed with moms and dads who came out to watch their children play one form of ball or another. Some ran from field to field to catch glimpse of each child they were blessed to have. I listened to them cheer and chant the name of said child. I remembered doing that. I remembered watching one play a game and chasing another around the playground. I remembered drippy ice cream kisses and bouquets of dandelions.

I felt the warm squeeze of Tom's hand, "Hey, where'd ya go?"

"Remembering when we would come here to watch the girl's games."

"I remember us laying a blanket over there," he pointed to a cool spot beneath a cover of branches that shaded the area below, "and having a picnic dinner. We ate fried chicken and cole slaw before one of Lily's softball games and she threw up all over short stop."

I snorted in laughter, "It started a chain reaction with the kids and Lily almost got kicked off the team for it. It was sad, but so frickin' funny."

Tom gave me a slight nudge, "I also remember lying in that very spot, much later in the evening, and not having a picnic," he winked and gave a very knowing nod.

"I have no idea what you are referring to, sir. Are you accusing me of doing the unspeakable in public? Certainly not, sir." I fanned my face in mock shame.

"Ms. Liv, I know what I know and I know you."

"That you do, Mr. Carpenter." We wondered around the park hand in hand and watched families and children building memories they didn't know would mean so much to them later. I petted dogs and said hello to strangers. I inhaled deeply the wondrous smells of flowers, grilled hot dogs, and life. "What do you think about planting my tree somewhere in here?"

"In the park? Can we do that?"

"I don't know but I can call and ask. Only way to find out, right?"

"Where would you want to be planted?"

I tugged on his hand, "My favorite spot in the park." I led him along the sidewalk and veered off to the left toward a bank of large bushes. There was my bench and the fountain that bounced cool water droplets out of its pool and onto warm skin. I used to stand very close for that reason. "Here, I want to be planted around here. Maybe over there," I pointed to a small clearing across from the bench seat on the other side of the fountain. "I've never seen the park crew plant anything over there, no flowers or bushes, so maybe they could plant...me."

Tom sat down on the bench and looked around, "Why is this your favorite spot? It's so secluded."

I slipped into the space beside him and sighed, "That's why. Lean back and close your eyes," he did, "What do you hear?"

"I hear everything."

"Tell me each thing."

"I hear...a ball hit a bat and the crowd cheering...I hear...a dog and...is that the ice cream truck?"

"Now, what do you smell?" I breathed into his ear.

A shiver rolled up his back, "I smell Dove soap."

"That's me, but what else do you smell?"

"Hot dogs, I smell something sweet...I smell...what is that?" he pondered, "It smells dirty, like..."

"Like soil?"

"Yeah, maybe," he opened his eyes and looked at me, "It still doesn't explain why you like this spot."

"I love this spot because while you were listening and smelling no one saw you. I love this spot because I can watch and listen but not be a part of what is happening around me. I can watch life unfold. I like to lay on this bench and look up," I pointed to the canopy of leaves over head, "and watch the light try to peek through the leaves. It's beautiful."

"Yes, it is," Tom murmured beside me. I looked over at him as he turned his head to look at me and we shared a smile. We sat for a while and watched the world move around us. We laughed at the antics of people who had no clue we were there and witnessed their acts of stupidity. We talked about what was and what would be. We held hands and just were.

"We should head back. I'm being eaten alive by skeeters," I sighed.

I know what you're thinking...she gave up. Just because I was planning for "after" didn't mean I had given up. I had come to realize there were some battles worth fighting and this wasn't one of them. I didn't want to waste precious time fighting to live when it wasn't going to happen. Only an act of God or a mystical event could save me. What I could do with my remaining time was to make it valuable to the people I loved more than air. If there were a shot in hell of surviving then you could have bet your life on me fighting tooth and nail to live. I was no stranger to battle, but all I wanted then was a little more time so I could make my passing...tolerable. I hoped we could all make peace with the eventuality of what was going to come to pass, to accept it and release some of the pain. I hoped for a lot.

Chapter Twenty Nine

"Oh, my fucking God!" I sat shocked, holding a single piece of paper with a ridiculous series of numbers typed across it, $62,473.42. "Holy shit," I released in a sharp gasp. It was the bill. Even with insurance our balance was well over twelve thousand dollars, but that didn't include chemo treatments, radiation, and the many orange safety capped bottles that lined the kitchen counter. I logged on to my computer and did some research into the cost of my treatments. I bounced around on a few medical web sites to try to get consistent numbers and what I found left me slack jawed.

So here's what I figured out:

We had 80/20 insurance, meaning they paid 80% and we got the rest: $62,473.42

Minus 80%   - $49,978.74

Left to us a whopping balance of: $12,494.68

Keep in mind that was only for the surgery. More math coming...each chemo session would cost approximately $950, that could easily be another $7,600 in costs we would share with the insurance company. Then there was radiation. Radiation treatments could cost upwards of $20,000. And...I was still gonna die.

Fuck THAT!

I was not going to leave behind a bill that would take a decade to pay off. Tom would have to mortgage the house or have to sell it and move. No, no, not going to happen. My days were numbered, but they weren't going to have monetary value. That was yet another cost in life. You come into the world costing money and go out costing more. But, somehow during a life span, you can be viewed as worthless. Which was it? Worthless or billable? Was I a worthless waste of skin, as my loving mother pointed out daily, or was I worth the thousands it would cost to keep me breathing a little while longer?

"Here ya go," smiled Tom as he slid a fresh cup of coffee in front of me. "What's that?" he jerked his head in the direction of the paper that lay on the laptop.

I picked up my mug and hugged it to me, "The cost of a boob-ectomy," I snorted and sipped from my cup. Tom took the paper and his mug to the chair across from me. He slid into the seat with ease, kicked his bare feet up onto the edge of the desk and perused the page of numbers. I waited for his reaction.

"Sssss," he hissed between his teeth, "well, we knew it wasn't gonna be free, but damn."

"I know and that doesn't even cover the rest of this shit," I ticked off the items on my fingers, "chemo every other week, enough pills to choke a goat on a daily basis, and radiation, if I live that long."

"You will live that long."

"Not if it's gonna cost twenty grand. I can't do this to you, babe. I can't leave you in debt. I won't."

Tom shifted his feet back down to the floor and leaned forward pinning me with his cool blue eyes, "You will and that's the end of that. You will do whatever it takes to ..."

"To what? Live? Would it be living? I have my first chemo in two days and I'm already seeing it as a waste of time and money."

"How is it a waste of time?" he roared, "Why do you get to decide if it's a waste? I don't think having my wife around for as long as possible is a waste. You don't get to decide what I think you're worth." He shoved away from the desk and stood staring at me, "keep in mind, you get to leave. I have to stay. You don't have to wake up alone and face each day with your heart ripped out. No, that gets to fall in my lap," before I had regained the ability to control my tongue he was gone. He had stormed from the room and slammed a door somewhere in the house.

What did he think I was worth? What was my value to Tom? I never had value before so I didn't quite understand its purpose. My entire childhood I was made to feel like I was less, less than in looks, brains, and abilities. I would amount to nothing, and no one would ever want me for anything more than a quick fuck. Thanks for that, Mother. I still believed these words, and they affected the way I did things. I couldn't bring myself to look into the faces of the people in her world. I cowered in corners and stayed on the periphery of her life. If they didn't see me, then they couldn't hurt me. I was so wrong on that point. What was clear was I had little worth.

But in school, I could be anything. I could have friends. I could be happy and I was. I lived through horrible nights to escape to school each morning. I was a different person within those halls. I was protected. I was liked. I was accepted. It was the one place I could go and feel normal. Even boys liked me, but I remained cautious around them. My Mother's words would ring in my ears telling me I was usable, but not keep-able. Boys would never love me, only use me for a little while, then leave me like the trash I was. Until HIM, HE treated me like a princess. HE protected me from the world. HE said HE loved me. HE was different.

How wrong I was. HE did everything Mother said except toss me to the side. HE said all the right things and treated me well to lure me in and then HIS evil peeked through. No, HE didn't toss me away. HE wanted to use me whenever HE wanted for whatever HE wanted. I became a punching bag, a sex toy, and a maid. It wasn't until HE wanted to "share" me with HIS buddies I drew my line in the sand. HE beat me bloody that night, which meant the buddies wouldn't get a shot at me until I healed up. It bought me time. Time to run. When HE wasn't looking, I was all asshole and elbows. I ran and didn't look back.

After that, I became very protective of myself. I did a complete 180°. I went from the shy coward to the bitch from hell. I snapped the head off of anyone who stepped over some imaginary boundary I put around myself. It took a very long time to build trust with people. It wasn't until I started working at Mr. Zinkman's diner I started to put things into perspective. Mr. Zinkman swore to protect me. He treated me with respect and kindness. He taught me it was okay to set boundaries, but to leave room to let others in. His wife, Mrs. Martha, taught me to be a B.I.T.C.H. She taught me that bitch could mean a lot of things, some good and some bad. She only saw the good. Martha taught me bitch was just short for beautiful, intelligent, tenacious, caring, and hopeful. She wanted me to see that beauty was more than the skin. You had to be beautiful through and through. Martha showed me intelligence was learned in school and in the world. But, to learn from the world around me, I had to let it in. Tenacious was to keep your chin up even when you felt like hiding, and I had hid my head in the sand enough. I needed to hang on for dear life to the things that mattered. I had to be caring. I had to be open to love, to accept it when it was given, and to give it freely to those who deserved it. Hopeful, was to hope for more, to want bigger and better things and believe they were possible. I really had to work on that one.

I learned to be that person. I learned to believe in my beauty, inside and out. I knew I was book smart. I had to open up to the world and let it teach me. I kept my chin up and pushed through the hard times and cared about those who cared about me. I hoped, I hoped for unconditional love and one day I found it. Well, he found me. Tom opened up the world to me and showed me the possibilities I never looked for. He protected me and pushed me. He helped me up when I fell and laughed when we fell together. I learned to love. I learned to trust. I learned my Mother was wrong because I was a B.I.T.C.H. and proud to be. I had worth but I also had the strength and wherewithal to choose my path. In the end, all things would be left to me to decide, so I had a lot of thinking to do. The question remained, what was I going to do? I was going to make this as easy as possible for all involved.

I went in search of the man I pissed off without intending to. I poked my head into each room looking for his slumped angry shoulders, but was greeted with a vacancy in every room. I made my way to the kitchen to see if he had taken refuge on the deck, but I could hear where he was long before I saw him. Tom sat at his work bench in the garage screaming along to Metallica and cursing the world. Metallica was singing a bedtime prayer and that was right about the time the wrench flew across the garage and smashed out one of the lift door windows only to be accompanied by a guttural wail from Tom.

"It's only a window, babe," I whispered gently as I placed my hands on his shoulders.

He straightened at my touch, "I don't give a fuck about the God damn window, Liv." He stepped away from me and went to gather up the glass that sparkled on the concrete floor. I dragged the trash can over to where the evidence of his hurt lay shattered on the floor. "I can do it. Go back in the house."

"I can help."

"Just go. Just go in the house," he growled. I could tell he was hanging on to his control with little more than will power and a jagged finger nail.

I gave a slight nod then turned away from my support. I had forgotten he needed support too. I pulled my cell from my pocket as I left my heart behind me and called Wayne.

"3C's garage, this is Wayne."

"It's Liv, are you busy?" I heard muted noises in the background and waited for him to deal with whatever it was that had his attention.

"Hold on a sec, Liv," Wayne grunted. I heard him lay the phone down and move away from the receiver. *'Yo, Miguel...take care of that minivan, will ya? Thanks,* man.'

"Liv?"

"I'm here."

"What's going on?"

I let out a sigh, "I think Tom needs his brother," I hesitated, "I...I think he needs someone to talk to and, right now, that isn't me." I felt a warm wet tear slip down my cheek and kiss my nose before landing on the screen of my cell. I could hear Wayne breathing on the other end of the line. I hoped he was trying to figure out what to do for Tom.

"I know it's early, but has he been drinking?"

"No."

"I'm gonna call him and tell him to come in to the garage. Okay?"

"Yeah, I think that would be good for him. Get his mind off of ...off of..."

"Yeah, I'm gonna call him." He hung up before I could thank him for stepping up for Tom.

Moments later Tom came through the back door with his phone between his ear and his shoulder, and had a red shop towel wrapped around his fingers, "Yeah, give me a few minutes. I need to clean up my hand...I was cleaning up some glass and cut my finger...No, I'm fine...No...No, stitches...Dude, I'll be there in a few. Fuck." Tom ended the call and tossed the phone on the counter and shoved his hand under the faucet in the kitchen sink. I hurried to the bathroom and gathered up the Band-Aids and anti-bacterial stuff.

"Let me see," I demanded.

"It's fine. No big deal."

I grabbed his shoulder and forced him to turn to the side so I could get to his hand. There was blood, but not as much as I had imagined. I squirted some dish soap into his hand then waited for him to wash away the grime.

"Where are you going?" I asked as if I didn't know what the phone conversation was.

"Heading into the shop."

I dried his finger with a paper towel, dabbed on some Neosporin, then wrapped a bandage around the jagged cut, "Oh, okay." I bent down and placed a kiss on his "boo-boo" then looked up into his sad eyes and placed a kiss on his lips, "I love you."

"I love you too." I could see the shine in his eyes as tears tried to form, "Okay, I gotta go," he grumbled as he looked away. "Don't know when I'll be back."

"Um, okay."

I found myself sitting alone in front of my computer scrolling through social media, trying to forget the words Tom left behind, realizing none of it mattered. I had comments on my Facebook wall and a few messages telling me how important juicing was to my well-being. Juicing? I read a lot of "What you need to do is" and "you should's." Oh and then there were the "God never gives you more than you can handle," "Everything happens for a reason," and my personal favorite... "It was God's plan." It was his plan to kill me in a slow painful way and have my family and friends watch as it happened. Well, ain't that just peachy. Blah, blah, blah. Did people actually read some of the shit they sent? Clearly they didn't, or they wouldn't have been stupid enough to send it. I wanted nothing more than to respond the way I truly *felt.*

Dear Dumb-ass',

Thank you for telling me God hates me so much He believes I must suffer terribly before I die WAY TOO YOUNG. Thank you for informing me my life was so poorly lived my children must suffer by not having a mother. I must be a vile, foul, despicable person for such hatred to be thrust upon me. Gee, thanks. Oh, and juicing is stupid. It's easier to just EAT the fruits and vegetables versus squeezing the shit out of them. Wouldn't I be getting the same "benefits" from said fruits and veggies by, I don't know...eating them?

I wish I could say the things that needed to be said. I wanted to do the things that needed to be done. I wanted the world around me to stop and think before they opened their mouths and spit out ridiculous comments and instructions for how I should live the rest of my brief life. I should live my life surrounded by love and joy, but what I got was fear and sadness. Fuck you, world, and all your stupid ideas.

I typed out some "Thank yous" and a few "Oh, reallys" comments then shut down the anti-Social Media that took up too much precious time. I opened the media player on my computer and let it play random music, then I went back to the documents I had been creating. I worked on scrapbooks, a cookbook, letters, and my story. I focused the words that needed to be said into a place where it would matter, not where people could "like" it, or could stir it into a big pot of steaming drama. Nope, I had better things to do with my words.

I sang along with Paolo Nutini as he sang of picking up pieces and rewinding the life he was given.

Why couldn't I just rewind? Because, as someone pointed out, it was God's plan.

It was late by the time Tom got home and he reeked of bottled spirits. Wayne poured him onto the couch, gave me a pity nod and walked back out of the door. I could only hope his time with his brother did him some good and wasn't just liqueur using his liver as a trampoline. I knew he wouldn't make it up the stairs on his own and I wasn't strong enough to even try so I stripped him of his shoes and socks. I emptied his pockets and covered him with the blanket I had been curled up under when Wayne threw the door open only minutes before. I placed a kiss on his lips and ran my fingers along his stubbled cheek, "No, I'm married," he grumbled and batted at my hand.

"Yes, you are...for now," I choked past the lump of emotion as it formed in my throat. I kissed him again then left him to his dreams as I went in search of my own.

Chapter Thirty

I woke to the sound of Israel Kamakawiwo'ole strumming his ukulele and Shell singing about how wonderful the world was. Did I agree? "Shell?" I hollered over her strained vocals.

She poked her head around the corner of the door frame, "Morning, Madre."

"Morning," I croaked, "what're you doing today?" I asked while crawling from my small, lonely bed.

"I don't have to work until later so I thought I would actually clean my room and do some laundry."

"That sounds...boring and tedious."

She shrugged her shoulders, "Meh, it's not like it'll get done by itself. What are you doing today besides nursing dad's hangover? Dude, he smells totally pickled. I could smell it when I got home last night."

"He had a rough day yesterday."

"Clearly."

I dug through my dresser in search of clothes, "I'm gonna shower then I'll make some breakfast. Any suggestions?"

"We could have greasy sausage and drippy under cooked eggs smothered in cigar ashes...that should start dad's day off well," she chuckled.

"Digestive pyro technics, lovely." I slipped into my bathroom and showered quickly. I decided that Shell's suggestions were not going to be on the breakfast menu. I tried to quietly slip down the stairs so I didn't wake him but he wasn't where I left him the night before. He sat at the breakfast bar clutching a coffee mug in one hand and his head in the other. I went and got him some Advil from the bathroom and laid them on the counter next to him. He downed them without acknowledging my existence. He dropped his head and stared into his mug as if he was searching for the lost city of gold.

"Are you hungry?" I asked while rummaging around in the pantry, "I'm gonna make breakfast."

"No, I'm not."

"Okay, well, if you change your mind..."

"I'm gonna go shower," he grumbled, then stumbled from the stool in the direction of the stairs with his coffee in hand.

I called Michelle down when I had finished making pancakes and sausage. We ate with little conversation. I caught her looking at me from time to time, "What? Do I have something on my face?" I asked.

She gave me another shrug, "Just wondering what's up with dad."

I lay my fork on my plate and gulped down some coffee. I wished it was something stronger but it lacked, "He's upset about everything and the fact we can't do anything about it." I looked into the sky blue of her eyes and saw the rain form.

"I know how he feels," she admitted.

"I know, sweetie, me too. All we can do is make the best of what we have, ya know?" I laid my hand on her arm and petted her softly, "When is your next day off?"

"Wednesday, I work the closing shift Tuesday and open on Thursday."

"Well, if you are game and I feel human after Monday's crap, how about we spend the day together? Just you and me, we can watch Disney movies and sing along to the songs or play video games and you can kick my butt," I hoped out loud.

Her smile was better than the sun shining in the window, "It's a date."

I had a date with my baby girl. At least that gave me something to look forward to. Unlike the conversation I was about to have with my husband. Shell and I finished up breakfast and made some solid plans for Wednesday. I cleaned up the evidence of our meal, then went to talk with Tom. He was sitting on the edge of our bed wrapped in a towel with cold droplets of water sitting silent on his skin.

"Hey, how ya feeling?" I asked as I slid onto the space next to him.

"Fine."

"Bullshit."

His head jerked to me and it was quickly clear that was a bad idea. His hand immediately went to his forehead and a groan escaped his lips, "Fuck."

"That doesn't sound so fine to me," I remarked. "We need to talk about what happened yesterday."

"What's there to say? You wanna go and I want to keep you as long as possible," he stood slowly to gain his balance then went to his dresser. "You forget, I'm part of this too and so are the kids. You aren't the only one that's got cancer here. We all have cancer."

We all had cancer. He was right. We were all suffering from the same life ending disease. "You're right."

He leaned against the dresser for balance and pulled on his briefs followed by roughed up jeans. Crossing his arms over his chest, "I'm right? Maybe we should mark that on the calendar. I don't think any woman, anywhere, has ever said those words to a guy."

I let a small smile spread across my lips, "Because it is so rare for a man to be right." We looked at each other. No...we saw each other. We saw fear, pain, and intense love.

He moved towards me, reached down, took my hands in his and gave them a squeeze, "We have to talk about all of this. You can't make decisions without me. You can't decide to take you away from me." I dropped my head in shame. I had removed Tom. I was taking on this disease alone when, as he said, we all had cancer. "Hey," he tucked his fingers under my chin and forced me to look him in the eyes, "We are a team and a team works together."

"I'm on this team, too," pouted Shell from the door. She was leaning into the door frame with her arms wrapped around herself, "I get a say, too."

I held out my hand to her, "I promise to talk to you two and Lily before I decide on anything."

She ignored my hand. Instead, she threw her arms around me and cried into my shoulder, "Decide to live forever."

*****

"Why don't we call everyone and have a barbeque tonight? Tomorrow is gonna be a shit day, but they said I should eat normally. Not like greasy chili dogs but something good. What do ya think?" I asked Tom as we sat quietly on the deck enjoying the flowers screaming look at me. Okay, I was enjoying the flowers. Tom was checking his eyelids for holes.

"M' kay."

"Are you awake? Did you hear what I said?"

"Hmm...barbeque stuff," he sniffed with his fingers laced over his chest and sunglasses firmly in place.

"So, do you want to?"

"Sure, give me a few more minutes here."

I huffed at him, got up and went inside to call Molly and Charlotte to see if they were interested in charred meat and store bought potato salad.

"Wayne said he would like that," chirped Molly, "Should I make something?"

"You cook?" I quizzed.

"When I say 'make something' I meant pick something up," Molly clarified. I could swear I heard a giggle in there somewhere.

"Sure, pick up whatever you are craving. I'm sure we will be more than happy to eat it with you. See you later."

"Bye, now."

I hit the speed dial on my cell for Charlotte, "Of course we are comin'."

"Wha...?" I stammered.

"Tom rang Miguel and invited us to yer barbeque." I laughed when I saw Tom pacing around the deck with his phone pressed against his head.

"Is he on the phone with him now?"

"He is, why?"

I shook my head and continued to watch Tom's pacing, "Just wondering."

"What do ya want us to bring?"

"Whatever strikes your fancy when you get in the store."

Charlotte sighed, "That could be many things, don't cha know."

We laughed and wrapped up the call so she and Miguel could get themselves ready and stop by the store.

I went upstairs to clean up and let Shell know we are going to have a barbeque. "Yum, who's bringin' what?"

"I have no clue," I shrugged, "I told them to bring what they want."

"OMG, Mom! Charlotte might bring haggis or something," she squeaked in horror.

I laughed heartily, "She's Irish, not Scottish, and I don't think they sell that in the grocery store. But, if that's what she wants then that's what she wants."

"Gross."

I plopped down on her well-made bed, "You don't have to eat anything you don't want. Besides," I added while pulling her down onto the bed with me, "you have to go to work so you can always eat something there." I cuddled up close to her and wrapped myself tightly around her.

"I guess," she mumbled and settled into the hold I had on her. We just lay there quietly for a few minutes. I wanted to enjoy the feel of her in my arms for a while. "Are you gonna make anything?"

"What would you like me to make?"

"Deviled eggs, I love your deviled eggs."

"You got it," I loosened my grip on her, "help me up, please." We got me righted, "I'm gonna get cleaned up and I will go make your eggs." She squealed in delight and gave that silly clap girls do. I gave her my *'what the hell'* look.

"What? I'm excited. I love your deviled eggs," she defended with her shoulders at her ears.

"Got it." I made a note to myself to make sure I added that to the cookbook I was working on. I got myself put together and headed to the kitchen to boil some eggs. Tom was on the deck running a wire brush over the grill.

I heard him talking and looked up to see he was on his *cell, "...I don't know why she wants to have a barbeque. Shit, yesterday she was talking about not doin' treatments and now she wants a fucking party...I don't know, man. What the fuck was I supposed to say, 'no, I don't want to have people over?...*" He wasn't whispering but his voice was very low. So, instead of hiding my interest I threw open the screen door crossed my arms over my vacant chest and looked at him with true anger. "Shit! I'll talk to you when you get here...yeah. Later."

I deleted the few spaces between us. I poked my finger in his face, "I asked you if you wanted to do this," I waved my hand over the grill, "I asked if you wanted to have people over. I asked and now you wanna talk shit to your brother. I tell you what, forget it. Call them all back and tell them you are a fucking asshole and we aren't doing it." Before he could spit out a syllable I threw my hand up in his face, "Don't. You told me this morning we were a team, well, teams work together. Teams tell the truth. You," I poked him in the chest, "are suspended from my team." I went back inside, grabbed my purse and called up to Michelle.

"Sup?" she asked when she reached the last step.

"I'm leaving. You wanna come?" I asked.

"I thought we were..."

"We were but your dad is an asshole."

"Got it. Let's go."

We were half way down our street when I saw Wayne and Molly pass us. I shot Wayne a look to make it very clear he was on my shit list for what happened. My team was crumbling on the very day it was declared.

Shell and I went out and had pizza. We talked about everything she wanted to talk about. I tried to be good company for her, but I had a feeling I was failing miserably, "I'm sorry I'm not much fun," I said, "I was hoping for some fun before tomorrow. I don't know if I'll get sick and I don't know how long it will last if I do. So, I wanted to spend time with everyone beforehand."

"Oh, that makes sense, I guess," Shell agreed while picking at the piece of pizza that sat, cold, on her plate. She glanced at the time on her phone, "I have to be to work soon. Can you drop me at home so I can change?"

I tucked some money under the bill and gathered up my stuff, "Come on."

Tom hadn't called off the barbeque, or if he did, they came anyway. I parked my car along the road since Wayne decided he could park in my space in the driveway. I hurried inside and up the stairs before anyone knew I was there.

Shell went to her room to change and leave for work. She stopped off in my room before she left for the night, "Mom, I gotta go. Do you need anything?" she asked.

"No, I'm gonna stay in here. Have a good night. I love you."

She placed a kiss on my cheek, "Love you, too." She gave me a wave from the door then vanished from sight.

I sat on my bed facing the window that led to the back yard. I could hear the voices drifting up from below...

"Why didn't ya just say ya didn't wanna have this?" asked Charlotte with a little heat behind her words. "We are all sittin' here not knowin' what's goin' on."

"I know, okay, I know! I should have just...fuck. I don't know what I should have done."

"You should talk to your wife, man. I know this is a messed up situation, but you still need to say your piece to her. I'm here for ya, brother."

He should have said something before I picked up the phone and called anyone. He should have voiced his opinion or concerns when I asked him if he would want to do this. No, he kept it to himself...no, wait...he didn't keep it to himself. He called his brother instead of talking to me, his team member. I stormed down the stairs and slammed the door open.

"Ain't that nice. Your brother is here for you. I guess he's on your team then, right? 'Mr. We are a team', 'Mr. We all have cancer.' You're an ass," I snarled. "All you had to say was 'no,' that's all it would have taken for this," I jerked my arms all around to encompass the whole fucked up situation, "to not have happened."

"But..."

"But what, Tom? I asked you more than once. I asked you and you said 'sure,'" I finished with air quotes.

"I know," he whispered, "I didn't know what else to say."

"No, you could have just said no or asked questions."

I heard a gentle clear voice and scanned the deck. Molly stood and walk towards me, "Olivia, why did you want to have this dinner? Maybe if you explain it," she stood before me with concern in her eyes, "maybe it would help."

I looked around at the faces that sat as audience to our private lives, "I wanted to do this because I didn't know when the next time will come around when I will be strong enough to do it. I don't know how I'm gonna react to chemo tomorrow. I don't know if I'm gonna be a puking mess. So," I turned to Tom, "I wanted to spend some time with people I care about before tomorrow comes."

"Dumb-ass," grumbled Wayne.

"You shut your mouth," barked Molly, "It doesn't help when you are helping Tom keep things from Olivia. You should have told him to talk to her," she finished with a light slap to Wayne's very hard shoulder.

"Yes, dear."

We all burst out laughing at their display. "Sorry, man, but you just lost your man card," joked Miguel.

"I keep it in my purse," sniffed Molly. The laughter came harder and snorts were heard from Charlotte's general area. Who would have thought Molly had a sense of humor?

During the uproar, Tom came to my side, "I'm sorry I didn't say what I was thinkin'. I didn't want to make you mad, but I guess I did anyway."

"Ya think," I snipped.

"Yeah, I'm sorry, really."

I really didn't want to talk about it anymore, at least, not in front of everyone. I shook my head and walked over to find a place to sit. I bypassed the empty chair next to Wayne. I wasn't ready to be close to him unless I could knock the shit out of him. I reached out to him for help with his brother and I felt like he turned his back on me. I didn't ask for any of this. I didn't volunteer for cancer to run rampant in my body and steal my life. It wasn't my fault the people I was closest to were getting hurt.

It isn't my fault.

Chapter Thirty One

My ears woke before my eyes.

"...are you even sure she wants you to go with her? After you shoved your head so far up your ass yesterday you might find it difficult to drive," Shell bit out.

"Watch what you say, young lady," Tom growled, "Your mom can't go alone, so I'm going with her."

"I bet she can't wait, then again, maybe she's planning on puking all over you."

With a grunt Tom mumbled, "You're probably right."

I opened my eyes and found I wasn't alone. Oliver was curled up next to me sleeping through the rampant stupidity echoing down the hall. I pulled the fuzz-ball close and petted his soft fur, "You wanna go with me? I'm sure you could comfort me more than he can today," I whispered. He answered with a long stretch. He moved closer to my face and nuzzled my chin. "I love you too." He replied with a purr and another nuzzle. I lay there for a few more minutes trying to push the fear out of my mind, *it's all in my head, it's all in my head, it's all in my head...* The question was, how did I get it out of my head? I was slapped back to reality. Really, I was slapped by Oliver. He was trying to get my attention and resorted to violence. "Dude, that wasn't cool," I grumbled. "Are you hungry? Is that your problem?"

"Meow, purr, purr, meow."

"I see. Well, let's go get you something to eat." I gathered up my Lolly Monster and took him downstairs for his breakfast and my attempt at food.

"Morning, um, do you want coffee?" wavered Tom. I guess he was a little embarrassed about what happened last night or the fact his sixteen year old handed him his ass this morning.

You really are a badass, Shell. :-)

"No, I think I'm gonna stick with things that won't hurt coming up, like water and oatmeal. Mm, gotta love planning a meal around vomiting it up later." I set Oliver down near his bowls and went to the pantry to get his food. Tom poured me and Oliver some water and proceeded to make me some sticky, gooey, instant oatmeal. Yum, not. I settled in for a bowl of baby food, a hand full of meds and a glass of delicious water. Breakfast of old, toothless, diet restricted champions. WooHoo! That was all followed up by a pep talk from the guy who severely pissed me off just hours before...

"You can do this. Not everyone gets sick from chemo."

"I'm well aware of that," I mumbled between spoonsful of gray mush.

He continued with his motivational speech, "I did some research..."

"You mean you Googled something," I snickered.

"Yea, I Googled the side effects of chemo and getting sick depends on..."

I interrupted again, "It depends on the meds, my age, if I'm a drinker and ...it's all in your head?"

"Um, yea. You already looked it up?" He looked as if I had popped his balloon.

"I have researched every step of this process. I want to go in prepared." I finished up my breakfast, took the dishes to the sink, rinsed them and loaded them into the dishwasher. "I gotta get ready."

Oliver sat at the front door waiting for someone to let him out. "You're leaving me? Just when I thought I had someone on my side," I sneered as I opened the door to let the fuzz-ball out. "Later," I bellowed as I watched his flag pole tail disappear off the porch.

I dressed as comfortably as possible in yoga pants and a loose-fitting tee. It's funny, I have yoga pants but wouldn't know a yoga mat if it hit me in the, well, yoga pants. Go figure. I decided to pack an extra set of clothes. Just in case. The websites I visited said I should bring something to pass the time, so I tossed a few magazines and my kindle into my bag. I headed down stairs to tell Tom to do the same. "Hey, you should bring something to keep you busy. I have a couple of magazines and my kindle. I downloaded a couple of movies onto it last night. But, if there is something else you would rather have then get it and put it in my bag."

"Do you want to play a game? I could pack…"

"I don't think I will be up for that, sorry."

Tom looked around for anything to take with us but came up empty, "I'll just watch movies with you then," he smiled. Yippee.

*****

"Today is going to be a test in patience," explained Dr. Fraiser, "We will be doing a few things that will take a very, very, long time before we even get to your actual treatment."

"Okay, so what do I have to do?" I asked and looked at Tom like *'Did you know about this? Cuz I didn't.'* Tom shrugged and looked as confused as I did.

Dr. Fraiser opened a pamphlet and handed it to me, "We will do a blood test first. We need to make sure your white count is good before we begin. Then we have to prepare the correct drugs and doses for you. To be quite honest, we need to poison you enough to stop or slow the cancer's growth without killing you."

I gaped at her honesty, "Let's not mince words, shall we? So, we need to get to third base without going all the way."

"Exactly, but it can take some time to get the dosages right. When we are all set with the drug prep we will get you settled into the room and get the drip started."

Tom leaned back in his chair, exhausted from the list before any of them were checked off. "How long, exactly, are we gonna be here?"

Dr. Fraiser looked at her non-existent watch, "I'd say...all day."

"All day?" Tom and I gasped in unison.

The good doctor leaned against her desk and pointed to the pamphlet in my hands, "The first chemotherapy treatment can often take all day. It's a lot of checking, rechecking and prep work. Once we get you started, the rest of your treatments will move along much faster and with a shorter list of 'to do's'." We all looked around the room at each other, "Shall we do this?" she asked.

"Let's do it," I said with not one lick of excitement.

And so it began...

"Oh, for fuck's sake," Tom grumbled, "How much longer do we have to wait?" It was nearing two hours at this point. I had sacrificed my left arm to a blood draw. It took nearly half an hour to get the okay from the lab. I guess my blood was stronger than my emotions. I had nearly rubbed the skin clean off my hands at that point. They were doing the drug preparation and it was taking a very, very, very long time which explained Tom's patience wearing out.

"Why don't you walk around and see if you can find a coffee machine or the cafeteria?"

"Yea, fine," he snapped. He had reached his point of annoyance. He stormed down the hall. The waiting was pissing him off and scaring the shit out of me. I was already nervous when I got there over two hours ago, at that point it has multiplied tenfold.

"Olivia?"

I lifted my eyes to the dreamy voice. "Dr. K, it's nice to see you again." Dr. Khudiadadzai stood before me in khakis and a long white lab coat. I could just make out the royal purple collar of his shirt above his coat. He was as beautiful as ever and I was too nervous to truly appreciate the perfection on display.

"It's nice to see you, too. How are you feeling?"

"I don't know, like I have cancer...or something," I joked, "I'm waiting to start my first chemo treatment. I'm waiting on the drug prep."

Dr. K pointed to the seat next to me, "May I?"

"Please," I waved my hand over the seat in offering to him.

"Thank you, prep can take a while. How long have you been waiting?"

"About two hours, it shouldn't be too much longer, right?" *Please agree, please.*

"I wouldn't think so. You will be in there," he pointed to a door halfway down the hall, "settled into a seat in no time at all."

"Not sure how thrilled I am with that idea. I would much rather be laid out on my couch, remote in hand, watching Dr. Phil."

He laughed at my admission, "Me too. I would love to be laid out, asleep, on my couch. But, like you, I am here for the day."

"I thought you came in today just to cheer me up," I gasped in mock shock.

"Alas, I had other reasons to be here today." I laughed at his false shame. We chatted for a few more minutes before he was called away to see to a patient.

"Mrs. Carpenter, we are ready for you now," announced a lovely young nurse in *Scooby-doo* scrubs. I gathered up my things and followed her to 'the room.'

"My husband went in search of a coffee machine. Will someone be able to let him know where I am when he finds his way back?"

Nurse -*Scooby*- gestured towards a large chair with light blue vinyl cushions for me to sit on, "Here," she held out a white hospital blanket, "the cushions can get sweaty after a while. This should help." I lay the blanket over the cushions for when it was time to settle in. "Someone will tell Mr. Carpenter where to find you as soon as he comes back."

"Thanks."

"My name is Cindy and I will be helping you out with your treatment today. Let's get you into a gown. You can leave on everything below the waist. Put the gown on backwards so we have easier access to your port-a-cath." She gave me a threadbare gown with a few of the ties missing, but what difference did it make, no one was going to see me and I no longer had anything to see. I heard a knock at the door while I was changing.

"I'm looking for my wife, Olivia Carpenter?" stammered Tom. He must have been upset to see I wasn't out there waiting when he got back.

"She's in here, Mr. Carpenter. Come in. Have a seat right over there." When I stepped around the curtain I saw Tom sitting in a less than comfortable chair next to the one I would be sitting in for a few fun filled hours.

I folded my top and stuffed it into my bag of tricks, "Did you find the coffee machine?"

"Yes, but I was worried the smell might bug you," he waved his hand in the direction of the nurse loading up a tray, "when all this gets started so I got a bottle of water instead." I smiled at him for thinking of me, even if it was just so I wouldn't get sick from the smell of his coffee.

I placed a much needed kiss on his head then climbed onto the chair I would be poisoned in. Nurse Cindy...Nurse –Scooby- rolled a small metal tray table over towards me. It had bags filled with clear liquid, needles, sponges, and other stuff I didn't want. "The doctor will be in shortly and we can get started."

We? Did she have a mouse in her pocket? Was she going to have bags of poison hooked up to her? No, I think not. The only 'we' in that room was me and Tom.

A single knock fell on the door... breathe, Olivia.

*****

I was nearly an hour into my treatment and I was faring fine, okay, not fine. I hadn't puked...yet. It was coming, but I was trying so hard to hold it. 'It's all in your head' my ass. It was all about to be in the puke basin.

"Babe, let it go. I can tell you want too. Your face is green," Tom whispered and stroked my arm. He glanced over at Nurse -Scooby-.

"He's right, Mrs. Carpenter. It's better to not fight it." I hugged the basin closer to me, turned away from Tom and revisited the light lunch I had eaten more than two hours ago. I revisited it a few times. Can you vomit a spleen? How about a shoelace? In between each purge, Tom and Nurse *-I don't like Scooby* anymore- forced me to drink water.

"You need to stay hydrated," Nurse Cindy explained.

Tom rubbed my arm, "It will give you something to throw up instead of dry heaves."

"Argh..." which was vomit *for* 'Screw you.' I wanted to yank the tube out of my chest and call it quits right then and there but I hadn't finished the treatment yet. How many more were in my future? How much of a future did I have left?

"How much longer?" I choked during a pause in my attempts at regurgitating what I ate last Tuesday.

Nurse *-Scooby* Sucks- checked the clear plastic bag that dangled from a pole above me, "About two hours, give or take."

"Give or take what? Me begging you to make it stop?"

Tom shifted my freshly poisoned body to the opposite side of the lounge chair then climbed on beside me. He reclined the back, turned us on our sides and cuddled closer with his chest to my back. Slowly and gently, he began to rock us and whispered encouragements into my deaf ears. I didn't want to hear it. I wanted it over, but he held me closer. "You can do this, babe." "You are so strong." "You got this." Bullshit. I was there because I was too chicken to let the cancer take over. I was afraid of saying goodbye. I was scared shitless of death. But the fact was, I was going to die no matter how many times I sat in that chair.

Nearly three hours later I was scooped up and put into the truck, buckled in, and driven home. I fought a battle to keep my eyes open but lost.

*****

"...I haven't seen anyone get that sick before," Tom whispered.

"She looks like crap. Can we do anything to make her feel better?" begged Michelle.

"Make sure she eats and drinks. The vomiting may continue so we have to watch what she eats. No bringing home crap from work for her, understand?"

"You know how she likes the fries."

"No fries, got it?"

Shell sighed and gave in, "Yea, I got it."

"Come on. Let's let your mom sleep."

I drifted in and out for a few hours. My stomach fought me every time I moved. I wanted to get up but was afraid the dam would break and I would start spewing my innards again. Problem was... I had to pee. I was mildly amazed I had enough liquid left in my body to need to pee. I opened my eyes to try to figure out how to get to the bathroom without making a terrible mess. That was when my love for Tom was renewed, again. On the bed side table stood a card that read, "Call me and I will come up to help you," and at its base lay my cell.

I tapped the speed dial number for my rescuer, "I'm on my way. Did you get sick, baby?"

"No, I have to go to the bathroom and am afraid I might not make it without getting sick." I hadn't gotten out the last words when Tom appeared in the doorway. "Hi."

"Hi, yourself," he smiled and slid his phone back into his pocket, "okay then, let's get you into the bathroom."

Tom helped me sit up slowly and waited until I got my bearings before he helped me stand. I was about as steady as a drunk on 'buy one get one free' night at the pub.

"I got it from here," I said as I stood hovering over the toilet, "I'll call you if I need you."

"What? I can wait."

"Yes, you can. On the other side of the door," I grumbled and pointed to the doorway.

"Fine, I'll be right out there. Do you want a shower? I'll get you some clean clothes."

"Oh God, yes, I would love a shower."

"Pee and I will get your stuff together."

I did what I had to do. By the time I was done Tom was back at the door. He sat me on the toilet seat and told me to strip while he turned the shower on for me. "Don't get in yet. I'll be right back." He was back a few minutes later with a plastic deck chair. "You can sit and shower and I won't worry about you falling over." I think I may have chuckled.

I was wrapped in fresh pj's, a blanket, and holding a cup of hot tea watching *August Rush*, Shell lay sleeping beside me. So much for a *Disney* filled date night with my baby girl. It was weird being in bed so early. Even Oliver seemed confused as he stared at me from the other side of the bed. "Don't blame me, bud. Tom said I had to rest." I patted the comforter to coax him a bit closer. Nope, he was quite content right where he was, "Brat."

I drifted during the credits to *John Legend* singing *Someday*. Reminding me that there would be a time in the very far off future when we would all be together again.

Maybe, maybe not.

Chapter Thirty Two

Oh, my fucking God, stay still, don't move. Oh my God, oh my God, oh my God, I wanna die. I opened my eyes slowly. I was living in fear I might vomit, again. Tom left my anti-nausea pills on my night stand which seemed so...faaar...awaaay. I reached my arm out in a feeble attempt to get them but it felt like that dream you have where the faster and harder you run the further away your destination got. I was stuck in that God-forsaken scenario. I didn't have the energy to keep reaching for something I wasn't going to get my hands on so I allowed my arm to drop back down to the bed and my eyelids to slam shut to block out the light. I struggled to fall back to sleep and even then I had to hang on to the peace with what little energy I had.

"Hey...hey...babe?"

"Huh?"

"Come on, babe. You need to wake up so you can take your medication. Come on, wake up," Tom coaxed, "I see your eyeballs moving around. Don't make me shake you."

"Argh...noooo, don't," I whined.

"I won't. Let me help you sit up."

I rolled very slowly, keeping my eyes closed tight. I prayed I wouldn't get sick. Once I was on my back, Tom leaned over me and put my arms around his neck, "Grab hold and I'll lift you up."

"You just wanted to hug me."

As he sat back up he took my upper body with him, "True, I was using your pills as an excuse. How's that? You okay?"

I opened my eyes, squinted into the light, "I'm...okay."

"Good, now let's shift you back so you can lean against the head board." He helped me work my body backward inch by inch until I was within leaning range. "All right, here ya go," he smiled as he handed me my 'please, don't puke again' pills and a bottle of water. I took what was offered and hoped for the best. "I'm going to go get your breakfast," I tried to put my two cents in but he held up his hand to stop me, "Stop...you will eat. You will drink. Doctor's orders, remember? You have to eat to stay strong. Calories are good."

I leaned my head back against the hard wood of the headboard, "I don't wanna," I whined. "You can't make me." I stuck out my tongue like a full grown eight year old.

With a menacing whisper Tom took the fight right out of me, "I can and I will." Well, all righty then. I guess I was gonna eat.

I was awakened again minutes later by Tom and Michelle bringing in my culinary delights...dry toast, oatmeal and hot tea. Mmmm...oh joy, can you say bland? I made the food disappear and I hoped it would remain out of sight for a long time. Tom took the dishes away as fast as he had brought them then appeared in front of me holding my toothbrush, "Do you want to brush here or can you make it to the bathroom?"

"I just wanna go to sleep," I murmured with my head resting on Shell's shoulder.

"What's the hurry? She just finished eating?"

"Look, the doctor warned us about side effects and one was chemo mouth and that makes it harder for you to eat and drink. So, here," he pointed to the bed, "or do you want us to help you to the bathroom?"

I looked up into Shell's face, "He is a meanie."

393

Shrugging the shoulder my head wasn't supported on, "Meh, not as bad as you've been known to be."

I gasped. Did my daughter just call me a meanie? I believe she did. "Am not," I choked as I reached out my hand for Tom to take and ease me out of bed. "Bathroom, I can clean up then go back to bed."

"Bathroom it is."

Shell held me steady while I brushed, flossed and brushed my teeth again. I couldn't get the taste of vomit and metal out of my mouth. I finished with a mouth rinse and hoped for the best. I washed the crud from my face and ran a brush through my hair. I checked to see if there were more hairs than normal left in the bristles. I couldn't tell and I didn't see any in the sink or on the counter. Tom interrupted my feeble attempt at hygiene when he set clean pajamas on the vanity next to me and wrapped his arm around my waist, "I got this, kiddo. I'm pretty sure you don't wanna see your Mom nekked," Tom chuckled as he took my body weight from Shell's shoulders.

"Um, no thank you, I have to get ready for work anyways," Shell placed a single perfect kiss on my cheek, "Love ya, Moms. I'll check on you when I come home to change later." She leaned in a bit closer and whispered into my ear, "I have a date with *'The Dude.'*" I felt her smile before I saw it. I smiled back. "Bye."

"Bye," I croaked, "I love you, too." Then she was gone.

"Let's get you changed and back into bed."

*****

I woke to the unrelenting urge to get rid of the breakfast I had eaten no more than an hour ago. As if he knew, Tom had left a bucket hanging on the knob of my bed side table and sadly, I used it. During my abdominal commotion I saw Oliver streak from the bed and Tom take his place. He rubbed my back and shoulders and told me he loved me and this would pass. He brought me a cool washcloth to wipe my face when my stomach finally emptied.

"Do you need the bathroom?"

I nodded my head, knowing I needed to brush my teeth. And so it continued for another 24 hours. Sleep, eat, vomit, brush teeth, and repeat.

I clung to the banister as I made my descent down the stairs, praying I had enough energy to make it without bouncing down them. I was finally in my living room, a room I hadn't seen in days. Huh, it looked the same, nothing noteworthy to speak of. I was feeling a little closer to human but far enough away to know I wasn't going to be doing anything too strenuous. I found Tom sitting on a stool at the breakfast bar. He was resting his weight on his elbows and staring down into a mug. His shoulders were hugging his ears. I could feel the stress pulsating all around him.

"Hi."

Tom jerked upright and spun around, "What are you doing down here?" he demanded as he walked toward me. He ushered me to a chair at the dining room table, "Sit. You shouldn't have come down the stairs alone." I got the distinct feeling he was pissed.

"As you can see," I began, "I am feeling better and stronger. If I needed help," I reached into my robe pocket and extracted my cell, "I would have called you." I smiled up at him, "Good morning. Can I have coffee?"

"Do you think you can handle coffee?" he asked with a questioning eyebrow.

"We won't know until I try, right?" I stood from the chair, "I'm gonna go out to the deck. Can you bring it out there, please?" I asked as I placed my hands on his chest, "I love you. You know that, right? You have taken very good care of me these last few days." I muscled up my energy and rose up on my tippy toes and kissed my husband. It had been days since I felt his lips on mine. I had felt them on my forehead, on my cheek, in my hair, and even pressed to my shoulder but not my lips. "I missed that," I whispered and made my way, slowly, to the back door.

Oliver made his way out of the door before I did. I shuffled over to my favorite seat which over looked the flourish of color bursting from the garden I had worked for years to create. It didn't disappoint. I saw a sea of color and could smell the perfume surrounding me. I lifted my face to the sun and felt warm.

"Your coffee, ma lady. What would you like to try for breakfast?"

I took the hot mug in my hands and inhaled the aroma, "Mmmm...how about...um...ooo, scrambled eggs. Let's try," I smiled then took a sip of my coffee...and spit it across the table. "Hot, hot, hot, wow."

Tom took my chin in his hand and wiped the coffee from it with his other, "You okay? What the hell was that?"

"It's just really hot. Why was it so hot?"

"It's the same as always."

We were both confused by the turn of events, "I'll let it cool a little before I drink it." I stared at the offending cup in absolute confusion. What the heck was that all about?

Tom headed back towards the door, "I'm gonna make us some eggs. Holler if you need me." I nodded my head and blew on my coffee. Moments later he appeared with an ice cube and plopped it into my mug. "There, that should help."

"Thanks, babe."

I sat quietly and waited for the ice to melt. I watched Oliver make his way through the flower beds towards the collection of bird feeders in the corner of the yard. He lay down at the base of the pole and watched the birds swoop in for breakfast. "Oliver, don't you dare. You leave those birds alone," I warned. It wasn't like he was going to listen or even understood me but he got up from his spot and wandered back in my direction. He made his way to the sun filled chair next to me where he finally came to rest. "Good boy," I cheered and petted his head.

The petting was interrupted by the banging at the door, "Can you help me out here?" Tom stood on the other side of the screen door with his arms loaded with plates, silverware and all the trapping that went along with scrambled eggs. I went and opened the door to release Tom from his confines. "Thanks, let's eat." I helped Tom set the table, "Do you want a refill on your coffee?" asked Tom as he went in search of the ketchup. "I'll put an ice cube in it for ya."

I handed him my mug with a 'thanks, please' then inspected the bright yellow mass on the plate in front of me. I picked up my fork and pleaded with my body to let me be able to eat without feeling like death warmed over afterwards. It was hot. Like my coffee, hot. What the hell? I dropped the fork to my plate and panic chewed my food until it seemed to cool enough to swallow.

"What's wrong?" asked Tom as he came up next to me with ketchup in one hand and my coffee in the other.

"Hot, damn. Did you use a flame thrower to cook this morning?"

Tom set my mug in front of me, reached out his hand and touched my eggs with a single finger then touched his own, "Babe, they're the same temperature and it isn't hot. Warm maybe, but not hot. What's goin' on?"

I shrugged in confusion, "Maybe it's from being sick and brushing my teeth too much. You know, that chemo mouth thing," I offered as an explanation.

"Yeah, maybe."

We settled in to breakfast. Tom ate while I waited for things to cool to the point I could eat. I wondered if this was another side effect. I would have to look it up.

*****

Tom called the doctor's office and was told my mouth was probably over-sensitive due to the vomiting but to watch for any sores. I was to rinse my mouth at least every two hours with baking soda and water and to brush with a soft-bristled toothbrush. Good stuff to have known before all of this started. I guess I didn't *Google* *eve*rything I needed to know. The list of things to look out for has become longer and longer: pain, burning, tingling, fatigue, weakness, fever, constipation, temperature sensitivity, blah, blah, blah, and in my case, drum roll...death. Ta-da, everyone's life ends with death, I'm just more aware of when it will happen than the average person. Tick, tock, tick, tock...

Oliver and I took a nap on the couch while Tom napped in his recliner. It felt like all I was doing was sleeping. I was wasting away my time with my eyes closed to the things around me. I forced my eyes open. I watched Tom as he snored softly from across the room. I owed him time. I owed him more than I had to give. He was getting short changed right along with me. I forced myself up. I forced myself to do something other than sleep. I forced myself into the office where I sat in front of the computer and worked on my connection with my family. I typed up each of their favorite recipes and copied and pasted pictures onto pages with my memories attached. I wrote letters and made cards. I made plans and designed ways to be a part of their futures. When I couldn't concentrate any longer I wandered around Facebook then Pinterest then my email, delete, spam, delete, trash, delete, Trish...*Holy shit.*

Dear Liv,

I heard the news from Alyssa. Now I want to hear it from you. How bad is it really? I know you and Alyssa aren't really talking much and I feel like it's my fault. I lied to both of you for so long but you saw through all the crap or at least doubted some of it. Alyssa believed everything I said. I could never really figure out if it was because she's naïve, blind, or was too focused on her to see me? Is there any way for the two of you to be close again? Is there hope for your friendship?

I'm so sorry, Liv. I'm sorry I'm not there with you. I'm sorry you got dragged into my crap life. I'm sorry Richard hurt you. I have started to build a new life here. It's great to be around family again and the boys are doing great. They don't ask about their dad much which makes it easier on me. I'm doing okay. I miss you and Alyssa and crazy dip nights.

Talk to me, Liv. Tell me what's going on. Tell me there is something I can do.

I love you,

Trish

P.S. I filed for divorce.

I cried. I cried because I missed her. I cried because she was doing better. I cried because she was one of the reasons Alyssa and I weren't talking. I cried because I had to tell her I was le*aving.*

To My Long Lost Friend,

I miss you so much, Trish. I am happy you, Gage and Warren are finding peace surrounded by family. You deserve it. I hope you build a wonderful life for you and the boys. Maybe, someday in the future, you will find love again. You will find a man who honors you and will understand how lucky he is to have you in his life. Mark my words, it will happen.

My story...I'm not sure what Alyssa told you so I guess I have to tell you...everything. I have Stage IV breast cancer. The easiest way to explain it is to say I am terminal. I had a double mastectomy a few weeks back and have started chemo but it's not to save my life. It is my feeble attempt to buy me some more time. The cancer spread beyond the breast. That means it invaded other areas of my body. They would have to turn me into Swiss cheese to try to get it all and even then, well...like I said, I'm terminal.

I don't want you worrying about this. There is NOTHING you or anyone can do to make it all better. I am not going to come out of this. I am happy to know you and those handsome young men of yours are safe and happy. That is all I ever wanted for you. I am using the time I have to make sure my girls and Tom have peace in the future, like you are building in yours. I am saying the things I need to say and doing the things I need to do. Please, do the same.

Be happy, friend. Be strong and know you deserve a good life.

I love you bunches and tons,

Olivia

I cried some more. It felt so final when I clicked the 'send' button on that email. That part of my life was completed. I needed to do the same with Alyssa so I sent her a text and hoped for the *best*.

I was wondering if I could see you. Can you come by my place? I think we need to talk.

Send...wait...*Beep.*

Tonight, 6:30?

Could I do it? I had to.

See you then.

Send.

I sat behind the desk and stared at nothing on the screen. I had so many things I wanted to say but none seemed to come to mind. I needed to get my thoughts straight before Alyssa came over. I went in search of the one person who could help me. "Tom? Are you awake?"

Chapter Thirty Three

"What do you want to talk to her about?" yawned Tom.

"That's just it. I want to talk to her about a lot of stuff but every time we see each other I want to slap the shit out of her."

Tom scratched his head and yawned again, "Why do you want to talk to her now? You haven't talked to her since the hospital, right?"

I sat on the couch where I had been asleep earlier in the day, "Yea. It's all the Trish stuff and Dr. Matthews and…"

"Who? Who's Dr. Matthews?"

Crap. "Dr. Matthews was my gynecologist, the one who found the lumps to begin with. Well, Alyssa is dating him and she hasn't had a very good track record with guys and I basically called her a slut."

That caused Tom to sit up in his seat and take notice. "How, wha?"

"She's a *'screw 'em and leave 'em'* kinda girl. She doesn't believe in wasting time on a relationship if the sex is subpar. Well, she did think that way. I don't know if that's still the case," I looked down at my hands as I picked at my nails. "I was mad at the idea she was using my doctor."

"So what if she did?"

I huffed in annoyance, "Okay, now you can't get mad."

He looked at me with doubt, "Okay."

"Okay, so, Dr. Matthews is...well, he's..."

"He's what?"

"He's smokin' hot. I'm mean drool worthy."

Tom leaned back into his chair, "Oh."

"I'm sorry, babe. I was kinda, I don't know."

"You were jealous your friend was banging your hot doctor."

"Yes."

Tom burst out laughing. What was so damn funny? "You were jealous?"

"Yes, what's so funny about that?" I whined.

"The guy could have had a girlfriend or been married, for God's sake. Why are you jealous he is seeing Alyssa?"

How the hell do you explain a woman's logic to a guy? "Look, if you and I broke up and you started dating one of my friends I would be pissed at her and you. You are mine just like he was my doctor. Does that make sense?"

"Nope, but I hope you can explain it to her better than you explained it to me," he laughed. He got up from his chair then moved across the room to me. He tucked his finger under my chin and lifted my eyes to him, "I am yours." He kissed me softly then released my face. "Come on, let's get you some lunch."

"You have gotten so bossy."

"Yup," he took my hand and helped me up from the couch.

"I got an email from Trish. She's why I want to talk to Alyssa. She feels like it is her fault all this happened with me and Alyssa."

Tom looked confused, "I thought it was the doctor thing? Why would she think it was her?" Tom escorted me to a chair in the dining room and went to rummage around in the pantry for something to eat.

"It did kinda start after Dick Head put Trish in the hospital. You know, when Alyssa accused us of causing the whole blow up between them."

"Yeah, I remember. I couldn't believe she thought we caused it," Tom said while holding up a can of tuna. "Tuna?"

"Not for me. I think we have macaroni salad in the fridge, I'll take some of that." He gave me a nod and began opening the tuna.

"So you need to talk to her about the fight and the doctor. What else?"

"Just those two things, I know it doesn't seem like much, but it broke my trust in her."

Tom got the salad out and fixed me a bowl. He carried his sandwich, chips and my lunch to the table, "I get it. What do you want to drink?"

"Iced tea if we have it."

"It seems like an awful big fight for it to only be those two things."

"It is. The doctor thing I can get over, it's the accusations about Trish and Richard that really pissed me off. She accused you, too. She wasn't there, how would she know other than through the lies Trish told."

Tom put the drinks on the table and sat in the seat next to me, "I guess you know what you need to talk about then." He took a bite of his tuna sandwich then slid my bowl closer, signaling it was time to eat.

"Yes, dear," I griped, but ate anyway. I'd never eaten a handful of screws before but I could tell you what they tasted like. They tasted just like macaroni salad.

*****

I stood in the bathroom after a shower and looked at the hairs in my hand. It wasn't a clump but there were definitely a lot more than usual. Maybe I was imagining it. Like, you will only get sick if you think you will. Maybe, you will only lose your hair if you think you will. What a load of shit. You get sick because of the meds, not because of your inner thinking. Your hair falls out for the same reason.

"Mom? Where ya at?"

"In here," I hollered to Shell, "I'll be out in a sec."

I heard the shift of my bed followed by, "'k."

I rinsed the hairs from my hand, dried off, and swung open the door. I was still a bit queasy from lunch and the smell of her uniform wasn't helping. I slapped a hand over my mouth and nose, "Oh Shell, please go change your clothes. The smell is making me sick." I stepped back into the bathroom to get some distance.

"Crap, okay, I'll be right back."

Twenty minutes later Shell poked her head in the doorway, "I took a shower to get the smell outta my hair. Can I come in?"

I patted the space beside me on the bed, "Of course, but don't bounce."

Michelle climbed onto the bed next to me, "Do I smell okay?"

A gave her a reassuring smile, "You smell purdy."

"How ya feelin'? Never mind, that was a stupid question."

"No, it's not. I'm doing okay. Still queasy but your dad has been making me eat so I have some energy." I nudged her with my shoulder, "I even made it downstairs today."

"Look at you, super mom."

"If that impresses you then you will love this, I had breakfast outside," I stated proudly and watched her smile like I had just run a marathon.

"Look at you, getting' outta bed and all."

We both laughed, and I reached out and took her hand, "Tell me, how was your date with 'The Dude?'" I asked with my eyebrows kissing the top of my forehead. "Don't leave anything out."

"There's not much to tell. We went for pizza and talked. Then we went to a party for a little while but his ex was there and she was being the extreme version of a bitch, so we left and walked around the park and talked."

"Extreme version of a bitch? I like it. I think I need to be that."

"No, you do not want to be that. She was nasty mean, for no reason." Shell rested her head on my shoulder and I rested my head on hers.

"She was nasty because her ex-boyfriend showed up at a party with a beautiful girl. A girl she couldn't compete with. Ever."

"Nope. She was just a bitch."

"We need to think of a different word than bitch. Bitch means something else to me. It's not an insult to me. You could call her a witch or nut-ball or a...shrew. I like that. Call her a shrew."

"Shrew? Why can't I call her a bitch?"

I interlaced our fingers and kissed the back of her hand, "Bitch to me means brave, intelligent, tenacious, caring, and hopeful. Those are words I would want people to use when they describe me." We sat for a moment while that settled into her brain. "I took the power out of the insult. You can't hurt me with a word I redefined."

"I love you, Mom."

"I love you too. Are you gonna see, what's his name, again?"

She chuckled then lifted her head from my shoulder, "Kyle, his name is Kyle and I need to get dressed because we are going to a movie tonight." She gave a full megawatt smile then left me to bask in her after-glow.

*****

Six o'clock found me in the bathroom trying to calm my stomach. I turned down dinner, which pissed Tom off, but I knew it would have come back up very quickly if I hadn't. I nibbled on crackers and pretzels to try to make him happy, but it didn't help my stomach at all. Alyssa would be there in half an hour and my nerves were on edge. There was so much to say and I had no idea how to say any of it.

"Hey," Tom tapped on the door, "Are you okay? Can I come in?"

I opened the door to see his concerned face looking back at me, "I'm okay," I said and rested my hand to his cheek. "I'm trying to settle my stomach."

"You didn't eat anything. What's making you sick? Did you drink something?"

"No, I think it's nerves. Every time Alyssa and I have seen each other in the last few months we have fought like teenagers." I laid my head on his chest prompting Tom to wrap his arms around me, "I don't know how this is gonna go. If it goes bad we won't have

405

another chance to clear the air between us." Tom stiffened at the mention of not getting another shot. He knew what I was saying and he didn't take kindly to it.

"Let's get you settled, and I will bring you some stuff to snack on. You need to eat, babe."

"I can get to the couch on my own. Can you bring me some water?"

"Sure."

He went one way and I went the other. Tom made it back to the living room just in time to answer the door. I could feel the sweat run down my back and the slight tremor in my hands. I really was nervous.

"Alyssa, Come on in," invited Tom, but I could hear the sharpness in his tone.

"Tom, it's nice to, um, see you again," stammered Alyssa as she stepped through the doorway. Tom closed the door behind her and waved his arm in my direction. I sat on the couch with a blanket tucked around my legs. I knew I looked nowhere close to healthy but the blanket made me look feeble. Tom put it there and because of that I left it where it was.

"Have a seat. Do you want anything to drink?"

"Um, whatever Liv's having is fine." Alyssa hesitated before she took a few faltering steps towards the loveseat. She was nervous too.

"I'm nervous too," I volunteered.

"You are?"

I bobbed my head in agreement, "I don't want to fight but we do have something we need to talk about." I finally worked up the nerve to look her in the face. She looked like hell.

"We do. I don't want to fight either," her voice hovered barely above a whisper, "I've had a rough enough few days."

I tilted my head and looked at her from head to foot. She was off. There was something else going on besides my request to talk. "What's going on, Alyssa? You seem more than nervous about talking to me."

She covered her face with her hands and dropped her head in anguish, "He dumped me."

"What?"

She lifted her head to look at me, "He dumped me a couple days ago."

I was shocked, "Why? What happened?"

"He said I didn't trust him and he couldn't be with someone who didn't trust him," she garbled out between tears.

I was confused, "Why don't you trust him? Did he cheat on you?"

"No, I don't think so. It's just, women stare at him and he's so nice to all of them and he's good looking…"

"Good looking? He's hot, Alyssa, but that doesn't mean he did anything."

"Why wouldn't he? Like that nurse in your hospital room, he was really nice to her."

I chuckled, "You don't trust him because he is nice to women. You do realize he is a gynecologist. His entire clientele are women. He works in a hospital with nurses, who are typically women…unless you have some kind of proof he did something…I don't know." I sat in silence while my words bounced around the reasoning center of her brain. "Think about it this way, in the time frame you have been dating, has there ever been time for him to see another woman? Like, days without seeing him or not returning texts or calls?"

"No," she sniffled, "we've been together pretty much every night after we both get off work."

"Sounds like you have some groveling to do, Alyssa. That is if you still want to see him."

She bowed her head again and whimpered out a "yes."

"Then we better talk about what we need to talk about, so you can go over there and fix this. Go ahead and text him and tell him you want to talk after you leave here." I leaned back on the sofa and rubbed my head while she tapped out a desperate message to Neil. I was starting to get a headache from holding in anger. Tom noticed. Of course he did. He was at my side with two Advil and a refill of my water. I thanked him and downed the pills.

"I'll be in the office if you need me. I can hear you guys out here so if it gets loud..." he gave me a look that said he would toss Alyssa out on her ass if she upset me.

"Got it." I gave a smirk as he walked away. The beep of Alyssa's phone drew my attention back to her. "Is he willing to talk?"

Her smile eased the lines of worry on her face, "Yeah, he said he would love to talk and he's glad I am here talking to you."

"So am I."

I started. I told her how I felt jealous of her relationship with Dr. Matthews and how stupid it was to feel that way. She understood my reasoning better than Tom could. Duh. Woman to woman, we get it. The conversation about Trish was a lot more difficult to have. I told her Trish's email was what prompted me to reach out to her. I told her how I felt about things she said. She, in turn, did the same. It wasn't an easy conversation and it didn't correct all the ills but it was a start. I started to get very tired. It was draining both emotionally and physically to try to mend these busted-up fences.

"I'm sorry, Alyssa, but I am getting very tired. Can we talk again later?"

"Oh, yeah, um...I didn't realize."

"It's okay. I get tired really easy," I explained, "but we still have things to talk over. Can you come by again sometime?"

"Yeah, I can do that. Text me, okay?"

Alyssa gathered herself together and moved in the direction of the door, "Good luck with your next talk. I hope you guys work things out."

"Me, too, I want you to know I really do like him a lot. I might even be, kinda, in love with him."

I smiled at my friend, "Then you better get moving. You don't want to keep him waiting."

"Wish me luck," she begged then turned and walked out the front door.

I watched her pull away and wished her luck in a silent plea.

"You good?"

I was shaken from my silence by the guy who held my heart, "I guess. We still have things to talk about but I'm kind of tired so she left."

"I'm glad you told her it was time to go. You have to know your limits. Do you want to go to bed?"

I looked at the clock and chuckled, "It's only 8:20. I feel like a five-year-old being told it's bed time. No, I would like to sit here and watch the boob-tube with you for a little while. How does that sound?"

"Scooch over," Tom demanded, "What do you wanna watch?"

Chapter Thirty Four

It had been over a week since chemo and nearly as long since I heard from Alyssa. I got a text later that night telling me she and Neil were trying to work things out. That was it. So much for trying to make amends. It was more for me than her anyway and I said what I had to say.

I had been filling my days with handfuls of meds and large quantities of naps. I liked to call them short comas. Naps last an hour or two, but mine ran around five or six. I was sleeping my life away. The only bonus was the vomiting had pretty much stopped. I still got nauseated but not enough to stress about. I was getting to break free from my prison. I was going out to meet up with Charlotte. Molly's doctor's appointment was only 24 hours away and Charlotte needed to talk final details about the gender party. It was nice to know I was going to laugh. Charlotte always made me laugh. Tom had finally gone back to work. He was driving me nuts following me around for a whole week. I knew he was worried and concerned and there was nothing I could do to ease it for him. I needed a break from my life...wrong wording there. I needed a break from...my reality.

I stood before my bathroom mirror and was not shocked by what I saw. My already short hair was filling the sink. It didn't even seem to bother me all that much. It was hair. It wasn't my lung or my heart. I didn't need it to live another day. I didn't need it to be me. It was hair. That was all. I cleaned up the hairball and tossed it in the trash then tried to brush the remaining offenders from my tee-shirt. I dabbed on a little makeup to try to give my face a bit of color. I avoided mascara in fear I would comb my lashes right off my face. Besides, the face I use to make to put on mascara made me giggle. Why did I find that funny?

I returned to my room to finish getting ready and was approached by a very demanding fuzz-ball, "Meow."

"Well, hello to you, too."

"Meow," Oliver demanded while rubbing his body around my ankles.

"What?" I asked while patting the bed to coax him up to my level. He sprang to the bed and purred as I rubbed his bulbous head. I traced the trade mark "M" pattern on his forehead. "What are your plans for the day? Charlotte's coming over. You can always chase her around the deck."

"Purr."

"I gotta get ready, lil dude," I gave him one last rub then left him to curl up on my pillow and nap.

Tom had taken to leaving post-it notes all over the place, everything from "I love you" to "EAT & DRINK" to "Don't forget your meds." I found one on the mirror reminding me to brush and rinse my mouth every two hours to stave off chemo mouth. Too late, I had already developed a few sores, nothing too bad but enough to annoy the hell out of me. I had to admit, the best part about the post-it's was Shell got into the game as well. I would find little messages in obscure places with funny comments or drawings. One read, *"Do you know why I love you?... Me neither, I was hoping you could fill me in."* I laughed for a good five minutes after that one. But I think the thing that made me the proudest was the tee-shirts she had made for her and Lily:

My Mom is a

Brave

Intelligent

Tenacious

Caring &

Hopeful

woman.

I guess our little talk hit home for her. Embrace the insult and make it your own. I had no idea where she or Lily would ever wear it but it was thoughtful and I was so proud to see it. It made me smile.

I sat at the breakfast bar drinking a cup of coffee. It was actually hot without burning me like before. My mouth had been irritated from the sores developing but since they were clearing up, it wasn't so bad. I heard the car before I saw her face. I went to the door to greet my friend.

"Hi, Charlotte," I squealed.

"Hey, girlie. Howya?"

"Oh, well, I'm okay. I feel like a can of hammered assholes. You?"

"Could be better, don'tcha know."

"Do tell."

"I 'ave a hang nail," she blurted then shoved her hand in my face too show me the offending nail. "It bloody 'urts."

Laughter erupted from both of us, "And you wonder why I love you." I threw my arms around my friend and gave her a tight squeeze.

"Ye ready ta go? I could eat a baby's arse."

"Do I even want to know what you just said?

Charlotte looked at me in confused amusement, "I'm hungry. I been goin' like a blue-arsed fly fer days. I could use a good laugh and lunch."

"Um, okay. Let's go and you can explain what the hell you just said," I grinned. She nearly ran to the car. I guess she wasn't kidding when she said she was hungry, that, or I was moving slower than I thought. Nope, she was running. "Geesh, slow down, will ya? There will be food when we get there. Where is there?"

"Where is what?" she asked as she buckled herself in.

"Where are we going for lunch?"

"Flannigan's, they have Colcannon, that's mashed spuds and cabbage."

"What are you waitin' for? Let's go get some Colcannnnn...stuff." I hadn't been to Flannigan's since our last dip-n-drinks night. Come to think of it, it was the last normal event I had. Since then my life had been in a controlled chaos, a whole lot of crazy on a schedule.

We ordered and sat sipping drinks, "So, what have you done for the party? What's left to do?"

I should have seen it coming, Charlotte pulled a binder from her shoulder suit case and flipped it open, "Okay..." Our food arrived twenty minutes later and she was still talking about the to-do list and the plans for Saturday's extravaganza. The moment her plate hit the table her focus shifted to the mountain of potatoes and buttery cabbage. "I saw they 'ad this on tha menu and tha's all I thought on fer days." She took a large scoop and stuffed it into her mouth and melted into her seat, "So, good."

We sat in silence and enjoyed the meal in front of us. Well, she did, mine wasn't nearly as palatable. I stuck with things that wouldn't upset my stomach: chicken breast, steamed broccoli, and rice...plain rice. I've seen Weight Watcher's meals with more flavor than what sat before me. "That looks really good, Charlotte. I wish I could eat food with flavor again," I mumbled and cut another bite of the pale meat.

Charlotte offered up her plate to me, "Do ye want a taste?"

I sighed and inhaled the aroma, "I better not. I don't want to get sick."

"Olivia, is that you?" came a voice I knew, a voice that clawed at my ears.

"Hello, Nadine."

"Oh, sweetie, you're not looking so good. Oh, and your hair," she fake gasped, "I'm so sorry."

I smiled and looked up into her sour face, "It's only hair, Nadine. You should understand considering you walked out of your house lookin' like that." Suck it, you gap-toothed troll. Calm, Olivia, find your calm.

A smile snaked across her face and flared in her fangs when she opened her mouth to spit more poison, "I saw Tom the other day. He's looking...quite well. Do tell him I asked about him, will you?"

"Are ye thick? Tom wouldn't touch ye with another man's tool, ya scrubber."

"Pardon? What did you say?"

I waved a hand at Charlotte, "Allow me. Charlotte just told you Tom wouldn't fuck you with another guys dick and she called you a ..." I leaned to Charlotte and whispered in her ear to make sure I was right, "basically she called you a slut."

Nadine's face got redder by the second. Her gob flopped open and closed like a fish gasping out of water and I smiled. "Have a nice day, Nadine, preferably somewhere else," I flicked my hand at her, effectively shooing her off. She stomped back to whatever hole she slithered out of and I released the breath I had been holding.

"Who was tha' arse? She seems as useless as tits on a bull." I nearly spat my tea across the table at her.

I roared with laughter, "Tits on a bull...bahahaha...priceless. Oh, oh, oh my God."

Charlotte looked back in the direction Nadine slithered in, "I'd like to eat the head off that slag. What's her story?"

"Eat the...never mind. I get it, I think," I wiped the tears from my eyes and the spit from my chin. "Nadine wants Tom. She's waiting for me to fall over dead. She won't get it through her thick skull he thinks she's nasty."

"She be quite the scab of a woman. It's almost unfortunate. She wouldn't have a prayer as a bean-flicker let alone gettin' her paws on Tom."

"Ta hell with her. Let's enjoy our lunch," I demanded, then stuffed a piece of broccoli in my gob and smiled.

*****

Charlotte and I sat on my back deck drinking iced tea and chatting about everything and nothing. We were just enjoying each other's company. We talked about the garden and I told her about the flowers yet to bloom. We watched Oliver for different reasons. I watched him out of love and she out of fear.

"You do know Oliver won't hurt you, right? He's a very sweet cat."

A shiver shot through her body, "I find cats to be vile creatures. He may be a brilliant cat to ye but I will keep my distance, thank ye very much."

"That may be harder than you think," I pointed to the orange mass bouncing across the lawn, "cuz he's heading this way."

"I'll give 'im a toe in the hole if he comes ove' here. I'm tellin' ya,"

"I won't let him bother you." I caught Oliver before he could get too close to Charlotte. "You be a good boy now," I told him as I stroked his head. I walked over and opened the screen door then lightly tossed him in, "Go to bed."

"Thanks."

"You bet, friend."

I heard a slam then, "Moms, where ya at?"

"Deck," I screamed back. I followed Shell's footsteps with my ears and knew the moment she reached the screen door, "Hey, kiddo. How was work?"

She stepped out onto the deck but kept her distance for fear the smell would make me hurl, "Grilling, ha, get it? Grilling."

"I don't. Wha?" admitted Charlotte with a bemused look on her face.

"I work at a burger joint where we 'grill,'" Shell air-quoted. "So my day was grilling." The blank look on Charlotte's face was a clue to Shell to give up, "Aw, never mind. What are you two babes up to?"

Charlotte lit up like a Roman candle, "Oh, I like ye. Would ye like to come home with me and teach Miguel to call me babe?"

Shell rubbed her chin in consideration of the offer, "How much will you pay me? I ain't cheap, ya know?"

"Hmm...no, can't pay ye but I'll love ye forever. Will that do?"

Shell slammed her hand over her heart, "Are you tryin' to tell me you didn't already plan to love me forever?" She inhaled a shaky gasp, "That hurt, Charlotte. That really and truly hurt." Shell followed it up with a big pouty face and sniffles.

...and the Oscar goes to...

"Come sit down, girlie, so we can chat."

Michelle looked at me then Charlotte then me, "I better not. I smell like bad fast food and it tends to turn mom's stomach."

"I'm good. I can't really smell anything. Why don't you grab a soda and come hang out with us for a bit?"

"On it," she was out of sight then back again in no time at all.

Charlotte eyed Shell as she sipped her tea. Barely lowering the glass from her lips, she challenged, "Well, wee one, tell me about boys. Do ye got one?"

Shell threw me a look of disbelief. She thought I told. I threw my hands up in surrender, "I didn't say anything. Swear."

"So there is a boy," Charlotte rubbed her hands together, "What's he like? Cute, I'd bet."

Michelle's face shaded red. Her head tilted and a slow sweet smile coasted over her lips, "Maybe."

Charlotte snorted, "I'll bet. Purdy girl like ye, he's a looker for sure. He's not a dodgy wee cub is he?" She leaned across the table to lap up every detail Shell was willing to share.

Shell looked at me to translate what Charlotte asked. "She thinks he has to be cute because you're beautiful and...I think she asked if he is a good guy, right?" I asked looking to Charlotte for confirmation.

"Tha's right. Is he?"

"He's a good guy. We've been talking for a few weeks and have gone out a few times."

Charlotte looked at me and cocked her eyebrow, "She don't give up much, does she?"

"Nope, good luck," I chuckled. Charlotte spent the next hour pokin' and proddin, as she would say, to gather intel on Michelle's young man.

Charlotte exhaled in defeat, "Good Lord that was like safe crackin'. I feel like I would be a better burglar than a mum. I couldn't get much outta her at all."

I patted her hand, "You will be a great mum. Shell is simply a private person. She keeps things to herself, that's all. I have to do the same thing to get her to talk about stuff. It's even harder now."

"Harder now? Why?"

"Because, I won't be here much longer, why talk to someone who won't be around?" I just ripped the light from our light-hearted conversation. "Anyway...I think she likes you. She told you more in this last hour than she has told anyone since Lily left." Maybe Shell will be able to turn to Charlotte in the future. Hopefully.

"I had fun talkin' to 'er. She's a sweet girlie."

"That she is."

*****

I had dozed on the couch when my phone went off.

"Hello," I whispered in my 'yes, you woke me up' voice.

"Hi, mom, did I wake you up?"

"No, no, I'm up. How are you? What's going on?"

"We are in our fourth week. Half way, mom."

"I know, baby. I'm so proud of you. What amazing thing did you do today?"

"We finally went to the range and learned to shoot M-16's. I was kinda scared. I never held a gun before and this thing was as big as a bat, but easy to handle. I did pretty good. I'm not an expert but not bad. What's going on at Carpenter Manor?"

"Not much. I had lunch with Charlotte today. It was nice to get out of the house for a few hours. We will know in a few days what Aunt Molly and Uncle Wayne are having. Um, your dad finally went back to work," as I was talking Shell came and sat down beside me, "and your sister is right here and wants to talk to you. I love you, kiddo, bunches and tons."

"I love you too, mom." I handed the phone to Shell then she was gone in a flash. It was strange how Lily leaving made their bond stronger. I was glad it was. They would need it, sooner rather than later.

417

Chapter Thirty Five

I woke to the sound of moaning. Turned out to be me, "Shhhhh, I got ya, babe."

"Nooooo, sick," I groaned.

"Okay, easy," Tom eased me back down onto the bathroom floor where he found me. I purged again. I swear I barfed up something I ate at our wedding. It had to have an end. The only thing I had left were organs. I thought I saw a kidney earlier in my porcelain adventure. Tom sat behind me and rubbed my back and shoulders, "You are really hot. I think we need to get you into a cool bath."

"I'm okay," I mumbled with my head face down in the toilet.

"You are the picture of perfect health," Tom griped, "I think not. Your nightgown is soaked through." Tom stood up and went to turn on the water in the tub. "I'm gonna get you some clean clothes."

I lay back down on the bathroom floor to try to cool off. Tom was right, I was hot, really hot. I didn't understand why this was still happening. I was doing so well, only to start vomiting again. What the hell? I needed to pull out of this, fast. The gender party was at two o'clock. I couldn't miss it. It would crush Charlotte if I missed it.

"Let me help you up," Tom slid his hands under my shoulders and helped me to sit up. "Arms up," I did as I was told while Tom pulled my nightgown over my head. "Up we go," he slipped his hands under my armpits taking on my body weight as I got my feet under me. I wasn't steady but with his help I was able to climb into the tub.

"C..cold," I squeaked. "Why so cold?"

Tom dropped his pajama pants and stepped into the water, "It's not cold. It only feels that way because you are so hot." He sat down behind me and pulled me back against his chest. He grabbed a wash cloth, dipped it into the water and began squeezing water over my shoulders. "Lean forward a little bit. I want to run some water over your neck and back." I raised my knees, wrapped my arms around my bent legs and leaned into them for support. "Are you going to fall over?"

"No, I'm okay."

Tom started scooping water from the tub and pouring it down my neck and back, "I need to wet your head." Crap, which meant more hair down the drain, literally.

"Go ahead. What do you think about buzzing it off?"

He scooped more water into his hands and poured it over my head, "Yeah, I think it would be easier for you. You know, instead of watching it come out one at a time."

"Do we have clippers?"

"No, but I'll go with you when you decide to do it."

"Tomorrow...er, today."

Tom slid his arms around my non-existent chest and pulled me back against him, "I'm there, babe."

I jerked away, beached myself on the floor in front of the toilet and puked up my ovaries. What else was left?

*****

Tom and I managed to crawl back into bed for a few hours of sleep. I felt so bad for him. He got up every time I got sick and cleaned me up the one time I didn't make it. Something had to give. He needed his sleep. He was working all day long then taking care of me all night. I had my good days but even those sucked. I woke before him, which was rare and a true indication of how tired he was. I went down stairs to make coffee and take another collection of pills. I didn't even bother to try to figure out their names. There were more letters than the alphabet and not enough vowels to make sense to the average brain and mine was very average indeed. I took what and how much I was told and found more important things to do with my time, like live.

I sat sipping my coffee when I heard Tom thumping down the stairs. He skidded around the corner from the living room and came to a stop in front of me, "Are you okay? Why are you up?" he placed a hand on my forehead, "You don't feel hot."

"Stop. I'm fine. I woke up before you and wanted to make sure there was coffee when you got up." I reached out and took his face in my hands and kissed him, "I love you too."

Tom exhaled and leaned his forehead to mine, "It scared me when you weren't in bed. I thought you might have been in the bathroom but..."

"But, I was down here making coffee and taking my pills and doing fine."

"Right," he stepped away, "What would you like for breakfast?" he asked as he poured himself some coffee.

"How about we go get my head buzzed, then get breakfast at Maria's?"

Tom's eyes searched mine, "Are you sure you want to do it?"

"Yup, it's only hair and I'm tired of cleaning it up off the bathroom floor," I stated, smiled, and continued to sip from my mug.

"Let's do it."

"Do what?" asked Shell as she made her way to the fridge. "What are we doing?" she yawned.

"Well, your mom wants to go get her head buzzed. Maybe, even go for breakfast."

Shell peeked up over the fridge door, "Really? You wanna do that?"

My mouth slanted as I thought for about…two seconds, "Yup, I want to. Wanna come with?" I asked then raised my cup back up to my lips. She seemed hesitant.

"I don't know. It's kinda weird."

"How's it weird?" asked Tom as he leaned against the breakfast bar beside me. "Mom's hair is already falling out," he quipped while running a hand across my shoulders in support, "so what difference does it make if she has the rest buzzed?"

I thought for a moment, "We could just buy some clippers and do it right here. You each could have a turn wielding the clippers."

"You don't wanna do that, babe. It can hurt if you use 'em wrong. You want someone who knows how to do it."

"Okay, so are we all going? Then breakfast," I added to coax Shell into joining in.

Tom raised his mug, "I'm in."

We waited for Shell. She closed the fridge and looked at me, "Can I take pictures to send to Lily?"

"I think that would be a wonderful idea." It was decided. I was getting my last haircut.

I had tucked a zip-lock bag and three pieces of pink ribbon in my purse. I gave them to the hair stylist with instructions to tie the ribbons into three of the longest sections of hair then snip them off so I could save them for Tom and the girls in the baggie. "I would be honored to do this for you," the young girl choked, "This is my first…"

"Cancer cut," I joked to help ease her emotions. "Hey, at least you know you can't possibly mess it up." I gave her a great big smile and nodded for her to begin. After the three ribbon-tied pieces were safely in my purse I had Tom and Michelle come and hold my hands, "Let's do this." Shell snapped a few pictures and wiped away tears and Tom's face was blank. He showed no emotion as we watched my hair fall to the floor.

The young girl brushed away the wayward strands from my shoulders, "There you go, sweetie. It's on the house."

She removed the cape that draped my shoulders. I stood and ran my hands over my freshly buzzed head, "Thank you," I choked then gave her a hug.

With her voice laced with tears she tightened the hug for a moment, "You're welcome."

I looked down at the hairs on the floor one last time. I was born bald and I was going to go out bald. Full circle and all that shit.

We sat at a booth and pretended to look at the menus in our hands. "Come on, guys. It's only hair," I whispered.

"People are staring, Mom. It's kinda weird, ya know."

"It's only because they have never seen a more perfect specimen of a head," declared Tom as he ran his calloused hand over my bald skin.

Shell gasped, "Dad, don't."

I took her hand in mine, "It was going to go anyway. I wanted it to go on my terms. I wanted to turn it from a bad thing to a good one. Understand?"

She thought for a moment, "Like bitch."

"Just like bitch."

"What?" Tom asked in absolute confusion. So Michelle and I clued him in on claiming the ugly and making it beautiful.

*****

We stood in a sea of white. Wayne's and Molly's back yard was stunning. It looked ethereal. It looked like something out of a fairytale. Charlotte had done an amazing job. As we entered the wonderland of white we chose our prediction of boy versus girl by donning a bow tie or a hair bow. I chose a bow tie because, clearly, I couldn't wear a hair bow. The tables were covered with white table cloths, piled with white napkins, cups, and white plastic silverware. Even the trash bags in the strategically placed garbage cans were white. Food was laid out buffet style with a small table at the end that held cupcakes frosted in white. From the trees hung, you guessed it, white streamers and a large white box with a rope hanging from it. I had to admit I was not only shocked, but quite impressed with the style and sophistication with which Charlotte pulled it off.

"You're here," Charlotte squealed as she barreled towards us. She stopped dead three feet short of me. "Wha' 'ave ye done? Yer hair..." she gasped.

"I donated it to the trash at Quik-clip in town. They needed more hair in their trash. There was a shortage," I joked. "It's no big deal."

"Can I touch it?"

I bent slightly at the waist and pointed my head in her direction, "Knock yourself out."

Charlotte ran her hand over my head, "It's not prickly like Miguel's. It's more like cotton balls."

"Fuzzy," Shell clarified, "I thought so, too."

I straightened myself and my top, "Now, let's not make a big deal about this. Today is about the parents, okay?"

"Too right ye are. Come look around," Charlotte grabbed my hand and led me around to show all the decorations and plans for the event.

"You are really good at this," I said in awe of her handiwork. "Have you ever thought about doing this professionally?"

"What? Plannin' parties? It was fun, don'tcha know. I would love doin' it all the time." The pure joy radiated from her face like a sunbeam breaking through a cloudy day.

"Then you should. Ya never know, maybe people here today will ask you to do parties for them."

"Ye think?" Her smile said it all.

The party was wonderful. I actually had a great time for the most part. I did have to excuse myself a few times to sit down or cool off inside in the air conditioning. Molly glowed. Her little bump was more visible in her white shimmering sundress. She looked so happy as she made her way around to the guests to chat with each one. I sat quietly under the protective shade of a tree and watched the celebration of life all around me.

"How are you feeling, Olivia?"

I looked into the face of a mom to be, "I'm doing okay. You look lovely, Molly."

"Thank you, Charlotte did a wonderful job. It's all so beautiful. I'm impressed and surprised," She smiled.

"I have to admit, I'm kind of surprised, too. She really loved doing it and would love to do more."

"Really? Then I will be passing on her number to a few of my friends."

I laid my hand over hers on the table, "That would be great. Thank you for being good to her. She really is a wonderful soul."

"She is," was all Molly said as she sandwiched my hand between hers. We sat for just a moment before she was called over to another table.

I watched the party progress around me. Charlotte was working the crowd like a pro. At moments she would pull out her phone, as would the guest she was talking with. She was booking more parties. She was finding her joy. I felt the joy with her. She glanced up and caught me watching, so I gave her a nod and a smile. Told ya, friend, I thought as she continued to move through the mass of future clients. Ya done good.

Charlotte excused herself from the person she was talking with to move to the front of the crowd, "Hello everyone, attention," she waited a moment for the crowd to quiet. "I want to thank ye all for comin' out today to celebrate with Molly and Wayne." A round of applause sounded while Molly and Wayne made their way to the front to stand with Charlotte. "Now, please go to yer tables and get the cans of spray string but do not spray them yet." The crowd fumbled around as people claimed their cans. "Does everyone 'ave a can?" Cans were raised up in the air. "Wonderful," Charlotte turned to Molly and Wayne and instructed them to stand below the white box that hung from the tree branch. As they took their places Charlotte explained what would happen. "On the count of three, I will pull the rope," she pointed toward the rope on the other side of the tree, "Ye all will know the gender of the baby the moment ye see the color. That is when ye can let yer string fly. Are ye ready?" The crowd erupted. Charlotte looked over at Molly and Wayne who were holding hands under the box, "Are ye two ready?" They nodded with excitement. "Okay, anyone wantin to get pictures, move over to the side." She waited while people situated themselves. "Okay, here we go," Charlotte took the rope in hand, "One…Two…and Three!" Screams and string flew through the air as bright blue balloons and glitter fell over the delighted parents to be. "Yer havin' a boy," yelled Charlotte as she came running around the tree to the waiting parents. Molly and Wayne were wrapped in a tight hug when

Charlotte threw her arms around them. It was then I realized I was crying.

Tom touched my shoulder and kissed my fuzzy head, "Are you okay?"

"Oh yes. Wasn't it amazing? There's gonna be a little boy in the family," I laid my hand over his, "A boy...you should go over and congratulate them."

"You don't want to come?"

"I don't want to fight the crowd. I'll wait 'til it dies down a bit."

Tom took the seat beside me taking my hand in his, "Then I'll wait with you."

The party started to clear out about an hour later. Molly, Wayne, Charlotte, Miguel, Tom, Shell and I sat around a table and enjoyed the after-glow of such a wonderful day. Wayne couldn't stop touching Molly's baby bump and declaring, "That's my boy in there." She would just smile at him and place her hand over his.

"Charlotte, you will have to help with the baby shower," demanded Molly. "I found you first so my parties take precedence."

"I would love ta. I can't believe how many of yer friends asked fer my number." Charlotte grinned from ear to ear then placed a wet, happy kiss on her husband who couldn't stop looking at her with pride.

The day was a success. A baby boy would join the Carpenter clan. But, I would never meet him.

Chapter Thrity Six

Round two sucked just as much as round one. The only differences were they increased my anti-nausea medication, so the vomiting didn't start until hour two and my partner in crime wasn't Tom. Molly sat next to me as I threw up my breakfast. She continued reading some parenting magazine without blinking an eye. *Note: explain to Molly she must have compassion for her son when he is puking.* When I stopped barfing, Molly took baby wipes and cleaned up my face without flinching. She handed me a bottle of water and told me to rinse out my mouth. "Who are you and what have you done with my sister-in-law?"

"Please don't speak until after you rinse, your breath is vile." I couldn't help but laugh, "Argh, rinse for God's sake," she hissed then turned her head and held her nose.

I swished the water around in my mouth and spit it into the barf bucket. "Why did you volunteer to come, Molly? If this bothers you so much you shouldn't have come," I grumbled.

Molly ear marked the page she had been reading then closed the magazine. "I have seen all of this before, if you recall. I know what is happening to you. I know what comes next. I've been on this journey before whereas, Tom has not. I'm quite sure you don't want Michelle sitting here watching them slowly poison you."

"God, of course not, it's hard enough being sick in the same house with her."

"Drink," Molly nodded toward the water bottle in my hand, "Has she asked to come with you?"

I forced myself to swallow the metallic liquid, "God, that's awful. Blah," I shivered as my tongue hung from my lips.

"Michael had trouble with things tasting like he was sucking on a nickel," she said wistfully. "Mom would bring him Kool-aid. It seemed to mask the bad taste."

"Michael, was he your brother?"

"He is my brother. Here or not, he will always be my brother," she corrected. "Do you have Kool-aid at home?"

I thought for a moment while doing a mental inventory of my pantry, which made my stomach turn, "No, but I have some Mio. Do you think it will work?" Flashes of runny pork and beans, under cooked eggs, and greasy sausage ran through my head...and I puked again. "Don't talk about food. No food."

Molly rested back in her seat and reopened her magazine. She flipped to the dog-eared page and was back in her own little world with me hovering on the outside vomiting around the perimeter.

Dr. Fraiser stopped by as the oncology nurse was cleaning and taping the small tubes, which were used to inject the poison into my body, onto my chest. "I would like to do another MRI before your next treatment," she pulled out her prescription pad and scribbled across it. She handed the paper to Molly, "Call and make an appointment. You'll want to go on an empty stomach so you don't get sick while in the machine. Whatever time of day you seem to feel at your best is when you should schedule the MRI."

I smirked at the last comment, "I'm supposed to feel better at certain points in the day? Wish I had known that."

"Feeling like crap, huh?"

"Yup, warm and squishy and according to Molly, my breath smells like ass."

Dr. Fraiser and I both laughed while Molly looked on in amusement, "Well it does."

The doc pulled out her prescription pad again and scribbled across it, "This is for a mouth rinse to help with the Mucosis. The sores can cause an odor." She handed the sheet to Molly who slipped both into my bag. "Okay, well, I will let you get dressed so you can go home. I'll see you next time and Olivia, call if you need anything."

I gave her an odd look but answered her anyway, "Okay." We said our goodbyes. "Can you hand me my top from my bag please?" I asked Molly.

"Let me help you. I know you have to be tired." She pulled my shirt from the bag and reached over to untie the gown I had wrapped around me.

"No, I can do it," I squeaked. "I don't want you to see."

Molly chortled, "See what, Olivia? You don't have breasts you have scars, and scars I have seen." My mouth gaped at her but she pulled the strings holding the gown tight to me. "Let go so we can get you dressed." I released my hold and leaned forward so we could slide the gown down my arms. "Here, put your arms in," directed Molly as she held the shirt in front of me. I put my arms through the holes as she carefully pulled it over my head and down my torso. "See how easy that was. Next time it will be easier." Molly pulled my shoes on my feet and tied the laces into perfect little bows. She offered me her hand, "Come on, I want to swing by the garage to see if Wayne would like to have lunch."

"Fine, but please don't talk about food or I will likely barf in your purdy car." I wasn't sure which was more of a shock to my system, chemo or Molly's about face in personality. I was leaning toward her personality shift.

*****

Molly parked in front of the garage, "Do you want to get out?"

"No strength."

"All right, I'll be right back." Molly got out of the car and strolled towards the open bay doors. She waved to Miguel without stopping and continued down the hall to Wayne's office. I saw Randy off to the side staring at her as she walked away. Miguel threw a rag at his head and seemed to yell a*t him. That's what ya get, ya c*reeper. Miguel was walking away when he saw me in Molly's car.

"Hey, little lady, how ya feelin' today," he asked as he bent down to look at me through the car window.

"Like I've been poisoned. How are you, Miguel? How's Charlotte?"

"I'm good. Char is great though. She has gotten, like, a dozen calls from people wanting her to do their parties. She's so happy. Thank you," he said as he placed his hand on the door, "it means a lot to me to see her so happy."

I smiled at my friend's husband, "She did all the work. I only pointed her in that direction." It was a blessing to see the smile on his face.

"Miguel," bellowed Tom, "You hittin' on my wife?"

"Damn straight, and a fine wife she is."

Tom slapped Miguel on the shoulder, "That she is. Hey, go hose Randy down, will ya. He's staring at Molly like she's lunch."

"Argh, don't talk about food, pleeease," I groaned.

Tom squatted down next to the door, "Sorry, babe."

"Later, Liv," hollered Miguel as he jogged back towards the garage. I threw my hand up in a half-hearted wave.

"How ya feelin', babe? Do you need anything?"

I slumped further down in the seat, "No, I just wanna go home. I'm fighting getting sick in the car. The smell is getting to me."

"I can take you to the bathroom," he said while grabbing the door handle.

"No, it's okay. I don't want to move and make it worse."

Tom looked at his hands and down at his clothes, "Is it me? Do I smell?"

I scrunched up my nose and drew my eyebrows together, "Yeah, you do kinda smell. It's the grease."

"Sorry, babe. I'll go get Molly so she can take you home," he leaned towards me then jerked back, "I was gonna kiss ya but I don't think it would help you."

"I love you too."

"I love you more."

"Never."

Tom gave me a sweet smile then turned back to the bay doors, "Quit looking at Molly's ass and my wife, ya asshole," he barked at Randy who only shrugged and smirked. Tom disappeared in the same direction Molly had minutes before. In no time flat, Tom and Wayne were walking Molly back out to where I waited. Wayne kissed his wife, "See you in a few." He opened her door and helped her into the car. He closed the door and leaned down, "Drive safe. Olivia, hope you feel better." I gave a weak wave then sent a kiss sailing across the parking lot to Tom. He reached his hand up into the air *and* caught the kiss and stuffed it into his pocket. We were such sappy people.

On the short drive to my house Molly told me Charlotte was going to come over and sit with me. "Wayne and I are going to lunch but I didn't want to leave you alone."

"She doesn't have to. Just get me to the couch and bring me a bucket and I will be fine."

"She's coming. Period."

We pulled into the driveway. Molly went to open the front door when Charlotte pulled up to the curb. "Help me get her into the house," said Molly. Charlotte joined Molly on the passenger side of the car. Charlotte opened the door then they both helped me balance myself while getting out. I was so tired. I wanted to sleep. "Keep those eyes open long enough to get to bed. Olivia, open your eyes."

"They're open."

"Good." We moved slowly across the lawn and up the steps of the porch. "Charlotte, can you help her up the stairs to her room? I'm going to go get a few things together for her."

"I can take 'er up." Charlotte put her arm around me, "Put your arms around my neck, girlie. We'll get ye in bed in no time."

I sat on the edge of my bed as they stripped me down. They carefully pulled a night gown over my head as I did my best not to get sick, again. Molly brought up water, the Mio from the pantry, pain meds, and my cell. She put everything neatly on my bed side table. Molly, ever the boss, barked out orders, "Charlotte, hand me the remote to the television," Charlotte passed it to her, "Thank you. There, you should have everything you need for a while. Oh, no. Where is your bucket?"

"Bathroom," I pointed in the general direction.

"Charlotte, can you get it please?" She went to get the bucket while Molly helped me get settled into bed. I was out before Charlotte came back.

*****

I woke to the sound of Donny Osmond singing about getting daughters instead of sons in one of my favorite Disney movies.

I snorted, *"Mulan?"*

"Who doesn't love a war with singing, where a girl is the hero?" chuckled Shell.

"And dragons."

"And little dragons."

I rolled over slowly, begging my stomach not to erupt. I blinked at the clock on my night stand, 6:16, Holy shit. I had been asleep for five hours. Damn it. I didn't have enough time to spend it asleep. "How long have you been home?"

"Um, about two hours, I guess. Did you know you snore?"

I snorted again, "Yup, I've woken myself up from it being so loud." I maneuvered myself into a sitting position then leaned back against the head board, "Is your dad home?"

"Yuppers, he went to take a shower downstairs. Weird."

I smiled at his thoughtfulness, "Not weird. The smell of grease nearly made me ralph earlier."

"Um, gross. Then it's good he hosed off down there."

"How are you doing? What's going on in the wonderful world of Shell?"

She bounced her head to the left then to the right in evaluation, "Not bad, working, hanging with ma peeps, and diggin' 'The Dude.'"

"Who's 'The Dude' and why are you diggin' him?" asked Tom as he buffed his head with a towel. Taking the towel in both hands he wound it up tight and snapped it out at Shell, "Do you have a boyfriend now?"

She yelped and jumped from the bed, causing a wave of movement to slam into me. I dug my fingers into the comforter and white-knuckled the night stand as I bent over and almost missed the bucket. "Shit, dad, see what you did." Michelle screamed. "Mom, are you okay?"

I waved her off, "Don't come over here. I'll be okay, just don't."

"Here," she slid something across the bed, "Aunt Molly texted me and told me to get you these." It was a package of baby wipes. "She said they were better on your skin than a wash cloth."

"Thanks," I wiped my face then sat back up, "Babe, can you help me to the bathroom?"

Tom draped the offending towel around his neck then offered me his arm. He walked with me to the bathroom where I brushed my teeth. I felt like I was always brushing my teeth. The mouth rinse the doctor prescribed sat on the vanity, "Did you get this?" I asked Tom.

Tom looked at it in confusion, "No, what is it?"

"It's a rinse to help my mouth. Dr. Fraiser gave me a script for it today. Molly must have filled it." That woman had her moments. I made my way back to bed and Tom took the bucket to the bathroom and cleaned it out. What a sucky job. "As much as I don't want to, I have to eat something. I haven't eaten all day."

I had piqued Shell's interest, "What do you want?"

"Hmmm...I think I would like a bowl of mashed potatoes."

"That's it? No meat or veggie?"

"Potatoes are a veggie. Have you eaten?"

"Yeah, dad and I had spaghetti Nadine brought over. It kinda sucked balls but it was better than a burger."

I looked at Tom who was standing in the bathroom doorway. "So your future wife brought you dinner, huh?"

"Gross, Dad would never...with Nadine...ew."

I laughed at Michelle's outrage, "No, no, no, it's a joke. She came over here a while back to inform me she would be here for your dad, oh, and you and Lily if you ever need a shoulder to cry on." The disgust on my face mirrored the look on Shell's.

"I won't be leaning on any shoulders," Tom asserted, "especially hers." He shook off a shudder and sat at the foot of the bed. "So, you want mashed taters, huh?"

"Yes, please."

"Done."

Tom made me a lovely bowl of plain mashed potatoes and the three of us settled in and watched *Mulan*.

"You never answered my question," Tom said while poking Shell with his toe.

"What question?"

"The boyfriend one."

"What was the question again?" she snickered and me right along with her.

"Do...you...have...a...boyfriend?"

"Y...E...S."

Tom looked over at me, "Looks like I'm gonna have ta start cleaning my guns. Yup, definitely need to do that." We smiled at each other then laughed at the look of horror on Shell's face.

The day may have started like shit but it ended in laughter.

Chapter Thirty Seven

Have you ever had a feeling that was so strong you had to follow through on it?

I did. I had the feeling it was imperative I move on things. Now. I gathered up the strength then went to my closet. None of my clothes fit anymore so what I was about to do wouldn't be a great loss. I collected all my favorite pieces, folded them, and placed them in a bag. I managed to lug the bag down the stairs with way more effort than I could afford. I went to the office and pulled up my 'To Do' list and dialed a number I had saved.

"Hello?"

"Um, yes, hello. Is this Quinn's Quaint Quilts?" I asked.

"That's me. What can I do for you?" asked the cheery voice.

I cleared my throat and began, "I need three quilts made. I found your number online and saw you had wonderful reviews."

Quinn squealed, "Oh, wonderful. It's nice to know people are pleased with my work. Now, what exactly are you wanting done?"

"Okay, well, I have terminal breast cancer and I would like quilts made from some of my clothes for my family."

"Oh my," she gasped.

I knew I was going to have to soften the blow for her. It was odd knowing I was dying but was afraid to tell people in fear of hurting them. "It's okay. I've made my peace with it. I just want to make things easier for my husband and daughters. Can you help me?"

"O...of course, of course I will help you. Um, besides the clothing is there anything else you want specific to the quilts?"

"Yes, as a matter of fact there is..." I proceeded to explain what I wanted and asked if there was any way the bag of clothes could be picked up.

"I'll send my husband by to collect them in a little bit. Would that be all right?"

"That would be fine. I will give him the payment as well. Quinn?"

"Yes?"

"Thank you for doing this, the sooner the better," I choked past the lump that had overtaken my throat.

I could hear the lump she had formed, too, "It will be my honor, Mrs. Carpenter."

Mr. Quinn stopped by about an hour later and collected the bag of quilt material, a few notes I jotted down, and the check for the hard work at hand. That was another thing checked off my list. I went back to the office and knelt down in front of an old steamer trunk Tom and I had found in the early days of our marriage. It was the time in our lives when money was tight but our love brought us closer together. I loved the old battered box and saw its possibilities. I saw it as a coffee table and then as a toy box. Tom saw an old battered box he paid a whopping fifteen bucks for. That money went a very long way. It was now going to fill yet another purpose. I pulled out the key from around my neck and opened the trunk. I needed to run an inventory of what it held so far and what was yet to fill its emptiness.

There wasn't much in there yet, but the items and plans were growing. The tree urn had come a while back. I slipped it in the trunk so Tom didn't have to look at it. Next to it lay a stack of addressed envelopes to be mailed when I was no longer there. There were some people I didn't want to see ever again, even knowing there wouldn't be another chance. Next to the letters sat four boxes, one for each of my loves and one for Molly. I was going to need Molly to step up and be a good Aunt and follow my final wishes with the items in her box. There were three 'Your Favorite Recipes' cookbooks I made for them. They could still have the things they liked the most. I added some of my memories I had cooking with them to the recipes so I would be there with them when they cooked the things they loved. I made scrapbooks for each of them chronicling our time together from the moment I found out I was carrying each of our girls until the end. Tom's was filled with pictures and memories from long before babies. It spanned our time in high school, to when we reconnected while I waited tables at Zinkman's, to our wedding, then babies, backyard barbeques, and the love. Love that built our family. Once the quilts were completed they too, would find their way into that old battered box. I had plans and I needed to get on them before...

I tried to sit out on the back deck, but the heat of the summer was far more than I could handle. I use to love the hot rays of the sun beating down on me while I tended to my gardens, but my body couldn't handle it anymore. I stood at my kitchen window and looked at the flowers blooming and was saddened I couldn't sit amongst them and inhale their perfume. Oliver lay under the rose bush over-flowing with bright pink ornaments. I planted it the year Lily was born. It had bloomed and flourished as she had over the past eighteen years. Shell had her own rose bush at the other end of the yard that screamed with vibrant red blooms. It too, has grown and become stunning along with the precious girl I planted it for. The bleeding hearts and forget-me-nots I planted early on in this fucked up journey were standing strong and reminding me I wasn't. I was weak and wilted. My color was fading with each passing day. My hair was gone, my eyebrows and lashes had joined in evacuation of my head. I had lost that pesky weight I was battling at the gym and more. My skin was the color of day-old oatmeal and the flakiness left much to be desired. So much for going out beautiful.

"Hey, Moms...whatcha doin'?"

I turned around to see Shell standing at the breakfast bar, "Just lookin' at the garden. It came in really nice, don't ya think?"

She crossed the kitchen, placed her arm around my shoulders and turned us back around to look out at the wonders growing within our fences. "Beautiful, as always. Why aren't you out there sniffin' everything?"

"Can't handle the heat."

"Oh," she turned us back toward the island, "what are you doing today?"

"Hmmm," I tapped my chin with my index finger, "My grand plan was to breathe in and out and maybe blink when the urge hits and to top off my day, maybe vomit once or twice. How 'bout you? What's on the agenda?"

"That depends on you. Are you up for a matinee? We can go sit dead center and do a running commentary of what we think of the movie. Chances are no one will be there cuz it's a week day. What do ya say? You game?"

"I think I can work that into my rather busy schedule. It shouldn't interfere with my existing plans. I may have to hold off on the vomiting until later."

Shell grimaced, "I think that would be for the best. Yes, definitely. We have about 45 minutes before it starts so I'm gonna eat something. Figured you wouldn't want to smell popcorn."

I shrugged and pouted, "I won't know until I get there, sorry."

"'s all good."

"I'm gonna change. You eat and I'll be right back." I went up to put on pants and grab a sweater. I could never tell if I would be hot or cold. It was summer and I was dragging along a sweater everywhere I went. Ridiculous. It was just another thing that made my so called life difficult. My newest battle was toothpaste. I could no longer stomach the taste of it. Tom had bought eight different kinds in hopes of finding one I could handle. No luck. As of late, I had been restricted to baking soda and water but I wasn't sure how long that would last.

I found Shell stuffing the remnants of what smelled like a peanut butter and jelly sandwich in her mouth. She chugged a glass of milk to wash it down, "Ahhhh, sometimes, nothing beats a good ol' pb & j. Am I right?"

"So true."

"Are you ready?" I gave a quick nod and grabbed my purse. "Cool, I'm gonna go brush my teeth then we can go dominate the seats."

"Are you driving?" I hollered out before she got too far to hear me.

"Yup."

Thank God. I wasn't sure if I had it in me to drive anywhere or if I was allowed to drive. Michelle bounded back down the stairs with her purse over her shoulder. Just as she grabbed ahold of the front doorknob the doorbell rang. With no hesitation at all, she pulled open the door and was accosted by the over-abundance of Nadine's perfume. "Well, hello Lily," cooed Nadine. "Aren't you pretty."

Shell sneered at the vile person standing before her, "It's nice to know that even after all these years you still haven't learned our names. I'm Michelle, not Lily." She gained her composure, held up her hand to keep me out of sight. She was going to be my protector. That was my job, not hers, but I wasn't strong enough to defend a kitten from a grasshopper. "What can I do for you, Nadine?"

"Oh, I came to see how your father...and you, liked the spaghetti last night."

Shell gave a snort, "Let's just say it was a good thing we have more than one bathroom in the house, if you get my drift?" I could imagine the face Nadine was sporting at the moment. I was picturing the full on lemon-pucker. I had to slap my hand over my mouth to prevent a belly laugh from escaping. "I'll leave the dish on your porch after I chisel out the burnt parts."

"There were no burnt parts and you know it. I'm sure your father enjoyed it and that's all that matters to me."

"You're right, Nadine. He enjoyed it well enough and then we made jokes about you while he and I lay in bed with my mom. She really enjoy*ed the 'her nose is so hooked she could catch a fish just by walking by water' line* he tossed out. It was hysterical."

I heard Nadine gasp and take a step closer to the doorway. "You listen here, ya little bitch, you better keep your mouth shut or I'll...

"You'll what, Nadine? Go on...what will you do to my daughter?" I snarled. I was shocked at the amount of energy I could still build when it came to protecting my children.

"Well, I...um...she..."

"I've been standing here," I pointed to the other side of the door, "the whole time. How dare you threaten a child? I should call the cops on you for that but someone is already on my phone." I held out my phone to her, "Take it. Say 'hello.'" She looked at the phone then back at me. She saw the photo icon of who was on the phone, "Don't you want to ask Tom how he liked the dinner you prepared for *him?*"

"...*put that bitch on the phone...she wants to threaten my kid she's got another thing coming...*" Tom growled.

"Don't you want to talk to him?"

Nadine looked at the phone one last time then glowered at me and Shell. I thrust the phone out a little further. She jerked, spun on her heel, and stormed away.

Michelle stepped out onto the porch and yelled across the yard, "Don't bother coming back, ya bitch. And didn't your mama ever teach you to not walk on other people's grass?"

"Hi," I smiled into the phone, "sorry."

"What the fuck was that all about?"

"She came by to see how much you liked her cooking but Shell kept me away from the door. I wanted you to hear what she was like when you weren't around. That's all."

I could hear the laughter in Tom's voice, "I would have loved to have seen Shell rip into that nasty piece of work."

I smiled at Shell, who was closing the door, "She was pretty awesome." Shell perked up at my words and proceeded to strike a few of her best body builder poses.

"You're okay then?" he asked with a touch of concern.

"Are you kidding? I have an awesome bodyguard and she's taking me to a movie. I might even eat popcorn."

"I love you, woman."

"Love you, too.'

Shell joined in with, "I love chocolate."

Tom laughed at her admission, "Have fun. I gotta get back to it."

"'k, see you later. Bye."

"Bye." I tossed my phone into my bag, "We still going?"

"Yup, but we are stopping at the store and filling your massive bag with every candy I can fit in it." She twirled her keys around her finger and opened the front door for me, "Ma lady," she smiled and bowed.

"You're a keeper, kiddo. You are definitely a keeper."

*****

Forty pounds of candy, two large drinks and a bucket of popcorn later we had successfully viewed a movie and eaten a week's worth of calories. Calories I needed and Shell would work off in no time flat.

"Ya know, Mom, it would be sacrilegious if you hurled. Puking chocolate is unacceptable."

I opened the passenger side door and slid into her car, "I'll do my best to honor the sanctity of the chocolate."

"Where to, Madre? Is there anywhere you wanna go?"

"Ummm...Zimbabwe."

Shell turned the key in the ignition, "Geography ain't my thing but I don't think we can drive there."

"Bummer," I thought for a moment, "You up for a short and I mean very short, walk in the park? I'd like to show you my favorite spot."

"To the park." She put the car in drive and made her way to shady trees and secluded benches.

It was hot to the average person, but to me it was a sauna. I peeled off my sweater before we left the car. I had guided Shell to the parking area closest to the bench I liked to rest on. Shell came to me and offered me her arm for support then I pointed us in the right direction. We walked in silence until we rounded the hedges to the fountain. I stepped closer to it and let the spray cool my scorched skin. "This is my spot," I said. I pointed to the bench, "I like to lay there and look up into the canopy of leaves," I pointed up. "The sun seems to turn them all kinds of colors. It's beautiful." Michelle went to the bench and lay back to see what I was talking about. The smile that stretched across her face was proof she saw it too. She saw the kaleidoscope.

"Wow, it really is cool," she jerked up, "the fountain is splashing me."

"I know. That's one of the other things I like about this spot. I could cool off after a walk," I smiled and ran my fingers through the cool water. I flicked the droplets from my fingers in her direction, "It's only water."

"Yeah, nasty water birds poop in, dogs drink from, and kids play in," she gagged.

I couldn't argue with that, "True, but I love it none the less." I walked over and sat next to her, "That is where I want to be planted," I pointed to the clearing across from the bench.

"I still think it's kinda weird you want to do that."

"What? Be a tree?"

"Yeah," she nodded her head then stared down at her hands that rested in her lap. "Why don't you want to be buried? You know, have a head stone with your name..."

"I told your dad I wanted to be able to hold my grandchildren some day and, at least, as a tree I could." I turned to face her taking her hands in mine, "There are so many things I won't get to do with you and Lily. This way, I would be alive. You could come here and, I don't know, hug me and I could hug you back." I watched a tear slip down her cheek, "Hey now, none of that. I didn't mean to upset you."

Her tear-filled azure blue eyes met mine, "Upset? Mom, I've been upset from the moment you told us. How could I not be?"

"I'm so sorry, baby. I really am."

"It's not your fault. It's not like you volunteered for this, ya know."

"There is no way on Earth I would ever volunteer to leave you, your sister and your dad," I shook my head stubbornly, "No way in hell."

"I know," Shell stood and took my hands with her, "Come on, it's too hot out here for you. Let's go home and have some watermelon."

I used her strength to stand. We walked back to her car the way we walked from it: arm in arm.

"Hey, is that Oliver?" Shell pointed to an orange cat lounging under the hedges that hid my bench.

"Huh, it wouldn't surprise me if it was," I looked toward the cat and hollered, "Oliver, go home." The great fur-ball looked at me, got up and walked off in the direction of home. "Come on, you. Let's go get some of that watermelon you were talkin' about."

Chapter Thirty Eight

The days were starting to bleed into one another. Time was moving faster than I could keep up. I had the MRI Dr. Fraiser had ordered a few days ago and was sitting in the waiting room to talk with her about the results. Tom sat next to me, filled with nervous energy, his leg bouncing a mile a minute. I reached a hand out and rested it on his leg to steady it and to calm him. His leg stopped. His hand shot out to mine and held it to his leg. I gave him a gentle squeeze, telling him I was still there.

"Hello, Olivia, Mr. Carpenter."

I looked up into the eyes of a man I used to fantasize about, "Hello, Dr. -*You are so not hot to me anymore-*."

"I was, um, I was really happy to hear you and Alyssa spoke recently."

I had to calm myself before I snapped at him, "Yeah, I'm glad you two were able to fix whatever was going on between you. Too bad I haven't heard from her since." I gave him a smug look and was blessed to hear my name being called. "If you will excuse me," I said as Tom helped me up.

"I'll talk to her."

I stopped and looked over my shoulder at him, "Don't bother. I've made peace with everything. Have a nice day, Dr. Matthews."

He dropped his gaze from my eyes to the patient folder in his hands, "You too, Olivia."

I walked away with the knowledge that chapter in my short life was closed and I had no intention of reopening it.

Tom and I were escorted to Dr. Frazier's office and to our surprise she was already in there waiting for us. "Olivia, Tom, come on in. Have a seat," she said waving us in the direction of the chairs we had become far too familiar with.

Tom and I took our seats. He took my hand in his, and looked at Dr. Fraiser, "What's going on, Doc?"

Dr. Fraiser opened the file in front of her, folded her hands over it, and looked up into our faces, "I wanted the new MRI to see if the chemotherapy was making any headway in stopping or even slowing the progression of the cancer," she looked down at the pages, then back up at me, "I do believe it is slowing the growth, slightly, but beyond that, I'm not seeing any marked improvement."

She wasn't telling me anything I didn't know. We knew this was only to buy time not save my life. "So...what's my time line look like now?" I asked, not wanting her to say the words.

Dr. Fraiser looked from Tom to me and back again. I could hear the tremor in her voice when she launched her response that hit so hard I nearly collapsed, "Weeks."

Not years. Not months. Weeks.

"I recommend you do one more chemo treatment. I think it could get you to a month."

"I want to see Lily graduate from Basic Training."

She came around and stood before me. She leaned back against the desk and folded her hands so they hung in front of her, "When is the graduation?"

"Three weeks," said Tom, "We were gonna fly out the day before."

"I'm sorry but I would not recommend you going. You will be extremely weak and highly susceptible to infection. It wouldn't be safe for you, Olivia."

I felt like I was being strangled. I couldn't breathe and my words were trapped below the hitch in my throat. I was screaming but no sound could be heard except in my head. I gasped for air then a wail tore through me like a howl released from an injured animal. Why was my world being ripped out from underneath me every time I thought I had my footing?

"Liv, baby, breathe. Breathe," Tom begged while rubbing my back and shoulders. "Baby, please..."

My face was in a scream as the torrent of tears poured from my face. Dr. Fraiser knelt in front of me and tried to calm me. "Olivia, you need to calm down and take a deep breath." She rubbed my hands and uttered encouragements to try to soothe my broken spirit. "Come on, Olivia. I don't want to give you a sedative. That's it. Breathe, slow, deep and slow." I managed to get myself into a calmer state but words remained elusive. "That's better." She stood up, rounded her desk and took a seat.

Tom held my hand like there was no tomorrow. There wasn't really. "Okay, so it's gotten worse. Will she hurt more than she does now? What should we expect?"

"Yes, there will be more discomfort as it progresses. I will write you a prescription for a stronger pain reliever. You shouldn't drive while taking it," she added as she scribbled on her prescription pad, "Also, you may develop a shortness of breath and dizziness. The cancer has spread throughout your body, Olivia. It is aggressive and we will do the best we can to give you..."

"Time? You just took away a large chunk of what I had left. How can you give me more?" I whispered.

"I can't. We can only try."

We left her office in a daze. I sat down in the waiting room for no other reason than I needed something solid under me. Tom stood next to my chair and I leaned my head against his hip. I wrapped my arms around his leg and held on. He cupped the side of my head with his warm hand. I stared at nothing. I felt nothing. I was nothing. I was a temporary thought. A breeze that disappeared as quickly as it came. I would soon be dust.

"Mr. Carpenter? Is everything all right?" asked Dr. Matthews.

"Weeks," was all that fell from Tom's lips.

Dr. Matthews placed his hand on Tom's shoulder, "Is there someone I can call to come and get you? You don't look in any condition to drive."

"I'll call my brother. I can call my brother," Tom mumbled as he reached into his pocket for his cell.

Neil slipped into the chair beside me, "Olivia, is there anything I can do for you?" I turned my head to see who was talking to me. I blinked in recognition and shook my head. What could he possibly do to help me?

"Do you want Alyssa to stop by?"

I shook my head.

"Can I tell her?"

I shrugged. What did I care who knew. It wouldn't stop it from happening. It wouldn't give me time. It wouldn't reverse it. Sure, tell her. It didn't matter.

Wayne and Randy flew into the waiting room like their hair was on fire. Wayne reached his brother and grabbed his biceps in his large hands, "What's going on?" Tom looked at him with a vacant stare. "Hey," Wayne gave him a little shake, "Tom, what's going on, man?"

"Sir, I'm Dr. Matthews. Tom and Olivia received some," Neil looked down at me then back to Wayne, "to be blunt, they received some pretty shitty news and neither is in any mindset to drive."

"Dude, what happened to her hair," whispered Randy to Wayne.

"She has cancer you fuck head. Did you think it was a fashion statement? Idiot." Wayne looked at Tom, "Hey, man, where are your keys? Randy will drive your truck back to the house and I'll drive you two home." Tom stuffed his hand in his pocket and pulled out his key ring. Wayne took it and passed it to Randy. Wayne stuck his hand out to Neil, "Thanks for staying with them." They shook hands, and they both helped me to my feet. "Come on, Liv, let's get you and Tom home."

Tom trudged along in front of us and climbed into the front passenger seat of Wayne's car. Wayne helped me into the back seat, and drove us home. Randy pulled the truck into the driveway and ran back to the car to help me out.

"Sorry about the hair thing back there," he mumbled, "Didn't know the story."

"Wish I didn't know."

Randy and Wayne got us into the house and settled on the couch, "Tom, I'm gonna take Randy back to the garage and I'll come back, okay?"

"Yeah, okay," Tom grunted and leaned back taking me with him.

Wayne and Randy left. We didn't move. We didn't speak. We didn't have too. I told him with my tears I was heartbroken and he responded with his. I told him I felt defeated with the shuddered breaths I took. His arms wrapped around me told me he loved me, no matter what.

A short while later our house was full of people. Wayne called Molly and went by the burger joint and told Shell to come home, now. Molly called Charlotte and they all ended up sitting in our living room waiting for an explanation. Michelle had claimed her spot on the couch with Tom and me.

"Ye got ta tell us what's goin' on, loves," coaxed Charlotte.

I straightened myself, wiped my nose, and scanned the faces staring back at me. "I have weeks. The cancer is spreading quickly. Chemo hasn't slowed it as much as they hoped." There was a collective gasp that seemed to echo off the walls followed by a mournful howl from the child in my arms. I pulled her tighter to me and rocked her like I did when she was a baby. She was still my baby. She would always be my baby. But my arms felt light, I was missing a piece. A very important piece and I might not get to see her before it was all over. I wouldn't get to hug her, to kiss her, to say goodbye. My Lily was out there and I couldn't see her. I fucking hated cancer so much. I was given a death sentence but had done nothing to deserve it. I was being short changed. My family was being made to suffer for no good reason. Some pissed-off cell in my body pissed off a bunch of other cells and they all decided I shouldn't live anymore. Where was the logic in that?

Then, as if the Universe knew I needed it, my cell rang. "Hello?" I choked from behind tears.

"Mom?...Hey, are you crying? What's goin' on?"

"Oh, Lily, it is so good to hear your voice. I miss you so much."

"What's wrong? Mom, tell me, please," she pleaded, "I can tell something's wrong."

The tears started fresh with each brutal word I had to force over the telephone lines to Lily. I suffered more listening to the suffering of those around me. My babies were in pain and all I was doing was dying. They had to live with it. "Dr. Fraiser said I won't be able to come to your graduation. My immune system will be too weak to travel."

"I understand," she whispered. I could hear the sadness in every syllable. "I'll ask and see if there is anything I can do here."

"I love you. I want nothing more than to give you a great big hug."

"I could use that right now. I really, really could." I passed the phone around the room so everyone had a chance to share some love with the chunk of my heart that had wandered off and decided to become a hero. We talked to her as long as she was allowed. I continued to talk to her long after the call ended. She was in my wishes and dreams.

Molly and Charlotte cooked for everyone and Miguel came over after he and Randy closed the garage. He brought Homer with him. Homer came right to me and I hugged him and petted him and kissed his nose. In return, he curled up close to me and laid his large head on my chest. He sniffed at me as if he could smell the disease that was eating its way through me, but he loved me anyway. They all loved me anyway. I was one lucky bitch. If, to hell with if, when I had to go at least I was surrounded by people who loved me openly and without hesitation.

I ate watermelon. It was the only thing that didn't taste like the bottom of a litter box, not that I actually knew what a litter box tasted like. The anti-nausea meds seemed to be working. It was kind of difficult to throw up when you hadn't eaten in days. The best I could do was water with a ton of Mio in it. We sat around the table and played the "remember when" game. We talked around the topic or avoided it completely. We could avoid it all we wanted it didn't mean it was gonna just up and leave. Till death did we part. Even in death it got to go with me. Selfish prick.

Homer and I curled up on the couch when I could no longer hang on to the conversations swirling around me. Sleep had been banging at the back of my eyelids since the trip to the medical center. I could no longer ignore it. Tom pulled the blanket off the back of the couch and draped it over me. "Do you want me to move Horror?"

"Homer can stay."

"Horror," he chuckled then bent down and kissed me. "Get some rest, babe. I'll be right here when you wake up, 'k?"

"Hmmm," I sighed and drifted off into oblivion.

I hovered over Lily as she graduated from Basic Training. I watched her march and salute. I saw her in her dress blues looking like a soldier. I tried to hug her but passed through her instead. I tried to talk to her, to tell her how proud I was but the words came out as a breeze that barely brushed her hair. I watched as she cried alone while the other soldiers' families beamed with pride at their sons and daughters. Lily was alone because of me. She didn't know I was there with her. I was nothing more than a breeze.

I cried out for Lily but found Tom instead. "Don't let her graduate alone. You promise me right now you will go and be by her side," I begged as the fog of my dream started to drift away.

He pulled me tight into him, "I can't leave you and you can't come."

I pushed him away and soothed Homer when he growled. I looked Tom in the eyes and with all the strength I had I said the things we all danced around. "I may be dead by then. I may die that day or I may live to see the pictures, but you will not let her face it alone. You are the only parent these two girls will have. They need to know they can count on you. Promise me."

"I'll stay here with Olivia," declared Molly.

Charlotte's arm sprang into the air, "Me too."

I begged him with my eyes and I clutched at him with my hands, "Promise."

"I promise."

I wrapped my arms tightly around him and sobbed at the thought that I wouldn't see her complete the journey, but there was no way in hell she would be alone when she did it. "Molly and Charlotte are my witnesses. You promised and I will hold you to it."

"Can I go too?" asked Shell from somewhere behind me.

"I think that would be wonderful for your sister to have you there with her. You can take pictures and text them to me."

"I can video it for you."

I reached out my hand in search of her. She took my hand, then came around so I could see her, "That is a great idea. Lily will be able to have a copy. You are one smart cookie, ya know?"

"I think I take after you on that one."

We were interrupted by the doorbell, "I got it," bellowed Wayne as he crossed the room. "Can I help you?"

"Yes, sir, I'm looking for Michelle."

Wayne poked his head back around the door, "Shell, it's for you."

Michelle went to the door then stepped outside with the mystery guest. "Who was it?" demanded Tom.

"Some kid."

"Boy kid or girl kid?" asked Tom.

"Boy kid," smirked Wayne.

Tom was up and at the door in a heartbeat. "Hey, you gonna introduce us to your friend?" Tom asked Shell. "We taught you better manners than that."

"But...mom," was the only explanation Shell could give.

"I'm sure your mom would like to meet him, too."

Michelle took her mystery guest by the hand, and led him into the lion's den. I almost felt sorry for him. "Everyone, this is Kyle. Kyle this is...everyone."

A choir of voices sang, "Hi Kyle." Shell proceeded to introduce him to individual people. Tom came and helped me to sit up and straighten myself as best as possible so I wouldn't embarrass her with the way I looked. What I said or did would be a different matter altogether.

"These are my parents, Tom and Olivia. This is Kyle."

Tom stood and puffed up. His voice became a few octaves lower and he jutted out his hand to shake the boy's. I'm sure it was tighter than it needed to be. "So, you're the guy she's been seeing."

"Y..yes, sir," the young man yelped.

"Oh, for God's sake, leave the poor boy alone and sit down," I tugged on Tom's shirt tail. "Hi, Kyle, it's nice to finally meet you."

"Okay, well, now that you have all scared the crap out of him he can go," Shell hissed.

"Go? Why?" I asked.

Shell gave me a sad smile, "We had made plans but, you know, things changed."

"Sweetie, if you want to go, then go. I promise I will be here when you get back," I gave her a bright smile to encourage her to live her life. "It's okay, really."

"Um," Kyle interrupted, "how about we walk down to the park and get an ice cream cone. You won't be gone long and we'll be close."

They both looked at me wondering what to do, "Now that's a wonderful idea," I gave Kyle a sly smile, "Her favorite flavor is cookies-n-cream. Go. Have fun. Oh, wait a sec, would you mind taking Homer? He needs a walk."

Shell perked up a tiny bit, "Sure, come on Homer," she patted her leg, "wanna go for a walk, boy?"

Homer was off the couch in a flash and at Miguel's side waiting for his leash. "Here ya go, boy. He likes to drink out of the fountain," Miguel explained as he hooked the leash to Homer's collar.

Shell looked at me in mock horror, "See, I told you." We both laughed at our inside joke.

"Have fun."

Have fun. Live life. Be carefree. Never limit yourself.

Chapter Thirty Nine

Summer had slipped from our fingers with no fun to show for it. No vacation. No barbeques. No laughter-filled memories. Michelle would be starting her junior year in high school in a week and we had done nothing to get ready for it. I decided that had to change. I knew she had the day off and I wanted to steal her away for the day. I slipped from my bed and tip-toed down the hall to her room. I poked my head in and saw her curled up with her teddy bear. My breath caught at the sight. That bear was the first thing I made when I found out I was carrying her and there she lay with it held close. I needed to get a grip if we were gonna have fun. I slithered my way from her doorway to the bed and slipped in next to her. I swaddled her with my arms then covered her face with kisses.

"Wake up. Come to the mall with me and spend money...on you."

A yawn took over her face, "Wha?"

I slapped more kisses on her sweet face, "Let's go buy you school clothes, but you have to drive cuz your mama's on drugs," I shook her, "You game? Wanna go?"

"Sure, I wanna go. Can I eat first?"

"Um...yup, that would be why I had your dad get donuts this morning. Your fav."

She was up and out of bed before I could even roll over, "Come on, mom. We have donuts."

"Go, I'll catch up," I laughed and waved her off. The truth was I needed a moment to catch my breath. I sat on the edge of her bed and listened to her bound down the stairs on a direct path to the box of doughy goodness. I took several deep breaths and tried to get it together for a day filled with walking.

When I finally made it down the stairs Shell was on her second donut, "You should see if Charlotte and Aunt Molly want to come," she smiled then stuffed another bite into her mouth.

"You don't want to spend the day with me? I'm hurt. You wounded me, Shell."

Shell set the sad remnant of her breakfast down on a napkin then brushed off her hands, "Look, mom, I know you want us to have fun. I also know you are weak and will have trouble walking around the mall all day. I know you think I'm a kid and shouldn't be worried or anything about everything that's going on but I'm not blind." I didn't know what to say. She wasn't wrong. "I love you, mom, and I want to hang out at the mall with you, but I will feel better if someone else was there in case, you know... just in case."

"Yup, I was right. You are a smart cookie, Michelle. So, who do you want me to call?" I asked as I picked up my cell. "Charlotte or Aunt Molly?"

"Both."

I called both. Molly was always up for a mall run. She loved it even more now since she could baby shop. Charlotte said she would meet us there after an appointment she had. Plans were set and I needed to put on some clothes. I wondered up to my room in search of something that wouldn't hang off me like a sack. I had lost a lot of weight and nothing fit. Shell came in a while later dressed in a cute sundress and sandals and I stood there still in my jammies.

"Nothing fits," I whined.

Shell looked at the sad collection of clothes and smirked at me, "Hold that thought." She was gone in a flash. She came back a few minutes later with an arm full of clothes that ended up tossed on my bed. "We should be able to find something in this pile that'll work," she said while digging through the mass. She held up things to my body then would toss them back into the pile until she settled on a bright yellow sundress. "That's the one. You should wear it," she declared, handing me the dress. "It's a happy color. I like yellow." She gathered up the rest of the mess from the bed, "You change and I'll throw these back in my closet." When she said 'throw' I knew she meant 'throw.' I shook my head and laughed. There were some things that just weren't worth stressing over. A year ago, I would have popped a cork if she did that. Now? Not so much.

I stood in front of the mirror and marveled at the fact I could wear anything Shell owned. But the more I analyzed what I saw the more I realized how bad I looked. No hair, no eyebrows, no color, and yes, I was too thin. Women joke you can't be too thin or too rich. I disagreed. Shell came in holding a little white cardigan, "You look great, Mom. Here," she said then handed me the sweater, "I know you get cold easy and the mall has the AC on."

I pulled the sweater over my shoulders, "Thanks, it makes the outfit." I looked at myself in the mirror again. I ran my hand over my very bald head and caught Michelle's gaze in the reflection, "Do you want me to wear a scarf or hat?"

"Why? You look fine just the way you are."

I shook my head, "If you think so then it must be so."

"I say so. Let's go. The mall awaits."

Shell drove and only tried to kill us...twice. The girl was insane behind the wheel. When we arrived at our destination, safely, I texted Molly to see where she was.

Are you here?

The response I got was no surprise.

Baby store

Of course she was. Where else would she be.

On our way.

Shell and I made our way through the teenager infested stores of the mall. "Wow, there are a lot of people here. I should have known being so close to school starting. Are any of your friends here today?" I asked as we squeezed through another group of girls drooling over another group of boys.

"Probably, but I'm here with you and that's who I want to be here with."

We found Molly holding at least a half dozen outfits in her arms while flipping through more baby clothes on the racks. She was so happy and...pleasant. Since finding out she was having a baby, then knowing it was healthy, and being blessed it was a boy, she had become sweeter as the days passed. She was nearing the five-month mark and glowed. She looked like one of those pregnancy models I always thought were fake. You know, they were wearing a fake belly for all the ads then whipped it off and went out partying with their friends later.

"Hey, Aunt Molly," called out Shell, "This baby is gonna have more clothes than you if you're not careful."

Molly held up the items she had been clutching, "There aren't that many here. Besides, I'm buying things in different sizes for him to grow into."

"He is one lucky little man," I grinned as I placed my hand on her belly, "Aren't you, lil guy?" He kicked me. "Oh my goodness, Shell, come here. He kicked."

Shell came closer but wouldn't put her hand over Molly's baby bump. "Thanks but I'm not diggin' the idea of feelin' up my Aunt so her fetus can kick me."

Molly and I stopped and stared at Shell and before I knew what was happening Molly was roaring with laughter, "When you put it like that it does sound kind of creepy."

"Leave it to my kid to point out the obvious."

We wandered around the baby clothes then on to toys followed by furniture. If I heard "What do you think of this?" one more time I was gonna curl up in a ball and hide in a crib. Just as I was reaching my breaking point my phone buzzed.

I'm here. Where u?

Charlotte to the rescue.

Baby store by the furniture.

All I had to do was wait for my hero and…there she was. Charlotte came breezing in with a look of pure joy on her face. "'ello, girlies. How ye be this beautiful mornin'?"

"We're good. How are you? You are looking mighty happy," I said. Something was up.

"Thank ye. I feel pretty great."

Molly looked at Charlotte from toes to nose, "Liv's right, you look amazing. What's going on, Charlotte?"

Charlotte looked confused, "Why must there be sumthin' up fer me ta look good? Can't I just look good?"

Shell threw her arm around Charlotte's shoulder, "You can look awesome whenever you want and I won't ask ya why."

"That's mighty kind of ye. I like ye."

"Hey, now, we love you too," I whined and snaked my arms around Charlotte too. "You can look awesome anytime you want."

Charlotte pushed us off, "Okay, then, I look good and tha's tha." We all laughed at our ridiculous outburst then went on searching for the perfect rocking chair for Molly's nursery. It was a mind numbing ordeal which I was more than ready to leave behind.

"I'm gonna take Shell over to *Hot Topic* to find some things for school. We can catch up after. Just text me, okay?"

Charlotte and Molly were completely engrossed in the details of a certain rocking chair, "Sure," was all I got as a collective response. Shell and I didn't wait for anything further before hightailing it out of there.

"Were you like that when you were pregnant with me and Lily?"

"No, we didn't have the money to be silly with. I hunted every sale I could find. I even learned to sew. You know that teddy bear you have on your bed?"

"Yeah?"

"I made it when I found out about you. It was how I told your dad we were pregnant again."

Shell stopped mid-stride, "Really? My teddy? You made him?" I nodded my head and grinned. Something she held precious was made at a very precious moment for me. "Wow."

"I made Lily's bunny, too."

"Huh, do you think it's weird those are our favorite toys?"

"I think it's great." I laced my arm with hers, "Let's go get you some clothes."

"Shop til we drop."

I dropped a lot quicker than I had hoped. I made it through a couple of stores before I had to find a place to sit down. Molly and Charlotte joined in around store two and were still going strong with Shell. They got me set up at the outer edge of the food court where I could still watch them make their way from store to store. Shell would bring things to the windows and would call to ask what I thought. She tried to keep me in the loop even when I wasn't anywhere near the loop. When Molly got tired she came and joined me at our table. When Charlotte got tired she dragged Shell with her. "I need lunch, girlies. Who's with me?" We all raised our hands.

"What do you want, Mom? I'll get it."

"Um, fried rice and a Sprite."

Michelle gave me a tilted look, "Is that all you're gonna eat? You need some meat in there somewhere."

"She's right, Liv. You need protein to keep up your strength," Molly interjected.

"Fine, chicken, nothing fried...please. I don't want to take any chances of getting sick. Not here." They seemed to understand. "Leave your stuff with me and go get your food," I said and shooed them away. I watched as they separated and got into different lines. Molly stood with her hand resting on her belly. Charlotte was in absolute concentration while she decided what to order and Shell...was watching me. I waved at my girl then she waved back.

"Um, excuse me."

I looked up into Kyle's smiling face, "Oh, hi, Kyle. Does Shell know you are here?"

"She's here?" he looked around.

"She's in line right over there," I pointed to the beautiful girl with long blonde hair waiting for my rice. I saw the smile of recognition spread across his face. "Why don't you go talk to her?"

His feet were already moving, "Yeah, I will."

"Was 'at Michelle's fella?" asked Charlotte when she sidled up to the table holding a platter of pizza and the biggest soda cup I'd ever seen.

I watched as Kyle made it to Shell's side. Her smile was quick to respond to him. "Yeah, look at her. She is grinning like he is the sun."

Charlotte scanned the crowd until her eyes fell on them, "She sure does look happy." She did and I was so happy for it. "How ye feelin'?" asked Charlotte as she cleared a spot for her lunch tray.

"Better."

"Glad ta hear." She rubbed her hands together then tore into the pizza as if she had a grudge against it. Molly joined us with her salad, fruit and green tea. She really needed to learn to have fun and I knew she would the moment that baby boy demanded chicken nuggets. Shell and Kyle came back to the table once the order was completed.

She slid a plate of rice and chopped chicken in front of me, "They cooked it while I waited. There is nothing on the chicken so hopefully you won't get sick or anything."

I beamed up at my baby girl for thinking of me and my needs, "Thank you, it looks really good." She and Kyle sat at the table next to us and shared a lunch and a lot of shy looks. We enjoyed light conversation about babies and parties and planning while we ate our lunches. I mostly listened and watched the young couple next to us get to know each other better. "Hey Shell?"

"Yeah?"

"Come here for a sec."

Shell came and squatted down near me, "Are you sick?"

"No, I'm good," I reached into my purse and dug around for my wallet. I opened my wallet then handed Shell some cash, "Here, why don't you two go do a little shopping together and I'll shop a bit with Molly and Charlotte."

"But, Mom, we…"

"I know. You can come and find me whenever you want. I can't leave without you. You drove, remember?" I patted her hand, "Go and have some fun with 'The Dude.'" She kissed my cheek, took Kyle by the hand, and left us to watch her go.

I managed to hit a few more stores with the ladies without crawling under a rack and going to sleep but by the time Shell found me, I was exhausted. I was thankful she was as ready to go as I was. Kyle walked with us to her car. He was a gentleman and carried the bags while Shell kept an arm around me.

"Thank you for helping us, Kyle," I said as I lowered myself onto the seat. "You are welcome to come to the house and spend time with Shell if you want or whatever. I'm gonna go to bed when we get back," I chuckled, "The joys of getting old." Sadly, that had nothing to do with getting old.

"Um, well, that's up to Michelle."

"Sure, see you when you get there," she said as she closed her door. "I want to get mom home or I would wait."

"That's cool. I'll be there soon." Kyle tapped the top of the car and stepped back while Shell backed out of our spot.

I looked over at my driver, "He's very nice."

She grinned, "And cute."

"Yes, very cute."

"And smart."

I shrugged, "I wouldn't know."

"I would and he is."

"I'm glad you found a good guy who is cute and smart. As long as he is good to you, your dad won't have to string him up in the back yard and build a fire under him."

"He would, wouldn't he?"

"Yup, I have no doubt in my mind he would."

Shell pulled into the drive, "Stay," she instructed and took off up the steps to unlock the door. She came back to help me out of the car and into the house as Kyle pulled up to the curb.

"Hey, toss me your keys and I will bring in the stuff you got."

Shell tossed her keys to Kyle then helped me into the house. "Do you want your room or the couch?"

"I think my room. That way you and Kyle won't have to listen to me snore." I grabbed onto the railing and proceeded to climb the steps. "Hey," I stopped and turned to her, "Thanks for today. I'm sorry I got wore out but I still had fun."

"Me, too."

I nodded and continued my climb. You would have thought I was climbing Mount Kilimanjaro instead of thirteen steps. I was breathing hard by the time I made it to the top and had to rest against the wall to clear the dizziness that had crept in to steal my vision.

"Mom, are you okay?" shrilled Shell when she found me on my knees at the top of the stairs. "Kyle! Help me!" I heard his heavy steps thunder up the stairs and the two of them carried me to my room.

"I'm okay. I just got kinda winded. I'm okay, really." I sat on the side of the bed to gain some control over my uncooperative body.

Michelle shoved her hand in her pocket, "I'm gonna call dad.'

I reached out and caught her hand just as her phone was in sight, "Don't. There is nothing he can do. The doctor said this would happen. I'm going to rest for a while, okay?" It was true. Tom couldn't change anything by being there. "Go on. There are sodas in the fridge. Thank you, Kyle, for helping," I nodded in his direction, "I appreciate it."

"You're welcome."

"Come on, let's get outta here so mom can get some sleep," Shell said as she took Kyle by the elbow and led him from the room. I heard them whispering as they made their way back to the staircase:

"...*Is she okay*..."

"...*No*..."

I wasn't.

I muscled my way out of clothes and into a tee-shirt and shorts and dragged my sagging ass into bed. I was so tired but the sun still shone through my windows. I could still hear birds chirping. I heard them chirping as I fell asleep.

Chapter Fourty

Naps were turning into sleeps and sleeps into mini comas. I felt like I spent more time in bed than out. I had gotten to the point I was bringing my laptop to bed with me and writing whenever I was awake long enough to turn on the blasted thing. The main ingredients in most of my meals came from little plastic bottles Tom picked up from the pharmacy. Was that living? I was really beginning to wonder. I was already becoming obsolete. Tom took Shell to enroll her in school. I used to do that. Tom and Shell went grocery shopping. I used to do that. They hung out together and watched TV. I used to do that, too. They were finding each other and in a weird way, I felt jealous. I felt unneeded. Which was what I wanted, wasn't it?

I lay in bed for as long as I could. It was the day of my last chemo, not because I was cured but because I was sentenced to death. Was this how death row inmates felt? It was strange to have a general idea of when it would happen. I forced myself out of bed. The loss of breath I was experiencing was the scariest part of all. I felt as long as I could breathe I was good. Once it became difficult to walk to the bathroom, I got scared. For real. I shuffled into the bathroom and did what I could to look less like the walking dead. I needed help with the simplest of things. You knew the end was creeping up on you when you couldn't wipe your own back side anymore. I hadn't gotten that bad...yet. It wasn't far off, though.

"Where ya at?"

I grabbed a breath and wheezed, "Here."

Tom stepped into the bathroom holding my meds and a glass of Mio-laden water, "Breakfast," he joked, and set the glass on the vanity. He lowered the toilet seat then helped me to sit. "Here ya go," he said as he put the collection of capsules and pills into my frail hand. "Mmmm, my favorite," I sighed and slowly ate my breakfast.

Tom stepped back into the bedroom returning moments later holding my shoes, "Are you about ready?" he asked as he stooped down to slip my shoes on for me. I tossed the last of my pills into my mouth, nodded at him then drank down my pomegranate flavored water. Tom finished tying my shoes and looked up at me with a bright, fake, smile, "Come on, hot stuff, you gotta date with an IV bag."

"You're a sweet talker, ya know that, right?"

He extended his hands to me so I could use his strength to get up, "I know." Once on my feet, Tom stepped in closer, "Take a deep breath." I questioned him with my eyes. "I'm going to kiss you. Take a deep breath." I smiled and took as deep a breath as I could without coughing giving him permission to kiss me. He hadn't kissed me like that in a long time. I didn't mind being lightheaded after that. "I may have to do that again," he whispered against my lips. He waited for me to gasp for more air and then took it all away.

"Wow."

He cupped my face in his hands and ran his thumb over my bottom lip, "It was definitely a 'wow' kinda kiss."

"Yeah," I couldn't catch my breath enough to say much more but what more could I say?

Tom took me by my hand and led me out of the bathroom and toward the stairs. It was time to go and be poisoned for no good reason at all. It might give me a day it might not. All I wanted was to see, or at least be alive, when Lily graduated. Beyond that, I was ready.

*****

I went through the motions. Weight, temperature, blood, blah,blah, blah. I put on the gown. I assumed the position in the big vinyl chair. It stung a bit more than usual when the oncology nurse hooked up my poison of choice to the tubes dangling from my chest. What was a little more pain in the grand story of my demise? That time I brought my laptop and worked on more of my wonderfully morbid tale. I still had a lot I wanted to get done and even less time to do it in. The quilts had been delivered already and stored away in the trunk. If I were gonna live forever I would scream to the roof tops about how wonderful Quinn's quilts were. She finished them early and gave back all the money. Sometimes people really did amaze me. I clicked away at the keyboard and poured out what little was left for me to tell, to share, or to hope for. When the sickness came I closed the laptop and rode out the storm, again. This was the last time I was going to have to deal with it. That was the only bright side to a very dark reality.

By the time it was all over I was too weak to go on foot so I was taken to our waiting truck by wheelchair. I sat in the waiting room while Tom pulled around and saw Tracy Pearson signing in at the desk. She was smiling and had a healthy growth of hair atop her head. She had a glow about her I no longer had. Our eyes met and it was as if she remembered the first time we saw each other. She won. I would lose. The nurse wheeled me out to the truck after she saw Tom pull up to the front of the building.

"Let's get you home and back into bed."

"I don't want to go to bed."

"Really? Okay, do you want to be on the couch?"

I drew in air and voiced my desire, "No, I want to go to the park. I want to sit on my bench. One last time."

"I don't know if that's a good idea, babe. You just had chemo."

"I know what I had. I don't care if it's a bad idea. I want to go to the park." Tom sat silent but changed the trajectory of the truck. We were heading toward the park whether he liked it or not.

"Happy?" he grumbled.

"No."

"Then why the fuck are we here?"

I closed my eyes and inhaled the summer breeze, "To say goodbye," I whispered.

Tom held on to me as I slid out of the truck. He held on to me as I made the trek to the bench. He held on to me as I looked around at all the amazing life within inches of where we sat and said goodbye. I rested my head against his chest and listened to the life beating within. "This is such a beautiful place," I whispered to no one. "I would be lucky to be planted here."

"You will only make it more beautiful, babe."

"Will you visit me?"

His arms came tighter around me, "Every day."

I looked up into his ocean blue eyes and begged, "Not every day. Do other things. Go places you've always wanted to go. Learn to kayak or water ski. Don't spend your life on this bench." He kissed my forehead and I tucked my head under his chin and listened to his heart beat some more. We sat for what could have been minutes or hours. It didn't quite matter. We were together in a place I would be forever.

I felt a nudge and a shake, "Liv, babe, wake up."

"Um up. Wha?"

"Time to go home. Come on, you fell asleep." I let him pull me to my feet and I shuffled back to the truck. I fell back to sleep the moment I was safely inside the cab.

*****

I woke to yelling from the front of the house. How did I get on the couch? What time was it? Who was yelling? I tried to sit up but had to fight with Oliver's weight holding me down. "Oliver, move, fat man." He did little more than lift his head at the mention of his name then plopped it back *down*.

"*...No, you get the fuck off my property or I swear to God I will call the cops...*"

"*...I have every right to see her. You can't stop me...*"

Who was *that*?

"...You have no rights here. Get out..."

"...I know she's sick. I want to talk to her..."

"...You should have thought of that before now. It's too late, Karen..."

Karen? Karen...my mother?

I shoved Oliver off and attempted to push myself up and off the couch, twice. I fumbled my way to the front door and pulled it open. I stood staring at the person who gave me life fight with the person who made my life worth living. "Tom," I said in a steady but firm voice. His eyes met mine, "Please, come in." They both started moving towards me, "No, I said Tom. I did not ask you in."

"But, I wanted to see you."

"You've seen me, now you can go." Tom made it to my side and held me as I defended my home from the evil that stood before it. We were locked in a staring contest when Shell pulled her car into the driveway. I broke eye contact with her. I sent Tom to put a block between Michelle and the woman I trusted the least with the people I loved most. "You need to leave and not come back," Michelle took hold of my hand when she made it to the doorway, "Take a good look at her, Shell. If you ever see her around, run. Get as far away from her as possible. She's a taker, she's greedy, she would suck you dry and leave you to rot if it would benefit her. You need to leave now." I stepped back into the security of my home. I slowly closed the door and felt the relief at the sound of the lock being engaged. Tom went to the window to keep watch as Shell and I sat down on the couch. "That was my mother," I said as my only explanation.

"Well, that was a whole lotta excitement to come home to. Half the neighborhood was out there with bowls of popcorn waitin' for a fight to break out."

"I guess they wasted a bunch of popcorn cuz they weren't gonna see anything."

Tom chuckled behind us, "Popcorn is never a waste. I can eat popcorn watching seeds sprout. As long as there's a ton of butter...I'm good."

We tried to laugh off the event and move forward with our evening. First came dinner, which I couldn't cook, or eat, or clean up after. Then came a movie I fell asleep during. I also missed out on a large bowl of popcorn which I probably wouldn't have been able to eat anyway. So, I was about as productive as a house plant. I was there but had no hand in the events that occurred around me.

Tom laid a hand on my arm, "You awake?"

"Yeah."

"Do you want to go to bed?"

I thought for a moment, "No, you go. I'll stay here. I'm too tired to move."

Tom slid down on to his knees on the floor next to the couch, "I'll carry you." He shoved his arms under my body with every intention of doing just that.

"No, don't," I winced, "Let me stay here."

"Why?" he begged, "I can carry you, you know I can."

"I hurt all over. Let me stay here, okay. Just...it hurts to move." My shoulders ached and a headache was moving in. It had to be the stress of seeing her in my front yard.

Tom rested his chin on the arm of the couch and dusted his fingers over my head. He sat with me for a few more minutes before he leaned in and kissed me, "Okay, I'm going to go up to bed."

"Good-night, I love you."

"I love you too."

"I love you more."

*****

Shell had to get permission to leave school for a few days to go to Texas to see Lily's graduation. They managed to give her what looked like a month's worth of homework for what would only be a three day lapse. I watched from my place on the couch while Molly helped Tom and Shell pack for their trip.

Tom was putting pressure on the suitcase to try to get it to close. "Damn Shell, how much crap did you pack? We're only gonna be gone three days."

"What do you mean? I have hanging out clothes, pj's, clothes for graduation, and travel clothes. Then there are shoes, my hair stuff, make-up, and..."

"Never mind," he grumbled and sat on the suitcase as Shell zipped it closed. "Don't touch it. Don't even look at it or it might pop like a friggin' balloon." I laughed at his feeble attempt at humor which triggered a coughing fit. I had been having them more often than not. "Hey, okay, I know I'm funny and all but you need to calm down." He rubbed and lightly patted my back to try to curb the cough. I tried to calm my breathing to stop the rumble. Tom sat on the edge of the coffee table next to me, "I can still cancel. We can stay with you," he pleaded.

"You promised," I hissed out with another cough.

Molly pushed Tom out of the way then slid more pillows behind me to put me in a more upright position which seemed to slow the coughs. Molly moved things around to get me into a good position, "Now you listen to me, Tom. You," she turned to him and stuck her finger in his face, "made a promise. You will keep your promise. You have a wonderful daughter who is about to swear an oath or something and you need to be there to witness it. Now, Shell?"

"Yeah?"

"Make sure you have everything you need. Your Uncle Wayne will be here in about twenty minutes to take you two to the airport. Tom, make sure you have the charging cables for your phones and don't forget the tablet so you can Skype with Olivia." Molly looked down at me, "Was there anything else?" My lips moved but no sound came out. "Oh, right, Shell, get the tin of cookies from the kitchen we made last night for Lily." Molly looked down at me and gave me a nod, "I think they are set." I agreed.

Wayne arrived right on time and helped Tom load their bags into the car. Shell smothered me in kisses and a few well-meant tears before she went outside to wait for her dad. "Okay, woman, it looks like we are ready to go. Do you need anything before I go?" I mouthed 'yes,' then puckered up my lips demanding a kiss goodbye. He gave me what I asked for with no complaint. When he pulled away he laid his hand on my forehead, "You're warm. Do you feel okay?" I shrugged. I hadn't felt okay in weeks. "Molly, I think she has a fever."

"I'll take her temp. If she does I will call the doctor's office," said Molly as she went in search of the thermometer. "You need to get going," she hollered from the bathroom.

"We have to go, babe. I would much rather stay home with you."
I grimaced at him. "Okay, okay, I'm going. I love you," he
whispered and sealed it with a kiss.

*****

"Wake up, Girlie, ye best wake up or ye will be missin' yer gurl
graduate," squawked Charlotte.

I peeled open my eyes to see the small screen held out in front of
me. It felt heavy in my hands but there was no way I was going to
miss this moment. Lily had somehow gotten permission for her
father to sit closer to the ceremony and Skype with me so I could be
there with her when she did something so amazing. I watched as a
sea of young men and women marched in parade formation onto the
graduation grounds. They were all decked out in their beautiful blue
uniforms and shiny shoes. A tear slid down my cheek as they played
the national anthem and all those soldiers saluted the flag with
pride. My baby girl chose to devote herself to her country and the
needs of the people. I was one proud mama. I watched as each
soldier's name was called. Each marched in turn to the podium,
spoke words no one heard with the officer, saluted, and marched
back to their spot holding a rolled up scroll.

"Airman Lily Carpenter."

That was my girl. I watched as she marched up to take what she
had earned all on her own. I watched her smile spread across her
face as her eyes slid over to where her dad sat holding the tablet up
so we could see each other. I threw her a kiss as she marched back
to her position. I couldn't control the big fat tears that rolled down
my cheeks. Molly wiped them away with soft baby wipes only to
have to wipe at them again.

"You are going to dehydrate yourself if you don't stop the water
works," she giggled as she continued to race the tears. I looked at
her to find that she, too, was crying. "What? Hormones, I'm going to
blame it on the hormones." She giggled again placing her mommy
hand on her growing baby boy. "Charlotte?"

"What can I do fer ye?"

"We need to take her temp again. Can you get the thermometer
from the medicine cabinet?"

I did have a fever the day Tom and Shell left for Texas and it
continued to stick with me more than 24 hours later. Molly and

Charlotte checked it regularly to keep track of it. The doctor's office gave Molly some magic temp number and if I reached it they should bring my bony ass into the hospital. Apparently I hadn't reached that number yet. But, my butt really was bony. I was going to see Lily in just over a day. Dr. Fraiser called the Red Cross and they arranged for Lily to be able to come home for a few days before she had to report to her technical training base. I would get to hug my soldier girl.

*****

My eyes opened and I saw the most glorious sight ever. Lily sat at the end of the couch holding my feet in her lap while she talked to her dad. She looked the same but different. She sounded the same but stronger. She was Lily but so much more. I wiggled my foot to let her know I was awake. Speech had taken an impromptu vacation. Between the coughing fits and the fever, my words went bye-bye. But, when you love and know people as well as we did then words weren't necessary. I reached out my arms and they were filled with a hug I had dreamt of for weeks. The hug I prayed I would live long enough to get. She felt good. She felt at home in my arms. My family was whole, one last time.

She told me all about her journey. I laughed and smiled at the story she spun. I felt pride and awe in her ability to be so strong. I let tears fall freely when I saw sisters hug and laugh together. I watched a father find respect for his child and his child understood the meaning of that respect.

Chapter Fourty One

So, I guess that catches you up on my tale of two titties. Here I sit faced with tomorrow and not knowing if it will come. See, I know how this story is gonna end. Tom and my girls don't want to face it, but I know this story ends with me. I have fought the battles up to now and have made a great showing, but I am low on ammo, energy, and hope. It is time I made peace with the past and give my blessings to the future that will move forward without me. So, here it is:

1.   To my mother: I forgive you for not being a mother. I forgive you for only seeing the world as a horror story and I was only a bit player. I forgive you for turning a blind eye to the nightmares that took

place one room away. I forgive you because you no longer have any control over me or my life.

2. To the "men" she brought home: I forgive you for ALL that you did to me. You will be judged, but not by me. Your vicious acts made me strong and taught me what I did not want in a man. You showed me the worst and I found the best.

3. To my ex-boyfriend: I forgive you for being weak. I forgive you for thinking you could raise your hand to me in anger. I forgive you for not knowing better.

4. To me: I forgive myself for judging people based on the things I experienced. I forgive myself for doubting genuine love and questioning the actions of others toward me. I learned. It was a slow process but the lessons were there and I learned them. I learned not to judge everyone based on what I lived as a child. I learned everyone has his own horror stories and nightmares. I learned life shouldn't be a competition but a journey worth sharing. I learned everyone you meet, good or bad, leaves something behind, something that will change you, mark you forever. These moments have been hard learned and long in lessons, but worth the effort.

To the ones I love:

Tom,

My love, my partner, my hero... you showed me not to judge one man by the actions of another. You proved to me over and over that I was worthy of love, worthy of your love. You taught me what a "daddy" is. You showed me unconditional love the moment you held your children. You taught me that moments can hurt but they don't have to be the end. You taught me to laugh at myself and at moments that others may have shed tears for. You taught me to dance, to throw my arms out and twirl in the sunshine and in the darkness. You taught me to sing, to sing because I wanted to or needed to and it didn't have to be to someone else's beat, but to mine. You showed me that being still can release the world around you. You taught me how to love by loving me. You said I had to love me as much as you loved me, but then you reminded me no one would ever love me the way you do. You loved me with and without breasts, with and without hair, with and without a tomorrow. I will love you with and without breath. I will love you beyond the edge of forever.

Lily,

My beautiful flower...a seed was planted, took root, grew and became a beautiful flower, my flower. You brought me joy and beauty from the moment I knew your heart was beating within me. You opened my eyes to the wonders around me with every discovery you made. You introduced me to the world. I watched you grow and bloom. I watched you become more and more amazing with every day that passed. I held your hands in mine and wondered what they would create. I looked into those doe eyes and wondered what they would see. Where would your tiny toes take you? The world was waiting for you and now you are on a journey of your own. I held your hand for as long as you would let me and watched from the sidelines. Now, I will watch you from somewhere out in the ether, out in the great wide nothing. Think of me when you hear a child laugh, and smile. I loved you long before we met and will love you long after I have drifted away.

Michelle,

Michelle my belle...my beautiful song. Every moment in life a soundtrack is created. As each day passed another song was added, you added music to my life. I felt the rhythm of your life with each kick and spin. You made me aware of you. You made me feel you. You made me love you. You challenged me and questioned me and defied me. You walked when you were ready, not when you were told. You touched everything and wanted to know "why?" You wanted to try everything and anything and did. You brought chaos and I love you for it. You pushed harder and loved stronger and wanted more than any person I have ever known. Your desire to be all, see all, feel all, do all and imagine more filled me with want. I want it ALL for you. Even now, I want you to do all the things you have ever dreamt of. You are only limited by you. I will be with you on a sunbeam. I will ride the breeze rushing through your hair. I will be that whisper you thought you heard. Do it, baby girl, do it all and then some. You gave me rhythm. You gave me desire. You gave me...you. I love you with every beat of my heart and with every beat of every heart everywhere. Go find them all.

*****

...the rest of the story.

Mom died two days after that last entry was made. It turned out the fever she had been fighting was something called Sepsis. She died from an infection that slowly started shutting down her organs until she passed on. I made it home from basic just in time to say goodbye to her. You may have guessed it by now but this is Lily. Dad gave me Mom's computer a few weeks ago to make it easier for me to keep in touch with him and Shell. I found this 'journal' as I was clearing off a bunch of stuff that wasn't important. This was very important. Dad didn't know about the trunk and all it contained. Mom didn't have a chance to let us know before she slipped into a coma and died. He has since sent me the quilt she had made for me and the charm bracelet she designed. Shell and I have a few of the same charms: a heart for our Mother's love, a crystal tear for our loss, and a pink ribbon to honor all those who had lived and died as a result of breast cancer. Mine also contained an Air Force charm. Dad got a key ring with the same three charms we got but he also got an infinity charm. It was Mom's way of saying she would love him for all time, I kind of wish I had gotten one of those. The box for Molly contained additional charms to be given to us as gifts in the future to mark special occasions. There was even a charm bracelet for Molly. It held a tiny baby shoe charm to mark the coming arrival of my first cousin. The quilts are another story altogether. Mom had the three quilts made out of her clothes but what she didn't say in this journal was she had photos of us printed onto pieces of cloth then sewn into the quilts. My quilt has pictures of Mom holding me when I was a baby, building a sand castle when I was seven, and teaching me to bake her apple pie when I was taking a cooking class my junior year. Michele's has a picture of Mom holding her while they both slept, one of Mom teaching her to ride a bike, and posing for her first Homecoming dance. Dad's, well, his made me cry. It was covered in pictures from when they were in high school, to their wedding day, each of our births, and a picture of Mom she took before she placed the order for the quilts. To be honest, I'm sitting here, right now, with mine wrapped tightly around me as I try to finish her story. She deserves an ending to the story she began and so I have taken it on as my last gift to her.

*****

Mom's passing was without drama. Her fever became much worse. By the time we got her to the hospital and into a room she had slipped into a coma. The doctor on call explained they found evidence of Sepsis and the infection was quite severe. Mom was too weak to fight it and left this Earth the following afternoon. I found it fitting that it was a dark, rainy day. Dad honored her wish to be cremated, but had no idea where the tree urn was. So, she sat in a sad little box on the book shelf behind their shared desk. We were kind of lost for quite some time. Mom always kept our schedules straight and planned out everything. She even planned out what to

---

do after she died. It took me a few weeks to find it all on her computer. So I started making some plans of my own.

*****

It started with an email.

To: Trish James, Alyssa Majors, Molly Carpenter, and 37 others

From: Lily Carpenter

Subject: Olivia Carpenter / Mom

Hey Guys,

I found this document on mom's computer a few weeks ago. I didn't know what to do with it so I thought I would send it on to all of you... because you meant something to her, or you're in it. Mom had been doing a lot of writing at the end and now you get to see it all from her side (if you read it). I know Dad mailed the letters Mom wrote for you guys. Maybe we can do the same and add them to the journal she wrote. Her birthday is coming up in a few weeks and I have decided to take leave to be home with Dad and Shell. I was hoping you guys would want to come and celebrate her just one more time. Mom made arrangements to have a tree planted in the park using her ashes. I thought maybe we could get together that weekend and ... well, I don't know what we can do. It's just an idea.

Let me know what you think.

Lily

hermommasflower@yahoo.com

A few weeks later...

"Hey everyone," Dad hollered above the drone of conversations that spread out around the back yard. There were at least fifty people spread out amongst the flowers. "Hey, so, I'm glad all of you could come to this...," he looked down at his left hand and shrugged his shoulders, "I don't know what this is but either way, I'm glad you are here. Lily told me she sent you the entire journal she found and asked you all to help us finish what Liv started." He looked off into the great wide nowhere and continued. "Ya know, I'm not really sure why Liv wrote this but I am glad she did." He looked around at the many faces that showed up to show their love for mom. "Did anyone think it was ironic that we called her 'Liv'? She did, ya know. She lived. It may not have been as long as I wanted, but shit, I'm selfish that way, ya know." Dad's tears ran a slow stream down his tired cheeks. "I wanted her to live. Live to see our girls graduate college and find husbands who would love them as much as I loved their mother. She should be here to hold and spoil grandbabies, but she's not." Tears fell all around his words. They poured from eyes looking back at him as he spoke. "I hate that she's not here. I hate that I have to face another day not hearing her laughter or her bitching or...her breathing as she lay next to me in a bed she hated." He raised his eyes to the stars and shook his head, "He took her from me, from us. I want to hate Him for it but I can't blame Him for wanting her back because I sure as hell do." Reaching into his pocket, Dad pulled out a crumpled up piece of paper. "I wrote my letter to Liv to add to the pages she wrote for all of us. She poured out her love and fears and anger in those pages and I needed to finish it." He gestured toward Lily and Shelley, "We need to finish it. We need to give her an ending that shows her as much love as she showed us."

Dad smoothed out the pages on his chest and began to read his love to the crowd.

My Beautiful Olivia,

There are no words pure enough to describe the love I have had for you for so many years. There are not enough ways to say I love you. So I will say it with every tear I have shed reading the words you left behind. Behind...why did you have to leave me behind? You were so good to me and our beautiful girls. You were the flavor in my life. You were the color in my world. You were the next breath I needed to take to live. Even at your worst you were the best thing in my life. Even through your pain you showed me love. You whispered it to me as your eyes would close and sleep would take you. You said it with your touch and your eyes. You said it before you left me forever. I will love you with every breath I take. I will honor who you were with every day I live. I will hold you in my heart forever. I will remind people of who you were and I will share your story because I love you and always will.

The Other Half of Our Whole,

Tom

A wave of tissues to eyes and noses rippled through the crowd. Dad stumbled back and rested his sobs in a chair.

Many others took the opportunity to say their peace to Mom and then slipped their envelopes between the pages of the bound copy I had made. Some chose to say nothing but left their envelopes just the same. Mom had missed so much in the few short months she had been gone. Wayne stood next to Dad to offer support while Molly rocked Michael in her arms. The baby count was growing around us. Charlotte was just now showing. She never got the chance to tell Mom she was pregnant, which saddened her greatly. Then there was Alyssa. She and Mom's old doctor were engaged and expecting. I don't know everything that happened between Mom and Alyssa but I hope they were able to let it go in the end. The only unexplainable event after Mom died was that Oliver disappeared. Dad said he never saw him again. We looked. Friends looked. No Oliver. Maybe he saw Mom's passing before us. She was his favorite person. Why stick around if she wasn't going to be there?

"Excuse me," I hollered over the crowd, "We are going to walk over to the park now to plant the tree urn that holds Mom's ashes. If you want to come then we will meet you all over by the fountain." The crowd milled around then gained momentum and moved along to the park. Dad, Michele and I walked alone carrying the Jerusalem Pine BioUrn. Kyle stayed near the back of the crowd to remain closer to Shell, but Shell stayed with me and Dad all the way to the park. Mom had talked to someone at Parks and Recreations while she planned where she would spend eternity. They honored her plans. All they were waiting for was a call from us and a date. They dug and prepped the hole before we got there.

The crowd had circled around the tiny hole and waited. Dad, Shell, and I circled around the plot of land. We each placed our hands on the urn then slowly lowered Mom into the ground. We pushed the cold wet dirt over her and watered her with our tears. There were hugs and kisses passed around. Some made their way home and others went back to our house for a celebratory barbeque.

"You coming?" asked Shell as she leaned into Kyle for support.

"In a bit." I sat next to the spot where my Mom would soon grow into a fine tree. I ran my fingers through the soil and begged that she be strong and healthy in her future life.

"Meow."

I was amazed to see the flick of an orange tail underneath the bench on the other side of the clearing. Oliver came out from his hiding spot and walked over to where I sat. He rubbed his head along my knee and moved to lie down on top of the freshly turned soil. "Huh, so were you just waiting for us to bring Mom out here? Is this where you have been all this time?" I asked the stubborn fur ball as I stroked his head.

"Meow." He rolled around on the mound of dirt and purred. He had been here waiting for Mom all along. Who could blame him?

"I love her, too."

Mom really was brave, intelligent, tenacious, caring, hopeful, but most of all, she was loved.

*****

The obituary of Olivia Carpenter.

I could never put words together quite like my wife, Liv, could. So, she wrote these words for me because she knew how hard it would be for me to say farewell. She said it needed to be important to some and mean nothing to others, because that's who she was.

I was born. I died. Somewhere in between

I lived. I loved. I laughed. I cried. But, I have

no regrets. If I loved you, you knew it, because

it would have been a waste not to show you.

If we were enemies, we are no more. I forgive

you for your faults as I forgive myself for mine.

479

I learned too late to live each day as if it were a gift. Live it large. Live life strong and live it with desire for more. I did in the end, but my more ran out. My love did not. Plant a seed, watch it grow. Nurture and love it. Never pluck it. Let it live. Let it live.

Be joy. Find joy. Enjoy.

I love you all.

Our Olivia loved us to her last sparkle. She loved us purely and honestly. I am proud to say I knew her. I held her. I love her, *today and* always.

The end.

Oliver passed away while I was writing O-B!tch-uary. He was the sweetest guy to love and snuggle. He always knew when I needed him. He had a cranky face but a puurr-fect heart. I miss my Lolly-Monster, but he is never far from my thoughts and will forever live in these pages.

In the story she was called Matilda, but in the real world, her name was Maggie. She was with me as each word was written and listened to me argue with some of the characters when they decided to do things I had not planned. Our ol' girl crossed the Rainbow Bridge in 2018 to hang out with Oliver and other much loved friends. She will live on forever with Oliver in this story and our hearts.

Enjoy them as we did. Love them as we still do.

About the Author

Ticia Rani is the proud mother of two amazing daughters, the blessed wife of a man she still can't resist, a veteran of the USAF, and a lover of words.

She finds peace in the stories she tells and looks forward to sharing more with you.

Other places you can find her are:

New Ink. Used ideas. Blog: https://ticia-rani.com/

Twitter: https://twitter.com/TiciaRani

Facebook: https://www.facebook.com/Nella-Warrent-1863744137235991/?ref=bookmarks

LinkedIn: https://www.linkedin.com/in/ticia-metheney-22181476/

Made in the USA
Middletown, DE
11 April 2019